Praise for the *Oscar Wilde Murder Mysteries*

'I don't know how he does it [*I do, actually: great talent and
damned hard work*] but Gyles Brandreth's Oscar Wilde Murder
Mysteries get better and better . . . positively dazzling. Oscar
is on sunny form, but the clouds are gathering. Like its central
character, *Oscar Wilde and the Nest of Vipers* is both witty and
profound. It's also devilishly clever' *The District Messenger*,
Newsletter of the Sherlock Holmes Society

'One of the most intelligent, amusing and entertaining books of
the year. If Oscar Wilde himself had been asked to write this
book he could not have done it any better'
Alexander McCall Smith

'Wilde has sprung back to life in this thrilling and richly
atmospheric new novel . . . The perfect topography for crime and
mystery . . . magnificent . . . an unforgettable shocker about sex
and vice, love and death' *Sunday Express*

'Gyles Brandreth and Oscar Wilde seem made for one another
. . . There is much here to enjoy . . . the complex and nicely
structured plot zips along' *Daily Telegraph*

'Brandreth has poured his considerable familiarity with London
into a witty *fin-de-siècle* entertainment, and the rattlingly elegant
dialogue is peppered with witticisms uttered by Wilde well before
he ever thought of putting them into his plays' *Sunday Times*

OSCAR WILDE

and the

Nest of Vipers

Gyles Brandreth

First published in Great Britain in 2010 by John Murray (Publishers)
An Hachette UK Company

First published in paperback in 2011

1

Map on page 423 drawn by Martin Collins

A CIP catalogue record for this title is available from the British Library

ISBN 978-1-84854-249-5
Ebook ISBN 978-1-84854-459-8

Typeset in Sabon by Servis Filmsetting Ltd, Stockport, Cheshire

Printed and bound by Clays Ltd, St Ives plc

John Murray policy is to use papers that are natural, renewable and recyclable
products and made from wood grown in sustainable forests. The logging and
manufacturing processes are expected to conform to the environmental regulations
of the country of origin.

John Murray (Publishers)
338 Euston Road
London NW1 3BH

www.johnmurray.co.uk

In memory of my mother
Alice Mary Addison
1914–2010

Freedom is the only law which genius knows.

Oscar Wilde (1854–1900)

Oscar Wilde and the Nest of Vipers

Drawn from the previously unpublished memoirs of
Robert Sherard (1861–1943),
Oscar Wilde's friend and his first and most
prolific biographer

Principal characters in the narrative

London, 1890

Oscar Wilde, poet and playwright
Constance Wilde, his wife
Robert Sherard, journalist
Arthur Conan Doyle, author and physician
Bram Stoker, theatre manager

HRH the Prince of Wales
HRH Prince Albert Victor, his son
General Sir Dighton Probyn VC, Comptroller
and Treasurer of the Prince of Wales's Household
Harry Tyrwhitt Wilson, equerry
Frank Watkins, page

The Duke and Duchess of Albemarle
Mr Parker, butler at 40 Grosvenor Square
Nellie Atkins, the Duchess of Albemarle's maid

Lord Yarborough, psychiatrist
Rex LaSalle, artist
Father John Callaghan, priest
Sister Agnes, nurse
Antonin Dvorak, composer
Louisa Lavallois, dancer

Professor Onofroff, mind-reader
Mrs Lillie Langtry, actress
Jane Avril, dancer

Inspector Hugh Boone, Metropolitan Police

Preface
Paris, 1900

'I remember nothing.'

'You must remember the nest of vipers.'

'I remember nothing. That is my rule.'

'Don't be absurd, Oscar.'

My friend smiled and ran his forefinger slowly around the rim of his glass of absinthe. He gazed at me, his eyes full of tears. 'What else should I be, Robert? I am absurd. Look at me.'

I looked at him as he sat slumped on the banquette like a debauched tart in a painting by Toulouse-Lautrec. His face was grey, blotchy, with patches of green and ochre beneath his eyes and starbursts of crimson where veins had broken in his cheeks. His auburn hair, once so lustrous, was lank. His uneven teeth were stained with mercury and nicotine. His body had run to fat. His appearance had gone to seed. Two years in prison, with hard labour, and three years in exile, without employment, had brought him to this.

'I remember nothing,' he repeated, 'as a matter of policy. The artist must destroy memory, Robert, and interest himself only in the moment – the hour that is passing, the very second as it occurs. The man who thinks of his past has no future.' He raised his now-empty glass towards the barman. 'Personally, I give myself absolutely to the present.'

We were in Paris, the city of light, sitting in semi-darkness at the back of the old Café Hugo on boulevard Montmartre. It was Friday, 16 March 1900 – five months to the day since his forty-fifth birthday; eight months and a half before his untimely death. We were having lunch: bread, cheese, salami. I had finished mine; Oscar had not touched his. He preferred absinthe. 'It makes the heart grow fonder,' he said, smiling and pressing his hand over mine.

Oscar Wilde and I were not lovers, but we were the best of friends. We met in Paris in the spring of 1883, when I was young and idolatrous and he was on the brink of becoming the literary sensation of the age. I was flattered by his friendship (I was twenty-one at the time), charmed by his generosity (Oscar was a profligate spender), and overwhelmed by the brilliance of his intellect and his way with words. From the day of our first encounter I kept a journal of our times together. In due course, I published *Oscar Wilde: The Story of an Unhappy Friendship* (1902) and *The Life of Oscar Wilde* (1906). In 1900 I hoped to publish the tale of Oscar Wilde and the Nest of Vipers.

'It is an extraordinary story, Oscar,' I said. 'Lurid, bizarre.'

'I don't recall, Robert.'

'You must,' I persisted. 'It's only ten years ago. If I write it up now and get it published, we can share the proceeds. You are in want of funds, Oscar.'

'That I do recall.' My friend laughed and gazed into his refilled glass of absinthe.

'Think how much Arthur Conan Doyle is making with Sherlock Holmes,' I continued, pressing home my advantage. 'He gets a pound a word, I'm told.'

Oscar swirled the green-gold liquid in his glass. 'I've not seen Arthur in a year and he rarely writes. I think he regards my condition as pathological. He pities me: he does not condemn. He is a decent fellow. You know that he has a sick wife to whom he is devoted and a young friend who is the love of his life – and they are not the same person. That is a difficulty for a gentleman like Arthur.'

'Arthur is part of the story, of course. That will add to its allure.'

Oscar put down his glass and looked towards me steadily, a sudden gleam in his watery eyes. 'You cannot publish the story, Robert. Not in your lifetime. Not in my lifetime. Not in the lifetime of the Prince of Wales. Nor for a hundred years thereafter. You know that.'

'You see,' I said, smiling. 'You do remember.'

'I remember nothing,' he insisted. 'But I do know that you can't disguise the Prince of Wales as the Prince of Carpathia or Bohemia or some such nonsense. That's what Conan Doyle does and Conan Doyle is writing fiction – while this is fact, is it not?'

'Yes, that's what makes it so remarkable. It is a murder mystery and yet it's fact, beyond dispute. I have gathered all the papers – the cuttings, the correspondence. Arthur will allow us to quote from his journals. I have LaSalle's diary and Bram's letters – and even one of the policeman's notebooks. I have included the telegrams from Marlborough House. It's all here.'

From the floor beneath my chair I produced a foolscap file, two inches deep.

Oscar was laughing at me now and, at the same time, lighting one of his favourite Turkish cigarettes. 'You cannot publish, Robert.'

'Who is to stop me?'

'In England? The courts.'

'And here? In France? In America? Doyle was paid ten thousand dollars for his last book.'

Oscar blew a thin plume of blue smoke into the air and grinned. 'Indeed. I had heard it wasn't very good.'

'I have all the papers,' I bleated, 'in chronological order.'

'I am sure that you do, my dear friend. Chronology has always been one of your longer suits. Keep the papers safe.'

'I have done that,' I said, tapping my file of foolscap with my forefinger. 'But I need your help, Oscar. I need to provide a linking narrative.'

'Oh no, Robert. Spare us the linking narrative! Present your evidence, lay out your material in chronological order, and leave it at that. Let the facts speak for themselves.'

'In that case,' I said, sliding the file across the table towards my friend, 'the book is done. Here they are – the facts. Make of them what you will.'

Oscar stubbed out his cigarette on a small circle of salami and sat forward to look me in the eye. 'You are proposing that I should read this material, Robert?'

'I am, Oscar – if you would be so kind.'

'It is a true story, you say?'

'It is – and you are part of it.'

'And you wish me to read it? Today? This very after-noon? When Dante calls and Baudelaire lies waiting?'

'Yes, Oscar, today – this very afternoon. Dante and Baudelaire will still be here tomorrow.'

'In that case, Robert,' he said, his fingers slowly untying the red ribbon around the file, 'I'll succumb to the temptation. Fetch me one more glass of absinthe, *mon ami*, and I will begin. As I remember nothing, the story will at least have the charm of the unexpected.'

Grosvenor Square
London, 1890

1

TO HAVE THE HONOUR OF MEETING
THEIR ROYAL HIGHNESSES
THE PRINCE OF WALES AND PRINCE ALBERT VICTOR

THE DUCHESS OF ALBEMARLE
AT HOME
THURSDAY, 13TH MARCH

RSVP   TEN O'CLOCK
40 GROSVENOR SQUARE, LONDON W.   DECORATIONS

HRH the Prince of Wales honoured the Duke and
Duchess of Albemarle with his presence last night at a
reception at Their Graces' London residence, 40
Grosvenor Square, W. HRH Prince Albert Victor, newly
returned from India, accompanied his father. General
Sir Dighton Probyn VC, treasurer and comptroller of
His Royal Highness's household, and Mr Harry
Tyrwhitt Wilson, equerry, were in attendance.

Among the many guests, representing the worlds of
art and science, were Lord Leighton, President of the
Royal Academy, and Sir George Stokes, President of the
Royal Society, as well as such notabilities as Professor
Jean-Martin Charcot from the Pitié-Salpêtrière Hospital
in Paris, Lord Yarborough, the physician and nerve
specialist, Mr Oscar Wilde, the poet, and Dr Arthur
Conan Doyle, creator of the popular detective, 'Sherlock
Holmes'.

From the notebooks of Robert Sherard

Oscar contrived to secure me an invitation to the Albemarle reception. I was, he told the Duchess, his 'confidential secretary'. 'If the Prince of Wales can come with a whole entourage – son, comptroller, equerry, valet, footmen – can a prince of words not be permitted an attendant scribe? Your beauty, Your Grace, may inspire a sonnet. I will need someone on hand to note it down.'

Her Grace obliged.

All evening Oscar was at his most ebullient. As we arrived, and he handed his hat and coat to the butler, he said to the poor man, 'Oh, Pierre, my usual table, if you please – away from the draughts and as far from the orchestra as possible.' When we were greeted by our hostess – an exquisitely beautiful young woman with huge eyes and a porcelain complexion – Oscar permitted her to kiss him full on the mouth and presented me to her saying, 'She is lovelier than a lily, is she not? She is Helen, late of Troy, now of Grosvenor Square.'

When we were presented to the Prince of Wales, Oscar was more circumspect, but only somewhat. I have always understood that with royalty one does not initiate a conversation: one waits to be spoken to. If that is the rule, Oscar ignored it. After he had bowed low before the prince, he stood at his side, towering over him, chatting away as though he and His Royal Highness were two old chums who had chanced to meet up for a drink before dinner at the club.

Where was the dear Princess of Wales?

In Denmark, visiting her parents.

Was she well? Oscar *so* hoped so. And how was the Queen? 'How *is* Her Majesty?' purred Oscar.

'Seventy and more robust than ever,' answered the prince drily. 'The air on the Isle of Wight appears to suit her. She goes from strength to strength.'

'I am happy to hear it,' Oscar murmured. 'We are all indebted to the Eternal Father. Your Royal Highness has the better of us. You are blessed with the eternal mother.'

The prince clapped his hands together and laughed out loud. 'I like that, Oscar. I like that very much. I'll borrow that, if I may.'

Oscar bowed obligingly as the prince's barking laugh turned into a wheezing cough. His equerry stepped forward and relieved the prince of his cigar. His Royal Highness fumbled for a handkerchief.

'And are you well, sir?' asked Oscar, solicitously.

'Mustn't complain,' spluttered the prince.

He is not yet fifty, but he looks much older. He has deep lines on his forehead and heavy bags beneath his eyes. He is fat and his hands shake.

'If I may say so, sir, you are looking remarkably well,' Oscar declared. Impertinently, he added: 'I believe that

4

an inordinate passion for pleasure is the secret of remaining young.'

'If you say so, Oscar,' replied the prince, pocketing his handkerchief and retrieving his cigar from the equerry. 'You say a lot of clever things.'

I said nothing. When Oscar had presented me to the heir apparent, I was offered a cursory nod of the princely head, but that was all. His Royal Highness neither addressed me nor looked again in my direction. His focus was entirely on Oscar. Oscar commands attention. And Oscar and the prince are well acquainted. According to Oscar, you cannot say they are friends. 'Royalties offer you friendliness, not friendship.' However, they have known one another for a number of years, since the late 1870s when Oscar, then in his early twenties, floated down from Oxford to be taken up by London society.

They met first, I believe, in Lowndes Square, at a tea party of Lady Sebright's, where the novelty of the afternoon was a demonstration of 'thought-reading' performed by the celebrated Professor Onofroff. They were last together in December just past at another of Professor Onofroff's interesting demonstrations. According to Oscar, the prince is a student of thought-reading. His Royal Highness is better known, of course, as a student of feminine beauty and, in the early days, the bond that really bound them was their mutual admiration for the matchless Mrs Lillie Langtry.

Oscar appeared to be reading the royal mind. 'Age cannot wither her, nor custom stale her infinite variety,' he said, apparently out of the blue. 'I hear Mrs Langtry is to play Cleopatra next.'

'How did you know I was just thinking about Mrs Langtry?' demanded the prince.

'Because whenever we meet, Your Royal Highness, we speak of the Jersey Lily. Besides, if I am not mistaken, Your Highness went to the St James's Theatre to see her give her Rosalind last night.'

The Prince of Wales drew on his cigar and looked at Oscar suspiciously. 'Remarkable. A moment ago Conan Doyle was telling me you'd turned detective – and here you are proving it. I did indeed see Mrs Langtry give her Rosalind last night and very fine she was too. But how did you deduce that?'

'I didn't. I read it in the court circular this morning,' replied Oscar, smiling.

'Ah, yes, of course,' mumbled the prince, momentarily thrown. He glanced about the room and nodded in the direction of Arthur Conan Doyle who was standing not far away, engaged in earnest conversation with General Sir Dighton Probyn. 'Conan Doyle's a good man. Solid. Improbable as it sounds, he tells me that you have the makings of a proper Sherlock Holmes. He has sent me his new story. It's even better than the first. Sherlock Holmes is a masterly creation.'

The prince was now shifting from one foot to the other. It was evident that our audience was drawing to a close.

'You've a new book coming, haven't you, Oscar? You'll send it to me, won't you? I want a first edition, mind.'

'As Your Royal Highness pleases,' said Oscar, with a modest bow, adding, as we backed away from the heir apparent, 'It is, of course, the second editions of my books that are the true rarities.'

The prince laughed amiably, raised a valedictory hand to Oscar and then, briskly, turned towards his equerry who was ushering Lord Yarborough and Sir George Stokes into the royal presence.

'I need a glass of champagne, Robert,' said Oscar, as soon as we had removed ourselves from the princely orbit. 'Would you be an angel and fetch me one?' He stood in contemplation for a moment, his eyes scanning the crowd. 'Arthur's in his element,' he murmured, smiling.

Dr Conan Doyle was now on the far side of the drawing room, standing on tiptoes, eagerly, at the outer edge of a circle of guests gathered about a small, stout, square-faced foreigner. The gentleman in question was clearly a foreigner: he was incorrectly attired – in a black frock-coat rather than evening dress – and wore his silver hair long at the back and heavily oiled. He was holding court, his right hand tucked firmly inside his coat-front in the manner of the late Napoleon Bonaparte, his left held out before him dramatically as if to arrest an oncoming train.

'*C'est le professeur Jean-Martin Charcot*,' explained Oscar, 'the great French physician, the "Napoleon of neuroses".' He laughed. 'He clearly has Arthur mesmerised.'

'Do you know him?'

'I saw him on stage at the Lyceum once, demonstrating his mesmeric powers. He holds your attention, but he doesn't make you laugh. Unlike Prince Eddy.'

Oscar's amused gaze had now fallen on the dapper

figure of Prince Albert Victor, the Prince of Wales's eldest son. The young prince was standing a few feet away from Professor Charcot's admirers, in the doorway to the ballroom. He was surrounded by wide-eyed, giggling women and obsequious, guffawing men.

'Now His Royal Highness should be on the stage. Look, Robert. As he tells his story, he is actually twirling his moustaches like a pantomime villain!'

'He looks remarkably swarthy,' I said, 'not at all as I expected.'

'Do you not read the papers? He is newly returned from India. He has been doing his duty, polishing the jewel in the Queen Empress's crown.'

'I hope you are going to present me to His Royal Highness?' I said.

'No, Robert. You are far too young.'

'I am older than the prince.'

'In years, possibly, not in experience. The boy is all corruption. It's well known – and plain to see. Sin is a thing that writes itself across a man's face. It cannot be concealed.'

Oscar turned away from Prince Eddy and his fawning entourage and surveyed the drawing room once more. 'When you have found our champagne,' he said, eventually, 'you will find me over there, Robert, by the fireplace, with that young man. He has no one to laugh at his jokes and he has rather caught my fancy. He has no sinister moustache and the most perfect profile, don't you think?'

Standing before the fireplace, alone, was a slender youth – tall, elegant, with a pale face and hooded eyes.

In his buttonhole he wore an amaryllis, Oscar's favourite flower. His head was held high, with a cultivated arrogance. With one hand he was brushing back his jet-black hair. With the other he held a Turkish cigarette to his highly coloured lips.

'Do you know him?' I asked.

'A little,' answered Oscar. 'I should like to know him better.'

'You have met him?'

'Once, just a few days ago. By chance. I came home and found him outside my house, standing in the street, looking up at the windows. It was gone midnight. He said he just happened to be passing, taking an evening stroll, but I think he sought me out. He is an "admirer". He knows all about me. He told me that his ambition is the same as mine – to be famous or, if not famous, at least notorious.'

'What is his name?' I enquired.

'Rex LaSalle,' said Oscar. 'He comes from the Channel Islands – like you and Lillie Langtry. He shares my birthday, the sixteenth of October. But he's your sort of age, I think. Twenty-seven, twenty-eight.'

'He looks younger.'

'Indeed.'

'What does he do?'

'By day, very little, it seems. He sleeps during the hours of light, apparently. He claims to be an actor – and an artist, a painter of sorts, but I've not seen any of his work. I have my doubts.'

'And by night?'

'By night? Oh, by night, he claims to be a vampire.'

I looked towards the beautiful young man with

the perfect profile, drawing slowly on his Turkish cigarette.

Oscar continued: 'I agree, Robert. He had already caught my attention. There was no need for that.'

4

From the diary of Rex LaSalle

'The first duty in life is to be as artificial as possible.
What the second duty is no one has yet discovered.'

I was on duty tonight – and on song. I now have
Oscar in my thrall. He was captivated. I know it. He
told me so. This was only our second encounter, but
he declared that he feels that he has known me since
the days when Zeus and Mnemosyne were lovers on
the slopes of Mount Parnassus! He adores my profile.
He admired my buttonhole – and noticed how
exactly it matched his own. 'One should either be a
work of art, or wear a work of art.' He was enchanted
with the way in which I quoted his own phrases and
philosophies back to him. 'To love oneself is the
beginning of a life-long romance.'

I have made a conquest.

When first I told him that I was a vampire, he was
amused. 'One should always be a little improbable,'
he said.

Tonight he took me much more seriously. He told
me that he had heard that vampires cast no shadows,
but he sensed that the shadow I cast over him would
be a long one. He made enquiries about my mode of
life. He asked where I lived and where I slept. He

asked about my parents. He asked what I did about money. He asked what I did about love. He said, 'Love and gluttony justify everything.' He was playful and earnest by turns.

When his friend joined us with two glasses of champagne, Oscar offered me his. I declined, politely. He pressed me to drink.

'You look pale,' he said.

'I am pale,' I replied, 'I am a vampire. Iced champagne is your drink of choice: blood is mine.' I looked him directly in the eye. 'Have you ever tasted blood, Mr Wilde?' I asked. 'Fresh blood, blood that is warm to the tongue. Human blood.'

'No,' he answered, 'the wine list at my club is dreadfully limited.'

We laughed and then his friend turned to me and enquired, lightly: 'Will you be drinking blood tonight?'

'Yes,' I said, 'I must.'

'And whose blood will it be?' asked Oscar.

I drew languorously on my cigarette and surveyed the crowded drawing room. At last I pointed across the throng. 'Hers,' I said.

'Who is that?' asked Oscar. 'I can't see.'

'Our hostess. The Duchess of Albemarle. She is very lovely, is she not?'

'She is indeed,' said Oscar. 'Helen, late of Troy . . .'

'Now of Grosvenor Square.' I finished his line for him – and we laughed once more. He has a most infectious laugh.

5

Letter from Arthur Conan Doyle to his younger brother, Innes Doyle

Langham Hotel,
London, W.
14.iii.90

Dearest boy –

I write as I had promised – but I write in haste. I am your older brother and I stand in loco parentis. *I am addressing you seriously now – sternly, even.*

These exams of yours are vital to your future. To be an officer in the British army is something noble. Pass these examinations and your future in the Sappers is assured. Fail them and where will you be? Adrift – with neither parents nor brother in a position to support you. You have lots of brains – all you want is steady undeviating industry. Think of nothing else, Innes, I beg you, until this is done. Put your heart and soul into it. You will find that work becomes a pleasure when you stick close to it. Achieve this and you will have all your life then for sport or riding or cricket or what you will.

I had hoped to say all this to you in more measured tones, but time is against me and it is perhaps no bad thing that I am obliged to be brief and to the point.

*There can at least be no misunderstanding. I am
writing in such haste because of a royal summons . . .
Indeed! I am in London on the morning after a
memorable night before. I was a guest last evening at
the Duke of Albemarle's reception for the arts and
sciences. I was presented to the Prince of Wales! HRH
was amiability itself. I wanted to speak of* Micah
Clarke *– ten thousand copies sold! – and my new
outrage,* The Captain of the Pole-Star, *but the heir
apparent wished to speak only of Sherlock Holmes!*

*I spent time also with HRH's private secretary, the
great Sir Dighton Probyn. When he was twenty-four
and a captain in the 2nd Punjab Cavalry, his daring
and gallantry during the Indian Mutiny earned him
the Victoria Cross. Let him be your role model!*

*I was furthermore presented to HRH's eldest, Prince
Eddy – a naval cadet in his youth and in the army
now, but a very weak-looking individual with a
sorrowful moustache quite unbecoming an officer and
gentleman. I doubt that he was required to pass
examinations to gain his present position! I will tell
you more when I see you next.*

*My friend Oscar Wilde was also of the party. He is
the wittiest man I know. He cannot stop talking. 'I like
hearing myself talk,' he declared last night, 'it is one
of my greatest pleasures.' He repeats himself
unashamedly, but there is a sweetness to him that I
find most endearing. And at Oxford, he won every
prize that was open to him. He affected indolence, but,
in truth, was the personification of* industry. *It is the
only way.*

Enough! I will send you something on your

birthday – you may be sure of that. And be a good fellow and drop me a line so that I may be sure you have hearkened to my words and are pegging to it. You have it in you. Onward! For our dear mother's sake.

Ever your loving bro.,
   Arthur

PS I have just seen today's newspaper. The Duchess of Albemarle – my hostess last evening – was found dead in her bed in the early hours of this morning. A heart attack is suspected. She was only thirty (my age), but had been in poor health for some time.

6

From the *Evening News*, London,
Friday, 14 March 1890

STOP PRESS

The sudden death was announced this morning of Her
Grace the Duchess of Albemarle. Born Helen Lascelles,
the daughter of Major Sir William Lascelles Bt, of
Welwyn, Herts, she married Henry, 7th Duke of
Albemarle, in 1885, when she was twenty-five and
His Grace was sixty. There were no children of the
marriage.

Noted for her beauty, philanthropy and devotion to
the arts, the duchess was a friend of the Prince of Wales
who attended a reception at her house in Grosvenor
Square only last evening. Her body was discovered by
her maid this morning. It is believed that the duchess
had been under medical supervision for some time, due
to the feebleness of her heart. The duke is reported to be
devastated by the death of his young wife.

A statement just issued from Marlborough House
reads: 'HRH the Prince of Wales KG, KT, is much
saddened to learn of the tragic death of Her Grace the
Duchess of Albemarle.'

The Metropolitan Police Commissioner has been
informed of the tragedy, but foul play is not suspected.

7

From the notebooks of Robert Sherard

What happened?

At midnight the Prince of Wales departed. I noted the time because, standing at the fireplace with Oscar and his curious new friend, I heard the distinct chimes of the ormolu clock that stood upon the mantelpiece behind us.

As HRH made to go, a hush fell on the crowded assembly. As the Red Sea once divided, so a path miraculously appeared in the midst of the throng. The prince, with his son and heir at his side, and their retinue in tow, proceeded through the drawing room and across the ballroom and out on to the first-floor gallery. Gentlemen bowed their heads and ladies curtsied to the ground as the royal party passed. The portly prince murmured benevolent farewells as he made his egress, wafting cigar smoke over his people as a thurifer wafts incense across his congregation.

Oscar, devoted to royalty as only a republican can be, whispered, 'Let's see him go,' and beckoned me to follow him. We slipped out of the drawing room by the nearest door and found ourselves, alone, at one end of the first-floor gallery as the prince and his party emerged on to it at the other. HRH noticed us and called out, 'Goodnight, Mr Wilde!'

Oscar, gratified, bowed low. 'Goodnight, sweet prince!' he responded.

We watched the royal party descend the stairs. Awaiting them, on either side of the front door, were two short lines of servants: to the left, representatives of the Albemarle household, headed by the butler; to the right, the prince's valet, two royal footmen and a young police constable in uniform. Alone, in the middle of the hallway, stood the Duke of Albemarle. He appeared fretful and looked up the stairway anxiously as the heir apparent moved towards him.

'No duchess?' enquired the prince.

'I have lost her!' laughed the duke awkwardly.

'No matter,' said the prince graciously. 'It has been a splendid evening. You will thank her for me, won't you, Albemarle?'

'I will indeed, sir. Thank you for honouring us with your presence.'

The duke bowed to each prince in turn, shook hands with Sir Dighton Probyn and Tyrwhitt Wilson, and accompanied the royal party out of the front door and into Grosvenor Square. We heard the clatter of hooves and the rumble of wheels as the princely carriages departed.

Oscar stood back, lighting a cigarette, while I remained in the gallery, looking down into the hallway. The Duke of Albemarle returned from the street and, as the front door was closed behind him, stood still for a moment, covering his face with his hands. He took a long, deep breath, as if both to calm himself and to gather his forces. He then turned enquiringly towards his butler who simply shook his head. The duke nodded and the butler went about his business.

The servants in the hallway began to scatter. The guests on the first floor began to emerge on to the gallery. I remained where I was for a moment longer, gazing down over the wooden balustrade, watching the duke below. Turning to his right, he stepped quickly and lightly across the hall towards a doorway in the corner. Without pause, he opened the door and, fumbling for a moment, removed the key from the inside lock. He then closed the door and immediately locked it from the outside. I saw him tuck the key into his waistcoat pocket.

I saw something else as well. Inside the door, immediately within it, I saw – only for a moment, but clearly, unmistakably – the standing figure of a young woman, her torso naked.

'Where's Rex?' asked Oscar, resting his right hand on my shoulder.

'He has gone,' I answered. 'He was complaining of a headache.'

Marlborough House

8

Telegram delivered to Oscar Wilde at 16 Tite Street, Chelsea, on Friday, 14 March 1890 at 8.15 a.m.

A CERTAIN PERSON URGENTLY REQUESTS AND REQUIRES YOUR PRESENCE AT TWELVE NOON TODAY FRIDAY AT SARAH CHURCHILL RESIDENCE. BRING ARTHUR CONAN DOYLE WITH YOU. TELL NO ONE. STRICTEST CONFIDENCE ESSENTIAL. SINCERELY OWL

9

Note from Oscar Wilde to Arthur Conan Doyle, delivered by hansom cab to the Langham Hotel at 9.15 a.m.

16 Tite Street
14.iii.90

Good morning, Arthur —

I trust you are still at your porridge and have not left for Southsea. If there is to be an outbreak of measles on the south coast, it must wait until tomorrow.

We have received a royal summons for today. You and I are commanded to attend upon the Prince of Wales at 12 noon. I will collect you at your hotel at 11.30 a.m. I do not know the nature of our business with HRH, but I conjecture — and I have fears. Robert Sherard — though not summoned — will come with us. If it is as terrible as I think it may be, he is a witness. For the time being, we are not to speak of this to anyone.

Ever yours,
Oscar

From the journal of Arthur Conan Doyle

What do I make of Oscar's friend, Sherard? He is pleasant enough, but there is something about the fellow that isn't quite right.

He is the son of a clergyman, the grandson of an earl and the great-grandson of William Wordsworth, but shows no sense of family pride. He went to a good school (Queen Elizabeth College, Guernsey) and a better university (Oxford), but failed to take his degree. He has travelled widely and boasts of his acquaintance with the likes of Emile Zola and Guy de Maupassant, but lives in a garret in Gower Street, earning his crust from cheap journalism.

Is he to be trusted? He has a weak face and a poor handshake. Is he a wrong 'un? Or simply one of those men destined never quite to hit his stride? Oscar I trust completely – he is a gentleman to the marrow – and his wife is an enchantment – but there is no denying that some of their circle leave me cold.

From the diary of Rex LaSalle

I did not sleep last night. I took the air. I needed it. When I left Grosvenor Square, as a black cat – an alpine lynx – why not? – I walked west until dawn. I took my time. The moon was full and my heart was heavy. I crossed the river at Hammersmith and went on, over Barn Elms, to Mortlake. I shall sleep here. I shall sleep alone. Other people are quite dreadful. The only possible society is one's own.

12

I slept at Tite Street, on the divan in Oscar's writing room. Mrs Wilde (who grows ever lovelier in my eyes) served what she termed a 'boys' breakfast' – poached eggs, bacon, grilled lamb chops and fried potatoes. Because her own boys were at the table – Vyvyan is just three and Cyril not yet five – we spoke not a word of the previous night's proceedings. As we feasted, Oscar, at his most gay, entertained his little ones with outlandish tales of faithless mermaids and dwarfish princes.

At eleven o'clock, a four-wheeler called to collect us from the door and drove us across town, in bright sunshine, to the Langham Hotel by Regent's Park. The smell of spring and straw were in the air. As we turned into Portland Place, Oscar said, 'Arthur will be on the pavement waiting for us, scrubbed and polished, eyes gleaming, moustache bristling. He is a good man.'

He was. He is. I like him.

'What's all this about?' asked the doctor eagerly, as he climbed aboard. He perched on the carriage seat facing us. Oscar passed him the telegram he had received. Conan Doyle inspected it carefully.

'"A certain person." is the Prince of Wales?'

'I am assuming so,' said Oscar.

'And the Sarah Churchill residence?'

'Marlborough House. Sarah Churchill was the first Duchess of Marlborough. It was built for her.'

'And who on earth is "Owl"?'

'"Owl" I take to be Tyrwhitt Wilson, the prince's equerry.'

Conan Doyle raised an eyebrow.

'"Tyrwhitt-tyrwhoo",' said Oscar, raising an eyebrow of his own. 'A schoolboy nickname. I am merely guessing. You know these English gentlemen – they never really leave their prep schools.'

Conan Doyle laughed and handed the telegram back to Oscar, who folded it neatly into his pocket book.

'But why the coded summons?' asked Doyle. 'Why the need for secrecy?'

'His Royal Highness fears a scandal. His mother does not like them.'

'Will the Duchess of Albemarle's death provoke a scandal?'

'It might.' Oscar turned to me and lightly flicked his lilac gloves across my knuckles. 'Robert, tell Arthur what you saw last night – after the prince had gone, when you were looking down into the hallway from the gallery.'

I told my story, as simply and briefly as I could. As I told it, Conan Doyle tugged furiously at his walrus moustache.

'Was she stark naked?' he asked.

'I saw only her torso.'

'Was she wearing nothing?'

'A tiara, I think, and ruby earrings.'

'Are you certain?'

'No. The door was open only for a moment. I caught

merely the briefest glimpse. I could not tell you whether she was alive or dead.'

'Was it the duchess?'

'I don't know. She was young. Her skin was white as snow. It might have been.'

'I don't recall the duchess wearing ruby earrings,' remarked Oscar, peering out on to the street, 'but I'm a man and men don't notice such things.'

Conan Doyle shook his head in disbelief. Our carriage was pulling off Pall Mall and into the forecourt of Marlborough House.

'Last night I thought little of it,' continued Oscar, straightening his waistcoat before adjusting his button-hole, 'horseplay in Mayfair, nothing more. Now I am less certain. And more anxious. We shall see.'

Oscar is a big man: more than six feet in height and well fleshed. He affects torpor and proclaims a disdain for exercise, but he is more alert, stronger and more agile than his detractors imagine. He jumped down from the four-wheeler with ease.

Harry Tyrwhitt Wilson awaited us inside the grey stone portico. He, too, is tall, but spare, thin as a whippet, with a long, mournful greyhound's face and an absurd waxed moustache that gives him the look of a comic villain in an Italian opera. As we climbed the steps towards him, Oscar whispered me a warning: 'Take care. He may not be the fool he seems.'

Tyrwhitt Wilson greeted us with easy courtesy and, if he was surprised to find me of the party, he did not show it. 'Robert Harborough Sherard, is it not?' he said affably as he shook my hand. 'I've been looking you up. Your father has a different name.'

'We had a falling out.'

'Say no more. I've not spoken with my papa in years. It's cost me a fortune.'

The equerry led us swiftly through the house, through mirrored doors, across hallways, along corridors, around corners, past chambers and ante-chambers, stairways, vestibules and drawing rooms. The house is a maze – and a wonderland. The chandeliers come from Venice, the tapestries from Gobelin, the taste from the Princess of Wales. We passed scarlet-coated footmen in powdered wigs at every turn and half-familiar paintings on every wall. Oscar named the artists as we sped by: 'Lely, Laguerre, Rubens, Gentileschi if I'm not mistaken . . .'

'You rarely are, Mr Wilde,' said Tyrwhitt Wilson, laughing. 'I think we'll find His Royal Highness is in the Chinese Drawing Room.'

As he spoke, a page (a Nubian in a dark-blue coat with golden buttons) pushed open the final doorway and admitted us to the royal presence.

It took a moment to discern the heir apparent.

The Prince of Wales was half hidden, lurking between a bust by Canova and a potted palm. His mouth was full. He held a substantial silver goblet in one hand and a cheese straw the size of a large cigar in the other.

'You have caught me unawares,' he mumbled, padding towards us. His genial smile revealed pastry trapped between his teeth. 'My secret is out. They call me Tum-Tum. And now you discover why. I take it as a term of endearment.' He chuckled, then sniffed and inspected us as we stood, bowing before him. 'Good morning, gentlemen,' he declared. 'I am grateful for your prompt attendance.'

Suddenly his brow furrowed. He looked at me and, grunting softly, raised a wary eyebrow.

Tyrwhitt Wilson spoke up at once. 'May I present Mr Robert Harborough Sherard, Your Royal Highness? I believe his father was the Anglican chaplain on the island of Guernsey, when last you were there, sir. He was presented.'

'Was he?' muttered the prince.

'Mr Sherard is my confidential secretary, sir,' said Oscar soothingly. 'My equerry, you might say. And my recording angel.' Oscar glanced in the direction of Conan Doyle. 'My Dr Watson.'

'Your Dr Watson, eh?' repeated the prince, turning to cast a nod in the direction of the two footmen who, mysteriously, had emerged from behind a Chinese screen, bearing trays laden with refreshment. 'That's apropos – though I want no record kept of any of this.' The prince looked back at us with a gimlet eye. 'Is that understood, gentlemen?'

'Without question, sir,' said Oscar, raising his beaker of champagne as if drinking a loyal toast. 'We are your liegemen and true.'

'You are an Irishman, Oscar, and a republican,' said the prince, laughing.

'Not at Marlborough House, sir,' purred Oscar ingratiatingly.

'I am happy to hear it. I am happy to have you here. I am grateful. I need your help, gentlemen. I have a case for you.'

'A case?' queried Oscar.

'Well – how shall I put it? I have some enquiries I'd be grateful if you might make on my behalf. Discreetly.' The prince smiled.

Arthur Conan Doyle cleared his throat. 'Sherlock Holmes is a figment of my imagination, Your Royal Highness.'

'Of course, I know that, Doyle. But, last night, you were telling me how you and Wilde had recently unravelled a mystery together. Is that not correct?'

'Yes, sir,' answered the good doctor, hesitantly. 'But—'

'Well, now I have another for you. That's all. It may amount to nothing.'

'We are at Your Royal Highness's service,' said Oscar emphatically.

'Indeed,' muttered Conan Doyle, with noticeably less conviction.

The Prince of Wales turned to the Scottish doctor. 'Do you not have time for this, Doyle? You told me last night that your medical practice is not very absorbing.'

'It is not, sir,' said Conan Doyle, quietly.

'It's in Southsea, sir,' said Oscar, by way of explanation.

'Southsea,' echoed the prince. 'I have been there. They looked fit enough to me.'

'They are,' said Conan Doyle, rallying. 'That is the problem.'

We laughed and then fell silent. The prince waited for the footmen to replenish our champagne and leave the room. 'Now, gentlemen,' he said, when they were gone, 'to business.'

We stood in a loose circle – the fat prince, the lean equerry, the anxious doctor, the ebullient poet and I: a motley fairy ring – and waited. Silence descended once more.

'Where to begin?' asked the prince, eventually.

'At the beginning?' suggested Conan Doyle.

'No,' said Oscar softly. 'The beginning is where we will end, I imagine.' I noticed the prince glance towards Oscar. 'Let us start with last evening,' Oscar continued, returning the prince's gaze. 'I take it the matter in hand concerns the late Duchess of Albemarle?'

'It does,' said the prince, with a small sigh, 'most certainly. Poor Helen.' He wiped some crumbs of pastry from his beard. 'It does indeed concern the duchess – and her untimely death.' He looked into our faces. 'Have you seen what the newspapers are saying this morning?'

'They are saying that foul play is not suspected,' said Conan Doyle.

'Exactly,' declared the prince, clapping the palm of his left hand against the knuckles of his right. 'And why are they saying that? For the very reason that foul play *is* suspected. Or if it isn't, they want it to be.'

'Journalism justifies its own existence by the great Darwinian principle of the survival of the vulgarest,' said Oscar, draining his goblet of champagne. 'The leading articles in our newspapers offer nothing but prejudice, stupidity, cant and twaddle – leaving the news reports to concentrate on scandal and scurrility. The very phrase "foul play is not suspected" is designed to arouse suspicion.'

'Precisely, Oscar.'

'And in this instance, sir,' asked Conan Doyle, looking earnestly into the now-troubled face of the Prince of Wales, 'do you suspect foul play?'

'I cannot answer that question, Dr Doyle. I am perplexed. I need to know more. I learnt of the duchess's death only three hours ago. The duke sent round a brief note containing the terrible news, but he did little more than provide the bare facts. I tried to contact him by telephone – to speak with him directly, to learn more and to extend my condolences. They have a telephone in Grosvenor Square. The duke is proud of it. But there was no reply. As matters stand, I know no more than you do.'

'Possibly less,' murmured Oscar, almost imperceptibly, glancing in my direction. I made to speak. Oscar shook his head.

The prince broke from the circle, smacking his hand against his fist once more. 'Gentlemen,' he said, 'I would be grateful if you would call at Grosvenor Square and discover what you can.' He nodded towards his equerry. 'Harry cannot go. The press men know him – and know how he arranges my affairs. His presence would certainly arouse suspicion. Yours will not.'

'What about the police?' suggested Conan Doyle.

The prince turned on the doctor in amazement. 'Good grief, man, what are you suggesting? This is a delicate matter. It calls for finesse and discretion, not the horny hands and hobnail boots of the lads from Scotland Yard.'

Oscar intervened, resting a hand on Conan Doyle's sleeve while offering the prince a gentle bow. 'We will call on the duke to extend our condolences,' he said smoothly, 'and we will discover what we can. It may be nothing.'

'Indeed,' said the prince, taking his hunter from his waistcoat pocket and inspecting the hour. 'It may be nothing. We can hope for that.'

He paused and adjusted the small pink rose that adorned his buttonhole. (As a gentleman of fashion, the Prince of Wales is even more fastidious than Mr Oscar Wilde.) Peering down at the dish of cheese straws that now sat upon a side table, he selected a large one.

'And yet she is dead,' he mused, 'and she ought not to be.' He looked back towards us. 'I will be candid with you, gentlemen. I am troubled. In his note to me, the duke spoke of his wife's enfeebled heart. I knew the duchess well. She never spoke to me of such a thing and we talked of her health on more than one occasion.'

Harry Tyrwhitt Wilson had moved towards the doorway. Evidently, our audience was at an end. Stepping backwards, slowly, we bowed our way out of the royal presence.

'Thank you, gentlemen,' said the prince, waving his cheese straw at us by way of farewell.

'My compliments to your new pastry chef, Your Royal Highness,' said Oscar, as we departed. 'He is just arrived from Madagascar?'

The prince laughed. 'Who told you?'

'No one,' answered Oscar. 'But Your Royal Highness's cheese straws have a new flavour – suggesting a new pastry chef. And it's a flavour I recognise. It is unique to a cinnamon from Madagascar.'

'You are extraordinary, Oscar.' The prince laughed. 'Doyle is right. You can out-Holmes Holmes. Bring your genius to bear on this matter, Oscar, and I will be much obliged. The duchess was my friend. I owe her this much.'

13

From the journal of Arthur Conan Doyle

Oscar is preposterous. As we climbed up into
our coach and four he freely admitted the
cheese-straw business was pure invention!
Laughing until his pale cheeks turned pink, he
declared: 'The prince will have no more idea
from whence his pastry chef comes than I do,
but the party piece reassured him – made him
feel that he did indeed have Holmes on the case.
Appearance is everything. It is only shallow
people who do not judge by appearances. You
know that, Arthur.'

I know no such thing. What I do know is that
already I have grave concerns about this. Why
will HRH not involve the police? He has
nothing to fear from them, surely? And why was
General Probyn not at our meeting? He is the
prince's private secretary. He is a man of long
experience and sound judgement. He has
bottom. And courage. His presence would have
reassured me completely. His absence leaves me
troubled.

The prince professes his concern for the late
duchess. That I accept. They were close. But how

close? Was their relationship as it should have been? Have Wilde and I been engaged to uncover the truth – or to assist in its suppression?

The Telephone Room

14

CERTIFICATE OF DEATH

Registration district: City of Westminster

Date and place of death: 14 March 1890, 40
Grosvenor Square, London W.

Name and surname: Helen Mary Alice ALBEMARLE

Sex: Female

Maiden surname of woman who has married:
LASCELLES

Date and place of birth: 11 October 1859,
Welwyn, Hertfordshire

Occupation and principal residence: Duchess,
Albermarle House, Eastry, Kent

Cause of death: Heart failure

Signature of certifying doctor: Yarborough MB
FRS

Date: 14 March 1890

15

From the notebooks of Robert Sherard

'I had not appreciated that Lord Yarborough is a practising physician.'

Arthur Conan Doyle spoke sternly. He is little more than my age, but his greying temples, bristling moustache, military bearing and fierce, piercing eyes combine to lend him an authority that belies his years.

'Lord Yarborough is many things,' replied the Duke of Albemarle.

'I know him by reputation,' said Oscar. 'He is versatile and unusually handsome, I believe.'

'I know him slightly,' continued Conan Doyle, 'as a specialist in nervous disorders. Not as a medical practitioner, but as a mind doctor. He's one of these modern men who like to call themselves "psychiatrists".'

'An ugly word,' said the duke.

'With beautiful origins,' said Oscar. 'It comes from the ancient Greek, *psyche* – the word for soul and breath and butterfly.'

The duke smiled at Oscar. 'I did not know. I have little Latin and less Greek.' He turned his attention back to Conan Doyle. 'Lord Yarborough is an old friend. He was a guest at last evening's reception. He stayed the night. We were fortunate that he was here.'

'Indeed,' answered Doyle, quietly.

We stood, the four of us, at the foot of the principal staircase in the main hallway at 40 Grosvenor Square, on the very spot where the Duke of Albemarle had stood the previous evening waiting to bid his royal guests farewell. The duke is sixty-five, of medium height, but well built, sturdy and broad-shouldered, with a round, red face, lined by wind rather than worry. His face reveals what the popular papers report: that he is a devotee of the outdoor life, a keen sportsman, one of those Englishmen who is only truly happy when he is riding to hounds.

He had found us by chance at the foot of the stairs. When the butler had admitted us to the hallway, we were advised that His Grace was resting and unable to receive callers. Oscar had pressed the servant to be so kind as to inform his master of our presence. The butler, pocketing the encouragement Oscar proffered, had made his way to the downstairs morning room. As the servant made his exit, the master appeared in the gallery above us. Oscar called up to him and the duke came down to meet us. He looked fatigued and ill-at-ease, dressed in heavy mourning.

'Good morning, gentlemen,' he said. 'Forgive me if I do not entertain you. It is a difficult time. You have heard the news?'

'We have, Your Grace,' said Oscar, gravely, 'and we have come to extend our condolences in person.'

In silence, briefly and without ceremony, as though we were estate workers come to pay our respects, the duke shook hands with each of us in turn. 'Thank you, gentlemen,' he said. 'Thank you kindly. Good day.' He turned to climb the stairs once more.

I made to depart, but Oscar and Conan Doyle, bolder spirits, stood their ground.

'We have come from Marlborough House,' said Oscar. The duke looked over his shoulder, surprised. 'The Prince of Wales asked us to call upon you to extend his condolences in person.'

The duke's brow furrowed. He held Oscar's gaze. 'But Sir Dighton Probyn has already called, Mr Wilde. He came on the prince's instructions. He came at noon.'

I caught my breath. Conan Doyle blanched. Oscar did not bat an eyelid. 'Quite so, Your Grace,' he continued. 'Sir Dighton Probyn's visit was the formal one. Ours is more personal.'

'Indeed?' enquired the duke, turning to face Oscar directly.

'His Royal Highness had hoped to speak to you by telephone,' continued Oscar, 'but found he was unable to do so.'

'The telephone is out of order,' said the duke.

'His Royal Highness was anxious to offer you the services of one of the royal physicians.'

'I'm obliged,' replied the duke, 'but there was no need. Lord Yarborough was already here.'

It was the mention of Lord Yarborough's name that provoked Conan Doyle. The young Scottish doctor began to cross-examine the elderly English duke with a severity bordering on effrontery.

'What does Lord Yarborough know of heart disease?' he asked.

'Lord Yarborough had been attending the duchess for some time. He understood her condition. He had warned me of the possibility of heart failure.'

40

'Did you not seek a second opinion?'

'I did not see the need. I know Lord Yarborough. I trust him. The duchess trusted him.'

'Do not think me impertinent, Your Grace. I am a doctor – in general practice. Might I be permitted to see the body of the deceased?'

The Duke of Albemarle made no response. He gazed at Conan Doyle impassively. An insect buzzed about our heads. The silence in the hallway was heavy. Outside, in the street, there was the clatter of hooves on cobbles and the noise of a carriage trundling past.

Eventually the duke spoke. 'Is that what the Prince of Wales would wish?' he asked.

'I believe so,' said Conan Doyle. His tone was gentler now. 'I understand Her Grace died during the night?'

'Yes.'

'At what time, do you know?'

'I do not know. We keep separate quarters. I did not see her before she went to bed.'

'She was discovered by her maid this morning?'

'Yes,' answered the duke, hesitating as he spoke. 'Yes, by her maid . . .'

'She was discovered by her maid in her bed?'

'Yes.' The duke faltered. 'No. No, she was not.' He looked directly at Conan Doyle. 'I discovered her.'

'In her bedroom?'

'No. No. I discovered her here – in the telephone room.'

The duke turned and looked in the direction of the corner doorway through which I had glimpsed the naked body of a young woman at midnight the night before.

'The telephone room,' repeated Conan Doyle. 'She died in the telephone room?' We all stood staring at the room's closed door. 'Why was she in the telephone room?'

'She must have come down during the night – to make a call. Or to receive one.'

'Where is her body now?' asked Conan Doyle.

'It has not been moved,' answered the duke. 'Lord Yarborough is returning with the undertakers. They are due at any moment.'

Conan Doyle took a small step towards the duke. 'Might I see her, Your Grace?'

'She is unclothed,' replied the duke, covering his face with his hands. 'She is dead.'

Conan Doyle pressed his hand on the duke's shoulder. 'It is quite in order. I am a medical man.'

16

From the journal of Arthur Conan Doyle

The duke remained outside the room, in the hallway with Oscar and Sherard. He unlocked the door, barely opened it to allow me to slip inside and shut it immediately after me. 'I must keep the door closed,' he said. 'Apart from Parker [the butler], the staff know nothing of this.'

The room itself was no more than a large cubicle, lit by a dim and flickering electric light. On the left of the door was a narrow wooden shelf on which stood the telephone apparatus. On the right was a tall wooden stool fixed to the wall. Perched upon the stool, leaning backwards into the corner, sat the half-naked body of the late Duchess of Albemarle.

It was a grotesque and pitiable sight. Beneath her velvet evening gown, the poor woman's legs dangled down from the stool. I brushed against them as I leant forward to study her face. Her eyes were open wide, staring, petrified. Her skin was pale grey, the colour of paving stones. Mucus had dried around her nostrils. Her white lips were twisted – contorted in pain, as I have sometimes seen on the victims of sudden, violent heart seizure. Her bodice and chemise had been ripped from her, exposing her full breasts, horribly disfigured with scratch marks. I touched her left arm and her naked belly. Her body was cold as stone but no longer rock hard. Rigor mortis was beginning to ease. She had not died within the past twelve hours.

I did not linger in the airless room. The horror was very great and the smell from the body already noticeable. Before I left, I made to close the dead woman's bulging, startled eyes. As I pressed my fingers against her eyelids to close them, her head lolled suddenly to the side and I saw some bloody marks upon her neck. They were of two sharp incisions, positioned below her earlobe, beneath her jaw, side by side, no more than an inch apart. The tears in the flesh were not wide – each was no more than an eighth of an inch in diameter – but they were deep. I took a matchstick from my pocket and carefully inserted it into each incision. The rupture was certainly deep enough to reach the jugular vein.

17

**Notes written by Oscar Wilde on the back of the
supper menu at Solferino's restaurant in Rupert Street**

When did the duchess die? Was she alive when Robert caught
sight of her at midnight? Or was she already dead? Did Robert
mistake the bloody marks on her neck for ruby earrings?

Why was she in the telephone room? What drew her there –
in the course of her own reception, at its very height, with
royalty present? If she was there to make use of the telephone,
why was the telephone itself apparently untouched?

When did the duke discover her body? He says it was in the
morning, at seven o'clock, when he went to use the telephone
himself – but Robert saw the duke at the door of the telephone
room at midnight. If his wife was missing at midnight – and
the duke knew that she was: she failed to say goodbye to her
guests – why did he not instigate a search for her then?

And once the body had been discovered, why was it left
hidden in the telephone room? Lord Yarborough – a mind
doctor, not a physician – examined her in the half-light and
concluded at once that she had died of heart failure. Why?
Why did he not order her body to be removed to the morgue
and examined properly there?

Is Yarborough to be trusted? Is he to be believed? Why did
he not examine the wounds upon her neck? In the gloom of
the room, did he not see them? And what caused those
wounds? _Who_ caused them? How exactly did the duchess die?

And _why_? Was it some unnatural horror? Was it murder? Was it suicide?

And which wine shall I take with my zabaglione? The Muscat de Lunel '87 or the darker Moscato from Sardinia? So many questions. As the divine Sarah [Bernhardt] says of the Ten Commandments: 'Zay are too many.'

18

From the diary of Rex LaSalle

To live is the rarest thing in the world. Most people exist, that is all. I live. And I rejoice that I am able to live as I do – freely, without fear and to the full. Tonight, Oscar came to my studio. Yes, I am now on intimate terms with Mr Oscar Wilde! He was alone. It was gone midnight. He had dined with a friend in Rupert Street. He had dined well. His cheeks were full of colour. His eyes sparkled. He sat on the edge of my bed and told me that he trusted me.

He took me into his confidence. He told me details of the death of the Duchess of Albemarle. He told me everything – so far as he knows it. Minutes before midnight, the duchess was alive and well. We saw her together across her crowded drawing room, entertaining her guests. At midnight, as the Prince of Wales departed, Oscar's friend, standing in the gallery, overlooking the hallway, caught sight of the duchess for the final time. He glimpsed her through an open doorway – the doorway to the telephone room. The unfortunate lady was already dead, said Oscar. She must have been. She was quite still and Oscar's friend saw stains of blood on her neck. At the time, he mistook them for ruby earrings.

It was the duke who discovered the duchess's body – but exactly when is not yet clear. Oscar's friend saw the duke at the door to the telephone room at midnight. He saw the duke open the door, remove a key from the inside lock and close the door. He did not see the duke enter the room or look within it. The duke claims to have come upon the body at seven o'clock this morning, when he went to make use of the telephone himself.

On discovering the tragedy, at once he alerted his butler, Parker, and his friend, Lord Yarborough – no one besides. Together the three men decided to leave the body in place – hidden in the locked telephone room – so as not to alarm the rest of the household. It was Parker's idea to tell the world that the duchess's body had been discovered in bed and by her maid. The maid is a simple-minded soul who can neither read nor write.

It was Lord Yarborough who signed the death certificate. He examined the dead woman as he found her and concluded that she had died of heart failure. Oscar does not believe it. Oscar told me – almost with relish, so it seemed to me – of the deep and bloody wounds in the duchess's neck.

'Are they the marks of a vampire?' he asked.

'I do not know,' I answered. 'I have not seen them.'

'But you are a vampire, are you not, Rex? You told me that you were.'

I made no reply. I sat next to him on the bed and turned my head so that he might better admire my profile.

'Who are you, Rex? What are you? What is your story? Will you tell me?'

As he laid his hand upon my knee, I turned back to him and smiled. As my lips parted to reveal the whiteness of my teeth and the sharpness of my fangs, he laughed and, throwing down his cigarette, made to kiss me.

Vermin in Grosvenor Square

19

Telegram delivered to Constance Wilde at 16 Tite
Street, Chelsea, on Friday, 14 March 1890 at 10 p.m.

CONSISTENCY IS THE LAST REFUGE OF THE
UNIMAGINATIVE. MY PLANS HAVE CHANGED.
FORGIVE ME DEAREST WIFE. DINING AT
SOLFERINO WITH ROBERT AND STAYING IN TOWN
AT THE CLUB. LOVE ME FOR MY DEFECTS AS I LOVE
YOU FOR YOUR PERFECTION. OSCAR

20

Letter from Arthur Conan Doyle to his wife, Louisa 'Touie' Conan Doyle

> *Langham Hotel,*
> *London W.*
> *14.iii.90*

> *7 p.m.*

Dearest Touie –

My own darling, forgive me. I shall not return to Southsea tomorrow as I had planned. I must stay in town until Tuesday now. All my arrangements have gone awry.

Today, as you know, I was due to travel to Muswell Hill to meet with the great Professor Charcot, to visit his clinic and to witness his experiments with hypnosis – but it was not to be. I was summoned instead to Marlborough House – for an audience with the Prince of Wales! You must not speak of it to anyone. I am bound to secrecy. I will explain all (or, at least, much) when I see you – in this matter, I may never be able to tell you everything.

I long to see you, Toodles. And Toodles Junior, too. Give my darling daughter a kiss. Give her one

thousand! No, give her one hundred and keep the rest
for yourself. No one deserves them more.

 Ever your loving husband,
  ACD

PS. Touie dearest – my heart is heavy tonight and for
two reasons. I miss you. And I am troubled by the
business in which I find myself involved. Oscar Wilde
is my companion in this adventure. That is something.
He is generous and a gentleman – and so witty. Today
he said, 'I like men who have a future and women who
have a past.' That is clever, is it not?

21

From the notebooks of Robert Sherard

It was mid-afternoon when we left the Duke of Albemarle. Parker, the butler, showed us out into the cool sunshine of Grosvenor Square.

'Do you think the butler did it?' mused Oscar, smiling, as we stepped into the street.

'It was undoubtedly murder,' said Conan Doyle, grimly. 'We must go to the police.'

'Not yet,' said Oscar, looking up at the cloudless sky and closing his eyes while breathing in the spring air. 'It is too soon. And nothing will be gained by it.'

'The police are already here,' I said.

'What do you mean?' snapped Conan Doyle.

I cast my eyes across the street. Standing on the corner opposite, beneath the gas lamp, were three men in dark overcoats and bowler hats. They had thick moustaches like Doyle's and were studying us.

'Those are not police officers in plain clothes, Robert. They are the gentlemen of the press.'

'How can you tell?'

'Look at their filthy boots. A policeman always polishes his. It's a matter of habit. A journalist never does, it's a matter of pride.' Oscar raised his hat in the direction of the three men. 'See,' he said. 'They are holding notebooks.' He gave a mock sigh. 'So it has come to this. There are now vermin above ground in Grosvenor Square.'

'I shall return to my hotel,' said Conan Doyle anxiously. 'I am troubled by all this, Oscar. Why did the Prince of Wales send us here this afternoon when he had already sent Sir Dighton Probyn this morning?'

'Because our mission was of a different nature, Arthur. More complex, more intriguing. And because the prince wanted Sir Dighton safely out of the way while he gave us his instructions.'

'Exactly,' sighed Conan Doyle. 'Where there are secrets, there are lies, and where there are lies, there is danger.'

'It's the danger that's half the excitement,' cried Oscar. 'Come on, Arthur. The game's afoot! There's been a murder in Mayfair and we can unravel the mystery.'

A hackney carriage, pulled by a handsome bay hackney stallion, rattled into view. Oscar raised his arm and waved his lilac gloves towards the coachman.

Conan Doyle rubbed his moustache uneasily. 'There's no doubt in my mind. I believe we should go to the police.'

Oscar laughed. 'To doubt is intensely engrossing, Arthur. To believe is very dull. To be on the alert is to live; to be lulled into security is to die.'

'Hmm,' grumbled Conan Doyle, shaking his head as he climbed into the hackney cab. 'The Langham Hotel, please,' he instructed the driver. 'Are you joining me?' he asked Oscar.

'No,' answered Oscar, cheerily. 'I shall give Robert a two-shilling dinner at Solferino and then begin on our enquiries in earnest. You go back to your hotel, Arthur. Write to your little wife in Southsea. Take supper in your room and do some work. Your paper is on histrionics, is it not?'

'Hysteria.'

'Quite so.' Oscar chuckled and slapped his gloves against the horse's flank. 'We shall meet in the morning, Arthur. Breakfast at the Savoy at nine o'clock? Don't be late. I want to introduce you to the world authority on vampires. You'll like him. He's Irish – like me. And the best of fellows – like you. He stole my first sweetheart from me, but I've forgiven him. She was too innocent. I like men who have a future and women who have a past, don't you?'

Conan Doyle smiled. The horse snorted. The hackney cab jerked into life and moved on. Doyle turned back and waved to us as the carriage left the square.

As our friend's cab disappeared at one side of Grosvenor Square, another four-wheeler – a fine brougham-landaulet, with a gold-embossed coat of arms on the nearside door – entered on the other. This elegant vehicle, pulled by a sprightly chestnut cob, was followed immediately by a second, more cumbersome one: a large, long, high-sided, enclosed four-wheeler, unmarked and all painted in black, drawn by a pair of heavy drays.

'A Black Maria,' I suggested.

'No,' countered Oscar. 'No windows. It's the death cart.'

He took me by the elbow and steered me across the cobbles, away from the trio of newspapermen, towards the gate leading to the gardens in the centre of the square.

'We can hide beneath the apple blossom,' he said.

The two carriages drew up outside 40 Grosvenor Square. Lord Yarborough stepped lightly down from the brougham-landaulet. Oscar describes him as unusually handsome – and so he is. He is around fifty years of age, but appears considerably younger. His profile is distinguished, his face is finely chiselled, his thick black hair is glossy, his walnut eyes shine. He wears no beard and dresses always in black and immaculately. In portraits, in photographs, at a distance, he looks magnificent. In reality, even in his riding boots, he is barely five feet tall.

'He is a pocket person,' whispered Oscar, as we closed the garden gate behind us. 'Handsome, versatile and dangerous.'

We watched as the gentlemen of the press approached his lordship. He waved them away dismissively. They shrank back, retreating without protest. A moment later, with a rattle and a clatter, the rear doors of the second vehicle were pushed open from within and five men, dressed in identical black serge suits, stepped out on to the pavement.

'The undertakers,' whispered Oscar. 'And what plain-looking fellows they are. Death, here is thy sting.'

Lord Yarborough climbed the steps to the front door of the Albemarle London residence. Even as he reached for the bell-pull, the door swung open. Parker's face appeared in the doorway, but no words were exchanged. His lordship swept into the house and Parker came down into the street.

Parker is easy to describe. He epitomises the caricature of the family retainer: he is sixty-five or thereabouts (and has been for ten years), silver-haired, ruddy-complexioned, clean-shaven with tufts of white hair growing from his cheeks; slightly stooped, a little slow, somewhat hard of hearing; utterly loyal, wholly unimaginative, thoroughly discreet.

'The hallmark of a first-rate butler is his readiness to commit murder for his employers,' observed Oscar, throwing a burnt match into the bushes and relishing a new cloud of cigarette smoke as it floated slowly through his nostrils.

Parker approached the undertakers and gave them their orders. Four of the men climbed back into the vehicle at the rear while the fifth joined Parker on the box seat with the driver at the front. The carriage lumbered off in the direction Conan Doyle's cab had taken.

'Where are they going?' I asked.

'Not far. I imagine to the mews behind the house. It seems that the unhappy duchess is to leave her home by the back door.'

'Shall we follow? The press men are going.'

'We don't follow the press men, Robert. They follow us.' He drew deeply on his cigarette and closed his eyes once more. 'Besides, there is no rush. I doubt that they'll bring out the body until after dark. Let us savour our smoke beneath the apple blossom for a while. Remember, pleasure is the only thing one should live for. No civilised man ever regrets a pleasure and no uncivilised man ever knows what a pleasure is.'

I smiled. 'Have I heard that before, Oscar?'

'You will hear it again, Robert, that's for sure.'

Oscar's gentle laughter was interrupted by the sharp clack of footsteps on the cobbles, followed by the dull screech of the garden gate being opened.

'Good evening, gentlemen,' said Lord Yarborough. His voice was light and high-pitched; his manner effortlessly courteous. 'I saw you standing here and thought I might take a moment to have a word. Would that be convenient?'

'Good evening, my lord,' replied Oscar, casting his cigarette into the bushes and offering the diminutive peer a lilac-gloved hand. 'I am Oscar Wilde.'

'Oscar Fingal O'Flahertie Wills Wilde,' responded Lord Yarborough. 'I know your name – and your reputation.' He smiled. 'I am acquainted with your friend, Dr Doyle. He speaks so highly of you.'

'And this is my friend, Mr Robert Sherard,' said Oscar.

Lord Yarborough turned and bowed towards me. 'Robert Harborough Sherard Kennedy,' he said. 'It is a pleasure. We are kinsmen, after all.'

'My lord?' I mumbled, confused, letting my own cigarette fall to the ground.

Lord Yarborough smiled at me. 'Your father is the natural son of the fifth and last Earl of Harborough, is he not?'

'He is.'

'My mother was Lord Harborough's legitimate daughter. She was born many years before your father, but our parents, Mr Sherard, were sister and brother. We are cousins.'

'My God,' I gasped. 'I had no idea.' I stood amazed.

'Bastard cousins, of course.'

'Of course.'

'My mother inherited everything. And your father . . . was given an education.'

'I had no idea,' I repeated. 'I knew none of this. We never spoke of my father's family at home.'

Oscar came to my rescue. 'Your mother is alive, my lord?' he asked.

'My mother is dead. And she was dead to me when she was alive. I did not care for her. She was a vain and ridiculous woman. Nor was she faithful to my father.'

'Your father was the late Earl of Yarborough?'

'Yes. My mother, Anne Harborough, married him not for love, but for reasons of euphony.'

Oscar laughed. Lord Yarborough stepped forward, bowed his head and shook my hand.

'Well, well,' said Oscar, opening his cigarette case and offering it around, 'this is a happy chance encounter.'

'Or would be,' said Lord Yarborough, standing back and selecting one of Oscar's Turkish cigarettes (the case contained three varieties), 'were it not for the tragedy across the road.' He rolled the cigarette between his fingers. 'That is heartbreaking.'

Oscar glanced back through the trees towards 40 Grosvenor Square. The front door was closed. The curtains were all drawn. Evening shadows were now falling on the house.

'We have just called upon His Grace,' he said.

'I know,' replied Yarborough. 'He has told me. We are old friends. He appreciates your concern and is grateful for your discretion.'

'What was the cause of death?' enquired Oscar casually, holding a match to the elegant earl's daintily held cigarette.

'Myocardial infarction. A heart attack.'

'Without a doubt?'

'Without a doubt. Without a doubt at all. I'd stake my professional reputation on it. The duchess had been my patient for a number of months. Her heart was enfeebled. Fatally so. I have been fearing this outcome for some while.'

'But the wounds upon her body?'

'Dr Doyle described them to you?'

'He did. In detail.'

'They are something else altogether.'

'I do not understand.'

'You do not need to, Mr Wilde. The Duchess of Albemarle died of a heart attack.'

'But the bloody wounds, my lord? The tears upon her body? The cuts upon her neck?'

'They are something else. They did not kill her. Those wounds are irrelevant, Mr Wilde. The duchess died because her heart gave way.'

'How can they be irrelevant, my lord?'

'They are not the cause of death.'

'How can you be so certain? Did you examine the wounds?'

'Yes.'

'Did you examine them closely?'

'No, not closely. There was no need. I knew the duchess. I knew her secrets.'

'What do you mean, my lord?'

'It does not matter, Mr Wilde.'

Oscar drew deeply upon his cigarette. Dusk was now falling about us.

'The wounds the duchess sustained,' he asked, 'they were sustained before her death?'

'I imagine so,' replied Lord Yarborough, his eyes narrowing. 'Shortly before.'

'They were not self-inflicted?'

'No.'

'Who caused them?'

'I do not care to speculate.'

'Why not, my lord?'

'Because no good or useful purpose can be served by such speculation, Mr Wilde.'

'But could not the infliction of the wounds have provoked the heart attack?'

Lord Yarborough – for the first time – hesitated. 'That is possible,' he said.

'Then the duchess's attacker is her murderer!' exclaimed Oscar.

'No, Mr Wilde. No. You do not understand.'

'Quite so, my lord,' cried Oscar, despairingly. 'I do not understand.'

'Then I will explain the matter to you as simply as I can,' said Lord Yarborough.

He spoke quietly now, almost in a whisper. Oscar and I gathered round him in the gloom. He stood, looking up at us, his eyes imploring us to understand.

'When I have told you what I have to tell you, we will not speak of it again. It is a matter of some delicacy. I am concerned to protect the late duchess's reputation, not for her sake but for the sake of the duke. I was the duchess's physician. I am the duke's friend.'

'Did the duke inflict those wounds?' I asked.

'Oh no,' answered Yarborough, 'but he knew of them – or others like them.'

'Ah,' murmured Oscar. 'I begin to understand. The danger was half the excitement.'

'Indeed, Mr Wilde. And the danger was very great indeed.'

I was lost. 'I do not understand you, gentlemen,' I confessed.

Lord Yarborough looked directly at me. 'The duchess was one of those unhappy women who become the victims of base carnal desires, unnatural appetites that they cannot control. My mother was such a one. It is a form of madness.'

'It is love gone mad,' said Oscar.

'The duchess sought satisfaction where she could – with whom she could – when she could. She gave her body to any man who chose to take it – she gave it willingly. She told me so.'

'This is horrible,' I said.

'It is not uncommon,' said Lord Yarborough, breaking away from our group and looking back towards the house. 'At the Charcot Clinic in Muswell Hill – it is my clinic, but, with permission, it bears Professor Charcot's name: we use his methods – we have other women similarly afflicted. We treat the hysteria with hypnosis. I had hopes that the duchess would submit to treatment. She could not be persuaded.'

'And the man who was with her in the telephone room last night?'

'It could have been anyone – a servant, a guest at the reception, you or me, Mr Wilde – it would not have mattered. The duchess, overwhelmed with desire, overcome by lust, wished to be taken – and taken violently. She was. If it had not happened last evening, it would have happened some other time. If it had not been one man, it would have been another. Whoever the man was, he was not a murderer. Pursuing him will serve no purpose. Bringing this sordid story to light will do no good. It will simply besmirch the duchess's memory and humiliate her husband. Let her rest in peace. And let the duke sleep more easily. He has suffered enough.'

The Savoy Hotel

22

Letter from Bram Stoker to his wife, Florence, delivered by messenger at 11.45 p.m. on Friday, 14 March 1890

Lyceum Theatre,
Strand,
London

Friday, 11 o'clock

Florrie –

Forgive me. The night has been unruly. We had drunken louts in the gallery again. I was called to deal with them personally and then obliged to submit a written report to the police. I pray that you have not waited up for me. I shall not be home.

You will not be surprised to learn that Mr Henry Irving presents his compliments to you, my darling, and asks that you allow him to keep his general manager at his desk and about his duties until the early hours – yet again! I have so much still to do here. I shall be working until two in the morning – at the very least. I have the books to do – business tonight was good: The Dead Heart once more – and then a letter to draft on behalf of my lord and master to the London County Council. They are threatening to impose a stamp duty on theatre tickets! Irving is incandescent. In civilised countries, well-conducted theatres are heavily subsidised by the state. In England, Kemble, Macready, Charles Kean and the rest have been driven to ruin through their commitment to their craft. Mr Irving does not wish to be laid to waste by the philistine members of the LCC.

Before I turn in for the night, I have to marshal his arguments for him – or he will be faced with penury and I with the workhouse! That's what he told me – before setting off, in full evening dress, for a late supper with the Prince of Wales. He is dining with HRH and the Duke of Fife at the Marlborough Club while I am enjoying a cheese sandwich, a pickled onion and a glass of beer at my desk. (I laugh that I may not weep.)

The good news is that this afternoon I made real progress with my book. I have 'the plan' complete.

Goodnight, Florrie dearest. I must be about my labours now. Sleep sweetly, angel. Think of me as dawn breaks, curled up here on the narrow divan beneath that old rug your mother gave us.

I shall at least breakfast well. Oscar sent me a wire tonight, summoning me to breakfast at the Savoy. He wishes for a master class on vampirism – and says that I am the man for the job. He will reward me with as much eggs and bacon and devilled kidneys as I can consume. He's an odd fellow. Witty, but wayward. Brilliant, but too strange. I think you did well to prefer me, my sweet. When I am not with you, I am here at my desk. When Oscar is not with his long-suffering Constance, there is no telling where he may be.

Goodnight, my darling. May your dreams be gentle ones.

Bram

23

Notes from the journal of Arthur Conan Doyle on the subject of 'Hysteria in Women'

Origins

Hippocrates gives us the word 'hysteria' – derived from *hustera*, the Greek for 'uterus'. Hippocrates teaches that the condition stems from uterine disturbance – a dislodged and wandering uterus exerts upward pressure on the heart and lungs and diaphragm, leading to sensations of suffocation and manifestations of irrational and lunatic behaviour. Hippocrates died in 370 BC.

Symptoms

Personally observed by ACD since January 1889 in female patients aged between fifteen and thirty-five (all English women from the Portsmouth and Southsea area):

> difficulty in breathing
> chest pains and chest constriction
> palpitations
> tumultuous heartbeats
> heaviness in limbs
> severe cramps
> swelling of the neck and jugular veins
> headaches

clenched teeth
tearfulness
involuntary sighing

In one woman (aged twenty-eight, married but childless), violent outbursts, convulsions, uncontrollable shrieks and cries, involuntary movements, including wild, windmill-like waving of the arms.

In another (aged eighteen, a virgin), the hysteric outburst involved severe chorea – spasmodic movements, repeated, rapid and jerky: her left hand beat upon her knee as though on a drum while her right scratched upon her left breast as though she was bent on tearing out her own heart. The sight was pitiful. The attack lasted upward of an hour and was followed by a trance lasting two days and two nights.

On examination (by ACD) all the women reported feelings of perpetual sadness, a craving for love and a need for sympathy.

Cause

No one knows! The most penetrating anatomical investigations have shown that Hippocrates was wrong. Hysteria is not brought about by a wandering uterus. It is as likely to be brought on by a full moon (there is some evidence to suggest as much).

Is hysteria a form of lunacy then? It leaves no material trace behind. Examine the internal organs of an hysteric and you will find no lesions. Is it (as many good men believe) a self-induced state conjured up in a disturbed mind? Or is it, as Jean-Martin Charcot – 'the great Charcot' – now tells us, an organic disease of the nervous system?

Treatments

The traditional treatments include the dousing of the reproductive organs with water and the application of physical pressure on the patient's ovaries – pressing hard upon the abdomen until the symptoms abate.

There are also *many* cases reported (notably from Germany and Holland) of a complete cure being effected by the physician introducing his line of life to the patient to satisfy her gross bodily appetites! (This remedy seems somewhat extreme for Southsea.)

Charcot is forcing us to reconsider all that we know of hysteria – the cause and the cure. At La Salpêtrière in Paris he has anatomised the malady – observed and analysed its 'four stages' – and developed the only reliably effective treatment reported to date: hypnosis.

24

From the diary of Rex LaSalle

Oscar spoke to me of his mother and I talked to him of mine, telling him of my mother's death. He said, 'All women become like their mothers. That is their tragedy. No man does. That's his.' He called Lady Wilde 'Speranza'. She, too, is a writer. 'Speranza' is her nom de plume. The word means hope. Oscar said, 'She is full of hope and life and rare intelligence. She has genius – and beauty. And beauty is a form of genius – is higher, indeed, than genius as it needs no explanation.' He loves her dearly and sees her often. Now that she is a widow, she lives not far from him in Chelsea, in Oakley Street – one of the streets I trawl.

Oscar spoke of his mother exactly as I speak of mine – with admiration and adoration and fierce, burning loyalty. I asked him whether she had any faults – even one.

'Yes,' he answered, earnestly, 'just the one. She is a dreamer.'

'Is that a fault?' I asked. 'Are you not a dreamer, also?'

'I am,' he replied, 'more's the pity – for a dreamer is one who can find his way only by moonlight, and his punishment is that he sees the dawn before the rest of the world.'

When he asked me about my father, I said nothing. When I asked him about his, he told me, 'Sir William Wilde was a great man, in his small way. He had genius without beauty. He was neither tall nor handsome. He had the energy of the little man and, in this world, energy is everything. And he had a special gift. He could make the blind see — in reality, not metaphor. He pioneered the operation to remove cataracts from men's eyes. In his time, as an ophthalmologist and ear surgeon, he was without equal. And not without recognition. He was oculist-in-ordinary to Queen Victoria in the early years of her reign. She was possibly the only young lady with whom he managed to behave respectably. Sir William Wilde had a weakness where drink and women were concerned. He was never led astray into the paths of virtue. Old wine and young girls were his temptations of choice. He littered Ireland with his natural children. Did you know that he was accused of the rape of a female patient anaesthetised under chloroform? My mother was well aware of his constant infidelities, but she survived by simply ignoring them. She rose above such things. She is a woman of stature, in every sense, and she knows that sins of the flesh are nothing. They are maladies for physicians to cure, if they should be cured.'

He spoke of Sir William easily, without rancour but with a casual, almost humorous contempt. 'Fathers should be neither seen nor heard,' he said.

'That is the only proper basis for family life. My mother gave me life and hope and my philosophy.'

'But your father gave you your name.'

'That cannot be denied. Nomen est omen. *And our fates lie in our names, we're told.'*

25

From the notebooks of Robert Sherard

S toker and I both chose the bacon, eggs and devilled kidneys. Conan Doyle, a true Scot, opted for porridge (with salt, not cream), followed by the kippers. Oscar settled for half a dozen Turkish cigarettes, coffee and Napoleon brandy.

'You must excuse me, gentlemen. I have spent the night with a vampire.'

'Who is this young man?' demanded Conan Doyle in a hoarse whisper, looking anxiously about him as he spoke.

We were seated at a large table by a bay window overlooking the river Thames. Henri, the Savoy's Saturday-morning *maître d'hotel*, had given us Oscar's favourite table and Oscar had given Henri a silver florin. (Oscar is absurdly generous – especially when he can least afford to be.) The tables adjacent to ours were both unoccupied. The waiters were well out of earshot. Nevertheless, throughout the breakfast, whenever Arthur spoke, he spoke in hushed tones.

'His name is Rex LaSalle. He is twenty-six years of age – twenty-seven on the sixteenth of October. We share a birthday – different years, alas. He hails from the Channel Islands – Guernsey or Jersey, I forget which. He had a dead mother without compare and a father he won't speak of. He appears to have no siblings and few friends. He is an artist – or so he says. But I saw no easel, paints or brushes in his room. There's none of the odour of turpentine about him – more the fragrance of roses. He lives above a Portuguese wine shop in a sordid side street in Soho, but he carries himself like a prince, he talks like a poet and he has the appearance of a Greek god.'

'Steady on, old man,' whispered Conan Doyle, skewering a shard of kipper and glancing nervously towards the waiters.

Oscar continued, unabashed. 'He is tall – six feet at least. Slender. Supple. Lithe. He moves with extraordinary grace, like a dancer – or a panther. He holds his head high. His profile is perfection. His hair is jet black, his eyes are cobalt blue, his skin as white as alabaster.'

Bram Stoker laid down his knife and fork. 'He doesn't sound like a vampire to me,' he announced, wiping his lips on his linen napkin. 'Vampires are swarthy, not pale. They gorge on blood. Their complexions are ruddy.' He pushed his chair away from the table and turned his ample frame towards Oscar. 'And they are very unlikely to find a berth above a Portuguese wine shop in Soho. The vintner and his wife are bound to live on a diet of garlic and malmsey – and vampires have an aversion to garlic, if not to fortified wine.'

He laughed jovially and scratched his chin through his ample, untrimmed red beard. Stoker is a big, shambling man, with an amiable, booming voice and a heart-warming, open face.

'How do you know all this?' I asked.

'Vampires are my passion,' he answered, turning his bright-blue eyes towards me. 'While Oscar pursues the youth and beauty of Soho, I pursue the blood-suckers of Transylvania. Each to his own.'

'Bram is writing a book,' explained Oscar, leaning back from the table and waving the smoke from his cigarette above his head. 'He has been writing it since we were boys in Dublin.'

'I have been researching it a while,' said Bram, ignoring Oscar. 'I haven't started writing yet. But the plan is fixed now. And the title too. *The Undead*. That's what they are, vampires – the undead who feed upon the living.'

Oscar raised his glass of brandy towards his old friend. 'Tell us more, Bram. Tell us everything. That's why we're here.'

'What do you want to know?' replied Stoker, looking around the faces at the table like an eager schoolboy ready to be tested on his homework.

'Are they real?' asked Conan Doyle, his voice still barely above a whisper.

'Did Our Lord turn water into wine at the marriage at Cana? Was the miracle of the loaves and fishes real? People believe these things. People have believed in vampires – or creatures like them – for millennia. In ancient Greece, in Mesopotamia, in Caesar's Rome, there were vampires. As I recall, the first *written* use of the word dates back a thousand years. A Russian priest transcribing the Book of Psalms for a Russian prince noted in the margin of his manuscript that his master was one of the undead – a *wumpir*.'

Stoker rolled the word around his mouth with relish.

As he did so, one of the waiters approached the table with fresh coffee. Conan Doyle flinched. Oscar soothed him. 'It's all right, Arthur. We are not in Southsea now.'

Stoker smiled and inclined his head towards Arthur. 'Dr Doyle's sense of discretion does him credit, Oscar. Not everyone's as comfortable with matters pagan as you seem to be.'

The waiter withdrew.

'These "undead",' I asked, looking into Stoker's broad, beaming face, 'who are they?'

'Souls that cannot rest in peace. Murderers and suicides, torturers, blackmailers, witches, warlocks, priests fallen from grace, princes mired in corruption, men – and women too – of every class, of every creed and culture and land, whose deeds of darkness are so vile that they follow them to the grave. They are evildoers in life who have not found absolution in death. They are buried, but not dead, no longer of this world, not yet of the next.'

'Are they always sinners?' asked Oscar.

Stoker paused. 'Good question, Oscar. You don't miss a trick.' He took his linen napkin and folded it slowly while he answered. 'There is a debate about that. Some say that every vampire was born a wrong 'un – they're all the devil's offspring. Others – and you can take it that I belong to this school of thinking – incline to the view that vampires are themselves *victims*, unfortunate men and women who in life have suffered a hurt that cannot be assuaged, a wound that will not heal. They bleed in life and, in death, they go on bleeding – through all eternity.' He took a sip of his coffee and mopped his beard with his neatly folded napkin. 'And it's because they bleed eternally that they require fresh blood on a perpetual basis.' He looked at Oscar teasingly. 'Blood's their eau-de-vie, so to speak. Each to his own.'

'And these people who are vampires,' I asked, 'are they easy to recognise?'

'Within their graves, most certainly. Their bodies neither decay nor decompose. After death, their teeth, their hair, their nails continue to grow. Shrouded in their coffins, the undead do not rest in peace – even as they sleep, one eye remains open at all times.'

Conan Doyle was now taking notes. 'They sleep?' he asked quietly.

'By day, they sleep,' answered Stoker, speaking more slowly to allow the young doctor time for his notetaking. 'They have an aversion to daylight. By night, they roam the world . . .'

'And would we recognise them as vampires then?' I asked.

'No. Not at all. At least, not by their appearance. Beyond the swarthy look – the purplish face that comes from drinking blood – there is no physical feature that distinguishes a vampire.'

'They cast no shadows,' suggested Oscar.

Stoker nodded. 'They cast no shadows because they have no souls.' He looked about the breakfast table and reached for the toast rack, the butter and the marmalade. 'They have no being – no existence – beyond themselves. They cast no shadows and give no reflection. You cannot see a vampire in a looking-glass.'

'But can they be prepossessing?' asked Oscar, an eyebrow lightly raised.

'Most certainly. On that score, Oscar, your young friend does indeed have vampiric possibilities. Vampires are handsome creatures on the whole. The devil hath power to assume pleasing shapes, you'll recall.'

'And fangs?' enquired Oscar, helping himself to a further libation of brandy. 'Do they have fangs?'

Stoker laughed. 'The better to draw blood, do you mean?' He lifted his slice of toast to his mouth and grinned. 'Who knows? There are no dental records for us to inspect, but it is possible and it's widely believed. Vampires can change shape, we are told, so why should they not also be able to sharpen and lengthen their teeth?'

'Who tells us that they can change shape?' asked Conan Doyle, looking up from his notebook.

'Oscar's sainted mother, among others,' replied Stoker, crunching his toast contentedly. 'Lady Wilde, *la bella* Speranza, is an authority on Irish and European folklore. Her books abound with tales of men and women driven by a lust for blood who have the gift of transformation.'

'You have read "A Wolf Story"?' asked Oscar.

'I believe that I have read every word that Lady Wilde has published, Oscar.'

Stoker turned towards Conan Doyle as if to demand that the doctor take a note of what he was about to say.

'Lady Wilde tells us of wild dogs who devour souls, of women who turn into serpents, of old men who become wolves – and of wolves who become youths, with long, sharp teeth and terrible, glittering eyes. She recounts tales of humans disguised as bats, of dead men becoming cats, of children who, as they sleep, turn into rats . . .'

'She is a good mother,' murmured Oscar, contemplating his brandy glass.

'And a fine writer,' said Bram Stoker, raising his coffee cup towards Oscar. 'If my book comes off, it will be in large measure thanks to her inspiration.' He turned back to Conan Doyle. 'Blood is the recurring theme in the work of Lady Wilde. In the world of which she writes, the dead who roam the earth are all sustained by blood – its colour excites them, its essence empowers them.'

'My women have been good to you, Bram,' said Oscar softly.

Stoker put down his coffee cup and pushed his chair farther from the table. 'It's too early in the day to become maudlin, Oscar,' he said reprovingly, then turned towards me and Conan Doyle. 'Oscar's mother was a second mother to me. And Oscar's first sweetheart is now my wife.'

'Florence Balcombe was the prettiest girl in Dublin,' said Oscar.

'And now she's the prettiest woman in London, I'm proud to say.' Stoker got to his feet. 'I must be about my business. We've a matinée of the Scottish play. Toil and trouble – that's my lot for today. Thank you for breakfast, gentlemen. I've enjoyed it. And I hope I've been of service.'

'You've been invaluable,' said Oscar, with feeling.

'Fascinating,' muttered Conan Doyle, closing his notebook.

'You didn't tell me what this was all about, Oscar,' said Stoker, straightening his waistcoat and buttoning up his jacket. 'Why does this handsome young friend of yours claim to be a vampire? Does he have a wound that will not heal?'

'I think perhaps he does,' replied Oscar, getting to his feet and taking his friend by the hand.

'I wonder if he belongs to the Vampire Club? Do you know? If he doesn't, you must bring him. You must all come anyway, since the subject so intrigues you.'

'The Vampire Club?' repeated Conan Doyle, reopening his notebook.

'You've not heard of it? It meets at midnight – on the third Sunday of the month. Come. I'm allowed up to four guests. I'm the convener. I'll wire you the details. It's at Mortlake cemetery this Sunday.'

'Who goes?' I asked.

'Scholars of vampirism – and souls in search of adventure. Gentlemen, mostly. Occasionally, we get a lady. We're thoroughly emancipated. And democratic. Servants come with their masters.'

'We shall be there,' said Oscar.

'I am not sure,' muttered Conan Doyle, rising from the table. 'I may need to be in Southsea.'

Bram Stoker put a large reassuring hand on Arthur's shoulder. 'It's quite respectable, Doctor, I assure you. There's a bit of hocus pocus, but nothing too alarming. On the whole, we prefer claret to blood. We picnic among the graves while one of our number reads a short paper by candlelight. We're a learned society in our way. We even have a royal patron – though I'm not supposed to tell you that.'

There was a moment's pause before Oscar spoke. 'Prince Albert Victor, I presume?'

Bram Stoker looked steadily into his friend's eyes

and smiled. 'You really don't miss a trick, do you?' He raised his hand to us all in a farewell salute. 'Good day, gentlemen,' he said cheerily. 'Until tomorrow then, at midnight.'

High Tea

26

Telegram delivered to Oscar Wilde at the Albemarle Club, Albemarle Street, London W., at 11 a.m. on Saturday, 15 March 1890

CERTAIN PERSON REQUESTS AND REQUIRES
PLEASURE OF YOUR COMPANY FOR HIGH TEA
THIS AFTERNOON AT FIVE AT CHURCHILL
RESIDENCE. BRING ACD AS BEFORE.
GRATEFULLY OWL

**Letter from Oscar Wilde to Rex LaSalle, care of
17 Wardour Street, Soho, delivered by messenger**

> *Albemarle Club*
> *15.iii.90*

My dear Vampire,

*Consider the date but ignore the omens. There
is no such thing as an omen. (Destiny does not
send us heralds: she is too wise – or too cruel –
for that.) Embrace the Ides of March! This is the
festival of Mars – god of war, son of Juno and
Jupiter, husband of Bellona, father of Romulus,
lover of Venus. You are he in other times. (Do you
know the Ludovisi Ares – the most beautiful statue
of Mars in all antiquity? You are he.)*

*Take your courage in your hands, dearest boy,
and dine with me tonight. Let us feast like gods
– or, at least, let us have oysters and champagne
at Simpson's. My carriage will collect you at nine
o'clock.*

*And, tomorrow, at midnight, let us go together
to Mortlake cemetery. The Vampire Club gathers
there, I'm told. You will be among friends – and
chief among them will be, yours most sincerely,*

Oscar Wilde

Letter from Arthur Conan Doyle to his wife, Louisa 'Touie' Conan Doyle

> Langham Hotel,
> London, W.
> 15.iii.90

> 2 p.m.

Dearest Touie, darling wife –

Thank you for your lovely postcard. It arrived this morning and, in answer to your kind enquiry, yes, I am indeed eating properly. In truth, I am eating far too well. I am forgoing luncheon today, because Oscar treated me to a magnificent breakfast at the Savoy Hotel (porridge, kippers, the works!) and this afternoon I am summoned once again to the presence of HRH the Prince of Wales – where, apparently, a right royal 'High Tea' will be served. So, you see, Touie, I can tell you, in all honesty, that I am eating like a king.

I am missing you most dreadfully, as you may imagine, and my lovely daughter, too, but there's no denying this visit to the great metropolis is proving memorable. At every turn, there is a remarkable encounter. In the corridor, just now, I bumped into Antonin Dvorak, the composer. He is staying at the hotel with his daughter. He told me that, in the interest of economy, he had asked if he might share a double room with the young lady. The hotel manager was outraged and forbade it absolutely!

At breakfast, I met Bram Stoker – a most congenial fellow. He is Irish, like Oscar, but, unlike Oscar, he has a wonderfully down-to-earth way with him. He is an older man and I felt oddly shy in his presence – possibly because he is business manager to Henry Irving at the Lyceum and, as you know, it is one of my abiding ambitions to write a play for Irving. I did not wish Stoker to think that I was interested in him solely because of his association with the great actor.

I shall be seeing him again tomorrow night. He is taking me and Oscar, together with two of Oscar's young friends, to Mortlake cemetery for a midnight gathering of 'vampires'! I have no idea what it will involve. I am both wary and intrigued. Oscar is anxious to go – one of his young friends affects to be a vampire – and there may be something in it that I could use in one of my stories. We shall see. (And, fear not, I shall wrap up warm.)

All being well, my postponed visit to the Charcot Clinic in Muswell Hill will take place on Monday and, on Tuesday, I will be back in Southsea where I belong. Now, I am going to do an hour of reading – Charcot on hypnosis in French! As you can tell, I am not idling – and I am eating – and, most of all, I am missing you, dearest girl.

Ever your loving husband,
    ACD

29

Letter from Bram Stoker to his wife, Florence, delivered by messenger at 6 p.m. on Saturday, 15 March 1890

Lyceum Theatre,
Strand,
London

Saturday, three o'clock

Florrie –

Good news. I will be home by midnight. Much to report.

Breakfast with Oscar was extraordinary. Our friend grows more eccentric by the minute. The talk was entirely of vampires! What is Oscar up to? Is he planning to write a comic opera about vampirism? It's possible – though he hated Gilbert and Sullivan's The Sorcerer, *as I recall.*

Arthur Conan Doyle was with him and another fellow whose name I didn't catch. Doyle is the young doctor who has created such a stir, first with his Highland adventure, Micah Clarke, *and now with his stories of the oddly named detective, Sherlock Holmes. Doyle made copious notes, but said little. (Do you think he is writing a novel about vampires? If he is, it will outsell mine. I know it. He is the coming man, while I have still to reach the starting post.)*

I have said that I will take them to the Vampire Club tomorrow night and now I am regretting it! There is something

*about Oscar's charm that is difficult to resist – though you
succeeded. And how grateful I am that you did.*

*Oscar said nothing of Constance or his boys. He spoke instead
– with embarrassing effusiveness – of a young man who –
according to Oscar – looks like the god Mars but is, in fact, a
vampire from the Channel Islands!*

*More of this anon. Banquo is about to be slain and I must
check the afternoon's takings.*

Your Bram

30

From the notebooks of Robert Sherard

I now understand why the Prince of Wales is the size that he is. I had expected 'High Tea' to include an omelette and cold meats alongside the cakes and scones and sandwiches. I had not for a moment expected the vast repast that was laid before us in the so-called Small Dining Room at Marlborough House.

Egg dishes and cold cuts were indeed on offer – to whet our appetites. There were breads and pastries of every description too – muffins and crumpets, macaroons and dainties – and an array of desserts – gateaux, tarts, baskets of spun sugar filled with fresh fruit and ice cream. But between the initial savouries and the final sweets came salver after salver, groaning with culinary riches: a salmon mousse decorated with caviar, cold lobster with brandy mayonnaise, snipe with foie gras, grilled chicken with asparagus.

'No turtle soup, Your Royal Highness?' said Oscar plaintively.

'This is merely High Tea, Oscar – a little something to sustain us until dinner.' The Prince of Wales looked towards me and Conan Doyle, adding by way of explanation: 'It was the late Duchess of Bedford's idea – High Tea. She was a good woman.'

'I shall remember her in my prayers,' said Oscar.

'Her Grace often felt a little low in the late afternoon,' the prince continued.

'Ah, yes,' sighed Oscar, 'that debilitating *crise de nerfs* that comes towards six o'clock unless a portion or two of pigeon pie and a plate of petits fours have been taken.'

The prince laughed and smacked his thin lips. He drew slowly on his cigar – he smoked throughout our repast – and fixed Oscar with moist, bulbous eyes. 'You are a funny man, Mr Wilde.'

We ate at one end of a large dining table. Oscar and Arthur were seated to the right and left of the prince; Tyrwhitt Wilson, the equerry, and I, just beyond. The prince's personal page – a boy with copper-coloured hair; Oscar says his name is Frank Watkins; he remembered him from the prince's entourage at the reception in Grosvenor Square – waited exclusively upon His Royal Highness. The rest of us were looked after by a trio of straight-backed footmen who circled round and round the table with one dish after another, bobbing up and down before us, like wooden horses on a fairground carousel.

'General Probyn is not here?' enquired Conan Doyle.

'He is at Sandringham,' replied the prince. 'I am allowed off the leash for a few weeks in March. I go to Paris and the French Riveria for a month or so while my wife visits her family in Denmark and our heroic comptroller stays in Norfolk. He is Capability Brown as well as Keeper of the Privy Purse. He is redesigning the gardens at Sandringham. Sir Dighton is an eager plantsman.'

'Paris in the spring,' murmured Oscar. 'Nothing is more delightful.'

'It's my constitutional duty, Mr Wilde,' said the prince sternly. 'I merely do what Bagehot says I must.'

'Ah!' exclaimed Oscar. 'The author of *The English Constitution* insists on Paris in the spring, does he, sir?'

'Oh, yes,' chuckled the prince, 'followed by a few weeks *en garçon* along the coast between Nice and Monte Carlo.'

Tyrwhitt Wilson piped up with a practised air: 'Bagehot is very clear on the point: "The role of the heir apparent is to taste all the world and the glory of it, whatever is most attractive, whatever is most seductive."'

The prince beamed. 'When Bagehot's book appeared I gave the Queen a copy – specially bound.'

'In fatted calf, I presume,' said Oscar.

The Prince of Wales banged the table with delight. 'You are very funny, Mr Wilde,' he wheezed, choking with laughter.

As the feast was laid before us, and the page and footmen hovered close by, the conversation remained general – if dominated by Oscar and the heir apparent. They talked of motherhood and Balmoral deer pie, of Irving's Macbeth and Mrs Langtry's Rosalind, of Cannes in April and Cowes in August, of happiness and hysteria (the Prince of Wales acknowledges a strain of madness in his family), of the value of hypnosis and the place of history.

'The one duty we owe to history is to rewrite it,' said Oscar.

For an hour we ate and drank and made merry and then, at six o'clock, as clocks, both within the dining room and without, began to whirr and strike and chime, the waiting staff, taking their cue from the hour and a nod from Tyrwhitt Wilson, discreetly bowed themselves backwards out of the room. When they had gone, the prince's equerry got to his feet and checked that the doors were securely closed. Once Wilson had resumed his place, silence fell.

The Prince of Wales pushed his chair a little from the table and drew heavily on a newly lit cigar. 'Well, gentlemen,' he said, in a businesslike tone, 'is it murder? Was my poor friend, Helen Albemarle, done to death?'

'Yes,' said Oscar, simply. 'I believe so.'

'Lord Yarborough thinks otherwise,' said Conan Doyle.

The prince raised an eyebrow. 'The "psychiatrist"?'

'He is also a physician – and a Fellow of the Royal Society. Lord Yarborough believes it was a heart attack.'

'A heart attack?'

'Myocardial infarction – a heart attack, possibly, but by no means certainly, provoked by sexual frenzy.'

'Good God, man,' cried the Prince of Wales, leaning forward, 'what on earth are you suggesting?'

'The duchess's body was found in the telephone room at 40 Grosvenor Square,' said Oscar calmly. 'She was half naked. Her torso was exposed. She had wounds about her chest and neck. She may have been the victim of a violent physical assault – or, as Lord Yarborough suggests, the willing participant in gross carnal activity that proved too stimulating for her enfeebled heart.'

'This is preposterous,' hissed the prince. 'Did she have an enfeebled heart?'

'Lord Yarborough says so,' said Conan Doyle.

'And what do you say, Doctor?' demanded the prince.

'A heart attack is certainly a possibility, sir. The cuts and scratches on her body were mostly superficial. The wounds in her neck were deeper, much deeper, but whether they were inflicted before or immediately after death, it is impossible to say.'

The prince was perspiring. He wiped his eyes and forehead with his napkin. 'This is most distressing. Not at all what I expected. Poor Helen.'

Oscar leant towards the prince. 'What did you expect, Your Royal Highness? Might one ask?'

'I didn't know what to expect. I suppose I hoped that it would be death by natural causes . . .'

'It may be,' protested Conan Doyle. 'Yarborough may be right.'

The Prince of Wales looked at Oscar. Tears pricked his round, protruding eyes. 'Or suicide.'

There was a moment's pause before Oscar asked, 'Was the duchess very unhappy?'

'No,' said the prince, 'but she was troubled.' He hesitated, before repeating, 'I did not know what to expect.' He found a handkerchief and blew his nose, then settled himself back in his chair once more. 'The telephone room? The duke said she'd been found in her bed.'

'No, the duke actually found her in the telephone room,' said Oscar.

'Why on earth was she there?'

'To make a call or to receive one,' suggested Conan Doyle.

'At midnight? At the climax of her party? At the very moment when His Royal Highness was about to take his leave?' Oscar shook his head. 'I think not.'

'Was she there by assignation?' I asked.

Oscar looked at me, as if surprised to hear me speak. Contemplating his cigarette, he spoke as if wondering out loud. 'Had she gone to meet someone by arrangement? A lover that she knew? A stranger who wished her harm? It is possible, I suppose, but the timing makes no sense. Why disappear at the very moment when your absence is most likely to be noticed? Midnight was the hour set for His Royal Highness's departure.'

'Now here's a thought,' said Conan Doyle, leaning into the table, his eyes suddenly glinting. 'Midnight approaches. The duchess comes downstairs to be in the hall ready to attend His Royal Highness's departure. When she arrives, the hall is empty. The duke and the servants are not yet there. The duchess waits, alone. And as she waits, her assailant appears and drags her into the telephone room.'

'She would have cried out!' exclaimed the prince. 'She would have called for help.'

'Her assailant could have silenced her,' said Doyle, pressing his own hand against his mouth.

The prince shuddered. Oscar stubbed out his cigarette on a small silver ashtray that featured the emblem of the Prince of Wales's feathers.

'Perhaps Arthur is right,' he said, slowly. 'Not long before midnight, the duchess was in her drawing room entertaining her guests. As midnight approached, realising the time, she made her way down the stairs and into the hall. She was alone at this point – with no thought of going into the telephone room, either to use the telephone or to keep an assignation. But, waiting alone in the hallway, something drew her into the telephone room. What was it? Did she flee there suddenly to hide

94

for some reason? To escape from someone – or something? Or did someone entice her into the room? Someone she knew?'

'The duke was waiting for me as I came down the stairs at midnight,' said the Prince of Wales.

I spoke again. 'That was when I saw the duke close the door to the telephone room. That was when I caught sight of the duchess's body.'

Oscar turned from me and looked directly at Conan Doyle. 'You are the storyteller, Arthur. In a traditional murder mystery, isn't the first person on the scene of the crime usually the chief suspect?'

Doyle tugged at his moustache and grunted.

Oscar went on: 'Perhaps it was the Duke of Albemarle who murdered the duchess?'

'Albemarle murder Helen?' exclaimed the Prince of Wales, throwing down his cigar. 'Impossible. I don't believe it. I won't believe it.'

'You may have to, sir,' said Oscar, calmly. 'It happens all the time. Men kill their womenfolk. It's the way of the world. Some do it with a single blow, others with a million cuts.'

'The Duke of Albemarle is no murderer,' protested the prince. 'He loved Helen.'

'Don't all men kill the thing they love?' asked Oscar softly.

'Why would Albemarle kill his young wife? *Why?*'

'Because he envied her her youth?' said Oscar.

'Jealousy, spite, revenge?' suggested Conan Doyle.

'Albemarle loved Helen,' repeated the prince.

'Well then,' said Oscar, 'if the duke adored his duchess, but the duchess was a wayward girl . . .'

'She was not "a wayward girl", Mr Wilde.'

'Lord Yarborough suggests that she might have been.'

'Lord Yarborough is wrong!' barked the Prince of Wales. Coughing and spluttering, he pushed back his chair and got to his feet. Immediately, we all got to ours. 'I knew Helen Albemarle. She was a lady, in every sense – I can assure you of that. Lord Yarborough's suggestion is outrageous – slanderous. You need give it no further thought, gentlemen.'

The prince, letting his napkin fall to the floor, walked away from the dining table, towards a large wooden globe that stood in the corner of the room and which showed the world as it was thought to be in Queen Elizabeth's reign. The prince made the globe revolve slowly and spoke with his back turned towards us.

'Lord Yarborough's disgusting suggestion beggars belief,' he said. 'Nor do I believe that the duchess's heart was in any sense "enfeebled". Had it been – had she had concerns of any kind about her health – she would have told me.'

'Then it is murder,' said Oscar.

'I fear so. I feared the worst, but I had hoped it would not be this terrible. I thought that perhaps she'd been poisoned – or strangled. But this . . .' He halted the gently spinning globe. 'It is murder of the most brutal kind. Poor Helen.' He turned and looked towards us as we stood at our places by the table. 'You must continue your investigations, gentlemen.'

'Very well,' said Oscar.

'I need to know the truth before I leave for France.'

'Is it not time to involve the police, sir?' asked Conan Doyle.

'No, Doctor. No. I forbid it.' The prince raised a hand to silence Conan Doyle. 'What can the police do, except stir up trouble and inform the press?'

'The press have not been generous to His Royal Highness,' said Tyrwhitt Wilson, stepping away from the dining-room table and moving towards the door. 'The Queen will be anxious to avoid a scandal. The Crown must be protected.'

'But if a murder has been committed—'

'Justice must be done,' said the Prince of Wales. 'I understand that. If you can establish, beyond peradventure, that it was the Duke of Albemarle who took his own wife's life, I shall speak to him. He will do what's necessary.'

Conan Doyle straightened himself and looked directly at the heir apparent. 'You mean, blow out his own brains?'

His Royal Highness made no reply.

Following Tyrwhitt Wilson's lead, we bowed and, stepping backwards, left the room. Oscar murmured words of thanks as we retreated, but offered no parting sally.

31

From the notebook of Inspector Hugh Boone of
Scotland Yard, Saturday, 15 March 1890

Sordid business. I feel it in my bones. I sense it. *I know it*. But, as yet, I cannot prove it.

Dr Jekyll and Mr Hyde

32

From the diary of Rex LaSalle

Oscar sent a hansom cab to collect me from my room and take me to Simpson's-in-the-Strand. I tried to tip the cabman, but the fellow said: 'You don't have to, guv. Mr Wilde has already taken care of that.'

I found Oscar at what he called his 'favourite table', in the corner, at the back of the main dining room on the ground floor. The room was hot and crowded, brightly lit (with electric light), filled with cigar smoke and hearty diners – the Saturday-night, mutton-chop brigade.

Oscar, in a silk evening jacket of midnight blue, seemed to be a creature from another planet. He was seated alone, reading. Before him, propped against an upturned drinking glass, was his open book. Next to it stood a saucer of champagne. His elbows were resting lightly on the table, his arms held out to either side of him. In his right hand, between his ring and middle fingers, loosely, he held a lighted cigarette. In his left hand, between his thumb and index finger, he grasped the stem of a crimson-coloured rose.

As I sat down beside him, he looked up with hooded, mischievous eyes and smiled. 'I am having Tacitus and a glass of Perrier-Jouët,' he said, as if our conversation was already in mid-flow. 'You are having this.'

He handed me the rose. I slipped it into my buttonhole and thanked him. He closed his book and let his eyes wander over me appraisingly.

'I like the knot in your tie,' he said. 'A well-tied tie is the first serious step in life.'

I apologised for my appearance. 'I have not changed for dinner. I—'

'Hush,' he silenced me. 'I knew that you would not. I knew that you could not. You have only one dress shirt and you wore it to the reception in Grosvenor Square two nights ago. It has not yet been laundered. I understand. You need not worry. You have nothing, but you look everything. What more could one desire?'

He put his hand on mine and told me that he was a little drunk and not at all hungry. He had been to Marlborough House, he explained, for High Tea, 'a curious feast that included every delight – except for tea itself, of course'.

He ordered me a dozen oysters and told me that we would have to sit together in silence because all that had passed between him and the Prince of Wales that afternoon was confidential and of 'a most delicate nature'. When the oysters were served, Oscar guzzled half of them himself and commanded a dozen more. When the first bottle of Perrier-Jouët was finished, he ordered a second and proceeded to tell me everything that had passed between him and the Prince of Wales.

I asked him whether the death of the Duchess of Albemarle had affected the prince. He told me that it had. Profoundly. I asked him whether the prince knew the details of how the duchess had died. He told me that he did and that the horror of the assault upon her – the incisions in her neck, the cuts upon her breasts – had distressed him very deeply.

I asked him to tell me about the wounds.

He said that he had not seen them himself. He said that it was his friend, Dr Doyle, who had examined the duchess's body.

I asked him whether Dr Doyle had described the incisions to him.

Yes, he said, he had. There were just two incisions, no more than an inch apart. They were to the woman's neck, to one side of her neck, just below her ear. They were not wide, but they were deep.

Had they killed her?

Dr Doyle had inserted a matchstick into each incision. In the doctor's estimation, the ruptures were deep enough to reach the jugular vein.

'And was there much blood?' I asked.

'The doctor did not mention blood.'

'Or vampires?' I smiled.

Oscar returned my smile and said, 'But you were with me at the time of the murder, Rex.'

I laughed. 'Does the Prince of Wales have any idea who might have done this terrible thing?' I asked.

'The prince believes that it may be the duke. He

was seen closing the door to the telephone room at midnight.'

'And why would the Duke of Albemarle wish to murder his young wife?'

'We do not yet know,' said Oscar. 'We are commissioned by His Royal Highness to make further enquiries.'

'Could it be,' I wondered out loud, 'that the duchess had taken a lover and that the duke was driven mad by jealousy?'

'Almost certainly,' said Oscar, his smile broadening. 'That is the usual story. Othello is my least favourite among Shakespeare's plays, but I am all too familiar with the green-eyed monster and his capacity for driving sane men mad.'

'And the late duchess's lover then? What of him?'

'Lord Yarborough – Fellow of the Royal Society, friend to the duke, physician to the duchess – suggests that Her Grace may have been on an intimate footing with a number of admirers – men from all walks of life.'

'Did the Prince of Wales tell you that he is generally counted among them?'

'No, he did not,' said Oscar.

'It's common knowledge,' I said.

'Perhaps that is why I did not know,' he answered.

'It was in the newspapers.'

'That explains my ignorance entirely.'

When we had had our fill of oysters and champagne, I helped Oscar to his feet. The heat of the room was overpowering. I held my friend by the arm and walked him slowly to the door. As we passed *among the tables, certain diners looked up at us. Some smiled or nodded to Oscar in recognition; others simply stared.*

Twice Oscar paused as we made our progress. He halted by a table at which an earnest young man was raising a young lady's hand to his lips and, gazing down at them both, remarked, 'A kiss may ruin a human life.' And at the doorway, as the head waiter wished us goodnight, Oscar produced a silver crown from his waistcoat pocket to press into the man's hand and told him: 'I have made an important discovery tonight, Edward. It is that alcohol, taken in sufficient quantities, produces all the effects of intoxication.'

When we reached the Strand, the street was busy, the pavement teeming with theatre-goers returning home and revellers still hungry for adventure, the gentry and the great unwashed, jostling with old soldiers selling matches, gypsy women plying sprigs of heather and ladies of the night touting for trade. I proposed a stroll down Savoy Hill to take the air and to watch the reflection of the moon in the high tide upon the Thames. Oscar was not for walking anywhere.

'Let's take a cab back to your room,' he said. 'I need a glass of wine and a cigarette. I have a question I want to ask you.'

Once we were back in Soho and Oscar was reclining on my bed, a glass of the roughest vino bianco *in one hand, his favourite Turkish cigarette in the other, I said to him, 'Well, my friend, ask me your question.'*

He looked at me through half-closed eyes. 'Why did you tell me that you are a vampire?'

'To amuse you. To intrigue you. To entice you, I suppose. And because I am.'

'But you are not,' he protested. 'I know that, Rex. You are exceptional, but you are not a vampire. You are something quite else.' As he said it, his eyelids closed and his breathing deepened.

I took the wine glass and the cigarette from his grasp, loosened his collar, unbuttoned his waistcoat and let him sleep. As I write this, it is nearly dawn and he is sleeping still.

33

From the journal of Arthur Conan Doyle

Saturday, 15 March 1890. An extraordinary day. Every encounter has been memorable.

Breakfast with Oscar Wilde and Bram Stoker at the Savoy. (Stoker is Henry Irving's man of business and an authority on vampirism, it seems. He referred to Irving as 'the old blood-sucker', which I thought interesting.)

A chance conversation here at the Langham with the composer, Antonin Dvorak. He is not at all happy with the hotel. They will not let him share his suite with his daughter. He has had to put her up in one of the servants' rooms, at a cost of 5s 6d a day. I told Dvorak how much I admire his 8th Symphony (the G Major). He said, 'Yes, it my simplest work and consequently dearly loved by the English.'

High Tea at Marlborough House with the Prince of Wales. The meal was gargantuan: there was so much on offer that none of it really pleased. A simple dish of tea and some Aberdonian oatcakes would have done me nicely. Neither was to be had. Wilde and his friend Sherard were also of the party, but of what passed between us and the prince I can write very little, alas. We are sworn to secrecy. I must be discreet – even to my own journal. Suffice to say, we were summoned to assist HRH with some 'enquiries' of a delicate nature.

This much I think I can record, however, because the nub of it is already in the public domain. When we left HRH, his equerry, Tyrwhitt Wilson, escorted us to our brougham by way of the equerries' sitting room. He said, 'I want to show you something,' and bade us follow him to a desk in the corner of the room. Unlocking the drawer of the desk, he produced from it a small leather attaché case. From the case he took a bulging paper folder, which he laid on the desk and opened out before us. It contained a mass of newspaper cuttings.

'None of this makes happy reading,' he said. 'These are newspaper reports of divorce cases.' He leafed through the cuttings and picked out one. 'Here,' he said, 'read this. It relates to Sir Charles Mordaunt's petition for divorce. Sir Charles was unsuccessful, but you may recall the case. The Prince of Wales was forced into the witness box to deny adultery.' He handed the cutting to me. 'Take it,' he said. 'Study it. It is from *Reynolds' Newspaper* – a publication read by half a million Englishmen each week.'

This is the cutting:

If the Prince of Wales is an accomplice in bringing dishonour to the homestead of an English gentleman, if he has assisted in rendering an honourable man miserable for life; if unbridled sensuality and lust have led him to violate the laws of honour and hospitality – then such a man, placed in the position he is, should not only be expelled from decent society, but is utterly unfit and unworthy to rule over this country.

'One day soon,' said Tyrwhitt Wilson, 'the Prince of Wales will be king. We must avoid another scandal – at all costs.'

And for the last of today's memorable encounters, I give you Dr Henry Jekyll and Mr Edward Hyde! In person. In the bar of the Langham Hotel. In the handsome form of Mr Richard Mansfield, the actor, who plays both roles in the stage version of Stevenson's fine story. I saw it twice when it came to the Lyceum. I have seen Mansfield play Richard III as well. He rivals Irving. The Americans reckon him greater than Irving. Certainly, he is more versatile. I have seen him in Gilbert and Sullivan too!

Tonight I scarcely recognised him. On stage, he is *magnificent*. In person, he is next to nothing. You'd think him a bank clerk in pince-nez. We were seated together at the bar, side by side, each nursing a whisky and water, and fell into conversation by chance. Mansfield heard the barman mention my name and turned to me.

'You are Arthur Conan Doyle?' he enquired. '*The* Arthur Conan Doyle? The creator of Sherlock Holmes?'

'The same,' I said.

The dear fellow told me that he has read all my work. He declared that after Stevenson and Shakespeare, I am his favourite author! He looked forward, he said, to the day when he might play Sherlock Holmes upon the stage.

Overwhelmed by all this, I mumbled an apology for not recognising him at once.

He said, 'Do not apologise. Nobody recognises me off stage. I am content with that. I am two people, after all. On stage, I have authority. I am bold, brave, daring – in complete command of all I survey. Off stage, I am as you see me now – an unassuming chap, somewhat shy and retiring, a little fearful of the world, to tell the truth. *The Strange Case of Dr Jekyll and Mr Hyde* is not a fairy tale, in my opinion. It is a story that grips the imagination because it speaks of a terrible truth. In varying degrees, we are all of us leading double lives, are we not?'

'We All Have Secrets'

34

From *Reynolds's Newspaper*, Sunday, 16 March 1890

The funeral of the Duchess of Albemarle is to take place at St George's, Hanover Square, London, W., on Thursday next, 20 March, at eleven o'clock. The duchess, noted for her beauty and charitable endeavour, died in the early hours of Friday morning.

Despite speculation in certain quarters, an inquest into the duchess's untimely death is not expected. The Metropolitan Police Commissioner at Scotland Yard has confirmed that foul play is not suspected and the duchess's physician, Lord Yarborough, MD, FRS, has issued a statement indicating that his patient died as the consequence of a long-established heart condition, 'possibly exacerbated by her arduous duties as a liberal and generous hostess'.

On Thursday last, at their mansion in Grosvenor Square, the Duke and Duchess of Albemarle gave an evening reception for 200 notabilities connected with the arts and sciences. The guest of honour on that occasion was HRH the Prince of Wales.

It is not yet known whether the heir apparent will be

among the mourners at the duchess's funeral on Thursday, but we think it likely. The young Duchess of Albemarle had the distinction of being a favourite with the Prince of Wales, much as Lady Mordaunt, Madame Bernhardt, Miss Chamberlayne, and Mrs Langtry, among others, had been before her.

35

From the notebooks of Robert Sherard

This morning (Sunday, 16 March), as arranged, I went to Tite Street at nine o'clock to take breakfast with Oscar. He was not there. Constance (looking ever lovelier) welcomed me sweetly. She said, 'Oscar often stays away. He needs his freedom. I understand.' She spoke without any bitterness. She has a generous heart and the gentlest of smiles. We spent the morning together, reading, while her boys played upstairs in the nursery.

At eleven o'clock Oscar appeared. He was unshaven and bleary-eyed, but in the highest of high spirits.

'I have just driven through the park,' he announced, 'and watched some young lads riding their bicycles around the lake. There is nothing like youth. The middle-aged are mortgaged to Life. The old are in life's lumber room. But youth is the Lord of Life.' He kissed Constance tenderly on the forehead. 'To win back my youth there is nothing I wouldn't do – except take exercise, get up early or be a useful member of the community.'

As we laughed, he caressed his wife's temples and then untied and tied again the blue ribbon in her hair. 'My wife is not so slim now as she was in younger and happier days – I blame our boys for that – but her face has all the intelligence and beauty of the young Apollo, don't you agree?'

'I do,' I said, as Constance blushed and, playfully, pushed her husband away from her.

Oscar stood square before us, stretching. 'I must shave and bathe, before putting on my lilac shirt and heliotrope tie. Spring is sprung and we have work to do, Robert. The Duke of Albemarle is granting us an interview on his return from church at half past twelve.'

'It is still Lent, my darling heart,' said Constance anxiously, 'and the Albemarle household will now be in mourning – do you think the heliotrope tie quite seemly?'

At 12.30 p.m., Oscar, cleanly shaven and dressed in a black velvet suit, white linen shirt and loose-fitting black silk tie, rang the bell at 40 Grosvenor Square. The front door swung open immediately.

'His Grace is expecting you, gentlemen,' said Parker, the butler, bowing slightly. 'Please follow me.'

He led us across the hallway, to the left of the grand staircase, towards the downstairs morning room. As I glanced back at the closed door to the telephone room, he added, 'I understand that when you have seen His Grace you wish also to see me.'

'We would be much obliged,' said Oscar genially.

We found the Duke of Albemarle standing alone, with his back to us, gazing out of the window into the garden. 'The daffodils are early this year,' he said. 'Helen so loved the daffodils.'

He spun round on his heels and stepped briskly towards us, extending a firm hand to each of us in turn. He is sixty-five, a big man, with thick and wiry silver hair and a farmer's face: broad and red and honest. He was dressed in full mourning, but he appeared fresh and bristling with energy. His manners are impeccable; his welcome was cordial.

'Your Grace did not go to church, I see,' said Oscar, raising an eyebrow. 'And you breakfasted late.'

The duke smiled. 'You have spent too much time with your friend Conan Doyle, Mr Wilde. You are trying to out-Holmes Holmes. But you are correct, of course. I rose later than I should. I have neglected my devotions and only just left the breakfast table. How did you know? Did Parker tell you?'

'Your butler is the soul of discretion, you may be sure of that. No. The perfect line of your trousers suggests that Your Grace has not been down on his knees and at prayer since they were pressed, while the breadcrumbs on your cuff indicate a slice of toast recently enjoyed.'

'Very good, Mr Wilde,' said the duke. He looked at Oscar with amused approval. 'I have received a note from the Prince of Wales asking me to co-operate with the enquiries you are making on his behalf. I am happy to oblige. I can well understand why His Royal Highness is ready to trust you as his new-found consulting detective.'

Oscar smiled. 'Because I have an eye for detail?'

'No. Because you are a man of the world, Mr Wilde. And you understand the prince.'

'I know His Royal Highness only very slightly,' Oscar protested. He did not protest strongly; he was flattered by the duke's suggestion. 'We met some years ago – as mutual friends of Mrs Langtry.'

'Yes,' replied the duke. 'The Prince of Wales and Mrs Langtry were very close once upon a time.'

'They are still friends,' said Oscar.

'And you understand such friendships, Mr Wilde. I know you do. The prince knows you do. He appreciates that. You are a lord of language and he is the Prince of Wales, but you have much in common.'

Oscar remained silent.

'The Prince of Wales is a happily married man. So are you. The prince's wife is a lady of quality and distinction. As is yours. Yet the prince enjoys a number of special friendships beyond his marriage – outside it – friendships that enrich his life but at the same time threaten his position. I am told that you might have a fellow feeling with His Royal Highness in this regard.'

Still Oscar said nothing.

'We all have secrets, Mr Wilde.'

A heavy silence filled the room. A bright ray of midday sunshine filtered through the window and fell on Oscar, isolating him as a spotlight might upon a bare stage. Dust danced about his head.

It was a curious moment. I have known Oscar for seven years. We have dined together, travelled together, lived together. We have shared digs – and adventures. I know him well. I have not seen him discomfited – and silenced – like this before.

The Duke of Albemarle, having secured the upper hand, moved to a sideboard and returned holding a large, silver cigarette box. 'A cigarette, gentlemen? It's American tobacco, I fear. We don't run to Turkish in Grosvenor Square.'

We each took cigarettes and, as he lit them for us, the duke indicated that we should now sit and make ourselves comfortable. I perched on a low divan. Oscar found a high-backed armchair out of the sunlight. The duke, who remained standing before the fireplace, put the cigarette box on the mantelpiece, beside a Meissen porcelain shepherd and shepherdess.

'Now, gentlemen,' he said, crisply, turning to us, 'to business. And to the point. The Prince of Wales wishes to avoid a scandal. So do I. A scandal would hurt me. A scandal could ruin him. But the prince, because of his profound fondness for my late wife, also wishes to know all there is to know about her death. This is where His Royal Highness and I differ. I believe I know enough already. I do not need to know more.'

Oscar looked up at the duke. 'You do not need to know more?' he repeated quietly.

'I know what Lord Yarborough has told me and that is sufficient. Yarborough is a man I trust. He likes to call himself a "psychiatrist", but by training he's a medical man. His judgement can be relied upon. He was my wife's physician. He signed her death certificate. He is convinced that Helen died of a heart attack – and so am I.'

'But what provoked that heart attack?' asked Oscar. 'What of the wounds about her body and in her neck?'

The Duke of Albemarle blew a great cloud of cigarette smoke across his morning room and laughed out loud. 'Oh, Mr Wilde,' he exclaimed, 'I thought that you of all men would understand! Are you not familiar with unnatural vice?'

Oscar made to speak, but stopped before he did so.

'Five years ago,' the duke continued, 'when I married Helen, I did so in good faith. I loved her dearly. By the time she died, I loved her not at all. There was residual affection, perhaps, but no love left.'

'And no respect?' asked Oscar.

'She had forfeited that.' The duke turned to gaze out of the window as he spoke. 'Lord Yarborough is convinced that she was mad. He wanted to take her to his clinic, to cure her of her cravings by hypnosis.'

'She craved other men?' asked Oscar gently.

The duke laughed once more – more gently this time – and looked back at Oscar. 'That's not a madness, Mr Wilde. Craving other men? That's commonplace. Half the wives in London crave men other than their husbands, so I'm told.'

Oscar smiled. The duke shook his head and drew slowly on his cigarette.

'No, what Helen craved was violence – the thrill of it and the pain of it. My wife was a woman who wanted to be thrashed – and went with any man who was willing to do her bidding.'

A different silence filled the room. The Duke of Albemarle sighed and threw the remains of his cigarette into the empty grate.

'I am sorry,' said Oscar.

'My wife brought her own death upon herself, Mr Wilde. Lord Yarborough had told her that her heart was enfeebled. She knew the risk that she was taking – but the risk, the danger, was half the excitement.'

'Whom was she with on the night she died? Do you know?'

'I do not. I neither know nor care. It does not matter. Whoever he was, he was not responsible for her death.'

'But he was responsible for the wounds about her person.'

'She would have welcomed those,' said the duke. 'It was the wounds she craved.'

The clock upon the mantelpiece struck one. The duke took a timepiece from his waistcoat pocket and inspected it. Oscar rose to his feet.

'How much of this does the Prince of Wales know?' he asked.

'All of it. I called upon His Highness last evening and told him everything.'

'Did you tell the prince who you thought the man might be?'

'It might be any man, Mr Wilde – any man at all. At least, any man who was in this house at about half past eleven last Thursday night.'

'Half past eleven?' repeated Oscar. 'But the duchess died just before midnight, did she not?'

'Helen was seen on her way to the telephone room at half past eleven. She went to receive a call. She passed Parker on the landing. She told him that she had been called to the telephone as a matter of urgency.'

'By whom?'

'She did not say.'

'At half past eleven?'

'At half past eleven. Parker is sure of that.'

'Yet she was seen in the drawing room after that,' said Oscar.

'I did not know that,' said the duke.

'And when did you discover her body, Your Grace? It was not on Friday morning, was it?'

'No. It was at midnight – just a moment before the prince departed. I expected Helen to join me in the hallway to bid farewell to the royal party, but she was nowhere to be found. When I asked Parker to search for her, he told me about the telephone call. I looked into the telephone room and there she was – half naked, bloodied, lifeless.'

'Why did you not raise the alarm at once?'

'And cause a scandal? I saw at once that she was dead. I knew at once what must have happened. Lord Yarborough had warned me of the possibility.'

'You should perhaps have called the police,' I suggested, getting up from the divan and standing alongside Oscar.

The duke looked at me directly. 'This is not a matter for the police,' he said. 'Or the press. This is a private matter.' He turned to look at Oscar. 'Make the private public and who knows what the consequences may be.'

'We will persist with our enquiries,' said Oscar carefully, 'unless His Royal Highness requires us to desist.'

'Nothing will be gained by knowing more, Mr Wilde. Persist if you must. I cannot stop you. Talk to whom you will. I will not stand in your way. But ponder as you persist: what is to be gained by what you are doing? My wife is dead. Her life cannot be recovered. Let her rest in peace.'

The door to the morning room opened. Parker, the butler, stood waiting to escort us from the ducal presence. We shook hands with His Grace, thanked him for his time and courtesy, and made our retreat.

As we returned across the hallway towards the front door, the servant looked up at Oscar enquiringly. 'And do you wish to speak to me now, sir?'

'No, thank you, Parker, your master has spoken for you. There will be no need.'

'I'm glad of that, sir,' said the butler.

'But the duchess's maid,' said Oscar, gently staying the butler's hand as it reached for the front door. 'Might we speak with her?'

'That won't be possible, I am afraid.'

'Why not? Is she gone away?'

'Oh no, Nellie's here, sir, but you can't speak with her.'

'Why not?' Oscar persisted.

'Because she's deaf and dumb, sir. Has been from a child.'

'But I saw her quoted in the newspaper, Mr Parker – at length.'

'So you did, sir. His Grace thought it expedient at the time. Nellie knew nothing of it. She's deaf and dumb. And she neither reads nor writes. She was one of the laundry maids until not long ago. Her Grace took pity on her and elevated her above her station. Her Grace was very fond of her.'

'Might we at least *see* her?' asked Oscar.

'Not today, sir,' said the butler, pulling open the front door and stepping aside to allow us to pass. 'She is in bed. She's in a bad way. She fell down the stairs.'

Mortlake

36

From the diary of Rex LaSalle

Last night, as we drove west out of London towards the churchyard at Mortlake, Oscar rested his hand on my arm and said, 'I never approve, or disapprove, of anything now. It is an absurd attitude to take towards life. We are not sent into the world to air our moral prejudices.' He pulled down the black blinds on the windows of our carriage. 'I never take any notice of what common people say,' he continued, 'and I never interfere with what charming people do.' He moved closer to me in the darkness. 'I have a feeling that Bram's vampires will prove to be charming people and that we will like them very much.'

'Do you think it's possible that the Duchess of Albemarle was attacked by a vampire?' I asked.

'Jules Verne tells us that one day soon men will fly to the moon. Mrs Langtry is to essay the role of Cleopatra. I shall have lost a stone in weight by Christmas. In this world, Rex, all manner of marvels are possible. The duchess may indeed have been attacked by a vampire – or by a man who believed he

was a vampire – or by a man pretending to be a vampire. Or the wounds in her neck could have been self-inflicted to give the impression of a vampiric attack – or they may have nothing to do with vampires at all . . . Who knows?'

I turned my head towards him. In the darkness I could barely discern his profile, but I felt the warmth of his breath, his face was so close to mine.

'Oscar,' I said, 'do you recall that on the night of the duchess's death, I asked you whether you had ever tasted blood, fresh blood, human blood, and you said that you had not?'

'I do recall it, Rex,' he answered, his voice barely above a whisper. 'It is not a conversation one is likely to forget.'

'When I told you that I had tasted blood, and would taste blood again that very night, you asked me whose blood it was that I would taste.'

'I did. I remember it well.'

'And, pointing towards our hostess, across the crowded room, I told you that it would be hers.'

'I have not forgotten.' I sensed that his face was turned towards mine, but I could not see it in the gloom.

'May I ask you something, Oscar?'

'Anything.'

'Since that night, since the duchess's death, why have you not questioned me about any of this? You have told me about the enquiries you are making, about your interviews with the Prince of Wales and Lord Yarborough and the duke, but you have not cross-examined me. Why not?'

'There is no need. You did not taste the duchess's blood that night.'

'How do you know?'

'Because, from the moment you spoke of doing so until the moment my friend Sherard caught sight of the duchess's dead body within the telephone room, you did not leave my side.'

'That is so.'

'Besides, as I told you last night, whatever you are, you are not a vampire.'

'And how can you be so certain of that?'

'Because a true vampire, as every folklorist knows, has an aversion to roses – and you, my dear Rex, do not.'

I felt his hand reach for my coat and lightly touch the buttonhole he had given me. I felt his mouth as it placed a gentle kiss upon my cheek.

I have him in my grasp.

37

Letter from Bram Stoker to his wife, Florence, delivered by messenger at 9 a.m. on Monday, 17 March 1890

Lyceum Theatre,
Strand,
London

3 a.m.

Florrie –

I am just in from the expedition to Mortlake. I am log-tired, but wide awake! We have rehearsals starting at ten in the morning (sharp – you know what the old man's like), so I shall kip down here and get what sleep I can.

I will give you a full account of our moonlit picnic among the gravestones when I see you. Suffice to say, Oscar and his young 'vampire' friend – a pale-faced Adonis by the name of Rex LaSalle – were in their element, and entered wholeheartedly into the spirit of the occasion, while the other two – Robert Sherard and Arthur Conan Doyle (good man) – were more circumspect.

At the finish, Doyle, I think, was frankly shocked. I had my reservations too. As you know, I go because the notion of the 'Vampire Club' amuses me and because there are true scholars there as well as rogues and vagabonds. (And royalty. Our patron was in attendance tonight – memorably so.) I believe that I learn something every time that I attend, but perhaps now I have enough research – the time has come to write the wretched book!

I will send this note to you by messenger at daybreak. The clock on St Clement Danes has just struck three. I trust you are sleeping sweetly, beloved one. May the blessed St Patrick watch over us both.

Bram

38

From the journal of Arthur Conan Doyle

I travelled out to Mortlake with Bram Stoker (Irving's man of business) and Robert Sherard.

South of the river, our cabman lost his bearings. Twice, he had to stop to ask the way: first at a public house in Barnes, and then, half a mile further on, at a deserted crossroads, where, at midnight, by moonlight, we came upon a curious scene: a man (heavily cloaked) and a stable lad, standing by the roadside, grooming a fine white stallion. (If I had a fancy for such things, I would have said it was a ghostly vision.) When our cabman called out to them, neither answered, but the cloaked man pointed west and our cabman drove on.

It was long past twelve when, eventually, beyond Mortlake village itself, down an overgrown and lonely track, we reached the churchyard of St Mary Magdalen. I had expected to find there a handful of hooded figures lurking between the graves. Instead, it was like a bankside party on Boat Race night.

There were upward of fifty souls in attendance: men of all ages and every class: young bucks in evening dress, clerks and tradesmen in overcoats and waterproofs, ruffians in little more than rags. They stood in small clusters, illuminated by lanterns and torchlight; some holding pint pots and uncorked bottles of wine, carousing; some engaged in loud and earnest conversation; a few, in the shadows, away from the rest, silent, seemingly wrapped in one another's arms.

'All manner of men come here,' said Stoker, as he led us through the throng.

'What brings them?' I asked. 'Do they all claim to be vampires?'

Stoker laughed. 'Far from it. This is a club without rules, open to all. Only one or two will call themselves vampires. Rather more will be like me – students of the subject. Most, however, will confess to coming mainly for amusement's sake, for the company, out of curiosity –' he glanced towards the figures in the shadows – 'or for reasons of concupiscence and carnality.'

'And the police make no objection?'

'The club secretary is the deputy commissioner for the metropolis.' He laughed once more. 'We are a long way from Southsea, Dr Doyle.'

Purposefully, he led us up the narrow pathway towards the porch of the church.

'You must meet tonight's presiding officer,' he said. 'He's a good man. From County Cork. He'll be giving the address.'

'He's a priest,' I murmured in astonishment.

'He is indeed,' answered Stoker. 'It's his church, his graveyard. We are his guests this evening.'

Beaming broadly, the priest, a stooped, elderly, white-haired man, dressed in a black cope and all the vestments appropriate to a funeral, stepped eagerly towards us with outstretched arms. Though his back was bent, his spirit was lively. He exuded bonhomie and smelt of whiskey and burnt incense. He embraced Bram Stoker as he might a brother, then shook Sherard and me warmly by the hand. His face was deeply lined, but his fingers were soft and delicate.

'Welcome, gentlemen,' he said in booming tones. 'Bram sent a note to tell me you'd be coming. I know all about you. Oscar is already here with his young friend. They've gone in search of wine. Welcome. You are among friends. We don't stand on ceremony. In a graveyard, all are equal. It's the democracy of death.'

We stood with the priest – Father John Callaghan is his name – as the whisper went round that the formal proceedings were about to begin. From all corners of the churchyard, the members of the Vampire Club and their guests moved slowly towards the church porch.

'It's a fine turnout tonight,' said the priest, with satisfaction. 'They look like carol-singers gathering around the tree on Christmas Eve, don't they? If you didn't know it, you'd not believe they were a band of brothers come to raise the undead.'

'Is that your purpose,' I asked, 'to raise the undead?'

Father Callaghan chuckled and laid his hand on my shoulder reassuringly. 'Don't worry, Dr Doyle.

I'm a good Catholic. I have my rosary and my crucifix about me. You'll be quite safe.'

I stood alongside him on the porch step as the men began to settle in a broad semi-circle before us. Beneath the yellow and orange light of the lanterns and wax candles, their faces glowed with expectation. As I sensed the priest was about to speak, I made to distance myself a little, but he put out a hand to restrain me.

'Stay,' he said. 'Don't go. You're young and strong. I may need you.'

He turned his head towards the interior of the porch and, with a brief nod, indicated a pair of gravedigger's spades resting against the doorway. I stood where I was, filled with foreboding.

I felt a hand touch my elbow. It was Oscar, holding an open bottle of wine to his lips and raising it to me. His face was shining; his eyes sparkled in the torchlight. Rex LaSalle stood at his side, impassively. I looked at the motley crowd ranged before us, then glanced back at the gravedigger's shovels resting in the doorway.

I leant towards Oscar and whispered into his ear: 'Is this wise? Is this sensible?'

Oscar laughed gently. 'I do hope not,' he murmured. 'Nowadays most people die of a sort of creeping common sense and discover when it is too late that the only things in life one never regrets are one's mistakes.'

As the church clock struck one, Father Callaghan raised his arms and addressed his congregation.

'In the name of the Father and of the Son and of the Holy Ghost, peace be among us.'

With his right hand held high for all to see, he made a sign of the cross.

'"I am the resurrection and the life," saith the Lord; "he that believeth in me, though he were dead, yet shall he live: and whosoever liveth and believeth in me shall never die." I know that my redeemer liveth, and that he shall stand at the latter day upon the earth: and though this body of mine be corrupted and destroyed – ashes to ashes and dust to dust – yet shall I see God.' He paused. 'That is God's promise. That is all that we have. We brought nothing into this world, and it is certain we can carry nothing out. The Lord giveth, and the Lord taketh away; blessed be the name of the Lord.'

The Irish priest turned out to be a powerful orator. He spoke, without notes and without pause, for nigh on half an hour and held his auditors throughout. He talked of life and death and the life hereafter – of the joy of life, of the gift of death, of the certainty of the life hereafter. He spoke of St Mary Magdalen and reminded us that it was she who first saw Christ on the day of His resurrection. He talked of the day of judgement and told tales of his travels around the cemeteries of Europe. He recounted how he was recently returned from Vienna where he found that the gravestones of unmarried women all featured the word *Fräulein*, meaning 'Miss', before the name of the departed. This, he explained, is because, at the sounding of the last trump, virgins will take precedence and it will be so much easier for Our Lord to gather them to him if their graves are clearly marked. He spoke with humour and heart and authority.

In the first half of his address Father Callaghan made no mention of vampires whatsoever. Then, quite suddenly, as the full moon appeared from behind the clouds and, in my ear, Oscar whispered a low 'At last!', the priest declared: 'I have spoken of the quick and the dead and the life everlasting. Let me now speak of the undead and let us pray for those who cannot rest in peace.'

He spoke of the undead as 'souls in torment', pitiful creatures trapped in limbo between this life and the next, destined to roam the world under cover of darkness, for all eternity, driven by bile and envy, and sustained only by the blood of innocents. He told us of our Christian duty to unearth the undead, to challenge and destroy them – for their sake as much as for our own.

He talked in wonderfully practical terms of how to set about this: of ways of identifying graves, of means of breaking into tombs and vaults and mausolea, of the craft of digging up coffins by gas lamp and candlelight, of the art of piercing and pinioning a vampire with a sword, a sickle or a scythe. He spoke of the uncorrupted bodies of the undead, of their open, wild and staring eyes, of their bloated features and their blood-soaked lips.

Finally, he told us that, on his travels in Europe, he had visited Albania where he had come across the most ancient and, he averred, the most reliable of all the rituals used to identify the graves of the undead. The method had the advantages of simplicity and beauty. It involved merely leading a virgin boy through a graveyard on a virgin stallion. With the youth on his bare back, instinctively the horse would baulk and rise up if he stepped over earth in which a vampire was buried.

'Will he show us, I wonder?' whispered Oscar at my side.

The priest turned to Oscar and smiled: 'I will.' He looked at me and enquired, 'What is the time, Dr Doyle?'

I checked my half-hunter. 'Half past one,' I said.

'Gentlemen,' announced the priest, stretching his hands out before him once more. 'Would you turn due north, towards the river, towards the track along which you travelled here tonight. Turn, gentlemen, and watch closely. Turn now, but make no noise.'

There was a brief murmuring as the men turned away from the church to gaze across the graveyard to the deserted track that led from the village. Silence fell. We waited. The wind blew gently in the trees. Somewhere in the undergrowth a fox or weasel stirred. Nothing happened.

'Wait!' said the priest. 'Be patient.'

The church clock struck the half-hour and then, from a distance, we heard the sound of a horse's hooves approaching. Out of the darkness it came, slowly, steadily, gently tossing its magnificent head from side to side. It was the pure white stallion we had seen at the crossroads an hour before. The horse was led towards us by the man in the cloak. His hat was pulled forward over his eyes, but as he approached, in the light of the lanterns, I recognised him – though I will not record his name here. On the horse's bare back sat the stable lad, a youth of no more than fifteen or sixteen years of age. Though the night was cold, the boy was naked.

'His skin is very white,' said Oscar.

39

From the notebooks of Robert Sherard

What happened? Nothing happened. The drama was all in the moment of revelation.

When the horse and the boy came out of the darkness there were gasps and cheers – and then complete silence. As the priest stepped down from the church porch to greet them, the crowd parted to let him through. When the priest reached the horse, the animal appeared to genuflect before him. More gasps, more cheers. The priest bowed towards the horse's cloaked minder – who, removing his hat with a flourish, returned the bow.

It was young Prince Eddy, the club's royal patron. More gasps, applause and loud hurrahs. The priest reached up to stroke the stallion's forelock. He blessed the animal with a sign of the cross and then, holding it by the mane, helped lead it through the graveyard. The men in the crowd fell back to create pathways along which the horse, the priest and the prince could pass. At three or four of the graves, the creature paused to graze a moment or sniff the air. At no point did it baulk or rear up – or even throw back its head and whinny.

Before the church clock struck two, the show was over. It would seem there are no vampires buried in the churchyard of St Mary Magdalen, Mortlake.

The crowd accepted the disappointment with a good grace. When the demonstration was done, the priest dismissed us with a brief farewell and a final blessing. All at once, the gathering, suddenly conscious of its collective weariness and the chill of the night air, began to disperse. Whistles blew and the cry went up: within minutes the deserted country track appeared as crowded as Park Lane. Bicycles were pulled from the undergrowth; donkey carts, pony-traps and carriages arrived from nowhere.

Bram Stoker and Conan Doyle reclaimed their hackney cab and hurried to take their leave. They were among the first to depart. Doyle could fairly be described as fleeing the scene! Oscar chose to linger. I said I would wait with him.

I lit a cigarette and, from the church porch, through the milling throng, I stood and watched as the naked boy, now shivering, dismounted his horse. The prince was with him. He took off his cloak and wrapped it round the lad. We had all recognised the prince at once, of course. It was only Oscar who recognised the boy.

40

**From the notebook of Inspector Hugh Boone of
Scotland Yard, Monday, 17 March 1890**

This sordid business grows more vicious by the hour. And more
entangled. Will what did for us last year in Beaufort Street defeat
us once again? The involvement of certain persons makes
hammering home the nail near impossible.

Duke of Clarence

41

From the notebooks of Robert Sherard

'You are Frank Watkins?'

'That's me.'

'Page to His Royal Highness the Prince of Wales?'

'One of them.'

'And friend to His Royal Highness Prince Albert Victor also, it seems.'

'Friend and bum-boy.'

The lad laughed and immediately blushed at his own cheek. Prince Eddy leant across the table to box his ears. 'Hold your tongue!'

The boy pulled back to avoid the blow. 'Mr Wilde understands, don't you, Mr Wilde?'

Oscar sat at the head of the table, complacently, his fingers intertwined and resting on his stomach, his eyes half closed, observing the scene as an Ottoman sultan might a catfight in his harem. He smiled, but said nothing.

'Mr Wilde's a man of the world,' the boy continued, leaning back on his chair, balancing it precariously on its rear legs. He grinned and slowly, deliberately, ran his fingers through his flop of copper-coloured hair. 'I knows that.'

The prince got to his feet. With his right hand he managed to land a glancing blow to the boy's left ear. 'Hold your tongue!'

The boy – still dressed in the prince's cloak – pushed back his chair and thrust his head up towards his assailant. 'My tongue's done you some service in its time!' he jeered.

The prince grabbed the lad by the scruff of the neck and held him hard. 'You are an impertinent whippersnapper.'

Frank Watkins looked up at the prince and snarled. The prince took the boy's hair roughly in both hands and wrenched the lad's head backward sharply. 'You are an impertinent whippersnapper. Admit it.' He pushed his own face down close to the boy's. '*Admit it.*'

'I am an impertinent whippersnapper.' The boy grimaced.

'You are a miserable and humble worm, unworthy even to tie my shoelaces. *Say it.*'

The prince tightened his grip on the lad's head, making him flinch.

'Say it!'

'I am a miserable and humble worm, unworthy even to tie your shoelaces,' whimpered the boy.

Prince Albert Victor let go of his victim and ran his hand roughly across the lad's thick and tangled head of hair. 'That's better,' he said. He started to caress the boy's neck. 'I'm happy, Frank, when you do my bidding.'

'And your bedding?'

The lad looked up at the prince and grinned. His face was round and brown and freckled; his teeth were small and white, but uneven. And one tooth – a canine on his upper jaw – was missing. When he smiled, Frank Watkins had the look of a small boy.

'He has a wonderful way with words,' murmured Oscar.

'And with horses,' said Father Callaghan, coming to the table with another bottle of wine and fresh pot of hot coffee. 'That's a fine white stallion he found for us – the real thing. Not a grey masquerading.'

'I've got to get him back to the barracks by eight,' said the boy. 'I promised the captain.'

It was now four o'clock in the morning and we were seated at table in the gas-lit parlour at the priest's house on the edge of Mortlake village. It was a small house (two up, two down): modern, cramped and dark. We were there awaiting the arrival of dawn when, by daylight, the royal prince and the royal page could return to town on horseback. Father Callaghan had promised to drive Oscar and me to Chelsea in his pony and trap. The priest had offered us armchairs, a settee and his bed to sleep on, but Oscar had asked for bread and wine and conversation.

'In my experience,' said Oscar, 'a good priest can perform miracles with bread and wine – and a good conversation is what makes life on earth worthwhile. Words are what define us, after all. It is only language that differentiates us from the animals and those whose hands do trail upon the ground. It is only by language that we rise above the lower creatures – by language, which is the parent not the child of thought.'

'I love to hear you talk, Mr Wilde,' said the boy, looking at Oscar and smiling.

'And I love to hear myself talk,' said Oscar. 'It is one of my greatest pleasures. I often have long conversations all by myself, and I am so clever that sometimes I don't understand a single word of what I am saying.'

He laughed and raised his cup of wine to the company. As he looked about the shadowy room, his brow darkened.

'I have just realised something quite shocking,' he said, sitting forward. 'There are five of us here. Four of us are seated and one is standing – and the one who is standing is a prince of the royal blood. We have forgotten all protocol, gentlemen. The moon is full and the world's gone topsy-turvy.'

'It matters not,' cried Prince Eddy. 'It matters not a jot. Stay seated, please. I love the freedom here.'

'Freedom is the only law that genius knows,' said Oscar.

'I know nothing about genius,' said the prince, 'but I know that in this room I can breathe. I can be myself.' He turned and, leaning over the boy, kissed the top of the lad's head tenderly. 'I am free here, to be who I am, to say what I please.'

'Yes,' said Father Callaghan. 'You may speak quite freely here. You may regard this room as your confessional. All your secrets are safe with me.'

'Are we to hear secrets?' cried Oscar. 'I adore other people's secrets,' he said teasingly. 'My own don't interest me, of course. They lack the charm of novelty.'

The prince looked about the small parlour, found a stool by the window and, bringing it to the table, sat down between the page and the priest. I was seated facing him. We were no more than two feet apart and, for a moment, consciously, I studied him. I tried to see beyond the pock-marked sallow skin, the black-rimmed eyes, the thin lips, the feeble chin, the villainous moustache – what Oscar calls the 'look of corruption' – but I failed. Appearances can be deceptive, but Prince Albert Victor has the face of a weak and vicious man.

As I studied him, he looked briefly into my eyes. As I gazed at him, he stared at me, then swung his gaze away, abruptly. Turning back to the page-boy, with a little show he lifted up the lad's hand, brought it slowly to his mouth and kissed it.

'Is our young friend your secret?' asked Father Callaghan.

'No,' replied the prince, letting go of the boy, 'my unhappiness is my secret. To the world I am the dissolute son of the Prince of Wales – irresponsible, totally spoilt, indulged beyond all understanding. I have everything that any man could want – everything that money and position can buy. Yet I have nothing – because I am not free.'

'We are all free in our hearts,' said Oscar.

'No!'

'Yes.'

'No. My heart is not my own, Mr Wilde. I am not a free man. I cannot marry the woman I love.'

'I thought you loved me,' said Frank Watkins plaintively.

The prince laughed. 'I do love you – but I cannot marry you. Men cannot marry men.'

'Why not?' asked the boy.

'It is not Nature's way,' said the prince.

'It's our way,' said the boy.

'It is not natural. I must marry a woman. I must have children. But I cannot marry the woman I wish to marry.'

'Why not?' asked Oscar.

'Because I am to be king! I am to be king of England one day. And Emperor of India. Therefore I must marry one of my German cousins. You see the logic?' He laughed and shook his head.

'It keeps it in the family,' said Oscar.

'Have you seen Margaret of Prussia, Mr Wilde? She has all the loveliness of a warthog.'

'That is uncharitable,' chided Father Callaghan.

'It is the truth – pure and simple,' cried Prince Eddy.

Oscar said nothing. The young prince turned once more to the page-boy and ran the back of his knuckles around the boy's chin. Playfully, the lad caught the prince's index finger between his teeth and held it tight.

'Your Royal Highness appears to be living a life that is relatively unconstrained,' said Oscar, looking at the prince over his cup of sacramental wine.

Prince Eddy pulled his hand away from the boy's mouth. 'I cannot live as I would wish to live.'

'But you wander the woods by moonlight, with your white stallion and your catamite. You trawl graveyards for vampires . . .'

'I take my pleasures where I can.'

'I am pleased to hear it,' said Oscar, bowing his head towards the prince. 'Pleasure is the only thing one should live for.'

'Is that true, Mr Wilde?' asked the priest, getting to his

feet and moving round the table to serve more wine and coffee.

'To realise oneself is the prime aim of life, and to realise oneself through pleasure is finer than to do so through pain. On that point I am entirely on the side of the ancients – the Greeks. It is a pagan idea. I apologise for raising it at your table, Father. I mean no disrespect.'

As he passed him, the old priest rested his hand on Oscar's shoulder. Oscar looked up at him and smiled.

'I have no problem with pleasure,' said the priest.

'Do you pursue vampires for pleasure, Father?' Oscar asked.

'No,' said the priest seriously. 'I regard the pursuit of vampires as a painful duty.'

'And Your Royal Highness? What brings you to the pursuit of vampires?'

'Porphyria,' answered the prince. 'The disease of vampires.'

'Ah,' exclaimed Oscar, 'of course.' A sudden look of anguish clouded his face. 'I should have realised. Porphyria – the disease of vampires . . . and of royalty.'

'Of Prussian royalty,' said Prince Eddy sharply. 'Of Hanoverian kings and princes.'

'And Stuart queens?' asked Oscar. 'Was Mary Queen of Scots not a victim also?'

'I've heard it said,' answered the prince. 'But there's no proof.'

'What's "porphyria"?' asked Frank Watkins, pulling his chair closer to the table and putting a hand out towards Oscar who was lighting another of his Turkish cigarettes.

'The word is Greek,' answered Oscar, throwing a

cigarette down the table towards the boy, 'as so often the best words are. It means the colour purple. Porphyria is a disease of the blood that drives men mad.'

'My great-great-grandfather, King George III, died of it. In our family, it is known as "the purple secret".'

'The faces of victims turn purple during an attack. Their faeces turn purple. Their urine runs purple.' Oscar leant forward to light Frank Watkins's cigarette.

'And no one knows the cause – or the cure,' said the prince.

'And vampires have this porphyria, do they?' asked the page-boy, puffing happily on his cigarette.

'Or could it be the other way around?' pondered Oscar. 'Could it be that in a world of ignorance and fear, victims of porphyria are mistaken for vampires?' He looked at the page-boy. 'You should know, Frank, that some people say that the vampire – like the werewolf and the unicorn – is no more than a myth.'

'But you believe in vampires, don't you, Mr Wilde?' asked the boy.

'I am a romantic, Frank. I believe in dragons and mermaids, too. I believe in Pegasus, the flying horse, and Pan, the god of shepherds. And when I am visiting Marlborough House or Buckingham Palace I am even ready to believe in the Divine Right of Kings.'

'I believe in vampires,' said the boy earnestly.

Oscar laughed. 'You are quite right. It is a good rule. Believe in anything, provided that it is quite incredible. To know the truth, one must imagine a myriad of falsehoods.'

'If I have porphyria,' said Prince Albert Victor, 'I will go mad – like George III.'

The boy, ignoring the prince, looked eagerly at Oscar. 'You've met a vampire, haven't you, Mr Wilde?'

'I have a friend who claims to be one, but he's not.'

'Is that the young man who was with you tonight?' asked Father Callaghan.

'Yes,' said Oscar. 'He is beautiful, is he not? Rex LaSalle is his name.'

'I recognised him,' said Father Callaghan. 'I have met him before. I am not sure where – perhaps at a meeting of the Vampire Club. I did not speak to him tonight. Where is he now?'

'Vanished into thin air,' said Oscar. 'When it was all over I looked for him, but he'd gone.'

'Rex LaSalle?' said Prince Eddy. 'I know him. I met him at the Duchess of Albemarle's reception. He introduced himself. He broke through Dighton Probyn's ring of defences and introduced himself! He was the only amusing man I met that night. Sir Dighton holed me up in a corner with the President of the Royal Society – the dullest man in Christendom.'

'I saw you there that night, Your Royal Highness,' said Oscar, smiling. 'Whenever I caught sight of you, far from being holed up in a corner, you were centre stage, entertaining the ladies.'

'Was I?' said the prince. 'I don't recall. Apart from your friend, it was a tedious evening. Full of grey old men and drab young women. Why were you there, Mr Wilde?'

'Because I was asked,' said Oscar. 'Why were you there, sir?'

The prince laughed. 'Because I was commanded. My father took me. He insisted. I had no choice. It was my "duty". I am being schooled for a life of "duty" – broken in, readied for an eternity of small-talk and ribbon-cutting.'

'There is more to it than that,' said Father Callaghan soothingly.

'So my father tells me. I am being groomed for great-ness – according to Papa. Soon I am to get a dukedom – did you know? I am to be Duke of Clarence.'

'Congratulations.' The priest rested his open palm on the prince's clenched fist. The prince pulled his hand away.

'It's a title with a ring to it,' said Oscar.

'And a history, Mr Wilde. I know that.' The prince got to his feet and moved impatiently towards the window, where he stood with his back to us. 'Am I, too, destined to end my days done to death in a butt of malmsey?'

'There may be worse ways to go,' said Oscar, sipping his cup of sacramental wine.

'Am I to be drowned like the runt of the litter?'

'You are the eldest son,' said Father Callaghan, 'and your father loves you.'

'My mother loves me,' said the prince.

'Your father loves you,' repeated the priest.

'Does he? When all I do is disappoint him? In the navy, in the army, at Cambridge – I failed. I couldn't cut the mustard. That's all I do – fail. And disappoint. And bring disgrace and scandal on the family. Papa is obsessed with scandal – and what the Queen will think.' He turned his head towards Oscar and looked at him unflinchingly. 'That, I assume, is why he has involved you in this Albemarle business, Mr Wilde –

my father wants to discover the truth so that he can suppress it.'

Oscar put down his cup of wine and returned the prince's gaze. 'Your Royal Highness knows about my informal "investigations" then?'

'I do. Owl told me. He tells me things. And how are these "investigations" proceeding? What is the mystery?'

'How did the duchess die? That is the question.'

'I thought it was a heart attack.'

'It may prove to be more complicated than that.'

'So she was not found in bed by her maid in the morning?'

'No. She was found at midnight, half naked, with blood upon her torso and deep wounds in her neck.'

The prince began to laugh. 'Are you going to tell me that the Duchess of Albemarle was the victim of a vampire, Mr Wilde? Is that it? Is that what you suspect?'

Oscar said nothing. The prince's bitter laughter turned to quiet fury.

'Or do you have something more sinister in mind? Do tell me. Do you know that imagining one is a vampire is a symptom of porphyria? Taking on the characteristics of a vampire is a part of the madness of porphyria – did you know that? Has my father asked you to investigate me? Is that why you are here, Mr Wilde? My father is always ready to believe the worst of me. Two years ago, when the whispering started that I was Jack the Ripper – God save the mark – my father was ready to believe it. Does he now think I murdered Helen Albemarle?'

'Did you?' asked Oscar.

The prince turned away to regain his composure. Having calmed himself, he stood by the little window peering out at the coming dawn. 'It's getting light,' he said eventually.

'Was the Duchess of Albemarle your mistress, Your Royal Highness? You were of an age.'

'I will not say another word.' He turned back towards the room and smiled. 'I must not make Frank jealous.'

Frank Watkins was asleep, seated at the parlour table with his head resting on his folded arms. Gently, the prince ruffled the boy's copper-coloured hair.

'It's time to go, Frank. We're no longer wanted here.'

Muswell Manor

42

Postcard from Arthur Conan Doyle to his wife, Louisa 'Touie' Conan Doyle, postmarked Monday, 17 March 1890, London W., 10 a.m.

A late night at Mortlake – searching for vampires! An unsatisfactory and unsavoury experience.

A good breakfast at the hotel this morning. I shared a table with James Tissot, a French painter, who told me an extraordinary story that has the makings of a novel – or possibly an adventure for one S. Holmes.

Now setting off for the clinic at Muswell Hill. This time tomorrow, I shall be home – God willing. Three cheers and amen to that.

I miss you, Touie.

Your ACD

43

Letter from Constance Wilde to her mother-in-law, Lady Wilde

16 Tite Street, Chelsea
17.iii.90

Dear Mother,

At last, I am sending you the copy of my book of fairy stories. I promised to send it to you weeks ago, I know, but so much has been happening here, that, I confess, I clean forgot! I only remembered this morning when I realised that it is St Patrick's Day and my mind went back to the good old days in Dublin. Do you miss them very much?

The stories are all the ones that my dear grandmother (Mama Mary) used to tell me when I was a girl. 'Puss in Boots' and 'Jack the Giant-Killer' are the two my boys like the best. I know, of course, that my stories are not so original as Oscar's, nor so exquisitely written (your son is a genius), but I think that for little people they are less alarming. Oscar can be quite alarming at times.

Last Sunday, my friend Lady Sandhurst came to tea – do you know her? She is the best of women and one of the leading lights of the London Missionary Society – and when Cyril asked, 'What are missionaries, Papa?' Oscar replied, 'Missionaries, my boy, are the divinely provided food for destitute and under-fed cannibals. Whenever they are on the brink of starvation, Heaven, in its infinite mercy, sends them a

nice plump missionary.' Lady Sandhurst (who is quite plump
herself) was profoundly shocked.

I love Oscar so much. He is as wise and witty as he is kind –
and he is the kindest man there ever was. He has garlanded
me with daisy chains and I am bound to him with hoops of
steel. We are more than man and wife – we are the best of
friends. People think it extraordinary that Oscar should have
chosen to marry me. I think so too. I am very blessed and so
very happy.

Ever your loving and grateful daughter,
Constance

PS. I do not know when I shall be able to take this parcel to the
post office. Oscar and his friend are just returned – with a
Catholic priest in tow! – and they are demanding both
breakfast and my complete attention. They have been out all
night, under the full moon, searching for vampires! Oscar tells
me that it was you, dear mother, who first introduced him to the
twilight world of the vampire and the werewolf.

44

Letter from Oscar Wilde to Rex LaSalle, care of 17 Wardour Street, Soho, delivered by messenger

> 16 Tite Street, Chelsea
> Monday morning

My dear Rex,

Where are you? How are you? What has happened to you, my precious, gilt and graceful boy? Why did you not say au revoir among the graves? Out of a complex night came a simple dawn – but you were nowhere to be seen.

Are you alone in your room? Or have you found some other Eden? Where are you hiding? What are you hiding? And why? I hope that you will want to share some of your many secrets with your admiring and devoted friend,

Oscar Wilde

This evening I am dining with Arthur Conan Doyle at the Langham Hotel. If you come by at ten o'clock you will find us in the Palm Court. Arthur will retire at eleven with a glass of warm milk and the collected works of Sir Walter Scott. You and I may then take a moonlit stroll and reflect upon the truth that every impulse we strive to strangle *broods in the mind and poisons us. The only way to get rid of temptation is to yield to it. Tonight, together, let us hear the chimes at midnight.*

45

Notes made by Arthur Conan Doyle following his visit to the Charcot Clinic at Muswell Manor, Monday, 17 March 1890

The Charcot Clinic is set in the east wing of a large country house on top of Muswell Hill. The house itself – Muswell Manor – is dark, covered in vines and cloistered by lime trees, but from the carriage drive leading to it there are fine views south towards the City of London. (There was a mist this morning, but even so I could see the dome of St Paul's Cathedral five miles away.)

Muswell Hill is an old English village fast becoming a suburb of the metropolis. Its name derives from the natural spring – the 'mossy well' – that has its source in the grounds of Muswell Manor and produces a pure drinking water famed for its curative powers.

Since medieval times Muswell Hill has been a place of pilgrimage for the sick in search of a miracle. Since the end of the last century, Muswell Manor has been a lunatic asylum. Since December of last year, the asylum has been under the direction of Lord Yarborough, MD, FRS.

My visit today – postponed from last Friday – was at the personal invitation of Lord Yarborough. He has approached a number of general practitioners like me – doctors who are members of the Provincial Medical and Surgical Association study group on hysteria. He has invited us to come to Muswell Manor, individually or in small groups, to visit the Charcot Clinic where he and his colleagues are exploring the pathology of hysteria. They are doing so under the guidance – and using the techniques – of the great Jean-Martin Charcot, professor of diseases of the nervous system at the Paris Medical Faculty and, indisputably, the leading neurologist of our time.

In his letter of invitation, Lord Yarborough expressed the certainty that I would learn something of value from my visit and the hope that it would lead to me recommending patients to him. He was candid: 'The clinic needs patients, both for their benefit and to assist us in our research.'

Foolishly, because I left my hotel in haste this morning, I omitted to take Lord Yarborough's letter with me to Muswell Hill. For this reason, on arrival I presented myself at the main entrance to Muswell Manor instead of the entrance to the east wing. When I rang the bell, I heard no sound, but the front door swung open almost at once. An old man – smiling, toothless, hairless, wearing nothing but a nightshirt, flimsy and soiled – beckoned me across the threshold and, in a thin, piping voice, begged to know my business. I explained that I had an appointment with Lord Yarborough. Solemnly, the old man told me that Lord Yarborough was not available, but that the Duke of Wellington would see me right away.

At once I realised my mistake, but it was too late. I was already surrounded by a dozen lunatics – mad men and women, bawling, screeching, laughing, pulling at my person, tearing at my clothes, demanding my attention and my sympathy. For minutes on end (or so it seemed) I stood locked in their midst, pleading with them, unable to free myself from their ghastly grip. Eventually, rescuers – in the unlikely form of two nuns, nursing sisters armed with heavy kitchen brooms – appeared from nowhere and, with alarming ferocity, set about my captors with their broomsticks, beating the hapless creatures into submission.

As my insane assailants limped and sloped away, some whimpering, some snarling angrily, some in tears, one of the nuns followed after them, shooing them towards the corridor that led out of the hallway, like a farmer's wife bustling after errant geese and chickens. The other nun, the older of the pair, stayed to reprimand me.

'This is not the public entrance,' she scolded. 'This is for patients only. They should not be disturbed. Some of them are dangerous. Did you meet the Duke of Wellington?'

'He is not the Duke of Wellington, surely?'

'No, but he is the Earl of Yattenden – the son of the Marquess of Truro. And he is capable of murder. He may have killed his own mother, but it was never proved. That's why he's here – and not down the road.'

'Down the road' is the Colney Hatch asylum

where more than three thousand lunatics are housed under one roof at public expense. 'Here' is Muswell Manor, a privately owned, fee-paying institution, where fifty deranged gentlefolk live in comparative comfort.

'Our patients are people of quality, all from good families – though we never see their families, of course. They are here because their families want nothing to do with them.'

When the nun spoke, I recognised her accent at once. She is an Aberdonian. When I introduced myself, she recognised my name, being herself an admirer of Sherlock Holmes.

The scolding done and familiarity established, Sister Agnes escorted me through the house to the east wing. Despite her forbidding features – an aquiline nose, a narrow mouth, a wart upon her chin – and her prowess with the broomstick, I took her to be a kindly woman. She told me something of the history of Muswell Manor and spoke with feeling of the pathetic creatures in her charge.

'We cannot cure them. We pray for them – and feed them and water them, and do our best to keep them clean and out of harm's way. They are not here to regain their wits. We have no treatment to offer them. They are here to live out their days. That's all. Some of them have been living here for more than sixty years.'

Most of the patients, as we passed by them, shied away from us, eyes cast down, cowering, saying nothing. Most wore nightshirts either covered with outdoor coats or dressing gowns.

There was but one exception that I saw. Outside the door that connected the main house with the east wing, sitting upright upon a hard-backed chair, gazing straight towards us, was a handsome woman of about fifty. Her hair was grey, her face was pale, but her dark-brown eyes burned fiercely. Though it was mid-morning she wore a full-length evening gown, of silk, plum-coloured with an edging of royal blue. As we came close to her, I noticed that the lace frills at her throat and wrists were worn and badly torn. She got to her feet and curtsied low before us.

'I must see Lord Yarborough,' she said.

'You cannot, Lady M,' said Sister Agnes. 'You know that. Lord Yarborough will not see you.'

'I must see him,' repeated the lady. 'I will see him. I will wait.'

She curtsied once more and resumed her seat. Her eyes never left us as Sister Agnes searched for her bundle of keys, found the one that she needed, unlocked the door to the east wing and escorted me through.

'Lady M has been with us for twenty years,' the nun explained, with a sigh, locking the door behind us. 'Every day she expects to be released. It will never happen.'

'And why will Lord Yarborough not see her?' I asked.

'Because my time is precious and there would be no point.'

Lord Yarborough's voice rang out along the corridor.

'Sister Agnes, kindly bring my guest this way.'

Lord Yarborough's office door was open. The nun took me to it.

'Thank you, Sister.'

The nun accepted her dismissal, bobbed a curtsy and went on her way.

'Welcome, Dr Doyle,' said Lord Yarborough affably. 'I am grateful to you for coming. You are our only visitor today.'

He did not rise from his desk, nor did he shake my hand. He simply indicated that I should take the seat facing him. I did so.

'I own the whole of Muswell Manor,' he went on at once, 'but I do not concern myself with the asylum. The patients there are beyond recall. I can do nothing for them. The asylum is Sister Agnes's domain. My work is all here in the clinic. This is what I want you to see.'

For almost an hour I sat listening to Lord Yarborough. He spoke swiftly, fluently, with passion and without pause. He is, he explained, both a physician and a psychiatrist, but, above all, he sees himself as a disciple of Jean-Martin Charcot.

'Of all men, he is the one I most admire. I was born to position and privilege. Charcot was not.'

He told me Charcot's story: how he had been born in Paris in 1825, the son of a wagon-maker; how all that he had achieved had been through his own endeavours; how, as a young man, he had secured himself a position at the notorious, sprawling Salpêtrière Hospital on the outskirts of

Paris, 'the Versailles of pain', 'the great emporium of human misery', where the lame and the halt, the lunatic and the senile, the demented and the depraved provided what Charcot called *'une sorte de musée pathologique vivant'* – a kind of living pathological museum.

Charcot, for over more than thirty years, found his specimens in that museum and did what no one in the field of neurology had done before: he studied them minutely, organ by organ, limb by limb, alive and dead. *Ante mortem*, he observed them in the closest detail, recording every symptom, noting every tic and twitch, every tremor and spasm; *post mortem*, he dissected them – without let or hindrance: the inmates of the Salpêtrière are society's detritus, so a doctor may do with them as he pleases. Through precise clinical observation and ruthless autopsy, Charcot made his great discoveries – anatomising upwards of a dozen significant conditions and diseases, from multiple sclerosis to cerebral haemorrhage.

'Charcot is a genius,' said Lord Yarborough, directing my eye to a framed photograph of the great man that stood upon his desk.

In the picture, Charcot was posed, like Bonaparte, with his right hand placed inside the front fold of his frock-coat.

'He is indeed the Napoleon of the neuroses. He understands the nervous system as no man has before him. Charcot can correlate plaques found on the brain to disorders of vision, speech and intellect. He can relate patterns of pathological behaviour to sclerotic patches on the spinal cord. And now, at the height of his powers, he is turning his attention to the study and treatment of hysteria – and it is with this work that we can help him.'

'Charcot is convinced that hysteria is a disease of the body as much as the mind?' I asked.

'He is. And so am I. Thus far the physical roots of hysteria have proved elusive, but we will discover them. In time. With patience.'

'And patients,' I added.

Lord Yarborough laughed. 'Indeed, Dr Doyle, we need patients. We have only four patients at present. We need many more. We need them alive and, alas, we also need them dead. We need to observe their hysterical behaviour with our own eyes and then explore their mortal remains beneath the microscope. There is no other way.'

'Your patients are all young females, I take it?'

'They are.'

'And they remain stubbornly alive?'

Lord Yarborough smiled. 'They do.'

'For their sakes,' I said, 'I am happy to hear it.'

'One of our patients did die recently. She took her own life. It was a tragedy, of course, but we were grateful to her.'

'You were able to conduct an autopsy?'

'With her family's permission. Professor Charcot undertook the autopsy. He came over from France. We did it here. I assisted. We have our own operating theatre and dissecting room.'

'And did the cadaver yield up any secrets?'

'None – none whatsoever – so the work goes on.'

Lord Yarborough got to his feet. He has the sheen of a man accustomed to command.

'Let me show you what we are doing, Doctor. We have not yet found the organic lesions we are looking for, but we are making progress, nonetheless. Come with me.'

I followed my host out of his office and along a series of deserted corridors. In the asylum the rooms were well appointed and comfortably furnished; there were prints and paintings hanging on the flock-papered walls and leafy plants in pots standing in corners and on windowsills. Here in the east wing there was nothing: the walls were bare, the floors uncarpeted, the gasoliers burnt low. The place felt quite empty.

I asked Lord Yarborough: 'Are you alone here? In your letter you spoke of "colleagues".'

'My colleagues are all in France. One of the nuns from the asylum is on the premises night and day, but I am the sole physician at the clinic and I cannot be here all the time. I have my practice in Harley Street to attend to – and, such as they are, my duties in the House of Lords. I need a junior here, but he'd have to be a specialist. Charcot promised me his assistant, Tourette, but he won't leave Paris. Would you consider leaving Southsea?'

I smiled but said nothing.

'I've looked you up, Dr Doyle,' said Lord Yarborough, pacing ahead, not looking back as he spoke. 'You're a Master of Surgery as well as a Bachelor of Medicine and you trained in Edinburgh – there's nowhere better. I know Dr Bell, your old tutor. You want to specialise in hysteria and you have an enquiring mind. I sense you have the right temperament, too. This job could suit you, Doyle – and it will be well paid. You have a young family. I imagine you are short of funds. You should think about it.'

He stopped, turned and looked at me. His eyes glittered. As he smiled, I noticed how white and sharp and pointed his canine teeth are. I thought to myself, absurdly: he has the mouth of a vampire.

We had reached the end of the farthermost corridor.

'Here we are,' he said and searched in his waistcoat pocket for a key. Having found it, he put it in the lock of the door on our right and turned it carefully, lowering his voice to speak: 'This is the patient I want you to see. She is already under hypnosis. I induced her before you arrived. Make no sudden movements, speak softly and speak only to me, and she will not know you are there.'

He turned the handle slowly and quietly opened the door.

The room we entered was much lighter than I had expected. There were curtains drawn at the window, but the fabric of them was thin and spring sunshine seeped both through and around them. The walls of the room were bare but whitewashed and clean. The only decoration was a simple wooden crucifix hanging above a plain chest of drawers. The only other furniture was an upright kitchen chair and a narrow iron bedstead.

Seated on the edge of the bed, with her feet touching the ground and her hands upon her knees, was the patient. Her head was bent forward and she appeared to be gazing down at a square scrap of Indian carpet that partially covered the floorboards and served as a bedside mat. She was a young woman of about twenty-five years of age. Her face was half hidden by her auburn hair, which hung loose down to her shoulders, but I could see that hers was the face of a lady. She had the most delicate features and the palest of skin.

She was also completely unclothed.

'Should we not dress her?' I whispered.

'There is no need,' replied Lord Yarborough. 'She is not aware of us and, seeing her as she is, we will more easily recognise the ecstasy when it takes her. Watch her neck and breasts and belly closely.'

'What am I to see?' I asked.

'The four stages of hysteria,' answered Lord Yarborough. 'At my command she will demonstrate each one in turn. What Charcot has discovered – and Louise will now demonstrate – is that every hysterical attack follows the same pattern, obeys the same rules.'

'Her name is Louise?'

'It is. She has been here for five months. Her family thought that her seizures were epileptic fits, but they were not. She is a true hysteric – and her hysterical attacks are exactly like those of every other hysteric Charcot has observed. It is their

164

uniformity, their universality, their mechanical regularity that tell us that hysteria is indeed an organic disease of the nervous system.'

'And I am to witness such an attack now?'

'You are. Observe it well. I shall trigger the attack with a simple command.' Lord Yarborough stepped into the centre of the room. 'Watch closely, Dr Doyle.'

I stood with my back against the door as Lord Yarborough positioned himself at the bedside immediately facing the naked girl. He stood at the far edge of the square of Indian carpet, about three feet away from his patient and, raising his voice, he called her name: 'Louise.' He spoke firmly. 'Louise, look at me.'

The young woman lifted her head. Her eyes were wide open and huge.

'Louise,' commanded Lord Yarborough, gazing directly down at the girl, 'when I clap my hands, the hysteria will be upon you once more and the attack will begin. Are you ready?'

The girl made no reply. Lord Yarborough clapped his hands.

At once her body began to shake. Her fingers twitched, her hands trembled, her knees shook. She rocked forwards and backwards on the bed. Her head turned from right to left and from left to right, at first rhythmically and, then, ever more frantically. As her head turned faster and faster, she ground her teeth, clenched her fists and began to beat one hand against her shoulder blade and the other upon her knee.

I stood watching the spectacle in horror. I wanted to reach out and hold the girl – release her from her frenzy. Lord Yarborough held out an arm towards me lest I be tempted to intervene.

'There's nothing to be done,' he whispered. 'The attack will take its course. We cannot stop it now – though we can speed it on its way. This first phase is what Charcot calls the *épileptoide* phase. Next come the *grands mouvements*.' He clapped his hands and called out loudly: 'Louise – move on!'

At once the girl stopped shaking and threw herself back on to the bed with a terrifying shriek. She swept her arms behind her head and lay on her back screaming, screeching, crying out with horrifying force. Suddenly she lifted her legs high into the air and, violently, repeatedly, obscenely, opened and closed them. I looked away and covered my ears as her piercing cries overwhelmed me. When I looked back I saw her body grotesquely contorted: she was bent backwards on the bed, her pelvis thrust forward, her spine arched, with only the top of her head and the base of her feet touching the mattress.

'This is depraved,' I murmured.

'This is the *arc-en-cercle*,' called Lord Yarborough through the girl's screams. 'It is what we expect. It happens every time.'

'Can you not stop this now?' I pleaded.

'We cannot halt the cycle, but we can drive it forward,' said Lord Yarborough. 'Next we have the *attitudes passionelles*.' Once more, he clapped his hands together and cried out: 'Louise, move on!'

Now the girl rolled on to her side and began to writhe upon the bed. She pressed the palms of her hands into the most intimate parts of her anatomy and, as she did so, yelped and moaned lasciviously.

'Move on,' I called out desperately.

Lord Yarborough laughed. 'Wait. Watch her torso turn scarlet first. See.'

I watched, embarrassed and ashamed, as the girl's skin displayed the stigmata of her ecstasy.

Lord Yarborough clapped his hands once more. 'Louise, move on.'

The girl threw her head to one side and spread her arms out wide, crossing her feet at the ankles in a grotesque imitation of Christ upon the cross.

'We have the final delirium now,' murmured Lord Yarborough. 'It will soon be over.'

And it was. The girl rolled to one side, brought her knees up towards her chest and tucked her hands beneath her chin. Her eyes were closed and her breathing slowed. As we watched, gradually she fell asleep.

'We can leave her now,' whispered Lord Yarborough. He leant over the girl and stroked her hair. With the back of his fingers, he caressed her cheek. Softly, he spoke into her ear: 'Well done, Louise. Sleep now, my child. Sleep.'

When we were outside her room once more, Lord Yarborough locked the door and returned the key to his waistcoat pocket. That done, he said to me: 'You should know that each of our patients would have demonstrated the effects of hysteria in exactly the same way.'

'Why did you choose to show me Louise?' I asked.

'Because she has been with us longest. We know her best. And I am her guardian as well as her physician.'

'Poor child,' I said. 'She is very lovely.'

'Yes, it makes her condition all the more tragic.'

'Somehow, I felt that I knew her. There was something familiar about her face.'

'You may have met her before,' said Lord Yarborough. 'You have certainly met her sister.'

'Her sister?'

'Yes, you met her sister quite recently – last Thursday evening, in fact. Louise is the younger sister of the late Duchess of Albemarle.'

'I am a Vampire'

46

From the notebooks of Robert Sherard

'A map of the world that does not include Utopia is not even worth glancing at. A wine list that does not include a Perrier-Jouët '84 should be dismissed out of hand.'

Oscar was in fine form tonight.

'Pleasure, gentlemen, is Nature's test, her sign of approval. When a man is happy he is in harmony with himself and his environment. Let us be happy, my friends. Let us set sail for Utopia. Let us drink the best champagne and agree that no marriage should last more than seven years and no dinner should last less than three hours.'

His putty-like cheeks were flushed; his hooded eyes were rimmed with tears. With a tremulous hand he raised his glass to us: 'This evening, let us pursue happiness with all the indolence at our command.'

'We are here to discuss murder, Oscar,' said Arthur Conan Doyle, sucking on his moustache and tapping his side plate with an impatient forefinger.

'Don't be serious, Arthur. Seriousness is the only refuge of the shallow – and you are deep.'

'And you are drunk, Oscar,' said Conan Doyle, reprovingly.

'A little intoxicated, perhaps. And tired, certainly. I did not sleep a wink last night. But not "drunk", Arthur. Never "drunk". "Drunk" is such an ugly word – and we are called to beauty.'

'We are called to business, Oscar,' sighed Doyle, shaking his head wearily. 'We have a case in hand. Whether you like it or not, there are serious matters to be addressed.'

'And we shall address them, Arthur, I do assure you.'

'Good.'

'– with every other course.'

Oscar sat back and looked around the Palm Court of the Langham Hotel. It was Monday night and the restaurant was not crowded.

'Man needs variety and contrast in his life – light and shade, prose and poetry, a wife and a mistress . . . It's no different with dinner. With each dish we shall have a different wine and a different topic of conversation. Over the soup, Arthur, you will tell us all about your day in Muswell Hill. With the fish, we shall discuss heaven and hell, and the curious fact that nothing makes one so vain as being told that one is a sinner. When the jugged hare arrives, Robert and I will give you a detailed account of the night we spent with the prince, the priest and the page-boy. You can rest easy, Arthur. Long before the angels on horseback and iced sorbets are set before us, we shall have delved deep into every nook and cranny of this murky affair.'

Oscar sipped at his wine. Conan Doyle seemed somewhat mollified.

'Perhaps you are not so drunk after all.'

'I am certainly sober enough to see that you are missing your wife quite desperately today, Arthur. I can tell you, too, that you arrived late for our dinner because you were upstairs in your room engaged in writing – and writing at speed. Probably an account of your adventures in Muswell Hill, followed by two letters – one of them, I imagine, addressed to your darling wife in Southsea, the other to Lord Yarborough.'

Conan Doyle sat open-mouthed in amazement. 'This is extraordinary, Oscar.'

'No.' Oscar grinned. 'Elementary thus far, my dear Arthur. Let me offer a final thought. This might impress and excite you.'

He ran his finger around the rim of his champagne glass and studied Conan Doyle with a beady eye.

'I have a feeling, Arthur, that you have recently enjoyed an interesting encounter with Monsieur James Tissot, the artist. I read in the newspaper that he was in London. I imagine that he is staying at this hotel. I have a hunch that you have met him, that he impressed you, and that, as you entered the restaurant tonight and walked towards our table, you were thinking of him. Am I correct?'

'In every particular,' answered Conan Doyle. 'I am utterly flabbergasted. Either you can read a man's mind, Oscar, or you have been spying on me.'

'Neither,' breathed Oscar happily, unfurling his table napkin with a satisfied flourish, 'but I have been reading the stories of Dr Arthur Conan Doyle and studying the methods of Mr Sherlock Holmes.'

Conan Doyle chuckled. 'Well then, take me through your reasoning. Where did you start?'

'With your tie, Arthur. It's hideous.'

'It's a gift from my wife.'

'Exactly. And you wore it today because you are missing her so dreadfully. Love drove you to wear it. There can be no other explanation. An orange tartan tie worn with a navy-blue business suit is a sartorial abomination, Arthur.'

'I apologise,' said Conan Doyle laughing. 'I should have changed for dinner, but as it's only Monday night—'

'You are a gentleman, Arthur. You would have changed for dinner, I know, had you not been so pressed for time. As it is, you arrived in the dining room and sat down at our table, in something of a fluster.'

'Again, I apologise.'

'Pray don't. It was an instructive fluster. As you took your place at table I noticed you hurriedly placing two envelopes in your inside coat pocket. I also observed ink marks on the fingers of your right hand and a red pressure mark on the left side of your right middle finger.'

Conan Doyle held out his right hand and examined it.

'The ink is still there,' said Oscar, 'but the pressure mark has gone. It was the redness of it that made me think you had been writing at length and at speed. I surmised that you would have made notes following your visit to Muswell Hill. You are a man who makes notes, Arthur: yours is a tidy soul – and I could see that you had written two letters because you brought them into the dining room with you.'

Arthur produced the envelopes from his jacket pocket. 'How did you know to whom they were addressed?'

'I guessed. You are in love with your wife – you write

to her three times a day. You are a gentleman – you send your thank-you letters promptly.'

Conan Doyle laid the two letters out on the tablecloth before us. They were indeed addressed to Lord Yarborough in Muswell Hill and Mrs Conan Doyle in Southsea.

Oscar turned to me and said, 'Robert, would you look at these envelopes carefully and tell me what, if anything, strikes you about them.'

I picked up the envelopes and examined them, then looked at Oscar.

'They appear to be identical – apart from the names and the addresses.'

'Are they the same weight?'

I took an envelope in each hand. 'They are.'

'And are they both stamped?'

I laid the envelopes on the table. 'They are.'

'And what do you make of that?' asked Oscar, with a note of triumph in his voice.

I was bemused. 'What do I make of it? I make nothing of it, Oscar. What should I make of it? Arthur wrote two letters, sealed them, stamped them and brought them with him into the dining room.'

'Exactly,' said Oscar. 'But *why*?'

'Why what?'

'Why did he bring the letters into the dining room – when each already carried a stamp, and to reach the dining room Arthur had to pass through the hotel foyer, directly past the letterbox that stands there at the foot of the main stairs? Arthur had been anxious to send his thanks to Lord Yarborough and his love to Mrs Doyle – he could have posted his letters on the way into dinner, but he did not do so. Why? I will tell you why . . . Because Arthur had recently made the acquaintance of Monsieur James Tissot and Monsieur Tissot had told him his story!'

'I am lost,' I said.

'I am dumbfounded, Oscar,' said Conan Doyle. 'I salute your genius. You should have sleepless nights more often.'

'You will have to explain,' I said pitifully. 'I have not the first idea what you are talking about.'

'It's very simple,' said Oscar. 'Tissot is a fine artist, but limited in his range. He has one style – and one story. The picture he paints is pleasing enough, but it is always the same picture. The story he tells is remarkable – but it is the same story. He is the French equivalent of the club bore. I have met him three times and heard the same story on each occasion.'

'And what is this story?' I asked.

'It is tragic,' said Conan Doyle.

'And it concerns two letters,' explained Oscar.

'Go on,' I said.

'Shall I tell the story, Arthur? Or will you? Or shall we ask the head waiter? He is bound to have heard it if Tissot has stayed here.'

Conan Doyle laughed. 'Tell the story, Oscar. Our soup is about to be served.'

'It's easily told. Once upon a time, Tissot had a mistress. An Irish girl, some years his junior. Kathleen was her name, as I recall. Tissot and the girl were inseparable. She had youth and beauty, energy and high intelligence. Tissot used her as his muse – and as his favourite model. The girl worshipped the ground on which the artist walked and he loved her dearly – for a time. But nothing lasts, and men are men, and novelty, by definition, has its day. So, as the years passed, and Kathleen's beauty faded and her health began to fade, Tissot's love for his mistress waned. What once had charmed him began to irritate. What had once delighted began to pall. And, eventually, the day came when Tissot knew that he must rid himself of this mistress.

'He wrote to a friend telling him what he planned to do – telling him how he had grown tired of Kathleen, weary of her conversation, bored by her company, depressed by her illness and her fading looks. He admitted to his friend that the woman he had once loved he now despised. On the same evening, at the same table, he wrote a second letter – a kinder, sweeter, softer letter – a letter telling Kathleen he was going to have to go away on business and might be away for some time . . . And yes, he put each letter into the wrong envelope. He sent the gentle letter intended for Kathleen to his friend – and he sent the letter that told the bitter truth to Kathleen. She read it and she killed herself.'

A waiter stood hovering at Oscar's side.

'Ah,' cried Oscar, 'the lobster bisque!'

As our soup was served, there was a moment's silence at the table. To my surprise, I found myself thinking of Constance Wilde. I first met her in Paris, six years ago, on the first day of her honeymoon. She was so happy. She and Oscar were completely in love. Constance loves Oscar still, and with a passion, but his love for her is fading. I see it. She does not. I fear what the future may hold.

Conan Doyle had his glass raised to Oscar. 'An affecting story beautifully told.'

'Well,' said Oscar, waving his soup spoon gaily, 'I've heard it often enough. Tissot is the Ancient Mariner – Kathleen is his albatross. He recounts the story to whoever will listen.'

'It's guilt, not grief that engulfs him,' said Doyle solemnly.

'And guilt does terrible things to a man. It's turned Tissot from a painter of charming narratives into an insufferable old bore who paints nothing but scenes from the Bible. When last I saw him he told me that he was depicting the life of Christ in seven hundred canvases! You might think that Our Lord had suffered enough.'

We all laughed and, following Oscar's injunction, Arthur opened the envelope addressed to Mrs Conan Doyle. It contained the letter intended for her.

'All's well,' he muttered, tugging at his moustache a touch shamefacedly.

'And all will be well,' said Oscar, looking at Conan Doyle benevolently. 'We'll get you back to Southsea, Arthur, and we'll solve this case into the bargain. Now, tell us, how was Lord Yarborough?'

As we finished our lobster bisque and embarked on our baked Dover sole, Conan Doyle gave us a full account of his day at Muswell Manor. While the fish was being served, Oscar laid his hand on Arthur's arm reassuringly.

'I am postponing our debate on heaven and hell and the significance of sin until we reach the savoury. Your tale, sir, would cure deafness. Take all the time you need.'

It took until the arrival of the jugged hare for Dr

Doyle to complete his story. When he had done so, he sat back and looked at each of us in turn, his eyebrows raised as if inviting a verdict.

Oscar prodded his food with his fork. 'So you now consider Lord Yarborough as suspect as this out-of-season hare, do you, Arthur?'

Conan Doyle said nothing.

'It doesn't look good for Yarborough, does it?' I volunteered.

'Why do you say that, Robert?' Oscar responded sharply. 'Lord Yarborough is a peer of the realm and a Fellow of the Royal Society. He is a model of respectability, a physician of distinction who is devoting himself, and his considerable means, to the alleviation of suffering – and doing so alongside the great Professor Charcot, one of the most regarded scientific figures of our time.'

'Two of Yarborough's patients turn out to be sisters,' I countered, 'one of whom is found murdered in a darkened room off a hallway in Grosvenor Square, while the other is discovered, naked, hypnotised and as good as imprisoned, in a darkened room in Muswell Hill.'

'I agree,' said Oscar, 'the address of the Charcot Clinic does not inspire confidence, but beyond that I don't quite see what Lord Yarborough has done to arouse your suspicion, Robert. He is a specialist in hysteria so one would expect his patients to include vulnerable young women of an hysterical disposition.'

'They were sisters.'

'What of that? These things run in families – and Lord Yarborough is a family doctor. Just as Arthur is.'

Oscar turned to gaze on Conan Doyle.

'Arthur has his practice in Southsea. Lord Yarborough

has his in Harley Street. Arthur looks after families fortunate enough to live in the purlieus of Portsmouth, while Lord Yarborough's patients are cursed with mansions in Mayfair. But both men have patients who may be sisters; both have patients who may be prone to hysteria; both have patients who will occasionally die in unfortunate circumstances. Why should one of these doctors be considered a more suspect character than the other? Aren't they both simply honest medical men, doing their best for the frail and ailing who pass their way?'

Conan Doyle leant forward and said quietly: 'There is a difference between us.'

'Is there?' asked Oscar, laying down his fork and reaching into his pocket for his cigarette case.

'There is,' continued Conan Doyle earnestly. 'Lord Yarborough is engaged in research and, by his own admission, for that research he needs access to the cadavers of former patients. This morning, when he told me that one of his patients had taken her own life, he said that he was grateful to her for her suicide.'

'Are you suggesting that he helped her to it?' asked Oscar, lighting a cigarette.

'No.'

'I thought not,' said Oscar, gently blowing a thin plume of blue smoke across the table.

'But could he have done so?' I asked, suddenly excited. 'Hypnotism is part of Yarborough's stock-in trade. Could he have persuaded this young woman to take her own life – under hypnosis?'

Conan Doyle considered his answer carefully. 'Yes,' he said, eventually. 'Hypnosis is a form of unconsciousness resembling sleep and some subjects are more suggestible than others. But, yes . . . under hypnosis, you can persuade people to do extraordinary things.'

Oscar contemplated his cigarette. 'Could you persuade a sophisticated woman hosting a reception for two hundred guests to abandon it at its height and make her way to a darkened room and there disrobe, first to mutilate herself, quite brutally, and, next, to stab herself to death in the neck before cleverly concealing the weapon she had used for the purpose? Could that be achieved with hypnosis?'

Conan Doyle frowned. 'I am not suggesting that Lord Yarborough murdered the Duchess of Albemarle, Oscar.'

'I am relieved to hear it. Are you suggesting that he might have been party to the suicide of this other patient? Or that he is lining up the duchess's younger sister for his cold marble slab?'

'No,' protested Conan Doyle, 'not for a moment. All I am saying is that Yarborough is obsessed with "the great Charcot" and, consequently, set upon finding *physical evidence* of the roots of hysteria, at whatever cost. Charcot identified multiple sclerosis in the morgue. Yarborough is determined to localise hysteria in the same way. To undertake his research he needs the bodies of former patients. How else can he put the nervous systems of known hysterics under the microscope? It is the only way. I am not suggesting he will have had any involvement in the murder of one patient or the suicide of another – but both deaths will have been useful to him.'

'Useful?' repeated Oscar.

'Yes, useful. He used the body of the girl who took her own life for dissection. He told me so.'

'And what did he discover?'

'Nothing – but that has not lessened his determination. The research goes on.'

'And you think he would have liked to use the body of the Duchess of Albemarle in the same way?'

'I do.'

Oscar studied Conan Doyle carefully, exhaled a cloud of smoke and smiled.

'In fact, Arthur, you think that he may even have succeeded in doing so.'

'I do.'

'But that's not possible,' I said. 'We saw the undertakers coming to collect the duchess's body. You remember, Oscar? We were standing in Grosvenor Square – in the gardens. We watched them arrive.'

'Oh, come now, Robert,' exclaimed Oscar reprovingly. 'Only the most literal believe the evidence of their own eyes. Poets and detectives need to do better than that. We saw a group of plain-faced, drably dressed individuals arrive at 40 Grosvenor Square with a hearse, that's true. I remember. I can picture them clearly. They arrived with Lord Yarborough, did they not? We took them for undertakers because we saw what we expected to see. Who is to say they were not body-snatchers?'

I was about to remonstrate with Oscar, but my protest was stilled by a hand on my shoulder. It was a pale hand, small and delicate like a woman's, but firm like a man's.

I looked up and there, behind me, stood Rex LaSalle. He was in evening dress, with a white silk scarf around his neck and a pale-pink carnation in his buttonhole. He leant on my shoulder as he bowed towards Oscar and then towards Conan Doyle.

'I am too early,' he said apologetically. 'I will go again.'

'You will stay, Rex. You are not early. We are late. But it does not signify. Punctuality is the thief of time. The waiter will bring you a chair. You will join us for our meat course – unless, of course, you've already feasted on some unsuspecting virgin you encountered on your way here.'

LaSalle did not rise to Oscar's sally. 'I have not eaten,' he said quietly. 'I will be pleased to join you.'

'Excellent!' cried Oscar, waving towards a waiter and shifting his chair around the table to make room for his young friend. 'You will sit here next to me and, over the collared beef, we'll tell sad stories of the death of duchesses.'

A waiter brought up an additional chair and LaSalle took his place at the table, between Oscar and Conan Doyle.

The young man's arrival had galvanised our host. Everything he now said appeared to be entirely for the young man's benefit.

'With the savoury, Rex, I shall be leading a colloquy on the nature of sin – you will have much of value to contribute. But first we are sharing our news.'

Oscar looked around the table, mischief in his eye.

'Dr Doyle has been to Muswell Hill today and lives to tell the tale. He tells it so well. Robert and I have been to Marlborough House this evening – on our way here – and enjoyed a brief audience with Tyrwhitt Wilson, equerry to the Prince of Wales. Tomorrow night, gentlemen, we are all invited to join HRH at the Empire Music Hall in Leicester Square. You are included in the invitation, Rex.'

'I shall be in Southsea,' muttered Conan Doyle.

'You will be in Leicester Square,' declared Oscar. 'It is a royal summons.'

'What's this about?' asked Conan Doyle, testily. 'Why did you not mention this before?'

'Patience, Arthur,' said Oscar, soothingly. 'I will explain in a moment – but, first, let us hear Rex's news.'

'I have no news,' said the young man.

'But you must have news,' insisted Oscar.

'I have none. I have been in bed all day. I have been asleep.'

'But last night?' said Oscar. 'What happened to you last night?'

'I came with you to Mortlake, to the cemetery.'

'And then you disappeared,' said Oscar. 'When the evening ended and the party broke up, and Arthur and Bram Stoker returned to town, and Robert and I joined young Prince Eddy and his companion at the priest's house, you were nowhere to be found.'

'I was there.'

'I did not see you. I looked for you.'

'I know. I saw you looking.'

'You saw me? Why didn't you call out?'

'I couldn't. I had changed my shape by then.'

'You are talking in riddles, Rex. Explain yourself.'

Rex LaSalle laid his hands upon the table, one placed carefully over the other. As he spoke, he turned his head sharply so that he could look directly into Oscar's eyes.

'I have a gift, Oscar. I have spoken to you of it before.

At night, after midnight, if I so choose, I can transform my shape. By effort of will, under cover of darkness, I can change from man to beast. I can transform myself from the person you see before you now into a creature of the night – a cat, a rat, a bat . . .'

Oscar narrowed his eyes and let the smoke from his cigarette drift up from his nostrils across his face.

'Do you turn yourself into a gnat now and again, Rex?' he asked, playfully. 'Is the rhyming element essential to this nocturnal transmogrification of yours?'

'Mock if you must, Oscar,' answered the young man, quite unperturbed by Oscar's teasing. 'I have the ability to change myself into any creature of the night – be it an owl or a wolf, a scorpion or a viper. Last night, when the charade with the naked boy on the white stallion was done, I chose to slip away. I went in the guise of a fox.'

Conan Doyle cleared his throat and shifted uncomfortably in his chair. The waiter was approaching with our tray of collared beef.

Rex LaSalle turned from Oscar and looked around the table. 'Forgive me, gentlemen. The truth is sometimes uncomfortable, but, as I have told Oscar more than once, I am a vampire. There it is.'

Oscar looked up at the waiter and smiled: 'Fetch the sommelier, if you'd be so kind. I think we'll be needing more claret.'

Leicester Square

47

From the diary of Rex LaSalle

It was a curious evening. I spoke only the truth and they believed not a word of it. Oscar offered joshing banter; Conan Doyle harrumphed and chewed on his moustache; Robert Sherard said nothing but looked on me with a mixture of disbelief and pity in his eyes.

We ate well and drank copiously. Oscar drank too much. He asked me about the taste of blood – how often I required it – in what amounts – at what temperature, etc. I was ready to answer him truthfully, but Conan Doyle would have none of it.

'Desist, gentlemen,' he said, 'or I shall be obliged to leave the table.'

We talked much of the death of the Duchess of Albemarle. Dr Doyle accepts Lord Yarborough's analysis: that the duchess died of a heart attack following a frenzy of carnal activity willingly entered into. Oscar believes that she was murdered, by a person or persons still unknown. Robert Sherard is convinced that Lord Yarborough is implicated in her death – that, under hypnosis, in a trance induced by

Lord Y or one of his associates, the duchess was persuaded to take her own life. Is such a thing possible?

'To know the truth one must imagine myriads of falsehoods,' said Oscar.

When dinner was done, Conan Doyle bade us goodnight at once and went up to his room. Sherard volunteered to get a cab to accompany Oscar back to his house in Tite Street, but Oscar would have none of it. He commanded Sherard to go to Tite Street in his place and make his excuses to Mrs Wilde.

'Tell her I am feasting with vampires and cannot come home tonight. Kiss my darlings for me.'

Sherard protested, but, realising how deep in drink Oscar had become, eventually agreed. At a little after midnight, we handed Sherard into a two-wheeler outside the Langham Hotel and waved him on his way. Arm in arm, and very slowly, Oscar and I then wandered down Regent Street towards Soho. I cannot be certain, but I sensed that we were being followed as we walked.

In my room I gave Oscar coffee while he told me that he loved me. He said: 'The only difference between a saint and a sinner is that every saint has a past and every sinner has a future. My wife is a saint, Rex, while you and I are sinners.'

This morning, before he left, he gave me five pounds.

48

**Letter from Arthur Conan Doyle to his wife,
Louisa 'Touie' Conan Doyle**

*Langham Hotel,
London, W.*

18.iii.90

Dearest Touie, most cherished wife –

*This is damnable, my darling. I have to postpone
my return to Southsea yet again. I am so sorry. I am
missing you so very much.*

*I am held here in town by royal command! This
evening I am obliged to join HRH the Prince of Wales
in the royal box at the Empire Music Hall in Leicester
Square. I am specifically asked for: I have no choice. If
not Leicester Square, then the Tower. Oscar Wilde will
also be of the party.*

*As I think I have already told you, Oscar and I are
engaged on some particular business on behalf of the
Prince of Wales – delicate stuff that need not concern
you. Of course, I wish now that I had never become
involved, but it is too late. ('Too late' – the two most
fateful words in the English language.)*

*And Oscar, I confess, I am beginning to find rather
'too much'. I dined with him again last night. He was
amusing to begin with, but became more preposterous*

as the evening wore on. He was heavily in wine – as he often is. He brought with him his friend Sherard (the great-grandson of William Wordsworth, but an insipid fellow nonetheless, colourless and too much the acolyte) and we were joined by a young 'exquisite' of Oscar's acquaintance who affects to be a vampire – and does so with the utmost seriousness.

When I protested that I did not consider 'blood-sucking' a suitable topic of conversation over dinner in a public restaurant, with waiters listening in, Oscar said to his friends, 'You must forgive Arthur, gentlemen. He hasn't a single redeeming vice.' Oscar is funny – and brilliant – and I am conscious of the honour of knowing him, but his prodigious capacity for food and drink as well as the doubtful nature of some of his associates trouble me.

Kiss my darling daughter for me. How is she? How are you? Has my young brother replied to my letter yet, I wonder? Is there news from the Mam? Send me some of your news if you get a moment.

Until I go out this evening, I plan to stay here at the hotel. My room, though costly, is comfortable. I have a desk. I can write. I propose spending the morning working up my notes for my study of hysteria. This afternoon I am planning to begin a new story – another adventure for Mr Sherlock Holmes. I am sad not to be at home, but I am content to be at work. I am more likely to hurt myself by idleness than by endeavour.

I shall return to Southsea tomorrow morning, come what may – I have my Wednesday surgery to attend to. Thursday, alas, will see me back in London once more, but only briefly. For reasons I will explain when I see you, I shall be joining the mourners at the Duchess of Albemarle's funeral.

Take care, my darling. Forgive my prolonged absence. To remind me of you, I am wearing the tartan tie you gave me for my birthday. It is being much admired.

Aye your loving husband,
ACD

49

THE EMPIRE THEATRE OF VARIETIES

LEICESTER SQUARE, LONDON, W.

Grand Vocal, Instrumental, Thespian and Terpsichorean Festival
The Most Powerful Programme Ever Presented Before the
Ever-Discerning British Public

TONIGHT, TUESDAY, 18 MARCH 1890
THE GREATEST NIGHT OF THE SEASON

For this night only

MR DAN LENO

The Funniest Man on Earth,
Clog-Dancing Champion of the World

Mr William Topaz McGONAGALL

Poet and Tragedian of Dundee
will recite his original poem 'Bruce of Bannockburn'

LES BALLETS FANTASTIQUES

present

A NIGHT IN ARABIA

PREMIÈRE DANSEUSE: MADEMOISELLE LOUISA LAVALLOIS

SCREAMING EXTRAVANGANZA

By the Irresistibly Funny Quartet,

Messrs DEVOY, LECLERQ
LOVELL & BUTLER

Introducing their amazing sagacious

BABY ELEPHANT

MISS HETTY MARENGO

'Always a Gentleman'

JOVIAL JOE JUSTINI

With his repertoire of entirely new songs

Not for the faint-hearted

THE TANK OF DEATH

CAPTAIN JOSIAH NEPTUNE brings the

ATLANTIC OCEAN to LEICESTER SQUARE with

'MIRANDA' THE MIRACULOUS MERMAID

Ludicrous tricks, antics and somersaults by

MONSIEUR PIQUET'S
PERFORMING DOGS AND MONKEYS

And for this night only

THE INCREDIBLE PROFESSOR ONOFROFF

Exhibiting MIND-READING SKILLS of the rarest order

ADDITIONAL NOVELTIES GUARANTEED

THE LYCEUM ORCHESTRA

Under the personal direction of Mr Samuel Trussock

ADMISSION: BOXES 2S DRESS CIRCLE 1S GRAND TIER 9D STALLS 6D
REAR STALLS & BALCONY 4D
THE ENTERTAINMENT WILL COMMENCE AT 7.15 P.M.;
DOORS OPEN HALF AN HOUR EARLIER

50

Extract from a letter from Bram Stoker to his wife, Florence, delivered by messenger in the early hours of Wednesday, 19 March 1890

> Lyceum Theatre,
> Strand,
> London

> Tuesday, 18 March 1890

Florrie –

It is midnight and I am just returned from the Empire Music Hall in Leicester Square. I am sitting down at once to send you this account of the events of the evening, not only so that you should read my record of what occurred before you see some garbled version in tomorrow's newspaper, but also because I know that you keep all my letters (dear girl that you are) and I believe I shall have recourse to this one when I come to write my memoirs. This has been a night of high drama, low farce – and tragedy.

Let me begin at the beginning. I arrived at the Empire at seven o'clock sharp – as instructed by Oscar. I went at Oscar's behest. He sent me a note this afternoon to tell me that the Prince of Wales was to pay an unexpected private visit to the Empire tonight – Dan Leno was top of the bill – and Oscar had been asked to make up an 'appropriate party' to entertain His Royal Highness during those items in the programme that might not entirely hold His Highness's attention.

The party that gathered in the ante-room to the royal box was a motley one. There were nine of us in all; besides Oscar and myself, two of Oscar's 'young men' were in attendance – the journalist, Sherard, who says little but 'knows' everybody, and the artist, LaSalle, who lays claim to being a vampire (he is a handsome youth, but he gets on my nerves). Oscar's friend, Arthur Conan Doyle, was there (I like him), with another medical man, Lord Yarborough, and Yarborough's friend, the Duke of Albemarle. (Albemarle is in mourning – his wife's funeral is on Thursday – but tonight he went to the music hall!) The last of the guests to arrive was the composer, Antonin Dvorak. He came with his very beautiful daughter. (At least, he told us she was his daughter.)

For an hour we stood about idly, gossiping, chatting, smoking, sipping champagne. (It was fine champagne. Albemarle brought it – at Oscar's suggestion – along with his own butler to serve it.) Though the champagne was good and the company congenial – I talked at length with Dvorak: he comes from Bohemia, and his father was a butcher – I would have liked to watch the performance from the start. First on the bill was a troupe of juggling monkeys! But Oscar said, no, that would be lèse majesté. We had to await the arrival of the prince.

HRH eventually appeared just after eight. He was immaculately kitted out – I don't think I've ever seen a man so perfectly attired, even Oscar – but stouter, shorter, older, much more out of breath than when last I saw him. (He is older: he is nearly fifty now.)

He arrived with his eldest in tow: Prince Eddy. The young prince looks better in the flesh than in the photographs: healthier, less saturnine. He is just returned from a tour of India. He said, 'I suspect I'm going to enjoy this Empire more than that one,' which I thought amusing. The princes were in evening dress, with matching white carnations in their buttonholes, but no decorations as this was very much a private outing. They came by brougham with just two in the royal retinue: the Prince of Wales's personal page and the equerry, Tyrwhitt Wilson. (If Irving revives his Malvolio, I'll get Tyrwhitt Wilson for Aguecheek.)

It fell to Oscar to present the party to the princes. He did it with his customary charm. (He is impossible at times, but still the most charming man I know.) It was all very easy and informal. I asked the heir apparent which of the night's entertainments he was most looking forward to – suggesting it might be the Great McGonagall.

He laughed. 'McGonagall is more to the Queen's taste than my own. The poor man hopes to succeed Lord Tennyson as Poet Laureate and keeps writing to Her Majesty at Balmoral to say so. Unfortunately he writes in verse.'

He laughed once more. I laughed. Oscar laughed. Dvorak – who'd not understood a word – positively roared. (In the presence of royalty I find there is always much forced bonhomie.)

It transpired that the performance HRH was most keenly anticipating was that of Professor Onofroff – the 'psychic phenomenon' noted for his feats of mind-reading.

'I have seen him in action before,' said HRH, eyes gently bulging. 'He is quite remarkable. He can reveal what you are thinking with uncanny accuracy. He can read your mood. He can see into your soul. After we've witnessed his act, I want you all to meet him. Did Oscar not tell you? I hope he's made the arrangements.'

'I have made all the arrangements, sir,' said Oscar smoothly, 'but I have told our friends nothing. I wished the evening to be a surprise. I did not want anyone putting up his guard before being subjected to Professor Onofroff's mental analysis.'

'Very good,' said the prince.

'Very bad,' muttered Dvorak. 'My soul is a secret place. It does not want visitors.'

'Never mind that,' said HRH dismissively. 'Time's getting on. Let's go into the show. Mademoiselle Dvorak can sit next to me.'

'She speaks no English, Your Highness,' said the composer anxiously.

'All the better.' The prince grinned. 'In we go.'

The prince's page and the duke's butler opened the narrow double doors that led from the ante-room to the royal box. Immediately we could hear the strains of the orchestra and the hubbub of the house. On stage Hetty Marengo (a male impersonator) was doing her best with 'The girl who knew a boy who knew a girl who knew a thing or two'. It's a strong song, but she was struggling.

I do not know how these music-hall artistes manage: the commotion in the auditorium is constant – patrons coming and going, talking, laughing, greeting their friends, hushing their neighbours, cadging cigarettes, ordering drinks, waving to the girls in the gallery. The Empire is a quality house – evening dress is worn – but there are long refreshment counters on every tier and, unless it's the top-liner on stage, the brouhaha and bustle around the bars and in the aisles never stop.

As the royal party entered the royal box, a solitary cheer rang out from the gallery, followed by another, and another. Within moments, the house was in uproar: cheering, applauding, whistling (they'd noticed the Dvorak girl), stamping their feet and raising their glasses. The Prince of Wales stood to acknowledge the ovation and Hetty Marengo proved her worth. She stepped up to the footlights, stopped the orchestra and embarked on a rousing chorus of 'For he's a jolly good fellow'. The entire audience joined in.

The song done, the prince took his seat, Hetty Marengo took her bow and the house began to calm itself. The theatre was hot and the royal box was crowded. There were just eight chairs arranged in two rows. We found ourselves seated like this:

D. of Albemarle Ld Yarborough A. Conan Doyle Self Dvorak
Prince Eddy The Prince of Wales Mlle Dvorak

Oscar and his young men stood at the back of the box, alongside the prince's equerry and the theatre manager. I sat almost immediately behind HRH and when, soon, he realised that Mlle Dvorak was unable to take on board anything more than a smile and a wink, he began addressing his remarks to me.

Throughout the performance he maintained a steady flow of comments, quips and asides. I can report that the vulgar comic songs of Jovial Joe Justini are much more to the royal liking than Henry Irving's Hamlet. And the four tumbling comedians who appeared on stage with a baby elephant scored a palpable hit. The Great McGonagall fared less well. As the Bard of Dundee launched into a spirited rendering of a very long poem about Robert the Bruce and the Battle of Bannockburn, the Prince of Wales stifled a yawn, lit a cigar and, muttering, 'I've never much cared for Scottish politics,' began to talk loudly about racing and his ambition one day to breed a Derby winner.

The next item on the bill, however, drew the royal eye back to the stage in no uncertain terms. Les Ballets Fantastiques featured a bevy of beautiful ballerinas decked out as Arabian slave girls. The provocative nature of their dancing and the boldness of their costumes – the young ladies were wearing tight-fitting beaded bodices and loose silk pantaloons – commanded full attention.

When the dancers appeared, HRH called to his equerry for his opera glasses. When the première danseuse took centre stage, the prince exclaimed: 'I know her. It's my Lulu. What a darling girl.'

The moment the ballet was done, while the dancers were still curtsying to the royal box, the prince called over to his equerry once more: 'Wilson, go and fetch her. Bring her up here. I want to see her. Now.' He turned to the rest of the party: 'The little dancer's an old friend of mine. This calls for a celebration. Gentlemen, shall we?'

The prince got his feet and, forgetting the Dvorak girl altogether, forged his way out of the royal box and back into the ante-room. When royalty rises, you rise too. Where royalty goes, you follow.

As the prince stalked ahead, Oscar bleated, 'Sir, we shall miss Onofroff's turn – he's next.'

'Onofroff be jiggered,' called out the prince gaily. 'We're seeing him later. We are going to have a drink with Lulu now.' He snapped his fingers at his page. 'Watkins, fresh champagne.' He looked around the empty ante-room. 'Isn't there any food? No titbits to keep us going? Where's the manager?'

'He's gone to fetch Miss Lavallois,' said Rex LaSalle.

'You know her?' boomed the prince.

'I know her name,' said LaSalle, 'that's all.'

'We all want to know her,' purred Oscar.

'You'll all adore her,' announced HRH. 'She's a poppet.'

We did. And she was.

Mademoiselle Louisa Lavallois – known to HRH the Prince of Wales as 'Lulu' and 'you naughty little wagtail' – was a complete delight. The moment she set foot in the room, she illuminated it like a ray of summer sunshine. A tiny bundle of joy, she exuded energy and a sense of fun. She was petite and not especially pretty, but her manner was so playful, her eyes so full of life and her voice so full of laughter, that she was, quite simply, irresistible.

When Tyrwhitt Wilson brought her in to us, she made a deep curtsy down to the floor in front of the prince. When HRH said, 'Get up, Lulu, and give your old uncle a kiss then,' she rolled head over heels, stood straight up and kissed the heir apparent on the mouth!

'Isn't she a marvel?' declared the prince, taking her by both hands and looking lovingly into her face.

(It was a common little face – with piggy eyes and a snub nose – but it was a happy one. It did you good to see it.) She was still in her Arabian costume, of course, out of breath and perspiring from her recent performance.

'It's lovely to see ya, Tum-Tum,' she said to the prince, caressing his shirt-front tenderly. 'I've missed ya.'

'And I've missed you, Lulu,' said the prince, 'very much.'

'I love you,' she said. 'And I always will.'

'And I love you,' said His Royal Highness.

It was an affecting scene, acted out without self-consciousness.

Prince Albert Victor was standing at his father's elbow. The Prince of Wales presented the little dancer to his son as though she were the Queen of Sheba. 'This is a very special lady, Eddy – one of my favourite friends.'

The young prince clicked his heels. Bowing, he took Mlle Lavallois's hand and kissed it. The little dancer giggled and bobbed a curtsy.

'We met in Paris,' continued the Prince of Wales, 'at one of the theatres there. Lulu was the star attraction.'

'I remember,' said his son, appreciatively. 'You introduced me.'

'Did I? I don't recall. Did you come with me to Paris?'

'Yes, Papa. Three years ago. I met Miss Lavallois then.'

'Very well. If you say so.'

'I'm going back to Paris soon,' said the girl. 'I'm only here for the season.'

'I hope to be in Paris next week,' said the Prince of Wales. 'I have my spring break, you know.'

The girl threw her arms around the heir apparent and, with a little gurgle, said, 'I know. I love your spring breaks. I love ya, Tum-Tum.'

The prince's page was now hovering with a glass of champagne for the royal guest. She saw it and squealed, 'I'd love to, dearie, but I can't. I've got to go. I'm back on stage in a tick.'

'More ballet?' enquired Prince Eddy.

'No. I'm Miranda the Mermaid next. In a fish tank. You'll like it. You get to see my titties.'

The girl was completely unabashed. She roared with laughter and kissed the Prince of Wales once more.

'Don't go,' he said. 'Not yet.'

'I must,' she said, pulling herself away. 'I'm on in a moment.'

'Come back later – when the show's over. Come back then.'

'I will,' she said. 'Promise.'

She separated herself from the prince and curtsied to the ground once more, then looked around the room at the dozen faces all gazing upon on her in rapt amazement.

'Goodbye, all,' she said, 'ta-ra for now. See you later.'

And, waving, she skipped out of the room. As she went, we all applauded.

'Isn't she extraordinary?' exclaimed the Prince of Wales.

I was standing with Oscar, Rex LaSalle and Robert Sherard on the far side of the ante-room, by the double doors leading back to the auditorium.

'Extraordinary,' echoed Sherard. 'I've seen her at the Moulin Rouge, with Jane Avril – dancing the cancan. She's an enchantress.'

'She's a free spirit,' said Oscar. 'I envy that.'

'She's wonderfully forward,' I said.

'She's wonderfully honest,' said Oscar.

'She and the prince don't hide the nature of their friendship, do they?' said Rex LaSalle.

'What is the good of friendship if one cannot say exactly what one means?' replied Oscar. 'The girl trades in happiness, not deception.'

'What about the Princess of Wales?' asked LaSalle. 'What about her happiness? I wonder what she makes of her husband's intimacy with the little dancer from the Moulin Rouge?'

'I trust she neither knows nor cares,' said Oscar. 'This is something else – somewhere else – in another world.'

Across the room, Prince Albert Victor was attempting small-talk with Dvorak's daughter while the Prince of Wales was still revelling in his reunion with his young dancing friend. He was talking exuberantly to the Duke of Albemarle, Lord Yarborough and Arthur Conan Doyle.

'Isn't she a delight? She gives herself some fanciful French name, but she comes from Bermondsey, of course.' He drained his champagne glass and looked about the room. 'I wish there was something to eat.'

Tyrwhitt Wilson stepped forward obsequiously. 'There will be, sir, after the performance, when Professor Onofroff is here. It's all in hand.'

'Good,' said the prince. 'Sandwiches, pies, cold cuts – nothing elaborate, but something.'

The theatre manager was now hovering.

'We've got to go back, have we?' grumbled the prince and offered up a barking laugh. 'They don't harry the Queen like this. What's next?'

'Miranda the Mermaid, Your Highness.'

'Oh,' purred the prince. 'Lulu's titties! This we mustn't miss.'

With a spring in his heel, the heir apparent led us back into the royal box. In the pit, the orchestra was playing a medley of sea shanties, while on stage an old man dressed as Neptune stood alongside a huge glass-fronted water tank on wheels. The central panel of the tank was covered by a tarpaulin sheet on which were painted gaudy pictures of assorted sea creatures – an octopus, a giant seahorse, a sea serpent, starfish and the like.

As drums began to roll beneath him, the old man waved his trident in the air and, in surprisingly stentorian tones, promised us a sight for sore eyes: the true wonder of the sub-aquatic world – fresh from the depths of the Atlantic Ocean where she had been caught by sailors fishing for shark – the only mermaid in captivity – the miraculous Miranda!

As he spoke her name, cymbals clashed below, and, with a mighty heave, old Neptune pulled the tarpaulin from the tank. Within it, under water, seated on a three-legged stool, her fine fish's tail laid out before her, slowly combing her thick golden tresses, was the Prince of Wales's Bermondsey paramour. (The tresses, I should add, were quite long enough to preserve the lady's modesty. We saw the outline of her charming figure, but nothing more.)

'Is she not a thing of beauty?' demanded Neptune. 'Is she not a living miracle?'

'She is indeed,' murmured the Prince of Wales.

'Watch!' cried Neptune, directing our attention with his trident. 'Watch as Miranda, breathing beneath the briny, performs her miraculous underwater feats.'

As the old man announced each 'feat' in turn, the young mermaid performed it and the audience, alternately, gasped and cheered. She abandoned her stool and swam to the bottom of the tank. She swam to the top. She executed an elegant somersault and disappeared to the back of the tank, returning a moment later and dragging a barnacle-covered strong box with her.

'See!' cried old Neptune. 'Miranda has discovered Davy Jones's locker!'

With much underwater pantomime, the mermaid threw open the strong box and revealed its treasures – gold doubloons, silver goblets and seaweed-strewn human skulls.

As she pressed her face against the front glass of the water tank and held up her trophies, a sudden cry of horror swept across the auditorium. A huge sea serpent, six feet in length, emerged from the darkness at the back of the tank and slithered slowly towards the girl. She was oblivious, facing the auditorium, playing to the crowd, until the hideous red-eyed creature reached her and swiftly entwined its long, black, scaly body about hers. She fell back, thrashing her tail wildly, clutching desperately at the serpent as it tightened its grip around her neck and torso. Locked together, intertwined, mermaid and serpent twisted, turned and struggled. As the pair revolved, waves of water splashed from the top of the tank on to the stage.

Old Neptune called out, 'Help! Calamity!'

The audience rose to its feet in alarm.

'In God's name, what's happening?' cried the Prince of Wales.

'It's part of the act, sir,' I hissed. 'All will be well.'

And, in a moment, it was. Beneath the turbulent waves, the mermaid and the serpent fought on. They fought to the death – and the mermaid won. Frantically tearing the sea creature from her neck, pulling it away from her body and throttling it with her bare hands, the mermaid swam up to the surface of the water and flung the dead serpent from the tank on to the stage. It lay motionless by the footlights, like a length of Mr Goodyear's vulcanised rubber tubing.

The audience roared its approval and the mermaid, bobbing about on the surface of the water, took her applause. Pulling herself to the edge of the tank by her arms, she lifted her torso out of the water to make a bow. As she leant forward, for a brief moment, from the royal box we caught a glimpse of her titties.

'All's well,' sighed the Prince of Wales. 'I knew it would be. Isn't she extraordinary?'

'I did not like the music,' said Dvorak.

Dan Leno was top of the bill – and rightly so. The little fellow is simply the funniest man on earth. As the curtains fell around the water tank, Dan hopped and skipped his way on to the front of the stage, dressed as a washerwoman! He apologised for being late, saying, 'I came by bus. It was so crowded, even the men were standing.'

What he offers is neither boisterous nor crude, yet he holds the entire house in the palm of his hand. I have met him. In the wings he is terrified. On stage he is fearless. And every audience loves him.

The show done, the national anthem played and the Prince of Wales gave a farewell wave to the Tuesday-night Empire crowd.

'Food!' he cried, leading us back to the ante-room. 'And Onofroff!'

Both awaited us. In the ante-room, on the sideboard, were trays of ham and egg sandwiches and assorted cold cuts: chicken legs, lamb cutlets, smoked oysters and lobster claws.

By the sideboard stood Professor Onofroff. He is a tall man, in his seventies now, with thick, snow-white hair and a full Russian beard. He has the Roman nose of the Duke of Wellington and the penetrating eye of the Emperor Napoleon.

As the Prince of Wales approached him, he bowed his head from the neck and whispered, 'Majesty, I am as ever humbled.'

He spoke at all times in a whisper, with a thick Germanic accent in almost perfect English.

The prince greeted him as an old friend. 'Thank you for joining us, Professor. Mr Wilde has explained everything to you?'

'He has.'

'Excellent,' rumbled the prince, with satisfaction. 'Most excellent.'

He helped himself to a sandwich from the sideboard, then turned to address the room.

'Gentlemen, before we tuck in, with your permission, we are going to undertake a small experiment in mind-reading. It's a particular interest of mine, as you know – and of Mr Wilde's and of Dr Conan Doyle's too, I believe – and I am grateful to you for indulging me in it.'

There was a murmur in the room (mostly of assent), broken by the theatre manager who was standing in the tiny vestibule that connected the ante-room with the entrance to the auditorium.

'Your Highness, please excuse me, but Mr McGonagall craves admittance.'

'Let him crave away,' declared the prince dismissively. 'We'll see little Leno if he wants to come up.'

'Mr Leno's on his way to Hoxton already. He has two more halls to play tonight. But Mr McGonagall is most anxious for an audience.'

'He's had one.' The prince laughed. 'We all heard his

bleatings on behalf of Robert the Bruce. I can't see him. Is Lulu on her way?'

'Yes, sir. Miss Lavallois is coming. She's just changing. She'll be here presently.'

'Good. Thank you. Kindly leave us in peace now.'

'But Mr McGonagall—'

'Enough! There's only so much Scottish blathering a Prince of Wales can take. My compliments to Mr McGonagall, but I have the toothache. Tell him to go pen a verse about that.'

I believe Oscar was the only one of us who did not laugh. He murmured to me, 'That was poorly done. I feel a fellow poet's pain.'

As the theatre manager retreated to break the news to poor McGonagall, the prince, helping himself to a second sandwich, sought to set the scene for the seance.

'Gentlemen, if you would kindly form a circle please – a circle around the professor. To see into your souls Professor Onofroff will need to look into your eyes. Isn't that correct, Professor?'

Onofroff smiled and, as his thick lips parted, his mouth revealed an array of gold and silver teeth. 'Yes, Majesty,' he whispered.

'Oscar,' called out the prince. 'You're in charge. Get the troops into a circle. Eddy, you come stand by me.'

'Who is to be included, sir?' asked Oscar.

'Everyone.'

'Including staff, sir?'

'Everyone – except Mademoiselle Dvorak. I think we can excuse the lady. She is too young for secrets.'

'What is this with secrets?' enquired Dvorak anxiously.

'Patience, Maestro,' said the prince cheerily. 'Let Mr Wilde put you in your place – all will be revealed. You have nothing to fear.'

This was the circle that Oscar arranged:

Door leading to stairs to auditorium

VESTIBULE

ANTEROOM

Parker (butler)   Watkins (page)

Bram Stoker   Tyrwhitt Wilson (equerry)

Oscar Wilde   Prince Albert Victor

Rex LaSalle   Professor Onofroff   The Prince of Wales

Robert Sherard   The Duke of Albemarle

Arthur Conan Doyle   Lord Yarborough

Antonin Dvorak

Door leading to stairs to street

---

*Once each man was in his place, the prince called for hush.
'We are in the professor's hands now. Gentlemen, please do as he
asks you.'*

*'What's all this in aid of, sir?' enquired Prince Albert
Victor.*

*'Clearing the air,' said his father. 'Now concentrate on the
professor.'*

*'Gentlemen,' whispered the professor, 'thank you for your
kind attention.'*

*As he spoke, he stood in the centre of the circle, revolving very
slowly, looking into each face in turn.*

*'His Majesty is correct. I am here to help clear the air – and
perhaps help clear the conscience, too. Look into my eyes,*

gentlemen, as I look into yours. Look directly into my eyes – look into my soul as I look into yours. Speak to me as I look at you – speak to me, not with words, but with thoughts. Share your thoughts with me. Let me read your minds.'

'If you can read my mind, Professor,' said Prince Eddy, 'you'll know I'm deuced hungry. Let's get on with this.'

'I can read minds, Your Majesty. I can read yours.'

'You're a professor, Professor,' said Lord Yarborough pleasantly. 'Are you offering us any scientific proof?'

'Who has a pen or pencil?' asked the professor.

'I do,' said Oscar, producing a small silver pencil and a visiting card from his waistcoat pocket.

'Kindly write down a word for me, Mr Wilde – whatever word is in your mind.'

Oscar scribbled briefly on his card.

The professor said at once, 'The word is "love", is it not, Mr Wilde?'

'It is,' said Oscar.

I looked over his shoulder. It was.

'I want to play this game,' said the Prince of Wales, breaking from the circle and coming over to claim Oscar's pencil and card. 'What's the word I am writing, Professor? What's in my mind? This'll test you.'

Onofroff hesitated. 'It does, Majesty,' he said, closing his eyes to concentrate. 'It is not a word I know. Or if it is, I think it is a card game. You are thinking of "Loo", of "Loo-loo". Is that possible? Does that make sense?'

The prince held out his card for general inspection. On it HRH had written the name 'LULU' in capital letters.

He laughed. 'That's proof enough for me, Professor – and I'm patron of the Royal Society. On with the experiment.'

'Thank you, Majesty. Let us all concentrate once more,

gentlemen. In complete silence. And as I look into your eyes, let me read your mind, let me learn your secret.'

Dvorak was on the far side of the room to me, but I could hear the composer's teeth grinding.

'We all have secrets,' continued the professor. 'And I sense dark secrets in this room. Everywhere I turn, I see a secret. Look into my eyes, gentlemen, and release your secrets. I will share your burden and your secrets will be safe with me.'

As the professor turned carefully from one pair of eyes to the next, speaking of sensing dark secrets in the room, it seemed to me that the room itself begin to darken: the gas lamps flickered and burned lower than before. Beyond the faint grinding of Dvorak's teeth and the slow, heavy breathing of the Prince of Wales, there was nothing to be heard but the steady hiss of the lamps.

At least two minutes of this profound stillness must have passed before the professor spoke again. When he did so, for the first time within my hearing his voice was raised above a whisper. He spoke, in fact, with a sudden, chilling authority.

'Gentlemen,' he said, 'enough. I know the truth.'

And as he said it, from within the vestibule, a terrifying scream was heard – long, piercing, pitiable.

'My daughter!' cried Dvorak, breaking from the circle and running across the ante-room to the vestibule.

Every one of us turned to follow him. Oscar and I pushed past the prince's page and reached the scene at once.

Dvorak's daughter was standing, unharmed. She flung her arms around her father and buried her face in his chest.

'My God,' cried Dvorak, his face contorted, 'look at that.'

The composer stood by the door that opened on to the tiny square room built into the corner of the vestibule, containing the water closet. There, thrown back against the wall, was the bloodied body of Mademoiselle Louisa Lavallois – the Prince of Wales's Lulu. Her bodice had been ripped open, her perfect titties scratched, torn and cut across. Her neck was twisted grotesquely to one side and punctured with two gaping, bloody holes. Her eyes were wide open, but she was undoubtedly dead.

A Duty to the Truth

51

From the *Daily Chronicle*, final edition, Wednesday,
19 March 1890

HORROR IN LEICESTER SQUARE

The mutilated body of a young female dancer was
discovered in a dark alley off Leicester Square in
London's West End late last night. The body is believed
to be that of Miss Louisa Lavallois, twenty-six, *première
danseuse* with Les Ballets Fantastiques, a French
troupe currently appearing at the Empire Theatre of
Varieties in Leicester Square.

The body was discovered shortly before midnight by
the Leicester Square lamplighter, William Higgins, as
he went about his business. According to Mr Higgins,
the body had been secreted behind dustbins beneath an
unlit lamp in Derby Alley, immediately adjacent to one
of the side entrances to the Empire Theatre on the
north side of Leicester Square. On discovering the
partly clothed cadaver, Mr Higgins immediately alerted
the police. Senior officers from Bow Street police station
and the Central Office at Scotland Yard were on the
scene soon afterwards.

The horrific nature of the attack upon the young dancer is reminiscent of the notorious 'Jack the Ripper' murders that have caused so much alarm in London in recent years. Since the assault on Emma Elizabeth Smith in Whitechapel in April 1888, eleven young women have been mutilated and murdered in London in similar circumstances. Most recently, on 10 September last, the torso of an unknown female was found under a railway arch in Pinchin Street, Whitechapel.

Inspector Walter Andrews of Scotland Yard, one of the officers investigating the 'Jack the Ripper' killings, attended the scene of the crime in Leicester Square last night and said afterwards: 'We are ruling nothing out at this stage, but at first sighting this does not look like the work of the man known as Jack the Ripper. Throat cutting and abdominal mutilation have been a common factor in the Ripper murders, all of which have taken place in and around the Whitechapel area of East London. In this case the physical attacks on the deceased, though similar, are distinctly different, and Leicester Square is a long way from Whitechapel.'

Top of the bill at the Empire last night were Dan Leno and the Scottish Bard, the Great McGonagall. The house was full for the performance and the audience is said to have included certain very distinguished persons.

Tonight's performance will commence at 7.15 p.m. as usual, but will not include Les Ballets Fantastiques as a mark of respect for the deceased.

52

From the journal of Arthur Conan Doyle

Yarborough and I examined the body together. We were left in peace to do so. The royal party departed at once – we agreed it was best. They took Onofroff with them and left, without ceremony, via the stairs that led directly from the ante-room to the street. Oscar and his young men took charge of Dvorak and his daughter, giving them brandy and sandwiches from the sideboard. Parker, the Duke of Albemarle's butler (a better man than I had realised), kept *cave* at the door to the vestibule, while the duke helped us lay out the dead girl's body on the floor.

She was only just dead: her flesh was still warm and soft to the touch. I closed her eyelids, but allowed Yarborough, the senior man, to examine her first. He proceeded exactly as I would have done – meticulously, with care and concentration, swiftly but not in haste – and reserved his judgement until I had examined the body also.

Our conclusions, when we shared them, proved identical. The poor girl had died not from her stab wounds, but from a broken neck. To the right side of her jaw were the impressions of finger marks, suggesting that a hand had been placed across her mouth. Her head had then been pulled from left to right with so mighty a force that the vertebrae at the top of her spine had snapped, severing her spinal cord and killing her outright.

'Is this the work of one man?' I wondered.

'One devil incarnate,' said Yarborough.

'Or of two men? While one brute held her down, the other broke her neck . . .'

'Either with his bare hands or smashing the neck violently against a solid surface – a step or the edge of a wall. The force used must have been considerable.'

'And what about the wounds to her chest and neck? Do you recognise them?'

'Yes,' answered Lord Yarborough. 'I do.'

We were kneeling on either side of the girl's body. The Duke of Albemarle stood at her feet, gazing down on us. He turned away.

Lord Yarborough continued quietly: 'The marks on the breasts are superficial, as you can see – cuts and tears executed with a knife and intended to disfigure and mutilate, not to kill. It is exactly as it was with the Duchess of Albemarle.'

'But the incisions in the neck are not quite the same.'

'No,' he agreed. 'They are not so neat, nor so subtle. This murder is more brutal, more brutish – more quickly done.'

'But the work of the same man?'

'Yes,' he said. 'Or designed to seem so.'

'Is she a patient of yours?' I asked.

'This girl? Miss Lavallois?' He sounded surprised by my question, but not affronted. Looking up from the bloody body that lay on the floor between us, he smiled bleakly. 'No,' he said softly. 'She was not a patient of mine. Alas.'

We got to our feet. 'We'd best alert the theatre manager,' I said. 'Where is he?'

'Drowning his sorrows with the Great McGonagall, I imagine,' replied Yarborough, with a chuckle. 'Leaving us be – as the prince requested.'

'We must find him,' I said. 'We must call the police.'

'Let us not be precipitate,' urged the Duke of Albemarle, glancing towards the ante-room. 'Let us send the others on their way first.'

'But they are witnesses,' I protested.

'Witnesses to what?' responded the duke. 'Not to the murder.'

'No, not to the murder – but Miss Dvorak discovered the body.'

'She went to the water closet, opened the door and discovered a body, yes – but what of that? Does it signify? Will knowing that in any way assist the police?'

'We were all here,' I said. 'We are all witnesses.'

'Witnesses to what? We saw nothing. We heard nothing. We were standing in a ludicrous fairy ring, playing some tomfool game at the moment when the body was discovered. What's it to do with us?'

Against my better judgement, and urged to it by

Lord Yarborough, I allowed the duke's view to prevail.

Leaving the Lavallois girl's corpse stretched out on the floor of the vestibule, we joined the others in the ante-room. Dvorak's daughter was no longer weeping, but there were still tears in her red-rimmed eyes and she clung pathetically to her father. Dvorak himself glistened with nervous perspiration.

'Are the police coming?' he asked anxiously.

'Not yet,' I said.

'No,' said the Duke of Albemarle. 'The police are not coming.'

'There were thirteen in the circle,' said Dvorak distractedly. 'Thirteen. It is a bad number. And that talk of secrets—'

'Forget it now,' said the duke. 'Return to your hotel. Look after your daughter. Mr Wilde and his friends will escort you.'

'I set sail for America on Thursday. I am fearful.'

'Do not be,' said Oscar gently. 'The Atlantic is much misunderstood.'

'But if the police have questions—'

'Go to America, Monsieur Dvorak,' urged the Duke of Albemarle, 'take your daughter with you – and put all this out of your mind.'

'But if there is to be an investigation—'

'It need not concern you. Return to your hotel, sir. Speak of this to no one. Pack your bags and set sail on Thursday as you planned. Who knows that you were here tonight?'

'Nobody – other than those who were present.'

'Then forget that you were here. Wipe this dreadful experience from your mind – entirely. It will be best.'

'And for your daughter also,' added Lord Yarborough.

'Very well,' muttered Dvorak. 'Another secret, but perhaps for the best.' Sighing heavily, he held his daughter close.

Oscar, I noticed, had broken from the group and gone into the vestibule to collect Dvorak's hat and cane and his daughter's evening cloak. As he returned I saw him look down at the body of the dead girl. He studied her face and did not flinch. I was surprised: Oscar is not one to lightly look on death. He makes a fetish of beauty. And he has a horror of the disfigured and the grotesque.

'Goodnight, gentlemen,' said the Duke of Albemarle. 'Goodnight, mademoiselle.'

Oscar, Sherard and LaSalle escorted the Dvoraks into the street. As they were departing, Oscar paused to pick up a small package from the sideboard. It was wrapped in a linen napkin. He held it up.

'My supper – lamb cutlets and lobster claws. There's nothing quite like an unexpected death for quickening the appetite.'

'Goodnight, Oscar,' I said.

'Goodnight, Arthur. I will call on you at breakfast. We must report all this to the Prince of Wales.'

'Why's that?' asked the Duke of Albemarle sharply.

'Because he was not here,' said Oscar, smiling. 'Because he left before the body was discovered – don't you recall, Your Grace?'

The duke laughed. 'Yes, of course. I had forgotten. Thank you for reminding me. Thank you, Mr Wilde. Goodnight.'

The moment Oscar and the rest of his party had gone, the Duke of Albemarle declared: 'Wilde is right. We must protect the prince at all costs – both princes.' He looked back towards the vestibule. 'We must move the body.'

'What?' I cried, dumbfounded.

'We cannot hide the fact that the Prince of Wales was here tonight. There are a thousand witnesses to his presence in the royal box. But we can hide the fact that a young woman's mutilated body was discovered immediately adjacent to the royal box. We can move the body.'

'I think not,' I said coldly.

'Think again,' said the duke. 'A scandal could ruin the prince. We have a duty to protect him.'

'We have a duty to the truth.'

'We are not hiding the truth, Doctor. We are protecting the reputation of the heir to the throne.'

'And of his eldest son,' added Lord Yarborough, 'our someday king – and a man once rumoured to be Jack the Ripper.'

Standing between Lord Yarborough and the Duke of Albemarle, I looked each man frankly in the eye.

'I cannot be party to this, gentlemen. Do as you think fit. Do as you think proper. So long as the course of justice is not perverted by your action, I will not speak of this to others – ever. But I will not be party to it. Forgive me. Goodnight, gentlemen.'

'Goodnight, Doctor.'

They spoke the words in unison.

7 a.m. Wednesday, 19 March 1890. I have barely slept. I have written up my journal, but now I think I must destroy what I have written – destroy it to protect the reputation of the Prince of Wales, and my own reputation, too.

How have I become enmeshed in this? I am sworn to secrecy. I cannot even whisper of it to my darling Touie. My hero was right: 'Oh what a tangled web we weave, when first we practise to deceive!'

53

Telegram from Arthur Conan Doyle to his wife,
Louisa 'Touie' Conan Doyle, despatched on
Wednesday, 19 March 1890, at 7.30 a.m.

UNEXPECTED BUSINESS. SADLY DELAYED IN
LONDON UNTIL FRIDAY. DEEPEST REGRETS.
KINDLY ASK CARTER TO BE LOCUM FOR SURGERY
TODAY. LETTER FOLLOWS. YOUR EVER LOVING
ACD

54

Telegram delivered to Oscar Wilde at 16 Tite Street, Chelsea, on Wednesday, 19 March 1890, at 7.30 a.m.

CERTAIN PERSON REQUIRES YOUR PRESENCE
AT TWELVE NOON TODAY WEDNESDAY AT
SARAH CHURCHILL RESIDENCE. REQUEST
BRING DOYLE. STRICTEST CONFIDENCE. OWL

55

From the diary of Rex LaSalle

> The night has been unruly: where we lay,
> Our chimneys were blown down; and, as they say,
> Lamentings heard i' the air; strange screams of death . . .

I pictured the girl's face and thought of my mother.

Oscar would not come back to my room. Once we had taken the composer and his daughter to their hotel, we went on to the Café Royal for a nightcap – brandy and champagne.

Sherard said little. Oscar said much – but none of it to any purpose. He said nothing of the horror of the night, nothing at all. He talked of Shakespeare (as he often does when in wine) and of love and death – and of the death of love in marriage. He quoted Macbeth. He spoke of Henry Irving's Macbeth and Ellen Terry's Lady Macbeth – and of his love for Ellen Terry and Lillie Langtry and Queen Victoria.

'I would marry any one of them willingly – or all three at once – if I believed in marriage. But I don't any more. Marriage ruins a man. It is as demoralising as cigarettes and far more expensive.'

He was, by turns, absurd and capricious. When it was gone one in the morning and the café was closing up about us, he said, 'I'll take a two-wheeler to Tite Street. How will you get home, Rex? Robert will walk to Gower Street, I know, but how will you travel? How does a vampire get about town these days – on foot or by wing?'

'Since you ask,' I said, 'I shall be an owl tonight.' I looked him directly in the eye as I spoke.

He returned my gaze and replied, 'You do not surprise me. "It was the owl that shrieked – the fatal bellman which gives the stern'st good-night." Goodnight, sweet Rex.'

What does he know?

56

From the notebooks of Robert Sherard

I reached the Langham Hotel at 9 a.m. and found Oscar and Arthur Conan Doyle seated alone at a quiet table in the farthest reaches of the Palm Court. Doyle, in a pepper-and-salt tweed suit, looked out of place and out of sorts. His eyes were rheumy, the dark bags beneath them swollen and creased.

Oscar, by contrast, appeared remarkably well rested and full of the joys of spring. His cheeks were pasty and pallid as ever, but his eyes sparkled and his costume was a riot of contrasting colours: a lime-green frock-coat (with sea-green silk facings), a rose-pink waistcoat, a lemon-yellow shirt, an azure-blue necktie, a pearl tiepin and, in his buttonhole, a daffodil.

He smiled as he watched me appraising his attire. 'Fashion is what one wears oneself,' he began, then glanced teasingly at Conan Doyle before adding: 'What is unfashionable is what other people wear.'

'Fashion be damned,' snapped Doyle. 'At the Empire Music Hall last night a young woman was brutally murdered.'

'Indeed,' sighed Oscar. 'And at the Savoy Hotel today, I understand they are introducing pink tablecloths to flatter the complexions of their female diners. What is becoming of the world?'

'Dammit, Oscar,' barked Conan Doyle, 'do you have to make a joke of everything?'

'Pink linen at the Savoy is no joke, Arthur.'

'Must you laugh at everything you encounter?'

'If I laugh at any mortal thing, my friend, 'tis that I may not weep. You know that. We must laugh before we are happy, for fear we die before we laugh at all.'

I took my place at table and, pouring myself some coffee, I looked at Conan Doyle's melancholy face. His eggs and bacon sat cold on his plate before him. His newspaper lay open on the table.

'What happened after we left last night?' I asked.

'I take it you've not read the paper?' he replied. 'It seems that the body of Miss Louisa Lavallois was discovered late last night – by a lamplighter – in a dark alley off Leicester Square.'

'Ah,' said Oscar lightly, buttering a piece of toast. 'You moved the body. Your conscience pricks.'

'I did *not* move the body,' hissed Doyle.

'Albemarle moved the body, then – or rather Albemarle got his butler to move the body, with Lord Yarborough assisting. I see it all.'

Conan Doyle said nothing.

''Twas well done. 'Twas necessary.'

'Was it?' demanded Conan Doyle tetchily.

'Yes, Arthur. The Prince of Wales is next in line to the throne of England. One day, probably quite soon, he will be king, ruling over a mighty empire that reaches across the globe. Protecting the royal reputation is in the national interest. To distance the prince from murder was the right thing to do – without question. To move the poor girl's body was a patriotic duty.' Oscar bit into his piece of toast. 'Besides,' he added, 'no harm was done.'

'Was it not?'

'I think we can safely assume that His Royal Highness was not personally involved in the girl's death.'

'Can we? Clearly he knew her. Clearly he loved her.'

'And all men kill the thing they love?'

'No, of course not. But Miss Lavallois's association with the prince may have had some bearing on her murder, don't you agree?'

'I do,' said Oscar, pushing his plate to one side and reaching for his cigarette case. 'That's why we are going to Paris – almost at once.'

'Paris?' Dr Doyle shook his head despairingly. 'If I am going anywhere, Oscar, I am going to Southsea.'

'By way of Montmartre, *mon ami*. Robert and I are off to the city of light, and you are coming too, Arthur. Not this morning – we have an audience with the Prince of Wales at noon. Not tomorrow morning – we are attending the Duchess of Albemarle's funeral. But tomorrow afternoon, Arthur, by the two o'clock train, we are going to Paris, to the Moulin Rouge. We are going for an evening of cabaret and detective work. We shall have solved this mystery before the police have got their boots on.'

'The police already have their boots on, and their laces tied,' said Conan Doyle, passing his newspaper across the table to Oscar. 'Scotland Yard have one of their top men on the case.'

Oscar drew on his cigarette and perused the newspaper. 'Inspector Walter Andrews,' he sniffed, 'not a name to conjure with.' He raised a supercilious eyebrow.

'And the officer's claim to fame appears to be an involvement with the Jack the Ripper murders – so the bright spark has at least ten unsolved crimes to his credit.' He dropped the newspaper disdainfully. 'I don't think we need be fearful of the competition, Arthur.'

'This isn't a game, Oscar. This is murder.'

'Yes, murder most foul. And Jack the Ripper isn't our murderer. As I recall, in the Ripper murders, throats were cut and stomachs eviscerated. Our man has a much lighter, defter touch – if our man be a man at all, of course.'

'What are you suggesting, Oscar?' I asked. 'That the murderer isn't a man but some strange creature of the night?'

Conan Doyle gave a hollow laugh and said mockingly: 'Such as a vampire?'

'No, not a vampire . . . but a *woman*, perhaps?'

Oscar returned Conan Doyle's newspaper to him.

'I observed the finger marks to one side of the dead girl's face. A hand had been placed across her mouth – to hold her down, to silence her. The bruising was considerable, but the impressions left by the assailant's fingertips suggested a small hand rather than a large one – a woman's rather than a man's.'

'But the girl's neck was broken with huge force.'

'Perhaps then we are looking for two murderers – a woman and a man.'

'Perhaps we should be letting the police look for the murderers, Oscar.'

'We can't withdraw from the case now, Arthur. We are too steeped in blood. We are committed. We must go on.'

'I don't think so,' said Conan Doyle, sitting upright and bracing himself. 'This is now a matter for the proper authorities.'

'In this instance, Arthur,' said Oscar, sitting up also, 'we are the proper authorities. We are best placed to solve this crime. We are ahead of the game. The police won't know where to start. They'll have a million suspects to eliminate – all of London, in fact. We have just thirteen.'

'Thirteen?'

Oscar smiled. 'Well, fifteen – if we include you and Professor Onofroff. Or sixteen, if we include Dvorak's daughter.'

'What on earth do you mean?' asked Doyle, rapping the table with his newspaper in exasperation.

'I mean that the murder of Louisa Lavallois was carried out by someone who was in the ante-room to the royal box last night.'

'Not necessarily,' said Conan Doyle.

'Necessarily,' said Oscar.

'No,' protested Doyle, leaning forward. 'The girl's body was discovered in the water closet in the vestibule. The murderer could have followed the girl from the auditorium into the vestibule, done the deed while we were in the ante-room, standing in Professor Onofroff's absurd mind-reading circle, and then slipped back into the auditorium unnoticed.'

'Except they did not do so. That is not what happened.'

'How do you know?'

'I know. The murderer was in the ante-room last night – with us. The murderer was in our midst.'

'You can be sure of that?'

'I can be and I am.'

'And what makes you so certain?'

'This.'

Oscar bent down and from the floor immediately beneath his chair picked up the small package that he had brought away from the theatre the evening before. He laid the parcel on the table before us and carefully unfolded the napkin wrapping to reveal its contents. There, lying between two cold lamb cutlets and three lobster claws, was a small oyster knife, its handle and blade covered in dried blood.

The Dark Penumbra

57

From the notebook of Inspector Hugh Boone of Scotland Yard, Tuesday, 18 March 1890

Important persons emerged from Empire Theatre of Varieties at 10.30 p.m. and departed in waiting brougham. Travelled in direction of Trafalgar Square, presumably towards Mall.

Suspect emerged at 10.45 p.m. approx, with regular companions, plus bearded gentleman (Russian?) and young female. Hailed four-wheeler. HB followed in two-wheeler. Trailed to Langham Hotel, brief stop, then returned to Piccadilly (Café Royal).

At 1 a.m. suspect returned to Chelsea – alone.

58

From the journal of Arthur Conan Doyle

Wednesday, 19 March 1890. Went with Oscar Wilde and Robert Sherard to see the Prince of Wales at twelve noon. We met in his study.

HRH was affable, but more guarded than at our previous encounters – and the hospitality was more modest. Watkins, the prince's page, offered coffee or sherry, and Tyrwhitt Wilson, the equerry, handed round cigars. HRH sat behind an ormolu writing desk while we stood ranged before him like errant schoolboys.

'There's no need to speak of last night,' he began, as soon as the refreshments had been served and the cigars lit. He looked at each of us in turn as he spoke. 'What occurred was a tragedy – of course it was. I knew Miss Lavallois a little and was fond of her, but she moved among an unsavoury crowd and these things happen. I had not seen her since I was last in Paris – a year ago. She was delightful, but some of her associates were not. I am afraid she mixed with a criminal fraternity. It would seem that her past caught up with her yesterday evening. I am sorry for it, but there's nothing to be done.'

He smiled a wintry smile before adding: 'I see from the morning's papers that her body was discovered in an alley off Leicester Square. I am grateful for that.'

I wanted to speak. 'With your permission, sir—' I began, but the prince anticipated me.

'I have no doubt the police will pursue their enquiries with their customary diligence,' he said, still smiling wanly. 'If I could be of assistance to them in any way, I would be, naturally, but in this instance I know nothing – nothing at all – and I cannot think that my intervention would serve any useful purpose.'

'Quite the reverse,' murmured the equerry.

The prince slapped the palms of his hands on his writing desk to indicate that the subject was now closed. Pushing back his chair, he drew on his cigar. 'Now, *revenons à nos moutons*, as the French like to say.'

'Professor Onofroff,' said Oscar.

'Indeed,' said the prince, seeming a touch disconcerted. 'How did you know?'

'Thought transference – this trick of mind-reading is catching, Your Royal Highness,' replied Oscar, with a modest bow.

The Prince of Wales narrowed his eyes.

'Besides,' continued Oscar, 'I see the note you have written on the desk before you, sir. It is upside down, but clear enough. Below the word "Lulu", I see the name "Onofroff".'

The prince picked up the sheet of notepaper and screwed it into a ball.

'Well done, Mr Wilde, but you can lay aside your Holmesian skills for the time being. I am most grateful to you – and to Dr Doyle – and to your friend [HRH never mastered Sherard's name] – sincerely grateful – but I have decided not to pursue the matter of the Duchess of Albemarle's death any further. I no longer require your "detective" services.'

It was Oscar's turn to appear disconcerted. 'And this is as a consequence of Professor Onofroff's reading?' he asked.

'In part, yes,' replied the prince.

'The professor has discovered the murderer?'

The prince laughed. 'No, but he has allayed my fears. He has put my mind at rest.'

'May one ask what the professor has told you?' persisted Oscar.

'Not a great a deal,' said the prince enigmatically, 'but enough.'

'Your Royal Highness is in a teasing mood today.'

The Prince of Wales got to his feet and moved behind his chair. 'I am in a mellow mood today, Mr Wilde – despite last night's tragedy. And, yes, it is thanks to Professor Onofroff.'

'Oh, sir,' pleaded Oscar. 'What did the professor uncover as he stood in our midst last night? What did he see through the miasmal mists of unconsciousness? What did his reading of our minds reveal?'

'Not much detail, that's for sure. His reading was interrupted, as you'll recall. But he saw enough. He saw the dark penumbra.'

'You tantalise us, sir. You must explain.'

The prince's equerry stirred uncomfortably.

'There's no "must" about it, Mr Wilde,' said the prince reprovingly, 'but I will try to explain, as best I can.'

I saw Oscar blush. I had not seen him abashed before.

The Prince of Wales drew heavily on his cigar. 'I am no authority on what people now call "telepathy",' he said, exhaling a cloud of pale purple smoke as he spoke, 'but this is my understanding of what Professor Onofroff was attempting to achieve last night. As you know, I had asked him to meet us to look into our minds. He asked me if I was seeking something in particular. I told him I was: guilt. He answered, "We are all guilty of something – I'll see guilt everywhere." But, I said to him, if you have a dozen men in a circle, and you look into each of their minds, will you see where the greatest guilt lies? He said, "I will. I will be guided by the dark penumbra. Those with the darkest secrets will be surrounded by the darkest shadows."'

The prince paused to draw on his cigar once more.

'And?' I asked.

'And so it proved,' said the prince with finality.

There was a moment's silence before Oscar, quite quietly, enquired: 'And may I ask, sir, which of us turns out to be the guiltiest party?'

'Not you, Mr Wilde – you may be disappointed to discover. Nor, indeed, you,

Dr Doyle. You are let off the hook, gentlemen, by virtue of your relative youth and the fact of not having beards.'

'I have a moustache,' I laughed nervously.

'But as he stood within that circle last night and turned about while letting his eyelids close, in his mind's eye Professor Onofroff claims to have seen the dark penumbra quite distinctly. It surrounded two men – older men – both men with full beards.'

'Did he name them?' asked Oscar.

'He was unfamiliar with the names of most of the men in the circle – but he knew my name.'

'And you, sir, were one of these two men surrounded by the dark penumbra?' I asked.

'Apparently so.' The Prince of Wales smiled.

'And the other?'

'The composer, Monsieur Dvorak. Onofroff was not able to name him – he did not know his name – but he identified him. By his beard. By his age. And on account of his daughter.'

'Did he name the daughter?' asked Oscar.

'No. The seance was too brief to establish any detail. As you know, it ended almost as it began. But what was clear to Onofroff was this: the two men in that circle with the guiltiest and darkest secrets were older men with beards and, in each case, the guilt – the secret – involved the man's eldest child, a child grown to adulthood. Onofroff saw their silhouettes in his mind's eye – each standing with its father. One was a daughter and one was a son.'

'Dear God,' I murmured. 'Dvorak and his daughter . . .'

'Calm yourself, Arthur. Incest is not the end of the world. In certain cultures – and some English counties – it's considered perfectly acceptable. Monsieur Dvorak and his daughter are bohemians. They must be allowed a certain licence.'

I turned on Oscar angrily. 'This is no laughing matter,' I protested. 'Incest is against the laws of God and Nature. It is a criminal offence in this country – and for a reason.'

'And Dvorak and his daughter are leaving the country tomorrow. Let them be. Let them go. He is a great composer and genius will have its way.'

'I am appalled by this,' I said. 'Shocked. I liked the man.'

'And Cleopatra loved her brother Ptolemy – and married him, as I recall. We cannot always choose whom we like and love, Arthur. If we avoided sinners at every turn, we would all lead very lonely lives.'

'Incest is wrong,' I repeated.

'It's inappropriate in Southsea, I grant you . . . but in Bohemia? They do things so differently on the continent.'

Oscar turned from me to address the Prince of Wales.

'I am sure His Royal Highness agrees. The Habsburgs, the Hohenzollerns, the Bourbons – but for a little light inbreeding, the royal families of Europe would have died out years ago.'

Tyrwhitt Wilson stirred uneasily. Robert

Sherard put out a hand to restrain our friend. But the prince appeared tolerably amused.

'Mr Wilde, you forget yourself,' he said. 'Professor Onofroff made no specific allegation. We can but conjecture as to the nature of the guilt surrounding Monsieur Dvorak, and how and why it involves his daughter. Do not get carried away.'

Oscar collected himself. 'I stand reproved,' he said, bowing his head to the prince. 'I did indeed forget myself, sir,' he went on, looking up once more and smiling. 'I cannot believe that Professor Onofroff was anything but woefully wide of the mark when he suggested that Your Royal Highness was one of those surrounded by the dark penumbra. His mind's eyesight must be failing him.'

The prince chuckled. 'You're very generous, Mr Wilde, but no. Onofroff was clear. He recognised me by my beard – and he saw the silhouette of my grown son at my side.'

Sherard spoke up. 'Bram Stoker has a beard, sir. He, too, was in the circle.'

'But does he have a son?' asked the prince.

'He does,' said Oscar. 'Noel Stoker – a charming child.'

'And the son's age?'

'The boy is ten, I believe,' said Oscar.

'Exactly.' The Prince of Wales held a match to a fresh cigar. 'I have no problem with what Onofroff saw, gentlemen. I am not as innocent as my mother would have me be. Indeed, I am guilty of many things – I confess it. I'm clearly more guilty than most.'

'Only by virtue of your age, sir,' quipped Oscar, raising his glass of sherry in the prince's direction. 'You've had more opportunity.'

'I'm not sure that's entirely helpful, Mr Wilde, but I take your point. Monsieur Dvorak and I were the senior men in the circle last night. We are of an age. We were born two months apart. We've lived and loved and bear the scars. We have our guilty secrets. But whatever my sins, I know that I am not guilty of murder . . .'

'Ah!' exclaimed Oscar, handing his glass to the prince's page. 'And you know, too, that Monsieur Dvorak was not in Grosvenor Square on the night of the Duchess of Albemarle's death.'

'Precisely so, Mr Wilde. Monsieur Dvorak was conducting a concert at the Royal Albert Hall last Thursday evening.'

'And this,' continued Oscar, warming to his theme, 'explains Your Royal Highness's sense of relief. If you and Monsieur Dvorak were the guiltiest men in that circle of thirteen, the two with the darkest secrets – and yet you did not murder the duchess and Monsieur Dvorak could not have done so, it follows that none of the others in the circle – all apparently less guilty men – could have committed the crime either.'

'Quite so, Mr Wilde. We are all off the hook.'

'Assuming Onofroff knows his business.'

'He does,' said the Prince of Wales with conviction.

'His Royal Highness places a lot of faith in Professor Onofroff,' murmured the prince's equerry.

'Tyrwhitt Wilson has his doubts,' declared the prince, 'but I don't – so case closed, gentlemen. Sherlock Holmes may return to Baker Street. I thank you for your endeavours on my behalf, but no further investigation is required.'

Evidently our audience was at an end. The prince's page relieved us of our coffee cups and sherry glasses. The equerry moved towards the study door. In unison, we bowed.

'Before we depart, Your Royal Highness,' said Oscar obsequiously, 'might I ask one final question? Who was it in the circle that you suspected of the crime?'

'It's irrelevant now,' said the prince, resuming his seat at his desk.

'Was it Lord Yarborough?'

'Most certainly not,' snapped the prince. 'Good day, Mr Wilde.'

Oscar persisted: 'Was it the Duke of Albemarle? Was it the jealous husband? Did Your Royal Highness fear that His Grace had been driven to it by his wife's repeated infidelity?'

'The matter is closed, Mr Wilde. Let it go.'

'Do you believe that the duchess died a natural death, sir?'

'I believe that Lord Yarborough is right – and has been all along. Poor Helen died of a heart attack. The heart attack may have been provoked because she was indulging in some foul practice –

playing some grotesque amatory game – but we do not need to concern ourselves with that. She had a weak heart. It failed her. She is dead now. Let her rest in peace. Good day, gentlemen.'

Do I burn these notes or keep them?

59

The funeral of the late Duchess of Albemarle will not now take place on Thursday, 20 March, as previously announced. The funeral service for Her Grace will now be held on Saturday, 22 March, at twelve noon at St George's, Hanover Square, London, W., and will be followed by private cremation. Further particulars are available from Messrs J. H. Kenyon, funeral directors of Rochester Row, Westminster, London, SW.

60

From the notebooks of Robert Sherard

We set off from Marlborough House in the four-wheeler that Oscar kept at his disposal all day. He is absurdly extravagant.

'Why don't we walk?' suggested Conan Doyle. 'Look at the sky. It's a fine afternoon.'

'Walk?' expostulated Oscar, as though his friend had quite taken leave of his senses. 'Look at the streets, Arthur – awash with horse manure.'

'We can walk on the pavements.'

'Awash with people! We'd need a street-sweeper to forge a path for us and he'd probably cost more than the brougham.'

Brooking no further argument, Oscar instructed the coachman to take us up St James's and along Piccadilly to the Café Royal.

'We are meeting Rex LaSalle for lunch.'

'Lunch?'

'A magnum of Perrier-Jouët '82. It's what we need to wash away the taste of His Royal Highness's amontillado.'

'I'm not drinking at lunchtime, Oscar.'

'And why not?'

'I'm resolved – absolutely. No alcohol during working

243

hours. It's one of my Lenten resolutions and I am sticking to it.'

'Don't be ridiculous, Arthur. Good resolutions are useless attempts to interfere with scientific laws – as well you know. Their origin is pure vanity. Their result is absolutely nil. They give us, now and then, some of those luxurious sterile emotions that have a certain charm for the weak. That is all that can be said for them. They are simply cheques that men draw on a bank where they have no account. You will have a glass or three of the Perrier-Jouët at the Café Royal, *mon ami. J'insiste.*'

At the Café Royal, Conan Doyle did indeed do as Oscar insisted – and did so without apparent regret. There is something compelling about Oscar. His charm is overwhelming. One does his bidding, whatever one's resolve.

We sat, conspicuously, at a round table in the middle of a crowded dining room on the ground floor. Oscar is always happy to be seen as well as heard. He placed his 'little vampire', Rex LaSalle, on his right hand and treated the young man as he might have done a favourite spaniel – petting and teasing him alternately.

As the wine flowed, so did Oscar's aphorisms. I noted the new ones – and the variations on the familiar ones. This one I had not heard before: 'If you pretend to be good, the world takes you very seriously. If you pretend to be bad, it doesn't. Such is the astounding stupidity of optimism.'

As we were finishing the magnum of champagne and Oscar was wondering out loud if he should choose a different vintage for the second, LaSalle asked casually,

'Have you seen *The Times* this morning? It seems the Duchess of Albemarle's funeral has been postponed until Saturday.'

This news galvanised Oscar. He drained his glass, extinguished his cigarette and pushed back his chair.

'Gentlemen,' he announced, 'we must proceed to Grosvenor Square. We must beard the Duke of Albemarle in his lair. We must discover the meaning of this.'

'Hold on, old boy,' said Conan Doyle, who was now enjoying his wine. 'I thought we were off the case. I distinctly heard a certain person say "case closed" – not an hour ago.'

'Has the Prince of Wales lost interest in the matter?' asked LaSalle, leaning forward.

'Hush!' hissed Conan Doyle, looking anxiously about him. 'No names. We are sworn to secrecy.'

'The Truth is our only mistress now,' said Oscar, getting to his feet. 'We are beholden to none but her.'

He took a five-pound note from his pocket and threw it on to the table.

'Come, gentlemen. To Grosvenor Square. The game's afoot.'

Our brougham made slow progress. The West End traffic was heavy and another carriage had turned over at Hyde Park Corner.

'We should have walked,' said Conan Doyle, adding, with his eyes half closed: 'I don't know why we are going to Grosvenor Square in any event. The duke won't see us.'

'He will,' said Oscar. 'He will feel an obligation. He knows that you know that he moved the body of Louisa Lavallois.'

'I know no such thing,' replied Conan Doyle, sitting upright. 'I have said not a word on the matter.'

Smiling, Oscar waved Conan Doyle's protestation aside. 'The duke will see us. A man always makes time for those who know his secrets.'

And so it proved. Within moments of our arrival at 40 Grosvenor Square, Parker, the butler, admitted us to the duke's presence. It was not quite three o'clock in the afternoon, but the duke was in the morning room, enjoying a post-prandial coffee, smoking a cigar and reading *Pride and Prejudice*.

'Ah, the comfort of Miss Austen,' murmured Oscar, as he bowed to His Grace. 'If one cannot enjoy reading a book over and over again, there is no use in reading it at all.'

The duke disregarded Oscar's pleasantry, got to his feet and stood facing us, his back to the fireplace. Evidently unamused by our intrusion, he invited us neither to sit nor take our ease. From inside his jacket, he produced a small ivory-handled pocket knife, which he used to cut off the lighted tip of his cigar. The unsmoked portion of cigar he laid carefully on the mantelpiece, then wiped the blade of the knife with his handkerchief and returned the knife to his pocket.

'I am surprised to see you, gentlemen,' he said bluntly. His eye rested stonily on Arthur Conan Doyle.

'We were surprised to read of the postponement of the duchess's funeral, Your Grace. We were concerned.'

The duke turned his gaze on Oscar. 'Is that why you are here?'

'It is,' said Oscar. 'It is the only reason.'

The duke's frown began to soften.

'So far as last night is concerned,' Oscar continued smoothly, 'I believe we are all of one mind. The theatre manager was wise to dispose of the poor girl's body in that alley by Leicester Square. Why entangle the heir apparent in a sordid murder inquiry when it is quite unnecessary to do so? The police can now be left to pursue the matter in the normal way of things.'

'Indeed,' said the duke lightly and smiled. 'Gentlemen, be seated, please.'

'No, thank you, sir,' said Oscar. 'We'll not linger.'

'A cigarette, then?' said the duke, taking the silver cigarette case from the mantelpiece and offering it to each of us in turn. 'It was an unfortunate ending to an otherwise enjoyable evening. Dan Leno was at his best, I thought.'

'And the Great McGonagall at his worst,' said Oscar. 'He is magnificent in his awfulness, is he not? He is an extraordinary national monument – like Monsieur Eiffel's new tower in Paris, splendid and pointless at the same time.'

The duke laughed, his demeanour now quite changed. Taking up the cigar he had just extinguished, he relit it.

'I am pleased to see you, gentlemen,' he said. 'Thank you for your concern about the funeral. There's nothing untoward in the postponement. The opposite, in fact. The Bishop of London wished to be one of those conducting the obsequies. He is an old friend. He was not free tomorrow. He can be with us on Saturday.'

'Ah, yes,' said Oscar, drawing on his cigarette with satisfaction. 'And I imagine the extra two days will be helpful to members of the late duchess's family who have farther to travel.'

'Helen had many friends, but no family to speak of. Her parents are both dead. She had no brothers, no cousins.'

'She was not an only child?'

'No, Mr Wilde. I think you know that. She had – has – a sister – a younger sister, Louise Lascelles. I believe Dr Doyle met her at Lord Yarborough's clinic at Muswell Hill.'

Conan Doyle grunted awkwardly. 'Yes, I saw her briefly. She is not well.'

'She is quite mad, Doctor. It is heartbreaking.'

'Indeed,' muttered Conan Doyle.

'I am grateful to Yarborough for all that he is doing for her. He is attempting to cure her through hypnosis. He wanted to admit Helen to the clinic also, but she'd have none of it. She was wilful, even when she was calm. And she was not often that.'

'Both sisters suffered from the same condition?' asked Conan Doyle. 'Both exhibited the same symptoms?'

'Yes,' said the duke, sighing heavily. 'I married Helen for her gaiety and discovered that I had married an hysteric.'

'I am sorry,' said Conan Doyle.

'Hysteria is a sickness – a disease – that's not yet understood. Charcot and Yarborough are exploring its pathology and I am helping them as best I can, funding their researches. But money alone cannot provide the answers. The human body must be ready to reveal its secrets. Progress is slow.'

He extinguished his cigarette in a small silver ashtray that bore the Prince of Wales's feathers and laughed bitterly.

'What am I saying? There is no progress.'

'None at all?'

'None at all – if Yarborough's to be believed. And he is. He's a good man. A great man.' The Duke of Albemarle looked directly at me. 'I believe he is a kinsman of yours, Mr Sherard. You are cousins, I think?'

'Bastard cousins,' I said, embarrassed.

'Cousins nonetheless,' said Rex LaSalle.

'Exactly, sir,' said the duke, smiling. 'Blood's thicker than water and all that.'

'Will the duchess's sister be able to attend the funeral?' enquired Oscar, putting out his cigarette alongside the duke's in the ashtray with the Prince of Wales's feathers.

'Oh no. She is far too unstable. Her lunacy is profound, her fits unpredictable. I fear she will live out her days in an asylum, as thousands do, as tens of thousands have before her. It is pitiable – horrible – and, as yet, there is no cure. My poor Helen may be the more blessed to be dead.'

'May she rest in peace,' said Oscar.

'Thank you,' said the duke. 'And thank you for calling, gentlemen. I apologise for not being more welcoming. I have been under some strain in recent days.' He glanced towards the novel he had put down on the side table. 'Hence the "comfort of Miss Austen", as Mr Wilde so neatly puts it.'

'Yes,' said Oscar, 'there is great consolation in known relationships.'

The duke smiled. 'They say Mr Darcy is loosely modelled on my grandfather.'

His Grace led us to the door of the morning room. As

he opened it, we found Parker, the butler, immediately awaiting us outside.

'Good afternoon, gentlemen,' said the duke pleasantly. 'On Friday evening, early, I am holding a small reception here in my wife's memory. The Prince of Wales does not attend funerals as you know, but he will be honouring us with his presence on Friday. He was very fond of Helen. I hope, gentlemen, that you will be able to honour us with your presence, too.'

We left him at the door of the morning room and, in silence, followed the butler along the corridor back to the front hall. Retrieving our hats, we bade the butler good day. He opened the front door for us and, as he did so, as we were lined up to depart, we heard a noise coming from the gallery at the top of the main staircase.

Looking up, we saw a young housemaid looking down at us. She had dropped a pile of linen and was kneeling down beside it, staring at us through the wooden balustrade. As her eyes met ours, her young face contorted in a silent scream. Hurriedly she grabbed the linen, scrambled to her feet and ran away.

'It's Her Grace's maid,' said the butler. 'The poor child has taken it very badly.'

The Jersey Lily

61

Telegram delivered to Constance Wilde at 16 Tite Street, Chelsea, on Wednesday, 19 March 1890 at 6 p.m.

BREAKFAST AND LUNCH WITH SHERLOCK HOLMES. SHERRY WITH A PRINCE. CIGARETTES WITH A DUKE. TEA WITH THE JERSEY LILY. DINING WITH VAMPIRES THEN TAKING THE NIGHT TRAIN TO PARIS. ALL TOO TEDIOUS BUT MUST BE DONE. FRESH WOODS AND NEWS TOMORROW. EVER YOUR LOVING OSCAR

62

Telegram delivered to Louisa 'Touie' Conan Doyle in
Southsea, on Wednesday, 19 March 1890 at 6 p.m.

DEEPLY DISTRESSED. UNAVOIDABLE FURTHER
DELAYS. PLEASE SECURE CARTER AS LOCUM
FOR FRIDAY SURGERY. RETURN TO SOUTHSEA
BY SATURDAY EVENING GUARANTEED. MY
LOVE AND APOLOGIES ACD

63

From the diary of Rex LaSalle

I looked directly into the eyes of the maidservant and she looked directly into mine. I saw fear there, bordering on terror, but it was not blind, animal fear. I saw intelligence and understanding, too.

Oscar asked: 'Is it possible that she is an hysteric also?'

'Yes,' said Conan Doyle. 'It's possible.'

'Can you "catch" hysteria – like the measles?'

'No, but you can observe it in others and learn the symptoms and imitate them – consciously or unconsciously. You can induce your own hysteric state.'

'And can hysteria render you speechless?'

'Hysterical paralysis is not uncommon. It can rob you of the power of speech, certainly – but for an hour, a day, months at most. Not for a lifetime. We were told the girl was deaf and dumb from childhood.'

'We were.'

Oscar's brougham took us from Grosvenor Square to St James's by way of the post office in Albemarle Street where Oscar and Conan Doyle stepped down for a moment to send telegrams to their wives.

When I said, 'The one advantage of not having a wife is that you don't have to tell her lies,' Oscar replied: 'But a perfect lie is one of life's most perfect pleasures, is it not?'

While Oscar and Conan Doyle were about their business, I remained with Robert Sherard in the brougham. I asked him about his grandfather, the last Earl of Harborough. Had he known him?

'No, he was already an old man when my father was born. My father was his natural son.'

'And his only son?'

'Yes, but conceived and born out of wedlock. My father might have been an earl, but for the small matter of his illegitimacy. Instead, he became a clergyman – and a poor one at that. He's spent his life as an itinerant Anglican chaplain.'

'Do you not resent the fact of your father's illegitimacy?' I asked. 'Would you not have liked to be an earl?'

'I would like to be a great man,' he replied, 'but not necessarily an earl. I would like to be like Oscar: extraordinary, original, unique.'

'I understand,' I said. 'It's what we all want – to be extraordinary, original, unique.'

'Is that why you claim to be a vampire?'

'I am a vampire,' I said.

He did not believe me. No one does.

The brougham took us on to the St James's Theatre and stopped in Duke Street, outside the stage door.

'Gentlemen,' declared Oscar, 'we have a treat in store. We are taking tea with Lillie Langtry.'

'How wonderful,' said Robert Sherard. 'But why?'

'Because few – if any – know the Prince of Wales so well as Lillie does. I wish to ask her something about His Royal Highness. It is something we need to know.'

With a spring in his step, Oscar led the way into the stage door.

'Are we expected?' asked Conan Doyle.

'No, but the Jersey Lily loves the unexpected.'

Oscar glanced up at the clock on the wall facing the stage-doorkeeper's lodge.

'It is half past five. The matinée finished half an hour ago. Mrs Langtry's kettle will be bubbling merrily on the hob. There may even be scones.'

He rattled the grille behind which lurked the dozing doorman. The old man sat slumped at his table; his gnarled, bald head lolled to one side; his near-toothless mouth hung open.

'Mr Oscar Wilde for Mrs Lillie Langtry.'

Oscar announced himself three times before the doorman stirred. He looked up slowly and grunted and smacked his lips. Without comment, he took the florin that Oscar held out to him.

'This way!' cried Oscar as we followed the shuffling doorman through an inner doorway and down a narrow flight of stone steps towards Mrs Langtry's dressing room.

As we went, over his shoulder, Oscar offered a hymn of praise to the object of our pilgrimage.

'As I am sure you know, she is the most painted woman of our age. Millais called her, quite simply, the most beautiful woman on earth. But Lillie's beauty has no meaning. Her charm, her wit, her

mind – what a mind! – are far more formidable
weapons. She is all fire and energy.'

The doorman knocked on the dressing-room door.
There was no answer.

'Allow me,' said Oscar. 'We are old friends.' Oscar
knocked on the door himself and opened it without
awaiting a reply. 'Lillie,' he called. 'My Lillie.'

We saw her at once: the gas lamps in the room
were turned high. She was lying on a chaise longue
next to her dressing table, wrapped in a heavy
woollen shawl. Her hair was swept up and pinned
tight against her head. Over her eyes she wore a
black harlequin's mask. There was little of her
celebrated beauty on display.

'Come away,' hissed Conan Doyle. 'The poor
woman's asleep.'

'She was,' murmured the slumbering figure. 'But
Wilde hath murdered sleep and Langtry shall sleep
no more.'

She pulled the mask from her eyes and sat up,
blinking. Gathering the shawl about her and shaking
her head, she got slowly to her feet. She wore no
stockings. On bare tiptoes she teetered towards Oscar
and accepted his embrace.

'If I didn't owe my entire career to you, Mr Oscar
Fingal O'Flahertie Wills Wilde, I would be quite cross.
I've just given three hours of As You Like It to a half-
empty house. The worse the business, the greater the
struggle. I have another three hours of it tonight. I
need my beauty sleep between performances. I'm
thirty-six now, Oscar. My God, do I need my beauty
sleep!'

Oscar broke away and stepped back to admire the lady. 'Isn't she wonderful?'

'Isn't he ridiculous?' growled the actress.

Her voice was deep and warm: she appeared to laugh as she spoke. She surveyed the trio of young men standing crowded in her doorway.

'Who are these people, Oscar? I can see that they are young and handsome.' She moved towards us. 'Robert I recognise. Robert I remember. But who is this?' She put out her hand to Conan Doyle. 'Is this an intrepid hunter newly returned from the Amazon jungle? He has the mark of the hero about him.'

'This is Arthur Conan Doyle,' said Oscar.

'I know him. I know his name. I know his work. Micah Clarke is quite possibly my favourite novel.'

Conan Doyle blushed and, shifting from foot to foot with pleasure, attempted to click his heels as he bowed to the actress.

'He is a gentleman – with the loveliest moustache I have seen in my entire life. I want to marry him, Oscar. I want to marry him at once.'

'He is already married, Lillie.'

'The best ones always are.' She sighed. 'How is dear Constance?' she asked. 'As patient as ever?' Without waiting for Oscar's reply, she turned to me: 'You are not married, are you, sir? You are far too young – and far too pale.'

'This is Mr Rex LaSalle,' said Oscar as Mrs Langtry took me gently by the hand.

She looked up at me and paused, narrowing her eyes and tilting her head to one side.

'I know you, too, I know your name. Have we not met before? Are we not old friends?'

'We have not met before, Mrs Langtry.'

'Are you sure? LaSalle – it's an old Jersey name. You come from Jersey?'

'Yes.'

'How old are you?'

'Twenty-six.'

'Is that all? I'm sure I knew you when you were a little boy. My father was Dean of Jersey.'

'I know.'

'We lived in St Saviour, at the old rectory, and your family lived in St Saviour, too. I remember. I remember you as a little boy, with corn-yellow hair and sea-green eyes – Reginald LaSalle.'

'That was my brother,' I said. 'He died.'

She squealed with distress and let the shawl fall from her shoulders as she took me in her arms. 'Of course,' she cried, 'in the fire. Your parents were killed, too. My poor, dear boy.'

'It was a long time ago – twenty years.'

'And Rex has risen phoenix-like from the ashes,' said Oscar. 'He's an actor now – and an artist – and a vampire.'

'By all that's wonderful,' cried Mrs Langtry, stepping back to gaze at me in rapture. 'I shall marry him, too. To be a vampire's bride: is that not every woman's dream?' She turned to Oscar. 'Now, I'm glad you came, Oscar. I adore your friends. I want to marry them all.'

Oscar looked about the little dressing room. 'No tea? No scones?'

'No Mrs Adler,' said Mrs Langtry sadly. 'My maid is not well. Matinée day and I'm having to make do and mend on my own. Sit, gentlemen, sit. I'll brew the tea myself.'

Side by side, Conan Doyle, Sherard and I perched ourselves along Mrs Langtry's velvet-covered chaise longue while Oscar and the actress crouched down by the hearth and fussed over the kettle and the teapot.

'Why are you here, Oscar?' she asked. 'To what do I owe the honour?'

'We wanted to talk to you about the Prince of Wales,' wheezed Oscar. (He was not comfortable on his haunches.)

'Oh!' cried Mrs Langtry with delight. 'Is there gossip? Is there news? Has Daisy Brooke fallen from grace at last? You know everything, Oscar.'

'I do not know the Prince of Wales so well as you, Lillie.'

'Perhaps not.' She snapped shut the malacca tea caddy and held it up for us to admire. 'This was one of His Highness's many gifts.'

'He was generous.'

'We were close.'

'None closer.'

Unsteadily, Oscar poured boiling water from the kettle into the teapot. The task done, he struggled to his feet and, motioning towards the chaise longue with his head, whispered hoarsely to his friend: 'They know your secret, Lillie.'

Mrs Langtry rocked on her heels with laughter. 'Everyone knows my secret, Oscar. And I don't care. I never did.' Taking the teapot and rotating it gently, she stood up and came towards us. 'We never did. The prince had a handsome house built for me in Bournemouth – the Red House, our house – and in the dining hall, below the minstrels' gallery, in letters large as life, we had written along the wall: "They say – What say they? – Let them say." We cared not a jot for what the world thought. We were so happy. We were so in love.'

'Did you meet when the prince first came to Jersey?' I asked.

She looked quite puzzled. 'When was that? The prince in Jersey? I don't remember that.'

'In January 1863.'

'I was ten, Mr LaSalle! I did not meet the Prince of Wales in 1863.'

She laughed, handed me a cup and saucer and poured me my tea.

'We met years later, in London, when I was twenty-four – at least. And married to Mr Langtry. I was safe.'

'But sensational,' added Oscar. He was now at Mrs Langtry's side, holding a jug of milk and a bowl of sugar. 'Beauty – with brains.'

'I'm not sure about that, Oscar, but I do know that I was fearless. I was not awed by the prince – in any way at all. I believe that's what he most liked about me.'

'And what did you most like about him?' I asked.

'Everything – except the stench of his cigars.' She laughed. 'He is a fine man, kind as well as generous. We are still friends, if not so close as once we were. I love him still.'

She steadied her hand as she poured Conan Doyle his tea. 'I hope you are not shocked by my chatter, Mr Doyle. You are very quiet.'

'Arthur is the kind of fellow you want in the orchestra stalls, Lillie,' said Oscar. 'He is a perfect gentleman. He never speaks when the leading lady is in full flood and centre stage.'

Conan Doyle smiled as Oscar dropped three lumps of sugar into his tea.

'And Arthur,' continued Oscar, 'is both newly married and happily married and may find some of your story a little disconcerting.'

'Oh!' cried Mrs Langtry, returning the teapot to the hearth. 'To be happily married is my life's ambition. I shall keep on marrying until I am.'

Through the laughter, I heard myself asking: 'Mrs Langtry, did you ever meet the Princess of Wales?'

As I put the question I thought it shocking – uncalled for, unmannerly. Mrs Langtry, however, appeared not the least discomfited.

'I know the Princess of Wales. I have met her. I like her very much. I admire her beauty greatly. And her good works.'

'And her forbearance,' added Oscar, stirring his tea.

'The princess is a woman of the world. She is wise to the ways of men. She has a father. She has brothers. She knows what these creatures are. Men – they are all the same.'

'All of them?' asked Conan Doyle, breaking his silence.

'In my experience,' said Mrs Langtry. She went over to the doctor and gently ran the backs of her fingers down his cheek. 'Perhaps you will be the one exception.'

Doyle blushed. 'I hope so,' he murmured.

'I hope so, too,' said Mrs Langtry, kindly.

'Did the princess know of your friendship with the prince?' I asked.

'You are very bold, Mr LaSalle, but yes. Yes, she did – and she looked the other way. She did not wish to cause a scandal. It is scandal, Mr LaSalle, that does the damage. Oscar's father was brought low by scandal. So was mine. My father was driven out of Jersey because of all the talk.'

'I know,' I said.

'I'm sure you do. People love to gossip. A hundred years from now, if people are still speaking of me it won't be because of my Rosalind – it will be because I was once a prince's paramour.'

Oscar smiled. 'There is only one thing in the world worse than being talked about and that is not being talked about.'

'As you say, Oscar,' Mrs Langtry said, laughing, 'so often. You are shameless in the way you repeat your own lines.'

'I like to give the public what they want.'

'And what do you want, Oscar? Why are you here?'

Mrs Langtry put down her teacup among the combs, brushes and powder puffs on her crowded dressing table and, going over to her old friend, placed her arms about his neck. I reflected that I had never before encountered a woman so intent on seducing every man she met.

'I am here to ask you a simple question. It is a serious question and I want you to think about it carefully before you give me your answer.'

'Very well,' she said, pulling his face close to hers and kissing him lightly on the lips. 'What is your question, Oscar?'

'It is this, Lillie. You know the Prince of Wales.'

'I do.'

'You know him well.'

'I do.'

'Do you think there are any circumstances in which His Royal Highness – either alone or in concert with others – would be capable of murder?'

She let her arms fall to her side and stepped back, looking at Oscar in amazement.

'No, Oscar, no.' She laughed. 'The question is absurd. The notion is absurd.'

'Think carefully, Lillie—'

'I do not need to think. I know the man. He has his faults, God knows. He is vain, greedy, restless, short-tempered, wilful, spoilt. He is obsessed with his appearance. He is self-indulgent beyond belief. He stinks of cigar smoke. But he is not a murderer. He is not capable of murder. He hasn't the courage.'

'To eliminate an enemy—'

'He would not think of anyone as his "enemy". He is too self-regarding, too self-absorbed.'

'To avoid a scandal—'

'He is the Prince of Wales. He has no need to murder anyone to avoid a scandal. He can simply walk away. That's what he does. When there's trouble *afoot, he simply walks away The Prince of Wales has not, will not, could not murder anyone.'*

Oscar took Mrs Langtry by the hand and kissed it. 'I think you have made your point, Lillie dear.'

She held Oscar's palm against her cheek and added playfully: 'Prince Albert Victor, on the other hand ...'

'What?' asked Oscar, his brows suddenly furrowed. 'What are you saying, you minx?'

'I'm saying nothing – nothing at all.'

'You are saying something of great moment,' said Conan Doyle, getting up from the chaise longue.

'No, I'm not. I don't mean to be. I'm just remembering something. The Prince of Wales has a weakness for fortune-tellers – as I do ... as Oscar does. And ten years ago, when our affaire was at its height, the prince and I visited a clairvoyant together. She lived in Mount Street, as I recall. She gazed into her crystal ball, she studied our palms, she felt the bumps upon our heads, and looked into our secret souls by means of tarot cards.'

'And what did she foretell?' asked Conan Doyle.

'Nothing but good fortune and long life for both of us!'

'I know the woman,' cried Oscar. 'Mrs Mountjoy – the mountebank of Mount Street. She tells you only what you want to hear.'

Mrs Langtry laughed. 'Exactly so. When the prince expressed his amused surprise that our prospects should be so uniformly golden, the good lady agreed to look again and dig a little deeper. She shuffled her tarot cards and invited His Highness to turn over three more himself – which he did. The cards featured the Page of Swords, the Devil and the Hanged Man. "What do these mean?" asked the prince. "They mean a great deal," said the clairvoyant. "They tell us that one day your eldest son may find himself in league with the devil and accused of murder." We took it as a joke, of course.'

Upper Swandam Lane

64

From the journal of Arthur Conan Doyle

I am an odd fellow. I acknowledge it. I am a man divided. I am a qualified physician, with special interests in diseases of both the body (consumption) and the mind (hysteria) – a family doctor with a general practice that I need to nurture. I am also an aspiring writer with a yearning for adventure – a hunger for danger and a thirst for the unknown. I am quite torn in two.

Part of me – the better part – wishes that, tonight, I was at home in Southsea, my little wife curled up in my arms, my darling daughter asleep in her crib at my side. The other part is grateful that I am where I am – in a dimly lit, smoke-filled, first-class compartment (which I cannot possibly afford), approaching the docks at Dover, on the night train to Paris, in the company of Oscar Wilde (dilettante, dandy, detective – and man of genius), his friend, Robert Sherard, and a complete stranger – an ugly individual with a twisted lip.

Oscar is reading our fellow traveller's evening

newspaper; that gentleman is fast asleep – and snoring fitfully; Mr Sherard is sleeping too. I am wide awake and making these notes in my journal. I have determined to keep a full record of my adventures with Oscar: they will furnish plentiful material for future yarns concerning Sherlock Holmes.

Tonight, for example, Oscar introduced me to the macabre delights of an opium den. Such places are unknown in Southsea. In East London, they abound. And Oscar, so at ease within the Marlborough House set and among the smooth club men of Pall Mall, appears equally at home amid the villains and ruffians of Limehouse – the East Indian sailors, the Lascars and the Chinamen who peddle opium and cocaine.

When we left Mrs Langtry, it was half past six. Rex LaSalle – Oscar's friend, the self-styled 'vampire' – took his leave of us. He had a sudden, throbbing pain in his temple, he said.

'Where we are going now will clear your head most wonderfully,' said Oscar.

LaSalle would not be pressed: he said he was confident that a quiet walk in St James's Park would be sufficient to do the trick.

We bade LaSalle farewell at the corner of Duke Street and St James's, then climbed aboard Oscar's brougham.

'Where are we going now?' I asked.

'To Paris by way of London Bridge.'

'To Paris? Tonight? I thought we were to go to Paris tomorrow. That's what I have told them at my hotel.'

'Our plans have changed. There's no time to be lost, Arthur. We need to get to the root of these mysterious deaths before another one occurs.'

'If Mrs Langtry is to be believed,' said Robert Sherard, 'our first port of call should be the court of His Royal Highness the Prince Albert Victor.'

'Indeed,' said Oscar, smiling slyly. 'Hence our *détour* by way of London Bridge. We are on our way, gentlemen, to "The Bar of Gold".'

'What's that?' I asked. 'A restaurant?'

'Of a kind, Arthur. It's a notorious den of iniquity where the only item on the menu is opium. According to Bram Stoker, Prince Eddy is one of the *habitués*. Bram told me so last night when we were at the Empire. If we get to the place between seven and eight Bram should be there with His Highness – they have Vampire Club business to discuss. Bram assures me that if we are to talk frankly with the prince, we will never have a better opportunity. At "The Bar of Gold" Prince Eddy is at his most unbuttoned.' Oscar called up to our coachman: 'Upper Swandam Lane, driver. Eastward ho!'

It took almost an hour for our brougham to reach the address – a vile alley lurking behind the high wharves that line the north side of the river Thames to the east of London Bridge. Between a slop-shop and a gin-shop, approached by a steep flight of steps leading down to a black gap like the mouth of a cave, we found the den of which we were in search.

'"The Bar of Gold", gentlemen,' announced

Oscar, leading the way. 'Will it live up to its promise, I wonder?'

We passed down the steps, worn in the centre by the ceaseless tread of drunken feet. By the light of a flickering oil lamp above the door we found the latch and made our way into a long, low room, thick and heavy with brown opium smoke, and terraced with wooden berths, like the forecastle of an emigrant ship. Through the gloom one could dimly catch a glimpse of bodies lying in strange, fantastic poses, with bowed shoulders, bent knees, heads thrown back and chins pointing upward. Here and there a dark, lacklustre eye turned upon the newcomers. Out of the black shadows there glimmered little red circles of light, now bright, now faint, as the burning poison waxed or waned in the metal bowls of the opium pipes.

Most of the denizens of "The Bar of Gold" lay silent, but some muttered to themselves, and others talked together in a strange, low, monotonous voice, their conversation coming in gushes, then suddenly tailing off into silence, each mumbling out his own thoughts and paying little heed to the words of his neighbour.

'Have you been to this hell-hole before?' I whispered to Oscar, as gradually our eyes began to accustom themselves to the gloom.

'Once,' he said, 'under the misapprehension that it was a gateway to paradise. I was particularly disappointed in the opium-master. I had envisioned a magnificent Chinaman, richly costumed as a mandarin – a figure from *Aladdin*, an emperor of poppy fruit. Instead, I was welcomed by a sour-faced Malay in a filthy smock who handed me a pipe without ceremony and left me alone to suck upon it until the fumes overwhelmed me. It was not a beautiful experience. It cost half a crown but was not worth sixpence.'

As he spoke, a sallow Malay attendant, exactly fitting Oscar's description, hurried up to greet us. He said not a word, but bowed cursorily and beckoned us to follow him. Shuffling along in down-at-heel slippers, he led us between the dismal berths to the far end of the long room where stood a small brazier of burning charcoal. Seated around it on low wooden benches were three figures – each just recognisable in the low, reflected firelight: Bram Stoker, Prince Albert Victor and Frank Watkins, page to the Prince of Wales.

None looked up as we bowed awkwardly towards the prince and crouched down to perch on the benches alongside them. The prince and the page were sharing a pipe. As we took our places, the prince claimed it from the youth and sucked on it slowly, his eyes closed, his head held back. We watched and said nothing. His Royal Highness sucked on until a faint gurgling in the pipe-stem announced that the opium in the bowl was spent.

'More?' muttered the Malay, leaning down by the prince's ear.

The prince opened his eyes and blinked. 'No more,' he murmured. 'I will talk with my friends.'

Handing the pipe to the page, he waved the Malay away.

'Gentlemen,' he said, breathing deeply and closing his eyes once more, 'good evening. Bram told me that you might drop by. Welcome to "The Bar of Gold". Be not too proud to be here. It's all part of the British Empire.'

'Good evening, sir,' said Oscar quietly.

The prince opened his eyes and smiled. His pupils were dilated: he had the stare of a man possessed, but his way of speaking – his manner – was all courtesy and gentleness.

'I am pleased to see you, Mr Wilde. You know some of my secrets and I trust you.'

'You can trust me, sir.'

'I am grateful. I am surrounded by those I cannot trust – and those who do not trust me. It makes a fellow feel quite lonely. And yet, wherever I go, I am never alone. There's always a policeman lurking – watching me from the shadows. Did you see him at the door? Did you spot him?'

'No,' said Oscar. 'I saw no one. Is he always there?'

'Always. I imagine he is in my father's pay – or the Home Secretary's. I trust he's well paid. He's dogged, I'll give him that. Day and night, he's always there. I can never escape his watchful eye. The devil knows, I've tried.'

He laughed and glanced down towards the pipe that the page was holding: a sixteen-inch length of black bamboo, as thick as a man's finger, with, screwed to its end, a tiny iron bowl the shape of a pigeon's egg.

'The opium here is sweet. I can at least escape from my policeman in "The Bar of Gold".'

The page – Frank Watkins: a handsome youth with bright hazel eyes and copper-coloured hair – leant across and kissed the prince's neck. The prince raised his right hand and buried his fingers in the boy's hair, clasping the lad's head close to him.

'I need you, Frank,' he murmured, and then, as if suddenly waking, startled, from a sleep, he released the boy and looked about him – gazing sharply at Oscar, at me, at Robert Sherard, as if he had seen none of us before. 'What are you doing here?' he asked.

'We remain concerned about the death of the Duchess of Albemarle,' said Oscar.

'Are you police spies, too?' demanded the prince. He seemed a man suddenly transformed.

'No,' replied Oscar soothingly. 'We are friends.'

'Are you working for my father?'

The prince's small eyes burned fiercely in a face wet with perspiration. In the glow of the brazier he had the look of a feral creature glimpsed by lamplight in the undergrowth.

'No,' said Oscar truthfully. 'When we spoke last of this matter, we were. But no longer, sir – I do assure you.'

'You "assure" me, do you, Mr Wilde? What's your assurance worth? Why should I trust you? In God's name, what business is Helen's death of yours?'

Oscar said nothing. Frank Watkins, the page, put his arm around the prince's back. Behind us, the Malay hovered with fresh pipes of opium.

Bram Stoker pulled a large, red handkerchief from his coat pocket and passed it to the prince. His Highness wiped his face with it and calmed himself.

'Helen Albemarle died of a heart attack,' he said. 'According to Lord Yarborough. Yarborough's a doctor, isn't he?'

'Yes,' I said, 'and a distinguished one. I am a doctor, too, Your Highness. With Lord Yarborough I examined the duchess's body some hours after her death and there were marks upon her body – cuts, abrasions—'

He did not look at me but continued to gaze at Oscar.

'Mr Wilde seemed to think they were the marks of a vampire. Mr Wilde, I recollect, wondered whether I might be the vampire in question.'

Oscar made to protest, but the prince continued speaking, laughing derisively as he spoke: 'Mr Wilde is said to be the most brilliant man of his generation. At Trinity College, Dublin, I'm told, Mr Wilde won every prize on offer and walked away with a First. At Trinity College, Cambridge, I failed to last the year and walked away with nothing. But I'm not so stupid as Mr Wilde. There are no such creatures as vampires. I know that. Stoker knows that. We *amuse* ourselves with vampires. We pursue them for our sport. We do not *believe* in them.'

'You believe in porphyria,' said Oscar softly.

'Porphyria is a disease of the blood that drives men mad, Mr Wilde. Porphyria is real. Vampires aren't.'

'The cuts on the duchess's body were real, Your Highness,' I said.

'I don't doubt it, Doctor,' said the prince, turning his gaze from Oscar to look at me. 'But they were not inflicted by a vampire. The Duchess of Albemarle's husband was in the habit of beating his wife. He beat her cruelly. He beat her *savagely*, to be precise.'

The prince paused and mopped his face. Returning the red handkerchief to Bram Stoker, he looked once more at Oscar.

'Did you not know that, Mr Wilde?'

'No,' said Oscar, quietly. 'I did not.'

'The Duke of Albemarle is a brute,' said Prince Albert Victor. 'He beat his wife. I imagine he beats his servants.'

'But the marks on the duchess's torso were not bruises,' I said. 'They were not the mark of a lash or a whip. They were *incisions*.'

'Yes,' said the prince. 'Incisions – cuts inflicted with a pocket knife kept for the purpose. I'm sure you've seen the knife. His Grace also uses it to cut his cigars. The Duke of Albemarle did not thrash his wife with a whip. He cut her quite precisely with a pocket knife.'

'How do you know this, Your Highness?' asked Oscar.

'Helen told me. She told my father, also.'

'Did you see these cuts?' I asked.

'No. His Grace was careful never to mark his wife's face or arms or hands. Helen told me that her husband was most particular about where on her body he marked her. I never saw the scars. But my father did.'

'Did the Prince of Wales tell you this?'

'No. My father and I don't discuss matters of an intimate nature, Mr Wilde. My father told his equerry – and Owl told me. And if he had not, Frank would have told me. Frank is my father's page. Frank hears everything and tells me all that he has heard.'

The prince reached out and took the page affectionately by the scruff of the neck. The boy paid no attention: he was busy sucking on a fresh opium pipe.

'And why did the duke mistreat his wife?' I asked.

'Because he loved her,' said Prince Albert Victor.

'A man can be happy with any woman as long as he does not love her,' said Oscar, softly.

'That is absurd,' I snapped.

'It is true, nevertheless,' murmured Oscar.

'Because he loved her,' repeated the prince, 'and because she did not love him. Because she loved other men.'

'That is why he wounded her as he did,' suggested Oscar.

'Yes,' said Prince Eddy. 'He cut her breasts and her belly because none would see the wounds except for Her Grace and her lovers.'

'And her lady's maid,' I added.

'Your father saw those wounds?' asked Oscar.

'I imagine so,' said the prince. 'I do not know for certain.'

'And he could do nothing about it because to admit that he had seen the wounds would be to admit to his own adultery . . .'

'Yes.' The prince laughed. 'And risk a scandal!'

'However much he might have loved her, the Prince of Wales could not protect the Duchess of Albemarle because the Duke of Albemarle, at all times, had the upper hand. The prince could do nothing to help his mistress – nothing at all – for fear that the duke would sue his wife for divorce, naming the heir apparent as co-respondent.'

Prince Albert Victor took the bamboo pipe from the page's hands and put it to his own lips. He sucked on it slowly, smiling at Oscar as he did so and closing his eyes as he breathed the poison into his lungs. Opening his eyes again, he offered the pipe to Oscar, who accepted it.

'They say that my father prefers men to books and women to either – but, above all, he wants to be king. He will let nothing stand in the way of that. He cannot afford another scandal. He will not allow it.'

'Would the Prince of Wales kill to be king?' asked Oscar.

'He has shot pheasant and partridge and grouse by the thousand, Mr Wilde. The deer at Abergeldie Castle quake at his approach. He has felled tiger and elephant. He slaughters animals with reckless abandon. But could he kill a man? I wonder. And could he kill a woman? I doubt it. And last Thursday night, he could not have killed the Duchess of Albemarle. He was on public view all evening.'

'His equerry was not,' said Oscar.

'His page was not,' said Frank Watkins, grinning.

'Why would the Prince of Wales want to murder his own mistress?' asked Bram Stoker.

'Because he could no longer trust her,' suggested Oscar. 'Because she was an hysteric, and he could no longer rely on her discretion. He could neither protect her from her husband nor protect her from herself. She was mad, poor woman – a danger to herself and to the throne. He could not help her, but he could put her out of her misery. And if he could not do the deed himself, others would do it for him. "Who will rid me of this turbulent duchess?"'

I looked at Oscar as he sucked on the opium pipe. 'This is somewhat far-fetched, my friend,' I said.

Oscar looked back at me and smiled. 'When you have eliminated the impossible, whatever remains, *however improbable*, must be the truth, Arthur. Remember that.'

'It's a lovely line, Oscar – one of your best – but we have not eliminated the impossible. Far from it.'

Prince Albert Victor raised his hand to silence us. 'Gentlemen,' he said, 'if anyone is responsible for the death of the Duchess of Albemarle, it is her husband. His cruelty provoked her madness and her heart attack. He mutilated her – that we know. She told us so. But he did not kill her. Lord Yarborough says her heart gave way – that was the cause of death – and there is no reason to doubt him.'

'And even if the duke had killed his wife,' I said, 'what could be done about it? If you threaten to bring His Grace to justice, His Grace will threaten to destroy the reputation of the future king of England. It cannot be done.'

'Case closed,' said Oscar, handing the opium pipe to Prince Albert Victor.

He put the palms of his hands on the bench on either side of him and attempted to stand. He could not do so. Sherard and I each took him by the elbow and, with an effort (Oscar is a large man), lifted him to his feet, standing closely at his side while he steadied himself.

Oscar looked down at the young prince and smiled. 'Thank you, Your Royal Highness,' he said.

'Thank you, Mr Wilde,' said the prince. 'I did not murder the Duchess of Albemarle.'

'I know,' said Oscar. 'I never thought you did.'

'And yet you came to see me here tonight to confront me with the possibility.'

The prince laughed. In the faint glow of the brazier, with his thin, waxed moustache and the sweat glistening on his saturnine features, he looked like a stage blackguard crouching by the footlights.

'I know why you came,' he said.

'Do you?' asked Oscar.

'You came because my father listened to a fortune-teller years ago and believed the gibberish he was told. My father believes me capable of murder.'

'And are you?'

Prince Albert Victor cast the opium pipe aside and sat upright. Looking up at Oscar and gazing steadily into his eyes, he spoke calmly.

'Yes. Yes, I am, Mr Wilde. I believe in capital punishment. I believe in taking a life – in war and at the gallows. I would fight a duel. And I would murder a man in cold blood – if it was just and right and necessary to do so. I did not murder the Duchess of Albemarle – why should I? I did not kill that little dancer that we met at the Empire last night – why would I? But, yes, Mr Wilde, I am capable of murder. And if, as my father believes, it is to be my destiny, I am ready for it.'

'You will be king one day, sir,' said Bram Stoker kindly. 'In the fullness of time, that is to be your destiny.'

'Oh no,' said the prince, shaking his head and putting his arm around the page-boy at his side. 'I'll not be king. I'll go mad before then. The porphyria will claim me. I shall never be king – and my father knows it. That's another thing the fortune-teller told him.'

65

From the *Evening News*, late edition, Wednesday,
19 March 1890

MURDERED MERMAID NOT RIPPER VICTIM
Louisa Lavallois, the French dancer who has been
appearing as Miranda the Mermaid at the Empire
Theatre of Varieties in Leicester Square, and whose
mutilated body was discovered in an alley adjacent to
the theatre late last night, was not the latest victim
of 'Jack the Ripper', according to the police.

The semi-clad body of Miss Lavallois, twenty-six,
principal dancer with the dance troupe Les Ballets
Fantastiques, was found shortly before midnight
hidden behind dustbins in Derby Alley, fifty yards from
the Empire Theatre stage door. The victim's throat had
been cut savagely and her body mutilated, leading to
speculation that the pretty young dancer was yet
another victim of the notorious 'Jack the Ripper'
who has so far claimed the lives of at least eleven
unfortunate females, mostly in the Whitechapel district
of East London.

However, we understand that the West End location
of the present murder and the particular nature of the
victim's wounds have led police to eliminate Jack the
Ripper from the list of possible suspects. We can
disclose that police now believe that Miss Lavallois

may have been the victim of a revenge killing undertaken by or on behalf of the leader of a French criminal gang based in the Montmartre district of Paris.

Well-informed and usually reliable sources close to the Metropolitan Police have revealed to the *Evening News* that, in Paris, Miss Lavallois had a reputation as a professional courtesan equal to her fame as a dancer and may have fallen foul of her paymaster.

According to the source, 'It seems that the young lady left Paris without the permission of her employer and had hopes of setting up in business independently in London. Her Paris paymaster, a man at the centre of an extensive web of corruption in France, and the owner of several houses of ill-repute in Paris, Lyons and Marseilles, was not ready to be crossed in this way and, as a warning to others, decided to make an example of Miss Lavallois. Either he murdered her himself or, much more likely, sent one of his henchmen to London to do the deed.'

We understand that Inspector Walter Andrews of Scotland Yard, who is leading the investigation into the murder, has been given the name of Miss Lavallois's former employer in Paris and will be contacting the French police as a matter of urgency.

However, according to our source, 'It is very unlikely that anyone will be brought to justice. The man in question is far too powerful to touch and what can be proved? He will have sent an anonymous miscreant to London to commit the crime, and that man will have slipped into the country yesterday afternoon unnoticed and then slipped out again as soon as the job was done.

There are a dozen trains a day to and from Paris and no passports required. Miss Lavallois's killer could be any one of a thousand French criminals ready to commit murder for money. Finding him will be no easier than finding a needle in a haystack.'

66

From the notebooks of Robert Sherard

As soon as the night train pulled out of Victoria station, I fell asleep. Our compartment was warm and dark, and the steady jolt and jar of the train's engine were curiously soothing. I let the locomotive's steam filtering through the carriage windows overwhelm me, like wafts of gas administered in the dentist's chair.

I must have slept for almost two hours for, when I awoke, I found we were approaching the docks at Dover. What roused me, I think, was not so much the clatter of the quayside as the sound of Oscar's lilting voice reading out loud paragraphs from the newspaper – and then laughing contemptuously. At first I was too befuddled to fully comprehend what I was hearing.

'"A professional courtesan", Arthur. What do you make of that? I'm surprised they didn't call her "a scarlet woman" or "a lady of the night".'

'So Miss Lavallois was a prostitute?'

'That's the implication – a jade, a hussy, a drab, a harlot, a wanton fornicatress, a common whore.'

'Steady on, old chap.'

'Unlike the *Evening News*, Arthur, I don't mince my words. When I see a spade, I call it a spade.'

'Have you ever seen a spade, Oscar?'

'Very droll, Arthur.'

Oscar sat with his coat collar turned up and a cigarette dangling from his lips.

'Well, *was* she a prostitute?'

'She was an actress, Arthur. What do you think?'

'I thought she was a dancer.'

'Yes,' said Oscar. 'You're right. She was a dancer. *Much* worse.'

Conan Doyle took the newspaper from Oscar and studied it reflectively. 'So Miss Lavallois was "a professional courtesan" in Paris who came to London to escape her "employer" . . .'

'Her pander, her pimp, Arthur. Read what it says. According to the paper, the blackguard has a string of houses of ill-repute.'

'And this "employer", outraged by the young lady's bid for freedom, sent a man to London to slit her throat.'

'*Pour encourager les autres*. And by way of revenge. That's the gist of it. What do you think?'

Arthur Conan Doyle sniffed. 'It seems plausible enough. Do you think the source is reliable?'

'What do you reckon to his way with words?' asked Oscar.

Conan Doyle raised an eyebrow and looked again at the newspaper. 'He has a poor turn of phrase. "Needle in a haystack" – I don't think much of that.'

'Exactly!' cried Oscar. 'Doesn't that phrase give the whole game away?'

'How do you mean?' laughed Conan Doyle. 'It's not very felicitous, I grant you. Even a trifle obvious.'

'*Precisely*, Arthur. It's far too obvious. The whole

cock and bull story is far too obvious. It's so predictable that it'd disgrace a three-volume novel.' Oscar pulled the newspaper from Doyle's grasp. 'This is all piffle, piss and wind, Doctor. Poppycock from start to finish.' Taking the paper, he flung it contemptuously into the corner of the carriage. 'I doubt there's a word of truth in it. Not a word.'

'Not a word?'

'Not a word, Arthur. This is Owl's doing. This has Owl's handwriting all over it.'

'Owl?'

'Tyrwhitt Wilson – equerry to the Prince of Wales. He went to Harrow, didn't he? Gentlemen go to Eton, scholars go to Winchester, cads go to Harrow. That's the rule. Owl's got perfect manners, but he's not to be trusted.'

Conan Doyle shook his head in bewilderment. I sat up, rubbing my eyes.

'What are you telling us, Oscar?' I asked. 'I have been asleep.'

'We've all been dozing, Robert, while a murderer has been running rings around us.'

'Is Tyrwhitt Wilson the murderer then?' I asked in amazement.

'I doubt it. He lacks the necessary style. No, Tyrwhitt Wilson is merely the source of the story that adorns the front page of the London *Evening News*. He's a cad and a bounder, but he is loyal to his master – I'll give him that. He placed the story in the paper to protect the prince. *Anything* to keep the gaze of the prying press away from the royal box at the Empire Theatre and down the dark alley by the dustbins beyond the stage door. When poor Lulu Lavallois's body was first found, all seemed to be well. The cry went up: "Jack the Ripper strikes again!" But, alas for Marlborough House, the Ripper theory wouldn't run. The wretched girl had been butchered in the wrong way in the wrong part of town. Even Inspector Andrews of the Yard was up to spotting that. Another diversionary tactic was called for – and Owl supplied it.'

'Are you suggesting Tyrwhitt Wilson invented this whole story?' I asked, retrieving the crumpled newspaper from the floor.

'I am,' said Oscar. 'Lock, stock and barrel – to use a phrase with which Owl would certainly be at home. Who else would need to or want to? Tyrwhitt Wilson conjured up the tale and then supplied it directly to the newspaper or to Scotland Yard or to both.'

'But wouldn't that be a risky enterprise in itself?' asked Conan Doyle. 'He's well known as the prince's equerry.'

'He won't have gone in person. They have a telephone at Marlborough House. He will have furnished his "information" anonymously, by telephone – and, knowing Owl, quite possibly in an assumed voice. An Englishman cannot speak French, of course, but, oddly enough, he can usually manage quite a convincing stage French accent.'

I was now reading the newspaper for myself.

'But the article says that Scotland Yard has the name of Miss Lavallois's former employer.'

'That's entirely possible,' said Oscar. 'Lulu was a dancer at the Moulin Rouge, whither we are bound. You saw her dancing there yourself, Robert, with your friend,

Jane Avril. They performed the cancan – memorably so. The Moulin Rouge is owned by one Joseph Oller – a Catalan of doubtful history, but a first-class tailor with a well-trimmed beard. I've met him. You've met him. No doubt, when the Prince of Wales and his equerry visited the Moulin Rouge, they met him, also. Monsieur Oller is well known in Paris. Indeed, he's notorious. And, I imagine, more than able to look after himself.'

Oscar peered through the carriage window: in the distance, lights flickered. 'If the Paris Préfecture question Monsieur Oller on behalf of Inspector Andrews of Scotland Yard, Oller will deny everything – and with reason. He is innocent. At least, he is not guilty of the murder of Louisa Lavallois. He is, however, a suspect character. He has served time in prison. He *might* be the murderer. Thanks to Owl's intervention, the Metropolitan Police and the gentlemen of the British press are now convinced that he is. But it cannot be proved. There's no hard evidence – and the man's in France – and who *really* cares about the death of Lulu Lavallois? There's nothing more to be done . . . Object achieved: case closed.'

The train had juddered to a halt. On the platform torches flared and in the half-dark station porters scurried back and forth with trolleys piled high with luggage.

'Our boat awaits,' said Oscar, getting to his feet, 'and we are travelling as one should – without encumbrance. No bags or baggage, only our hopes and dreams.'

'Did I dream it,' I asked, 'or was there another fellow in the compartment when we got on? An ugly little man in a black overcoat, with a warped face and a twisted lip?'

'He got off at Dover Priory,' said Oscar. 'Evidently, he's not joining us in France. I'm surprised. He's been following us for weeks. I think Arthur was quite struck by his appearance.'

67

From the notebook of Inspector Hugh Boone of
Scotland Yard, Wednesday, 19 March 1890

Suspect has left the country. The country is well rid of him.

68

From the diary of Rex LaSalle

'What man has sought for is neither pain nor pleasure, but simply Life. Man has sought to live intensely, fully, perfectly. When he can do so without exercising restraint on others, or suffering it ever, and his activities are all pleasurable to him, he will be saner, healthier, more civilised, more himself. Pleasure is Nature's test, her sign of approval. When a man is happy he is in harmony with himself and his environment.'

I am happy tonight. I walked through St James's Park and cleared my head. All is well. I am content. Oscar loves me. I am certain of that.

Jane Avril

69

From the notebooks of Robert Sherard

O scar says love is an illusion and that faithfulness is to the emotional life what consistency is to the life of the intellect – simply a confession of failure. Is he right? He usually is.

I am twenty-eight years of age and in my life, thus far, I have loved twelve women. None has made me so happy as Jane Avril. We met five years ago, in Paris, in the spring of 1885. I had just turned twenty-three: she was not quite seventeen. I was drawn to her because she was so beautiful. She was drawn to me, she said, because I was a poet and an Englishman, with perfect manners and famous friends and a fund of stories that she loved to hear me tell. Men fall in love with their eyes: women with their ears.

I first set eyes on her at the Bal Bullier, the exotic dance hall, designed like the Alhambra, on the rue de l'Observatoire. She was in a sea-green silk gown, dancing the polka. I was struck not simply by her youthful beauty – her fresh face, her wide eyes, her turned-up nose, her perfect figure – but by her extraordinary energy. She was so full of life and laughter: she was a ball of fire and a bundle of joy.

I introduced myself to her between dances, took her hand in mine and raised it to my lips. When I told her my name and that I was a poet, she giggled, kissed me on the nose and said, 'I like you. You're different.'

That night I bought her a bottle of champagne – Perrier-Jouët, Oscar's favourite. On the next night I bought her dinner – grilled lobster at Soufflot on the boulevard St Michel. On the third night we became lovers. She made me pay her.

'My heart you get for free. My breasts cost two sous apiece. I hope you think they're worth it.'

She was worth every penny that I spent on her that spring and summer, but I am proud to say that I gave her more than mere money and tales of my past adventures. I gave Jane Avril her name.

Her *real* name was Jeanne Richepin, but she was anxious to change it. She wanted a memorable 'stage name' because she knew in her bones that she was destined to be a famous dancer. She also needed a new soubriquet because, once she had made her fortune, she did not want her mother – who had abused her and whom she despised – pursuing her to claim a share of it. We chose 'Jane' together because – in my honour – she wanted an English version of her first name, and we chose 'Avril' because it was then April, the month of promise.

From April to September 1885, Jane and I were inseparable. She brought me only happiness: she was easy, carefree, uncomplicated – and funny. When we made love, she laughed, told jokes and chattered – I had known nothing like that before. We were good companions and happy lovers and, when our lust subsided, we remained friends.

We are close friends to this day. And today – Thursday, 20 March 1890 – I took Oscar Wilde and Arthur Conan Doyle to meet her. She is now the principal attraction at the Moulin Rouge, the vast, new cabaret on the boulevard de Clichy, by place Pigalle. She no longer dances the polka. The cancan is her speciality these days – and it is the dance that has made her and the Moulin Rouge famous.

She is not so pretty as once she was. Her long face is more drawn; her eyes have lost their sparkle; and her chestnut-brown hair – once so fine – is now coarse and the reddish-brown colour of henna. The glow of girlhood has gone (she is twenty-two), but her wonderful laugh and her sense of mischief remain.

We found her, as expected, at the Café Gump, just opposite the Moulin Rouge, sitting at a pavement table, drinking coffee and smoking a small Algerian cigar. She wore a red velvet coat, with black fur trimmings, and a bonnet piled high with ostrich feathers.

'Robert!' she cried as soon as she saw me. 'I miss you more and I love you more with every passing day. How are you? You look terrible.'

'I have not slept,' I explained. 'Not a wink.'

I introduced her to Oscar and Conan Doyle.

'*We* have not slept. We came over on the night train.'

'You are all unshaven and exhausted.'

She laughed, inspecting us with amused eyes and pointing to the three empty chairs around the table.

'Be seated, gentlemen. I will get you breakfast. You

are weak with hunger.' She reached out for Oscar's hand. 'Monsieur Wilde, you are quite green.'

'The English Channel was in Gallic mood last night,' said Oscar, closing his eyes as he slumped down on to the chair at her side.

She called out to the waiter who was standing in the doorway of the café.

'A calvados for Monsieur Wilde – and coffee. And ham and eggs – and bread. These are my friends. Look after them well.'

She turned to Conan Doyle. 'I like your moustache, Monsieur. Your moustache tells me that you are a good man – brave and strong. I have often told Robert that he should grow a moustache. It would suit him.' She blew a kiss to me across the table. 'I miss you every day, Robert,' she said. 'And every night.'

Conan Doyle coughed awkwardly before attempting a gallant response to Jane's compliment. He spoke in adequate French, but haltingly.

'May I say that you are even more beautiful, Mademoiselle, than Mr Sherard had led us to believe. I am sorry we are not able to stay in Paris long enough to witness your celebrated cancan.'

'I will dance for you any time, Monsieur,' she replied, taking both Conan Doyle's hands in hers and gazing steadily into his red-rimmed eyes. She glanced towards me. 'You must grow a moustache like this, Robert. I have never known anything so seductive.'

Conan Doyle flushed scarlet instantly.

'We have business to attend to, Jane,' I said, as the waiter arrived with a pot of coffee and a bottle of apple brandy.

'I know,' she answered, opening the bottle and pouring Oscar a libation. 'I got your telegram, Robert. Look, I am here – and I have barely slept either. I was dancing until two – but I am at your service, always.'

She dispensed our drinks and gave us coffee while the waiter brought us plates of ham and scrambled eggs.

'You said you wanted to talk to me about Lulu Lavallois. Apart from you, Robert, she is my dearest friend. We are like sisters. But she never writes. Has she had a triumph in England? What is her news? How is she?'

Oscar sat up and opened his eyes. 'She is dead, Mademoiselle. Did Robert not tell you?'

'Dead?'

Jane Avril put her hands to her face, rocked back in her seat and wailed. Her cry was pitiful.

'Dead? She cannot be dead.'

'She is dead, Mademoiselle,' repeated Oscar. 'I am sorry that we bring you such dreadful news.'

'I am so sorry,' I bleated. 'I did not wish to put it in a telegram.'

Arthur Conan Doyle was now crouching at Jane's side, with one arm around her shoulders and the other holding a small bottle of smelling salts to her mouth and nose. 'Breathe deeply, Mademoiselle,' he said. 'And slowly. Take your time.'

'How did she die?' gulped Jane. 'Why did she not write? What was her sickness?'

'She was murdered,' said Oscar. 'In cold blood, in London, on Tuesday night. That is why we are here.'

It was a full half-hour before Jane had recovered

sufficiently to answer our questions. Our scrambled eggs had turned cold; the ham was left untouched. Only the calvados served its purpose. We all took some and the waiter brought us more.

Eventually, once Oscar had outlined the circumstances of the murder, and when Conan Doyle had calmed and soothed Jane to the best of his ability, the poor girl said she was ready to tell us whatever we might want to know. Drying her eyes with clenched fists, and throwing back her head to face us, she said, with startling vehemence: 'I will do anything to help you – anything.'

'Why would anyone wish to murder Lulu Lavallois?' asked Oscar simply. 'That's what we need to know.'

'And because you were her best friend,' I added, 'you will know her secrets.'

'Lulu had no secrets,' cried Jane. 'She was all goodness.'

'We all have secrets,' said Oscar.

Conan Doyle rested his hands on Jane's and, leaning in towards her, almost as if to exclude Oscar and me from the conversation, asked her a series of questions in his imperfect, awkward French. He spoke softly, gently, as if trying to coax information from a sickly child.

Did Mademoiselle Lavallois have enemies in France?

No, none at all – everyone who knew her loved her.

Did she have family?

None that Jane had ever met – Lulu was an only child: she had never known her father; she had run away from her mother as soon as she was able; it was, said Jane, 'the usual story'.

When Jane had last seen her, did Mademoiselle Lavallois seem anxious, fearful or frightened in any way?

No, far from it – she seemed as happy as a lark. In fact, Jane had never known her happier.

Had Monsieur Oller, the owner of the Moulin Rouge, resented Lulu's departure?

Oh no, quite the reverse – Monsieur Oller had been more than content to see her go: Les Ballets Fantastiques had paid the Moulin Rouge a handsome fee for releasing Lulu from her contract.

As I sensed Conan Doyle struggling with his next question, I asked it for him. 'Did Lulu have lovers?'

Jane laughed. 'We all have lovers. Love is our life. Love is our trade. Love is what we do.' She regarded Conan Doyle seriously. 'Yes, Lulu had lovers – many lovers.'

'Was there one in particular?' I asked.

Jane smiled and looked at me kindly. 'No, my friend, she did not have a "Robert". She shared her favours, but not her heart.' She returned her gaze to Conan Doyle. 'She had many lovers, Doctor – and, no doubt, numbered doctors among them. And lawyers and bankers and soldiers and sailors. And artists – and even artisans. And villains, too. In our line of business, we meet all kinds and conditions of men. Some are generous, some are less so. Some are good and some are bad. We learn to look after ourselves.'

'And could Mademoiselle Lavallois look after herself?'

'Yes,' said Jane, raising her brandy glass, as if offering a toast in memory of her friend. 'Lulu was strong – and brave. She was fearless — and funny. She had only friends.'

She drank from her glass, then stared bleakly into it. 'Who could do this terrible thing?'

'One of just a dozen people,' said Oscar.

He sat forward as he spoke and breathed deeply, smiling directly at Jane Avril and narrowing his eyes to study her. The tinge of green had left his cheeks. His complexion had regained its customary yellow pallor – what he called 'the colour of cheap white burgundy'. His lips were purple and full. Oscar was himself again.

'My dear,' he said, in his impeccable French, 'talk of Monsieur Oller and Lulu's litany of lovers is neither here nor there. Whatever anyone tells you, whatever you may read in the newspaper, your friend was murdered in a cubicle attached to the ante-room to the royal box at the Empire Theatre of Varieties in London's Leicester Square. She was murdered by one person or, possibly, two. Whoever killed her left the murder weapon behind – in the ante-room, half hidden in a tray of sandwiches. There are just twelve suspects. There can be no others. I have the twelve names here.'

From inside his coat, Oscar produced a small pocket notebook, which he opened and laid flat upon the table.

'Here is a circle of names. One of these men murdered your friend.'

The names were written in pencil in Oscar's neat hand and arranged on the page as we had been standing on Tuesday night at the moment when Louisa Lavallois's body was discovered.

```
Parker (butler)    Watkins (page)

Bram Stoker            Tyrwhitt Wilson (equerry)

Oscar Wilde                    Prince Albert Victor

Rex LaSalle    Professor Onofroff    The Prince of Wales

Robert Sherard                  The Duke of Albemarle

Arthur Conan Doyle          Lord Yarborough

Antonin Dvorak
```

'There are fourteen names here,' said Jane Avril, looking at the notebook.

'Yes,' said Oscar. 'As you can see, mine is one of them and I know that I did not commit the murder. I think it unlikely that Professor Onofroff did, either. He is a mind-reader by calling – an elderly gentleman and quite frail. But, more to the point, he was standing in the centre of the circle conducting the seance – so that all eyes were constantly upon him. And even as the circle was forming, as we were milling to and fro, the professor was the focus of attention. Because we were concentrating on the professor, we paid little regard to one another.'

'Lulu was murdered during a seance?' asked Jane.

'Moments before it began, I think,' said Oscar. 'I imagine that Mademoiselle Lavallois arrived in the vestibule adjacent to the room where we were all standing just as Professor Onofroff was calling us to order and as the gas lights were lowered. I surmise that the murderer alone noticed her arrival. He saw her step into the cubicle to powder her nose and he seized his moment. He slipped away from the crowd and followed her into the cubicle. He committed the crime and returned to the circle – all unheeded. It was the work of moments. They say most murders are completed in fewer than ten seconds.'

Jane shuddered. 'What do you want of me?' she asked.

'I want you to consider these names,' said Oscar. 'I want to know if any of these names triggers a memory or a thought that might lead us somewhere useful. I want you to tell me if you recollect Lulu Lavallois ever mentioning any of these gentlemen. One of these men is her murderer.'

Jane considered Oscar's notebook, then looked up at him and smiled. 'Well, I know it is not Robert – and I am sure it is not Dr Doyle.'

Oscar smiled also. 'Moustaches can be cruelly deceptive,' he said. 'Remember that a smooth-faced man has nothing to hide behind.'

Conan Doyle cleared his throat and scowled. 'This is a serious business, Oscar,' he muttered in English.

'Let us assume Arthur and Robert are innocent,' continued Oscar in French, 'at least, for the time being.'

He leant forward towards his notebook and placed his finger on the page.

'Let me take you through the names, Mademoiselle, one by one. Let us start here, at the bottom. Antonin Dvorak. Does that name mean anything to you?'

Jane stared intently at Oscar's notebook. 'No,' she answered.

'Think carefully,' said Oscar.

'No, nothing at all.'

'Rex LaSalle,' said Oscar. 'Does that name suggest anything?'

'LaSalle,' she repeated. 'Is it French?'

'He comes from Jersey,' said Oscar. 'He speaks French. He is a very handsome young man. He's an actor or an artist – at least he's not gainfully employed. He claims to be a vampire, believe it or not.'

Jane laughed. 'Oh, I believe it,' she said. 'We get a lot of young men claiming to be vampires. They think it gives them a licence to do the most extraordinary things!' She held up the notebook and considered it carefully. 'I know the type, but I don't know the name.'

'Lulu never mentioned him?'

'Never.'

'And Bram Stoker? Have you heard his name before?'

'It is a strange name. I would have remembered it, I am sure. It means nothing to me, Monsieur.'

'I am pleased to hear it, Mademoiselle. I have known Bram Stoker since I was a boy. He stole my first sweetheart. He's a thief, with red hair and a beard as well as a moustache, but, even so, I'd be sorry to find he was a murderer.'

Oscar's finger moved to the top of the page.

'And how about Mr Parker? He is butler to the Duke of Albemarle.'

Jane shook her head. 'These names mean nothing, Monsieur Wilde. I am so sorry.'

'Mademoiselle Lavallois never mentioned the name of the Duke of Albemarle – you are certain of that? This is important.'

Jane sighed. 'I have not heard the name before. Of

course, that does not mean that Lulu did not know him. Not every lover tells you his real name. We have dukes who pay us court pretending to be nobodies – and, naturally, nobodies who pretend to be dukes. We meet rather more of those, but it hardly matters. A man is just a man when the clothes come off.'

She looked down at the notebook once more and smiled.

'But a prince is something else. As a rule, a prince is too well known to masquerade under a *nom de guerre*. Besides, he likes to be treated royally, whatever the circumstances. He is so accustomed to it that he cannot cope if you do not curtsy. It's in the blood.'

She ran her finger across the next four names on the list.

'These names, I know. Not the page, but the equerry – Monsieur Wilson – and the two princes. I have met them and Lulu knew them well.'

'Lulu was fond of the Prince of Wales?' enquired Oscar.

'She adored him – and he adored her. He came to see her every spring. He came here, to Paris, to Pigalle – to the Moulin Rouge. He loved Lulu – *very much*. He came five years in a row – at least.'

'They were lovers?'

Jane Avril laughed. 'They were lovers, Monsieur. There is no doubt of that.'

'And Prince Albert Victor?' asked Conan Doyle.

'They were lovers, also – but that was different. The father brought the son to break him in. That's not unusual. That happens all the time.'

'Good grief,' murmured Conan Doyle.

Oscar laughed and took a sip of calvados. 'Yes, Arthur. We're a long way from Southsea now.'

'The young prince came only the once,' Jane continued. 'According to Lulu, he is not the man his father is.'

She smiled. Oscar poured her another drink.

'And Tyrwhitt Wilson?' he asked.

'Monsieur Wilson made the arrangements,' said Jane. 'He brought the money – and the presents. The Prince of Wales was always generous – always a gentleman in bed and always generous afterwards. He has a fine reputation in France.' She raised her glass and said, in English: 'God bless the Prince of Wales!'

'And was there ever a falling out between the prince and Mademoiselle Lavallois? Were there disagreements? Did you hear of problems of any kind?'

Jane slammed her glass upon the table. 'No, no, no. Between Lulu and the prince there was only ever the most perfect *entente cordiale*. That's what he called it, I remember. Theirs was a wonderful friendship. When you saw them together you saw only happiness. The prince adored Lulu. He would not harm the smallest hair on her head. He worshipped her. He is not her murderer. I stake my life on it.'

'Which leaves us with Lord Yarborough,' said Oscar, picking up his notebook and holding it up for Jane to inspect. 'Do you recognise his name?'

'It is a peculiar name,' said Jane. 'I have never heard it before. Perhaps he is another English milord who comes to Paris under a different identity. Perhaps when he is here he calls himself "Monsieur Smith".' She laughed and sipped her brandy. 'One night, I recall, we had six Monsieur Smiths come to visit us in our dressing room.'

Oscar smiled. 'Lord Yarborough is a physician,' he explained, 'and very distinguished – a medical doctor and also what they nowadays call a "psychiatrist". I believe he comes to Paris regularly – to visit his colleague, Professor Charcot at the Pitié-Salpêtrière Hospital.'

'Ah,' said Jane, raising her glass once more, 'Professor Charcot – the *great* Professor Charcot. Of course. I know him well.'

Conan Doyle sat forward. 'Jean-Martin Charcot – you know him?'

'I know him *very* well. I know all his secrets.'

'You were his mistress?' asked Oscar.

'I was his *patient*, Monsieur Wilde. I was brought up at Pitié-Salpêtrière. Horrible as it is, for much of my girlhood the hospital was my home. Has Robert not told you my story?'

She looked across the table to me and shook her head sadly.

'Perhaps he was not listening. He is a man, after all.'

'I have forgotten nothing,' I protested – but, in truth, I had forgotten.

Jane turned towards Oscar and Conan Doyle. 'Professor Charcot was like a father to me – and to Lulu. We loved him, we feared him – eventually, we hated him. I never knew my real father. My mother said he was an Italian nobleman, but, in drink, my mother would say anything. In her cups, my mother was a monster. She beat me, so I ran away from home. I lived on the streets – a mad thing, a wild child, a beggar and a tart – until the authorities picked me up and put me away at Pitié-Salpêtrière.'

'And Mademoiselle Lavallois was at the hospital, too?'

'Yes, that's where we met. She was older than me – but her story was my story. She did not know her father and she despised her mother. Her mother was a dancer, from Lyons, but Lulu was born in England. Her mother worked at one of the big London theatres and took up with a young nobleman who promised her everything and gave her nothing – apart from a dose of the clap, a baby and ten pounds. When Lulu was eleven or twelve, her mother brought her back to France – to beg and work the streets. But Lulu ran away – and went mad – and, eventually, found herself at Pitié-Salpêtrière. There were hundreds of us there, all with the same story.'

'I remember,' I said.

'When did you leave the hospital?' Oscar asked.

'Six years ago, when I was sixteen. We were thrown out, Lulu and I – together. We broke the rules.'

'What rules?' asked Conan Doyle, his brow earnestly furrowed, his whole face a touching mixture of anxiety, pity and concern.

'Pitié-Salpêtrière is a municipal cesspit, Doctor. It's where the authorities dump the dregs – the lunatic and the lame, drunkards, prostitutes, opium-eaters and petty thieves, the homeless and the hopeless. Those who have nowhere else to go and are a disgrace to the fine streets of Paris are gathered up and deposited at Pitié-Salpêtrière.'

'Is it not also a hospital?'

'Of course it is, and the great Professor Charcot is the man in charge. The inmates are his patients and his creatures – and he can do with us what he wills. He uses us for his experiments. When we die, he cuts us up. While we live, he studies us as he pleases – he pokes, he prods. We dance for him.'

'I do not follow you,' said Conan Doyle. 'Did you dance at the hospital?'

'Yes, we danced. We loved to dance – in the refectory, on the tables – and at Christmas and on special feast days for the visitors and staff. But that's not what I meant. I meant that we danced to Professor Charcot's tune. We did his bidding. We did what he told us to do. We had no choice.'

'And what did he tell you to do?' asked Oscar.

'He told us to play our parts.'

'What do you mean?' said Conan Doyle. 'I am confused.'

'Professor Charcot treats madness with hypnosis. If you are having a fit of hysteria, he will calm you – he will *cure* you – by putting you into an hypnotic trance. He is famous for it. Every week the doors of the Pitié-Salpêtrière are thrown open for *les leçons du mardi* – when the great man demonstrates his skills. Young women – dressed in nothing more than night slips – are brought into the lecture theatre to entertain the crowd. We are his patients – girls gripped by hysteria. We dance for him in our bare feet. We cry, we scream, we shout. We contort our bodies and fling our arms into the air. The audience leans forward in silent, rapt attention, as we moan and writhe and lift our nightshirts to demonstrate the extremes of intimate ecstasy. And as we twist and turn and groan and sigh, the great professor describes what is occurring in the minutest detail – and then, with a few words softly spoken and the simplest gestures, he brings calm to our troubled spirits and, miraculously, restores our sanity.'

'And is this treatment all fakery? Is that what you are telling us?'

'No, the treatment does work – on some girls, sometimes. It does not work on all girls, always. But every Tuesday, the show goes on. The audience arrives – all Paris turns out – and Professor Charcot requires results. His favourites supply them, without fail. We do not let him down. We are mad to order. We counterfeit our fits. We act out our paroxysms. We make-believe our ecstasy. In short, we play our parts – and he rewards us.'

'With money?' asked Oscar.

'With sweets and food and wine – and softer beds and acts of kindness.'

'You say he was like your father,' said Conan Doyle, nervously holding the tip of his moustache between his thumb and forefinger as he spoke. 'Did he treat you at all times with respect?'

Jane laughed, letting her head roll back and closing her eyes. I could see that she was quite tipsy now.

'You mean – did he touch us? No, he never touched us – but he allowed others to do so. When we were on display, supposedly under hypnosis, supposedly in the throes of ecstasy, he would invite members of the audience to step forward to inspect us at close quarters. He would expose our breasts to them and allow them to place their hands between our legs to feel our ecstasy.'

'This is outrageous,' whispered Conan Doyle.

'This is France,' murmured Oscar.

'Did you not object to this disgraceful behaviour?'

asked Conan Doyle, his fingers now pressed against his temples in his distress.

'We did, but he would not listen. He told us to count our blessings. He reminded us that we were "under his protection".'

'What did that mean?'

'The professor's favourites – the girls like Lulu and me – were well treated at the hospital. The rest – "the unprotected" they were called – were treated no better than slaves. They could be taken by any man who wanted them: the hospital guards, the medical students, other patients, anybody. While I was at Pitié-Salpêtrière at least three of the young girls in our dormitory contracted syphilis. All three of them died – horribly. Professor Charcot would not allow them mercury treatment – he wanted to use their bodies for his experiments. And he did. And when Lulu and I threatened to report what had happened to the board of the hospital, he laughed at us and told us we had broken the rules for the last time. Then he threw us out, back on to the streets.'

'The man is a monster,' gasped Conan Doyle.

'And a national hero,' said Oscar. 'He is one of the great scientists of our time.'

'He is a murderer,' said Conan Doyle.

'But his English friend – how do you call him? – Lord Yarborough: he may be a very different kind of man.'

Curious Questions

70

Telegram from Oscar Wilde, Gare du Nord, Paris, to Lord Yarborough, 117 Harley Street, London W., despatched at 1 p.m. on Thursday, 20 March 1890

URGENTLY REQUEST MEETING TO DISCUSS
DEVELOPMENTS IN MATTER OF ALBEMARLE AND
LAVALLOIS. PLEASE ADVISE SOONEST CARE OF
CONAN DOYLE LANGHAM HOTEL. RESPECTFULLY
OSCAR WILDE

71

Telegram from Oscar Wilde, Gare du Nord, Paris, to
Constance Wilde, 16 Tite Street, Chelsea, despatched
at 1 p.m. on Thursday, 20 March 1890

I CAME TO PARIS AND FOUND YOU WERE NOT
HERE. AM RETURNING TO LONDON BEFORE
THE WEEK IS OUT. KISS OUR BOYS FOR ME AND
TELL THEM THE EIFFEL TOWER IS AS HIDEOUS
AS THEIR MOTHER IS LOVELY. OSCAR

72

From the journal of Arthur Conan Doyle

I am exhausted. I have barely slept in forty hours. And I have drunk too much.

The sky is dark and the English Channel at her least hospitable. Huge waves are crashing on to the deck above. I am sheltering below – wrapped in a blanket, wedged into a wicker deckchair in a corner of the first-class saloon. Around me, others with grey faces are tightly wrapped up, eyes closed, bent only on endurance. Oscar and Robert Sherard are rolled up in their blankets, lying on the wooden benches fixed to the saloon walls.

I am writing because I cannot sleep and I cannot see to read, but whether I shall ever be able to decipher what I am scrawling here only time will tell. My mood is oddly melancholy. Ten years ago, in the spring of 1880, on such a day as this, in such a storm as this, I set sail from Peterhead on the good ship *Hope* – a whaler bound for Greenland. I was twenty, a young ship's doctor hungry for adventure, and the worse the tempest grew, the more I relished it. Today all I feel is deep weariness and faint apprehension.

As we crossed from the railway train to the

steamer at Calais, I told Oscar of my whaling days. Walking up the ramp on to the SS *Dover Castle* I boasted of my six months in the North Atlantic pitted against the elements.

Oscar told me, teasingly: 'I went salmon fishing once, with my father, off the coast in Connemara. It was one of the most dispiriting days of my life. He talked of nothing but past triumphs and we returned home, cruelly sunburnt, with a desiccated bloater and an old brown boot.'

I said, grandly: 'To play a salmon is a royal game, but when your fish weighs more than a suburban villa it dwarfs all other experience.'

'I believe it, Arthur,' he replied, and, suddenly, he seemed in earnest. (I do not quite understand him yet: his tone can change as swiftly as the turning of a coin.) 'And when you caught and killed your Moby Dick,' he asked, 'what was it like?'

'Not as I had expected. Amid all the excitement – and no one who has not held an oar in such a scene can tell how exciting it is – I found that my sympathy lay with the poor hunted creature.'

'You were close to it?'

'Our boat was right alongside. We were roped to it – our harpoons embedded in its flesh.'

'Ah,' he said. 'And you looked into the creature's eyes?'

'The whale has a small eye,' I said, 'little larger than that of a bullock, and I will never forget the silent sadness that I saw in it as it dimmed over in death within a hand's touch of me.'

Before the wind rose and the rain came, while our ship remained moored, sheltered in the harbour, and Sherard went below deck in search of further refreshment, Oscar and I stood together at the stern, side by side, holding the ship's rail, smoking our cigarettes, watching the men working on the quayside.

'I wonder which is easier,' said Oscar, 'to kill a whale or send a man to the gallows?'

'That's a curious question.'

'Tonight or tomorrow, we shall look into the eyes of our murderer, Arthur. What shall we do then?'

'Hand him over to the police.'

'Do you think so? Whoever he is?'

'I do,' I said. 'Whoever he is. We will have no choice.'

'Oh, we will have a choice, Arthur. There is always a choice.'

'We will do what our conscience dictates,' I said.

'Oh, Arthur,' he cried, throwing the butt of his cigarette into the black and white water below us, and turning towards me despairingly. 'The spirit of Southsea really does run deep in you. In my experience, conscience and cowardice are the same things. Conscience is merely the trade-name of the firm.'

'Let's see if we get our man first,' I said, trying to deflect him. 'You imply that you know who the murderer is.'

'We have evidence still to gather,' he said, 'and

issues to resolve – but, yes, on balance, I think that I do. Don't you?'

'I do,' I said, emphatically. 'Jane Avril was a convincing witness, don't you think?'

'She was drunk, of course,' said Oscar.

'Only towards the end – and, as we know, what's said when drunk was thought when sober.'

Oscar laughed. 'You and Harry Tyrwhitt Wilson should get together to exchange wise saws and modern instances.'

He turned up his collar against the growing wind.

'But, yes, Mademoiselle Avril's testimony rang true, even at the end. I found it most affecting, especially the story of her loveless childhood – and that of little Lulu Lavallois.' He turned to look at me with the utmost seriousness. 'You and I have been blessed in our mothers, Arthur. They have never betrayed us, never let us down. They have loved us from the start – and will love us at the finish.'

I agreed. 'Mothers are everything,' I said.

'With good mothering, a man won't turn to murder,' he added. 'It's well known. It's why, in the long annals of crime, there have been so few Jewish murderers.'

'We are indeed blessed,' I said. 'We have good mothers – and good wives.'

'Oh, Arthur,' he exclaimed. 'Leave wives out of this. It's the wives that drive most men to murder. It's a good mother that counts. You get only one mother. You can always get another wife.'

I laughed. 'I will never get another wife.'

He put his hand on my shoulder and laughed, too. 'You will, Arthur, you will. Or, if not another wife, at least "a friend". It's that bewitching moustache of yours. In due course, some young filly will come along and seduce you from the path of righteousness.'

'No,' I protested. 'I am a happily married man. I will be good. Always.'

'When we are happy we are always good,' he replied. 'But when we are good we are not always happy.'

He tried to light another cigarette, but the wind would not allow him.

'Time will tell, Arthur. In my experience, all ways end at the same point – disillusion.'

'I hope not,' I said. 'Shall we go below? It's about to rain. The heavens are darkening. There's a storm brewing.'

Oscar looked up at the black sky and pocketed his cigarette case. 'Perhaps Robert will have found some rum to comfort us. We are on a ship, after all.'

'What time will we reach London now?' I wondered.

'Too late for dinner, too early for bed,' he said.

'I saw the telegram you sent from Paris. You are not going home to Constance tonight?'

'No, not tonight, Arthur. I'll come with you to the Langham. We'll drop Robert off at his digs on the way. If there's no word from Yarborough, I'll leave you to go to bed while I take a wander

317

through Soho, I am minded to call on Rex LaSalle. He keeps late hours – as we know. And he's very handsome – as you'll agree. And even men of the noblest possible moral character are susceptible to the influence of the physical charms of others – as you will discover one day. Note it in your journal, Arthur, lest you forget that it was I who told you so. I want the credit when it's due.'

73

From the diary of Rex LaSalle

'The English Channel is awash with French devils.
Our native sea nymphs have all swum south. The
crossing was hell.'

Oscar arrived at my room at midnight. His face
was grey as slate; he was unshaven; his clothes were
damp; he had about him the aroma of tar and soot
and sea. He told me that he had been to Paris and
back in under twenty-four hours and was too
exhausted to speak – and then took off his clothes,
lay on my bed, and spoke, volubly, with barely a
moment's pause, for at least an hour.

'Who would be a mere Nereid – anonymous and
tempest-tossed? One needs to command the tide, not
follow it. One needs to be Neptune or nobody. Am I
not right, Rex? Is that not your view?'

At first I thought he was delirious (he was
certainly a little drunk), but gradually a thread of
sorts became discernible in his meanderings.

'Wouldn't it be awful to be one of the chorus?' he
cried, reaching out and holding me by the wrist. 'I
could not bear it – and neither could you. You need to
be centre stage, Rex, don't you? In the limelight,
where it counts. Where they see you. Where you're

someone important, noticed, valued – different. That's why you affect to be a vampire, isn't it?'

'You don't need to believe that I'm a vampire, Oscar, if you don't want to.'

'I want to believe it,' he said, turning his head towards me on the pillow. 'I yearn to believe it. Who would not want a vampire among his close acquaintance? But I cannot believe it, Rex – not for a moment. You must remember that my mother is an authority on the folklore of the undead. She has already written one huge volume on the subject. A second is set for publication any day now. I was reared on tales of vampires and werewolves. I am a friend of Bram Stoker who talks of little else. I know about vampires, Rex – while you, dear friend, seem to know next to nothing. You have no hair growing in the palms of your hands. Even as I lie here I can clearly see your reflection in the looking-glass – and, if I turn this way, I can see your shadow cast against the wall. You have a crucifix above your bed and a rosary on your side table. Show me your teeth. Exactly – they are beautifully white and wonderfully even. You are no more a vampire than I am a Hottentot.'

I stood my ground. 'What your mother has written and Bram Stoker has researched are myths and legends, Oscar – tall tales and garbled half-truths. Might I not be the real thing – the whole truth, for once, unadorned?'

'I do not believe that you are a vampire,' he said simply.

'You do not have to,' I replied. 'A truth ceases to be true when more than one person believes in it.'

'That's another of my lines, Rex. You have adopted the persona of a vampire and the philosophy of Oscar Wilde. Why, I wonder? To make yourself somebody, I suppose. You don't know who you really are, do you?'

'I know who I am, Oscar.'

'You know who you think you are, but you don't know who you really are. Who are you, Rex LaSalle? What are you? Who made you what you are?'

He talked to me of his mother. He tried to talk to me of mine. And of my father.

His conversation was very strange. He talked to me of his own father – Sir William Wilde, oculist and philanderer. He spoke of his father's curious charm, of his casual cruelty to Lady Wilde, and of his kindness to his bastard children.

Then Oscar spoke – at length – of James II, King of Scotland, known as 'Fiery Face' because of the vermilion birthmark on his cheek and neck. He talked of the guillotining of Queen Marie Antoinette of France and of the executions of the Oxford martyrs – Hugh Latimer and Nicholas Ridley, burnt together at the stake.

He talked of the death of Pope Gregory XIV, 'the pope who laughed'. According to Oscar, His Holiness could not help himself: his laughter came unbidden and uncontrollably: it was a nervous affliction. On the day of his election he had burst into tears and said to the cardinals: 'God forgive you! What have you done?' Then the laughter started. It was said that he laughed at the very moment of his passing, on 16 October 1591.

Oscar talked and talked. At around two in the morning, he fell fast asleep. When I awoke, he was gone.

This morning, at ten, the man Boone came. I told him what I could, which was not much. He gave me ten shillings. I do not think he will come again.

74

Letter from Constance Wilde to Oscar Wilde, care of Arthur Conan Doyle at the Langham Hotel, Langham Place, London, W.

16 Tite Street, Chelsea
20.iii.90

My darling Oscar,

    I am not sure quite what to do. A telegram has just arrived for you. In your absence I opened it in case it was a matter of importance, but I am afraid it makes very little sense to me. It is signed 'OWL' and summons you and Arthur Conan Doyle to a meeting with 'A CERTAIN PERSON' on Friday at twelve noon. Is this the Prince of Wales? I think it may be and consequently the meeting will be important. I shall enclose the telegram with this note and send it to you care of Arthur at the Langham – that is where he is staying, is it not? When this reaches you, will you let me know?

    The doorbell has just rung again – another telegram. This time from you. You are in Paris! Did I know you were going to Paris? Did you tell me? Perhaps you did. You move about so much, my darling, I get quite easily confused. Why are you in Paris? Are you visiting Madame Bernhardt? I am not jealous. (Well, only a little bit.) Is Robert with you? When do you plan to return? You must be here on Sunday – your mother is coming to tea and Cyril has prepared a recitation in her honour.

    I am now suddenly anxious. Are you quite well, my darling?

You have had so many late nights, so many nights away, that I cannot help but worry. I am not scolding you – I know you must have your freedom. I am simply anxious for your health – for your well-being – for your work. *The proofs of* Dorian Gray *are here, but you have not yet touched them. I read the story again last night: it is the best thing you have ever done. I found one or two minor errors which I have corrected – in pencil. You can check everything thoroughly when you return.*

How I long to see you! I miss you very much. I am ever your loving wife,

Constance

PS. Do you have a change of clothes with you? I don't think you do. Buy new clothes in Paris. You must. I don't want Madame Bernhardt thinking I do not know how to look after my husband!

PPS. I shall write separately to Arthur CD. He will have to go to the meeting tomorrow in your place. I trust that one day you will tell me all about these mysterious assignations with the Prince of Wales. What a life you lead! And what a life we lead.

I am writing next to dear Bram Stoker. He has invited us both to join him and Florrie in their box at the Lyceum tomorrow night for Mr Irving's Macbeth. *I know you will be in Paris and cannot come, but, if I may, I shall accept the invitation on my own account – Bram says, sweetly, that I am invited on my own if you are not available. It is a dark play, of course, but the evening will be a happy distraction – and Bram may even flirt with me. I should like that. I believe the time has come for me to make you a little jealous, Oscar.*

75

From the notebooks of Robert Sherard

This morning – Friday, 21 March 1890 – I was woken at eight o'clock by an intrusive din: the sound of Oscar Wilde beating at the front door of my lodging house in Gower Street. I am three floors up and yet I heard the noise.

I struggled to open my window and, blearily, peered down into the street below. There was Oscar – resplendent in a sand-coloured summer suit, with a flamingo-pink tie about his neck and a matching carnation in his buttonhole – extravagantly beating a loud tattoo on the front door with his silver-topped malacca cane. He looked up and saw me.

'Robert! Come! Come at once. I need you now. Your carriage awaits. Hurry!'

As he climbed nonchalantly aboard the four-wheeler that stood at the kerbside waiting, I threw on my one clean shirt (still unpressed) and the suit that I had worn to Paris yesterday. (A shortage of properly laundered linen has been the worst aspect of my separation from my wife.) I pulled on my boots; I failed to find my hat; within five minutes of being roused, I was seated face to face with Oscar on my way to the Langham Hotel.

Oscar appeared immaculate: newly shaven, almost

pink-cheeked, his thick hair swept back across his large head, his eyes sparkling.

'New shoes?' I enquired, admiring the tan-coloured pumps he was sporting.

'Old shoes – and the wrong shoes for the season. I'm dressed for mid-May in mid-March – but I had no choice. These are the only clothes I had in town. I left them at the Savoy Hotel last September – and, at six o'clock this morning, I went to claim them and they were there: cleaned, pressed, brushed, ready to wear. The Savoy is a phenomenon, Robert: electric lights *everywhere*, electric *lifts*, its own artesian well bringing hot running water, *con brio*, to each and every room – and Frederick, the finest head porter in the western hemisphere. I arrived at six: by seven-thirty, I had bathed, shaved, dressed and breakfasted on a pair of lightly boiled pullet's eggs and a pot of perfectly brewed lapsang souchong tea.'

'They did you proud,' I said, laughing and looking down, dispiritedly, at the crumpled serge of my own suit.

'And I hope I did Frederick proud,' said Oscar happily. 'I gave him a guinea for his pains.'

'Where are we going now?' I asked, looking out on to the hustle and bustle of Oxford Street. The morning was bright. 'And why so early?'

'We are summoned to Marlborough House at noon. Tyrwhitt Wilson sent a telegram to Tite Street yesterday and my darling wife kindly sent it on to Arthur at the Langham. We found it waiting for us there last night.'

'Are we collecting Arthur now?'

'We are – and then we are off to Harley Street to

surprise Lord Yarborough in his lair. He is not expecting us. He did not respond to my wire from Paris. Of course, he is a very busy man.'

As he said this, my friend grinned gleefully, widening his eyes and revealing his uneven teeth. With elegantly gloved fingers – the gloves were kid and matched the shoes – he beat a jaunty rhythm on the silver top of his malacca cane.

'You are on form this morning,' I remarked.

'It was the bath, Robert – and the Savoy bath salts, scented with jasmine and bitter almonds. For thirty minutes as dawn broke I lay in foaming, fragrant warm water – and did nothing, bar contemplate my toes.'

'I envy you,' I said, feeling the rough stubble on my chin and cheeks.

'You should *admire* me, Robert. While, in the opinion of society, contemplation is the gravest thing of which any citizen can be guilty, in the opinion of the highest culture it is the proper occupation of man. I am hoping the fruits of my contemplation will be the resolution of our case.'

'You lay in your bath and saw your toes – and our murderer.'

'Exactly.'

At the Langham Hotel, Oscar remained in the four-wheeler and sent me to collect Conan Doyle. I found the doctor between the potted palms, crossing the hotel foyer. He looked weary and appeared flustered.

'Good morning. You are earlier than I expected, Robert,' he said. 'Is all well? How is Oscar?'

'Never better, it would seem. He is extraordinary. He wants you to come immediately.'

Doyle, sighing, came at once. He, too, was hatless. As he clambered aboard the four-wheeler, Oscar greeted him apologetically: 'Good morning, Arthur. Forgive me. It's earlier than I promised.'

Arthur grumbled a 'Good morning'.

Oscar continued smoothly: 'You have missed your breakfast, I see, and you are in a state of stress. Have you just been making a telephone call? I did not know the Langham had a telephone.'

Arthur Conan Doyle collapsed on to the leather seat next to Oscar and laughed out loud.

'You are amazing, Oscar – and correct. I have not had breakfast and I have indeed just come from the hotel's telephone room. How on earth did you know?'

'Your face is pale, but your right ear is red. Your moustache is free from crumbs, but there is a slight ridge across it – just a quarter of an inch beneath your nose. You are pale because you haven't eaten. You have a reddened right ear because it has been pressed hard against a telephone receiver. There is a light mark on your moustache because the telephone mouthpiece has been pressed up against it while you have been making your call – long distance, I take it – to Southsea, I presume.'

'Correct, in every particular.'

'I did not realise little Touie had a telephone at home.'

'She does not,' said Conan Doyle. 'But Carter, my locum, does. I telephoned to make my peace with him – he has gone beyond the call of duty this week.'

'You gave him a message, too, to pass on to your wife?'

'I did,' said Conan Doyle. 'I told him to tell her that I would be home tomorrow night – without fail.'

'That's quite possible, Arthur,' said Oscar, amiably, patting his friend lightly on the knee. 'Who knows what today will bring?'

'Cheese straws at Marlborough House, I hope,' said Conan Doyle, now mellowing. 'I'm famished.'

'We see the Prince at noon,' said Oscar. 'We are tackling Yarborough first and a keen appetite should sharpen your cross-examination of his lordship, Arthur. As you're the medical man, I think you should lead for us on this. Don't you agree, Robert?'

'I agree, Oscar.'

I smiled. (Oscar never asks me to lead on anything, but I do not mind. I have become accustomed to my role. As Oscar says, 'They also serve who only stand and wait to note down my quips for posterity.')

'I am ready,' said Arthur, smoothing out his moustache with the sides of his forefingers.

The journey from Langham Place to 117 Harley Street took only a matter of minutes, but it was in vain. Lord Yarborough was not at home. His manservant was uncertain of his lordship's whereabouts. When pressed, he conceded that the clinic at Muswell Hill was a possibility. He could not be certain. He advised us to leave our cards and wait for Lord Yarborough's private secretary to contact us to make a proper appointment.

'His lordship,' he repeated several times, 'is a very busy man.'

Our four-wheeler forged north, through Regent's Park and St John's Wood, up over Hampstead Heath, to Highgate and on to Muswell Hill.

As we travelled, Oscar smoked – and talked. By his own account, he had slept for no more than three hours last night, and none the night before, but he had found the Savoy bath salts quite 'transforming'. He was full of high energy and sly observation.

As we drove through St John's Wood, he pointed to one of the new suburban villas and declared: 'That's the house where Lillie Langtry's daughter was conceived. Ten years ago, when you, Robert, were being sent down from Oxford, and you, Arthur, were up in Greenland chasing whales, the Jersey Lillie gave birth to her first-born, a lovely little girl. They say the father was Louis, Prince of Battenburg. Who knows? This entire avenue was built on the back of adultery – every house in it was commissioned by a man for his mistress. The one charm of modern marriage is that it makes a life of deception absolutely necessary.'

'I laugh, Oscar,' said Conan Doyle, reprovingly, 'but I do not condone.'

'We need you at your most earnest, Arthur. We need you to put Yarborough to the test – and not take too long about it. We must set off for London again no later than eleven. We must not be late for the His Highness and your cheese straws.'

We reached the Charcot Clinic at just after ten. The village church clock was striking the hour as our four-wheeler turned into the carriage drive. The morning was bright – the sky was clear – and yet Muswell Manor, as we reached it, looked dismal and forbidding. The building is overshadowed by ancient lime trees and over-grown with vines. The upstairs windows all appeared shuttered and, downstairs, the curtains were drawn.

'The house is all shut up,' I exclaimed.

'My God,' cried Conan Doyle. 'Has he fled?'

'Or is he about to flee?' asked Oscar, peering down the drive towards the house.

There, half obscured in the shadow of the building, in a corner of the forecourt, was a pony and trap and, standing by it, two figures, dressed in black. One was a young woman, heavily veiled, unrecognisable in full mourning; the other was the diminutive yet dapper figure of Lord Yarborough. With one hand he held the woman tightly by the arm; in his other hand he held a coachman's whip.

'Stop!' cried Conan Doyle, jumping down from our moving four-wheeler as it drew up alongside the pony and trap. 'In the name of the law, stop!'

'What the devil do you mean, sir?' answered Yarborough fiercely. 'Explain yourself – and moderate your tone. This lady is not well.'

'You may not leave,' cried Conan Doyle, running up to Yarborough and his companion, and confronting them bodily, standing with his arms and legs akimbo to form a human barrier.

'I may do as I please, sir,' replied Yarborough coolly, lightly laying the tip of his whip on Doyle's right shoulder. 'I may have you thrown off my land as a trespasser if I so choose – and if I had not recognised you and your confederates, I'd do so without a second thought. What in God's name is the meaning of this?'

'You may not leave,' repeated Conan Doyle, breathing heavily as he stood his ground. He glanced towards Oscar and me as we came up beside him.

'I am not leaving, as it happens,' said Lord Yarborough, nodding towards Oscar by way of greeting. 'I am returning – with this young lady. She is not well. I had hoped she would be fit enough to accompany me to town – to pay her final respects to her late sister. But I drove her as far as St James's church in the village and it's clear that the journey to Grosvenor Square would be too great a strain for her.'

Removing his whip from Conan Doyle's shoulder, he turned to the woman at his side and, with both hands, carefully, lifted her veil from her face.

'This is Louise Lascelles, younger sister to the late Duchess of Albemarle. You may recall that you met her when you were last here, Dr Doyle. You were in a calmer frame of mind that day.'

Conan Doyle stepped back and lowered his eyes. The young woman – pale-faced and beautiful, with round brown eyes and auburn hair – gazed steadily at him. Her feathery white cheeks were stained with tears.

'She has been weeping,' said Oscar.

'Yes,' said Lord Yarborough. 'Uncontrollably. That's why I brought her back. I was wrong to think of taking her in the first place.'

He looked at the girl dispassionately, as though he were inspecting a marble statue at the British Museum, then shook his head and pulled her black veil down over her face once more.

'No,' whispered Oscar. 'Please. There's no need.'

'She does not see you,' said Lord Yarborough, crisply. 'Or, if she does, she is not aware of you. She is under hypnosis. She is in a trance.'

'And yet she weeps,' said Oscar.

'Yes,' answered Lord Yarborough.

'And you cannot stop her.'

'So it would seem. Hypnosis is an imperfect art.

Would it were a science. We have so much to learn about the treatment of hysteria, Mr Wilde. At this clinic, we are experimenting with hypnosis. Others are experimenting with the use of hallucinant drugs. In America, I am told, they are looking to pass an electric current through the skull of the patient to clear the madness from the brain. Who knows what's best? Who knows what lies at the root of the disease? We need to find out. That's why the research must go on – whatever the hazards.'

He turned to the young woman in black and took her by the arm.

'Meanwhile, we must do what we can to safeguard the afflicted.' He held out his whip to Conan Doyle, who took it from him. 'Thank you,' he said. 'I'll return Louise to the house and then we can talk.'

Clasping the young woman by the elbow, he steered her away from our group towards the main entrance of the building. There, standing in the portico, the door to the house half open behind them, were two other women. One was an elderly nun (a nursing sister, I presumed), ruddy-faced and bespectacled. The other was a younger woman dressed in mourning: a black-velvet bustle dress with a loose-falling skirt draped up at the back and a tight-fitting, waisted jacket. A sheaf of black swan's feathers swept from her imposing hat, but she wore no veil. She carried herself erect and gripped a large, white envelope in her black-gloved hands. She looked so formal and so elegant that she seemed quite out of place.

'Do you know them?' asked Oscar.

'Sister Agnes is in charge of the asylum,' said Conan

Doyle. 'And the other lady is a patient, as I recall. I met her only briefly.'

We watched as Lord Yarborough escorted Louise Lascelles to the doorway and gave the young woman into the nun's charge. She went without protest, as if in a dream.

'She walks as if she were a sleepwalker,' said Oscar.

The other patient, however, was anything but calm. The moment Lord Yarborough was within reach, she grabbed him by the arm. He tried to step aside, but she clung on. She pleaded with him. Her manner was pathetic – supplicatory, not irate. From what I could see, he spoke not a word to her, but shook his head repeatedly and, eventually, raising his arms, managed to break free.

As he turned back towards us, the woman followed him and caught his arm once more, pulling him to her. This time he looked directly at her and, suddenly, appeared to acquiesce to her demand. She laughed and, gratefully, pressed the white envelope she was holding into his hands. Stepping back, she made a deep curtsy in front of him, before finally turning to make her way into the house with Sister Agnes and Miss Lascelles.

Lord Yarborough watched the women go and then, briskly, walked back to us across the gravel courtyard where he reclaimed his whip from Arthur Conan Doyle.

'Thank you,' he said.

He threw the whip into the trap and slapped the pony on its flank, then looked at us enquiringly, one eyebrow raised, letting his beady eyes rest briefly on each of us in turn.

'Dr Doyle, Mr Wilde, kinsman Sherard – what can I do for you, gentlemen?'

'Answer some questions,' said Conan Doyle, sharply.

'If they are asked in a civil manner, I shall do so with pleasure.'

'I sent you a telegram, Lord Yarborough,' said Oscar. 'You did not reply.'

'I apologise. I am a very busy man. But you are here now and I am at your service. I'd invite you in, except that I am on my way to town and there has been a death at the asylum.'

Conan Doyle looked up at the shuttered house. 'A death?' he repeated.

'A natural death,' said Lord Yarborough. 'An elderly patient. A woman in her eighties. She had been here many years. It is a sadness, not a tragedy.'

'Is that why the curtains are all drawn?' asked Oscar.

'We keep the house in darkness on such days.'

'Out of respect for the dead?'

'No – to calm the nerves of the living. Death can unsettle us all. It can have a terrifying effect on those with troubled minds. At such times as this, we keep the patients subdued and pacified as best we can. We keep the house in darkness and encourage them to sleep. We give them laudanum – in small doses.'

Conan Doyle turned to Lord Yarborough. 'How did the Duchess of Albemarle die?' he asked.

Lord Yarborough did not seem surprised by the question and answered it at once – and simply: 'From a heart attack – provoked by the dangerous game she was playing or was about to play; provoked by it, but not caused by it, in my opinion.'

'With whom do you think she was playing this "dangerous game"?'

'I have no idea. None whatsoever. It could be any one of a dozen men – or more. The duchess was liberal in her favours.'

'Could it have been the duke?' asked Oscar.

'No. The duke and duchess were no longer on intimate terms and had not been for two years at least. She told me so quite frankly – and the duke, when drunk, would admit as much.'

'It would have been one of her regular lovers—' Oscar began.

'Or a complete stranger,' said Lord Yarborough, smiling. 'It could have been *anyone*, Mr Wilde – a gentleman or a servant, someone well known to her or someone quite unknown. Anyone. Nymphomania is the term we give her condition. It amounts to a lunatic desire for carnal relations with men – a desire, in the duchess's case, sweetened by danger and made more exhilarating by the infliction of pain.'

'The man will have used his knife on her at her behest?'

'The pain was part of the pleasure, Mr Wilde. It may even have been her knife.'

'He used it to cut her breasts,' said Conan Doyle.

'To mark them – to cause a sensation – to draw blood . . . If you examined her breasts, Doctor, you will have noticed how much they had been scarred. That episode in the telephone room was very far from being the first.'

'The man cut her throat,' said Conan Doyle.

'For the thrill of it – at her suggestion.'

'*He cut her throat*,' repeated Conan Doyle. 'Should he not be brought to justice?'

'He did not kill the duchess,' said Lord Yarborough

calmly. 'He was her lover and in all that he did I am certain the duchess acquiesced. She was the instigator, not the victim.'

'Are you certain of this?' asked Oscar.

'Absolutely. I was her doctor. She told me of her desires – without shame. She showed me her wounded breasts – with pride.'

'Were you her lover?' asked Conan Doyle.

'No, sir. I was her physician.'

'Were you her lover, Lord Yarborough?'

'Do not presume to repeat the question, Dr Doyle. We have both sworn the Hippocratic oath.'

'Do you remember it, Lord Yarborough?'

'How dare you, sir?'

Lord Yarborough's face was now whiter than ice. His small eyes narrowed; the veins in his neck and forehead began to pulse like the gorge of a toad. I saw his hands tremble, but they remained at his side – and his voice remained steady.

'I have the oath by heart, from my student days, as I am sure you do. "Whatever houses I may visit, I will come for the benefit of the sick, remaining free of all intentional injustice, of all mischief and, in particular, of intimate relations with either female or male persons, be they free or slaves."'

'I repeat the question, Lord Yarborough. Were you her lover?'

Lord Yarborough suddenly looked up to the sky and laughed. 'I almost admire your impertinence, Dr Doyle. I shall take it as an excess of zeal and shall put it down to youthful arrogance. And God knows why, but since you press me, and since, I take it, these exchanges are confidential, I will tell you frankly: I am no woman's lover – nor likely to be.'

He looked at the three of us in turn and smiled. 'But whoever her lover was is beside the point, gentlemen. The Duchess of Albemarle's lover is not guilty of her murder.'

'But he is responsible for her death,' said Oscar gently.

'Not so, Mr Wilde. Her weak heart is responsible for that.'

The storm-cloud had burst. The tension of a moment earlier was gone. Lord Yarborough and Conan Doyle no longer confronted one another as raging bull and defiant matador.

Oscar glanced over his shoulder to the four-wheeler that stood waiting for us at the far side of the courtyard and checked his watch. I checked mine. It was coming towards eleven o'clock.

Oscar turned back to Lord Yarborough. 'The duchess's heart gave way, but her throat was also cut. How can you be so certain that her heart gave way *before* her throat was cut?'

'Quite easily: because of the limited quantity of blood on her body and in the telephone room. There was much less than you would have expected to find, say, at the scene of a violent knife attack. If the jugular vein is cut during *exertion*, when the veins are engorged and blood is racing through the body, pumping wildly, then blood spurts and gushes everywhere. That was not the case in the telephone room at Grosvenor Square. It was the contained amount of blood there that led me to believe that the duchess had died at the outset of her sybaritic tryst, at the start, before the frenzy, before her blood

338

pressure was raised. The heart attack killed her almost as she met her lover. She died in his arms, but at first he did not know it. In the darkness, and in his excitement, he was unaware of what had occurred. Merely sensing that he was not getting the response from his *inamorata* that he might have expected, he sought to intensify the pleasure by intensifying the pain. He cut into her more deeply. He slashed her breasts and he cut her throat until he reached her jugular vein – and only then, as the blood poured out of her, did he realise what he had done.'

'And he fled the scene,' said Oscar, with a heavy sigh.

'We can take him for a coward,' said Lord Yarborough, 'but not a murderer.'

'Why do you not wish to know who he is?' I asked. 'Are you not curious?'

'I am curious, of course,' he answered easily. 'But I have thought the matter through and come to the conclusion that no useful purpose would be served by unmasking the man in question. Quite the reverse, in fact. If his secret is discovered, so is hers. How would that help the common good? If the truth were known about the private life of the Duchess of Albemarle, her reputation would be ruined. The duke would be humiliated. And the Prince of Wales would have been associated with yet another unsavoury affair.'

'But the man may do it all again, may he not?'

'Only if he encounters another woman anxious to play so dangerous a game with him – and I think that unlikely, don't you? Whoever he is, he is not a threat to the public at large.'

'But he killed again last Tuesday,' said Oscar.

'Did he, Mr Wilde?'

'He did – at the Empire Theatre of Varieties in Leicester Square. You were there.'

'I was there and I saw the body of the poor dead girl.' Lord Yarborough looked around the group. 'We all did.'

'And her wounds were the same wounds as those inflicted on Helen Albemarle,' said Oscar.

'They were similar.'

'They were the same,' said Conan Doyle.

'That does not mean that they were perpetrated by the same person. The second death could have been caused by someone who wanted it to appear exactly like the first.'

'But only four people saw the duchess's body after her death: you and I, Lord Yarborough, the Duke of Albemarle and, possibly, his butler. One of us is not the girl's murderer, surely?'

Lord Yarborough looked at Conan Doyle with gimlet eyes. 'A point well made, Doctor. But it could still be mere coincidence. The two women had little in common, after all.'

'They had an association with the Prince of Wales in common,' said Oscar casually, checking his timepiece once more.

'And a history of hysteria,' added Conan Doyle. 'One was your patient, Lord Yarborough. The other might have been.'

'What do you mean?'

'Did you know Louisa Lavallois?' asked Oscar. 'Or "Lulu", as the prince called her?'

'No. I had neither seen nor heard of the young lady before Tuesday night.'

'Did you know that she had been a patient at the Pitié-Salpêtrière Hospital in Paris – a "psychiatric" patient?'

'No.'

'Louisa Lavallois had been a patient of the great Professor Charcot – one of his favourites, in fact – one of those poor mad girls who was a star attraction at *les leçons du mardi*, exhibiting her hysteria under hypnosis for the edification and entertainment of all who cared to come and watch. Except she wasn't under hypnosis, of course. She was one of those who connived with the professor, who played the game, who acted her part and received her reward – until she rebelled and fell from favour and was thrown out.'

'I know nothing of this woman – and nothing of this story.'

Lord Yarborough tapped the edge of the white envelope he was holding against his chin and gazed steadily at Conan Doyle.

'Be careful what you say, Dr Doyle. Your excess of zeal could be the ruin of you. Remember the laws of slander. Jean-Martin Charcot is one of the great men of European medicine. His name will be remembered long after yours has been forgotten. He has his faults, I am sure, but he has one exceptional quality – genius. He is a giant. He is not a charlatan.'

'Is he a murderer?' asked Oscar, lightly.

Lord Yarborough's small frame rocked with self-conscious merriment. 'Very droll, Mr Wilde. Have you taken leave of your senses? Are you suggesting Jean-Martin Charcot murdered this girl to silence her?'

'To safeguard his reputation, perhaps,' said Oscar, smiling, his head tilted to one side.

341

'You *have* taken leave of your senses,' exclaimed Lord Yarborough. 'Professor Charcot was not at the Empire Theatre on Tuesday night.'

'No, Lord Yarborough, but you were. And Professor Charcot was at Grosvenor Square on the night that the Duchess of Albemarle died.'

'Good God, man, are you quite mad? Why should Charcot murder Helen Albemarle?'

'He doesn't murder her. He makes love to her – and in so doing provokes the heart attack that kills her. You have told him of her emotional frailty – of her "nymphomania", is that the word? – and of her vulnerability to cardiac arrest. He takes advantage of both – to your advantage. Charcot triggers the death of the Duchess of Albemarle and, in doing so, Lord Yarborough, helps furnish you with the cadaver of a known hysteric – one of your own patients; a cadaver you need – to dissect, to study, to assist you in your all-important clinical researches. Charcot helps kill the duchess for your benefit and you repay the favour by killing the Lavallois girl for his.'

Lord Yarborough threw back his head and roared with laughter. 'The notion is risible, Mr Wilde.'

Oscar grinned. 'Far-fetched, I grant you – not risible.'

'Risible,' repeated Lord Yarborough. 'It's the stuff of one of Dr Doyle's detective stories.'

'Now who's talking slander?' asked Oscar, chuckling. 'I believe Dr Doyle doesn't find the notion even far-fetched. I believe he thinks it's what may have happened.'

Conan Doyle said nothing.

'I am of a different opinion – for what it's worth. I do

not believe that Professor Charcot is implicated in the death of the Duchess of Albemarle in any way whatsoever. Why should he be? He was in her house on the night she died, but so were a hundred others. So were you, Lord Yarborough. Could you have murdered her? In your research work, you cut up cadavers. You have a surgeon's knife, I presume. You know how to use it, I am sure.'

Oscar folded his arms across his chest as he contemplated Lord Yarborough.

Lord Yarborough looked steadily at Oscar and appeared amused. 'Do I look like a man with a capacity for murder?' he asked.

'In your head, yes,' said Oscar. 'In your heart, also.'

'You flatter me.'

'I intend to. Ruthlessness is essential in a man who seeks high achievement. You have the capacity for murder, my lord, but – forgive me – do you have the physique?'

Lord Yarborough bridled slightly, but said nothing.

'Helen Albemarle, despite the weakness of her heart, was a tall woman – and she was young. You have neither stature nor bulk nor youth at your command. If you had attacked her, she could have resisted you. Would you have been able to drag her into the telephone room at Grosvenor Square against her will? I doubt it. And would she have gone with you voluntarily in anticipation of a romantic encounter? I doubt that, also. You have confessed to us that you are not a ladies' man. Helen Albemarle would have known that without you needing to tell her. Women have an instinct about these things.'

Oscar unfolded his arms and smiled.

'No, *pace* Dr Doyle, I do not think that you murdered the Duchess of Albemarle, Lord Yarborough.'

'I am relieved to hear it, Mr Wilde,' said Lord Yarborough, bowing his head towards Oscar.

Turning to the pony-trap, he opened the door to a container beneath the box seat, placed the white envelope inside the container and removed a pair of black driving gloves, which he began to pull on.

'But you might have murdered Lulu Lavallois,' said Oscar, still smiling. 'She was quite *petite* and you had the means and the opportunity . . .'

'But did I have the motive?' asked Lord Yarborough, examining his gloved hands with apparent satisfaction.

'I don't think you did,' said Oscar. 'I don't believe Mademoiselle Lavallois represented a threat to Professor Charcot. He is the Napoleon of neuroses after all, and she was nobody – an itinerant dancer, with a history of mental instability.'

'But "charming titties",' added Lord Yarborough, reaching into the trap to retrieve the horsewhip.

'There are worse epitaphs,' said Oscar.

'Personally,' said Lord Yarborough, climbing up on to the box seat, 'I think Dvorak did it. I was standing next to him in the circle. The man was sweating like a pig. His hands were trembling. His whole demeanour exuded guilt.'

'You think he murdered the girl to create a diversion? To prevent Professor Onofroff from reading his mind and revealing his dark secret?'

'Well, it's a possibility, you must admit.' Lord Yarborough looked down from the trap at Conan

Doyle. 'You are the writer of detective fiction, Dr Doyle. What do you think?'

'I shall keep my thoughts to myself for the moment,' replied Conan Doyle stiffly. 'I believe I have displayed enough "excess of zeal" for one morning.'

'That's all one now,' said Lord Yarborough pleasantly. Tugging at the pony's reins, he released the brake on the trap. 'If you'll excuse me, gentlemen, I must be about my business – if that is all?'

'One last thing,' said Oscar, looking back at the house, as in the distance the clock of St James's, Muswell Hill, began to strike the hour. 'I noticed that the letter that the lady pressed upon you just now is addressed to the Prince of Wales.'

Lord Yarborough laughed.

'You are very observant, Mr Wilde. Yes, it is a petition to the Prince of Wales. The lady knew him once. Harriet Mordaunt is her name. It's a sad story. Her husband wanted to divorce her on the grounds of her adultery. He tried to implicate the Prince of Wales.'

'I recall the story,' said Oscar. 'And the scandal. Why is Lady Mordaunt here?'

'To avoid the case coming to court – and to spare the Prince of Wales – Harriet's father declared his daughter mad. He had her put away – incarcerated. He had several other daughters. He needed to find them husbands. He felt he had no choice.'

'Is she mad?' asked Conan Doyle.

'She wasn't when she first came to the asylum. She feigned her madness then – to prove to the court officers that she was not fit to stand trial. She played the lunatic – throwing tantrums, breaking crockery, eating coal, crawling about on all fours, howling like a werewolf. It was pitiful to see her. But she was not mad then. That was twenty years ago. She is mad now, I fear. She has been locked away so long.'

'And she petitions the Prince of Wales to intercede on her behalf? To secure her release?'

'She believes the prince loves her still. She hopes that he will welcome her to Marlborough House and make an honest woman of her at last. It cannot be, of course. This is where she lives now. And this is where she will die.'

'We are on our way to see His Royal Highness,' said Oscar. 'We have an appointment at noon. Shall we deliver the poor woman's petition for you?'

'There's no need for that,' said Lord Yarborough. 'I'll destroy it later – as I have destroyed the others. The Prince of Wales has enough to worry him. I don't think we need trouble him with this.'

A Nest of Vipers

76

From the journal of Arthur Conan Doyle

Though the horse cantered much of the way, it took more than an hour for our four-wheeler to get us from Muswell Manor to Marlborough House. Heavily jostled and lightly bruised, with Oscar (the republican!) in a state of considerable agitation, we arrived for our appointment with the Prince of Wales fifteen minutes late.

In the event, it mattered not a jot. His Royal Highness was also running late, having had some urgent and unexpected business to attend to. He sent his apologies, was grateful for our patience and hoped to be with us shortly.

In truth, confided his page, HRH was in the process of changing his waistcoat and tie for luncheon. (He is notoriously fastidious about his clothes. According to Watkins, the prince changes costume as many as six times a day.)

As we stood waiting in the main hallway, our hands clasped behind our backs, our heels clacking on the parquet flooring, Oscar chattering inconsequentially about the paintings all around us (Oscar prefers Watteau to Van Dyck: 'Only an auctioneer can admire equally all schools of art'), we were joined by General Sir Dighton Probyn, principal private secretary to HRH and Comptroller of the Prince's Household.

He is a striking figure: tall, thin, spry, with aquiline features and a long white beard that give him the appearance of a goblin from a story by the Brothers Grimm. (They say that he keeps his beard so long to ensure that it hides his Victoria Cross on ceremonial occasions.) I was struck by how pleased I was to see him. I was more than pleased, I think: I was relieved. He is a good man – solid in a rackety world.

'Sir Dighton,' cried Oscar effusively, 'I am surprised to see you. We were told you were at Sandringham – planting.'

'I was,' said the general. 'And I will be again on Sunday. I've just come up to town to attend the Duchess of Albemarle's funeral tomorrow. I shall be representing the prince. And the princess.'

'I did not realise that the Princess of Wales knew the Duchess of Albemarle,' said Oscar.

'She didn't, or only slightly, but she likes to make her presence felt on these occasions. It goes a little way towards stifling the gossip.'

'His Royal Highness is not attending the funeral in person?' I asked.

'Royalties don't do funerals as a rule – other than family. Saves a lot of bother – deciding whose obsequies you favour and whose you don't. His

Highness is attending the duke's reception tonight, of course, but that's a private affair – behind closed doors. Not something for the court circular. You'll be there, I take it?'

'We will,' answered Oscar.

'A sorry business,' said the general, shaking his head. 'Best not dwelt upon. Draw a line, move on – that's my policy. I've told His Royal Highness – and Tyrwhitt Wilson: nothing to be gained by further enquiry, in my view.'

'Except, perhaps, the truth,' said Oscar lightly.

'In my experience, the truth can be a mixed blessing, Mr Wilde. Some stones are best left undisturbed.'

'But which stones, Sir Dighton?'

'Exactly. You never know until it's too late.'

The general twitched his beard, smiled benevolently and revealed a mouth of crooked yellow teeth. He nodded to each of us in turn.

'Good day, gentlemen,' he said.

I felt as his gaze met mine that there was an understanding between us.

'Good day, sir,' I said.

He waved a hand above his head as he departed, saying, 'I am lunching with the Danish ambassador. We shall speak of the Princess of Wales. No problems with the truth there. She is all goodness and straight as a die – God bless her. See you anon, gentlemen. Good day.'

As the general made his exit, Harry Tyrwhitt Wilson made his entrance.

'Royal apologies, gentlemen.'

He clicked his heels and bobbed his head. For a moment I thought he was about to twirl his waxed moustache.

'His Highness is lunching with Baron de Rothschild and Baron Hirsch. As money may be on the menu, he felt he was perhaps too gaily caparisoned for the occasion. I'm sure you understand.'

We murmured that we did – of course, we did – as the equerry led us along the corridors to the prince's morning room. He walked briskly, with a spring in his step. Oscar struggled to keep pace and provided no commentary on the paintings and statuary as we passed them by.

A footman and the prince's page opened the doors to admit us to the royal presence.

'Your Royal Highness,' declared Tyrwhitt Wilson. 'Mr Oscar Wilde, Dr Conan Doyle, Mr Robert Sherard.'

'Good afternoon, gentlemen,' said the Prince of Wales.

He stood in front of the fireplace, dressed all in black – save for a white shirt, a silver necktie, a pearl tiepin, a dove-grey waistcoat and matching spats.

'Please, come in. Be seated. No need to stand on ceremony. I'm afraid I'm running a little late today. I apologise.'

He sat himself down on a Louis XV armchair and indicated that we should sit on the Knole settee facing him. We perched side by side on the settee, like a trio of errant schoolboys summoned before the beak. Immediately in front of us – in between the settee and the prince's chair – stood a long, low, lacquered Chinese table. Apart from a large silver ashtray on which rested the prince's half-smoked cigar, the table was bare. Oscar looked along it hopefully, smiled at the prince and raised his eyebrows. I feared he was about to enquire after cheese straws.

The prince anticipated him.

'Forgive me if I don't offer you any refreshment, gentlemen. Time is of the essence, alas.' He returned Oscar's smile. 'And I mustn't keep you. Mr Wilde, you are clearly on your way to a picnic.'

'We are just returned from Muswell Hill,' answered Oscar, apparently puzzled.

'You look as if you are dressed for Margate,' said the prince playfully. 'Yellow and pink I always think of as seaside colours.'

Abashed (as he only ever is with royalty), Oscar glanced down at his apparel and muttered awkwardly, 'Ah, I see.'

'I will come straight to the point, gentlemen,' said the Prince of Wales, picking up his cigar and drawing on it slowly as he glanced about the room.

The page and footman had withdrawn. The equerry stood a yard or so to his right, at the far side of the fireplace, his head half bowed, his hands clasped behind his back.

'We are alone. We are among friends. I know that I can speak in confidence.'

He paused while we murmured our assent.

351

'A week ago,' he continued, 'in the immediate aftermath of the event, I asked you to make some enquiries into the circumstances surrounding the tragic death of the Duchess of Albemarle. I now think that was a mistake. I regret that I troubled you, gentlemen.'

'It was no trouble, sir—' Oscar began.

'Allow me to finish, Mr Wilde. I have made up my mind on this matter. Lord Yarborough has given us his settled opinion as to what occurred. I see no reason to question his conclusions. He was the late duchess's medical adviser and her confidant. I know him and I trust him. Nothing is to be gained by further enquiry.'

'But Your Royal Highness—'

'No, Mr Wilde. Let it rest now. It is the duchess's funeral tomorrow. Let her rest in peace. Let the duke get on with his life – and let us get on with ours.'

'If you insist—'

'I don't insist: I command, Mr Wilde. It is the prerogative of princes.'

'And Mademoiselle Lavallois?' persisted Oscar.

'I have read the newspapers,' said the prince, stubbing out his cigar in the silver ashtray. 'Tyrwhitt Wilson brought them to my attention. It appears that the poor girl was the victim of her erstwhile employer. I understand that the police in France are on the case. I trust that they will bring the man to justice – in due course.'

Oscar said nothing, but cast his eyes down towards his knees. I sensed our audience was at an end. I touched Sherard on the elbow and together we made to move.

'One final point, gentleman – and this is key. This is why I have asked you here today. I know you are all authors – and authors of distinction.'

The prince turned towards Robert Sherard for the first time.

'I seem to recall that Mr Wilde introduced you, Mr Sherard, as his recording angel – his Dr Watson.'

Sherard smiled and lowered his eyes.

'Well, I don't think we need a record of any of this business, do we, gentlemen? I don't want to see any of this in print – not in my lifetime, not for a hundred years after. Is that understood?'

'Of course,' I said at once.

'Is that agreed, gentlemen? Do I have your word on the matter?'

'Yes, sir,' said Robert Sherard.

'Yes, Your Royal Highness,' said Oscar quite distinctly.

The Prince of Wales clapped his hands.

'I'm glad. I'm grateful. The likes of Lord Henry Stanley are determined to bring about a republican party. We don't want to give any grist to their mill. The Queen will die one day and she will need an unsullied successor. And when I go, and I may not long outlast Her Majesty, Prince Eddy will be king. We must protect him – from himself and from the prying and pernicious press. The worst of the so-called gentlemen of Fleet Street are no better than vermin. They'd bring down the monarchy if they could.'

We were silent. The prince had said it all; there was nothing left to say.

From his waistcoat pocket, His Highness produced his half-hunter and checked the time. As he did so, there was a knock on the morning-room door. The prince looked up as Watkins, his page, entered the room and came towards his master. He was carrying what appeared to be a large basket of flowers – a wicker trug filled to overflowing with early-flowering white lilac. The fragrance of the flowers was sweet and almost overwhelming.

'This is charming,' declared the prince. 'Lilac is a favourite with the Princess of Wales. I am sorry she is not here.'

The page placed the basket on the table in front of His Highness.

'With the compliments of Mr Wilde, sir.'

Oscar looked up in surprise. 'No, sadly not. I cannot take the credit.'

'That's what I understood from the florist's boy,' said the page stoutly.

'Alas, no,' protested Oscar. 'Would that they were.'

'No matter,' said the prince. 'They're charming.'

He pulled a stem of lilac from the basket to admire it and to breathe in the scent. As he held the soft white petals to his nose, from the woody stalk at the base of the lilac stem something fell on to his lap – and slithered towards his knee.

The prince looked down, perturbed, and then, pushing back his chair, struggled to his feet.

'What in God's name—'

'It's a snake,' cried Oscar, rising from the settee and stepping away from the table in alarm.

The creature – about a foot in length, thick and scaly, black and tan in colouring, with a triangular-shaped head and slit-shaped eyes – fell from the prince's lap on to the floor. It twisted its head from side to side and slithered beneath the table.

'God Almighty!' cried the prince.

The page pulled the remainder of the lilac blossom from the basket to reveal a swarm of snakes – five or six of them at least, coiled and curled, one over another, intertwined, writhing, wriggling, twisting, turning. One had its large head held up towards the light, its jaws wide open, its fangs bared.

'It's a nest of vipers,' said the page.

'So I see,' said the Prince of Wales.

77

Letter from Bram Stoker to his wife, Florence, delivered by messenger at 6 p.m. on Friday, 21 March 1890

Lyceum Theatre,
Strand,
London

Friday afternoon

BE SURE TO READ THIS BEFORE SETTING OFF FOR THE
THEATRE TONIGHT

Florrie, dearest –

I shall expect you here at 7.30 p.m. – 7.40 p.m. at the very latest. It is Macbeth *again (I am sorry) but we have a new Macduff (young Mr Ringwold), a new Banquo (Mr Trewin) and an impressive new effect for the Weird Sisters' cauldron (real flames – despite the best endeavours of the London County Council) – and the Chief is anxious that I see it all from out front to assess the paying customers' reactions. (While you are looking at the stage I shall be gazing at the stalls!)*

The Chief is in fine form and Ellen Terry has never been more extraordinary (in her magenta wig and that dress: the 'beetle shell' one that Sargent painted) – and it is the Bard's briefest tragedy, so I believe (and hope and pray) that you will find it to be A Good and Memorable Evening. And, after the play and a moment with HI (one drink at most, I promise), I shall be taking you to supper at Rules. I have reserved our usual table.

You do remember that Constance Wilde is joining us, don't you? I invited them both, of course, but Oscar cannot come. He is impossible. Poor Constance believes that her husband is in Paris. That is what he has told her. In fact, he is London.

Indeed, he was in this very room with me not half an hour ago! He barged in, demanding sandwiches – and a bottle of hock – and a sober suit of clothes. He arrived dressed for a boating party on the Isis – a sand-coloured summer suit and a pink bow-tie! He explained that he was on his way to pay his last respects to the late Duchess of Albemarle and consequently required something more suitable for a man in mourning. I raided the wardrobe and furnished him with the chaplain's costume from The Lady of Lyons. It was a surprisingly good fit. (Oscar is now stouter even than I am. You chose the right man, Florrie dearest.)

Oscar arrived with his weak-chinned friend, Robert Sherard, and the admirable Arthur Conan Doyle in tow. All three appeared to be in a state of shock – the only one who talked any sense was Conan Doyle.

They had come directly here from Marlborough House. There they were closeted with the Prince of Wales – in his study or morning room or some such – when an elaborate basket of flowers was delivered to HRH. Hidden within the basket, lurking beneath the flowers, was a living nest of vipers! Would you believe it? I would not have done – except that Conan Doyle is a steady man – a prose man, not a poet – and swears it was so. He said he recognised the reptiles at once – Vipera aspis, long-fanged and deadly poisonous. Thankfully, no one was hurt. Only one of the snakes escaped from the basket and it was quickly retrieved by Doyle and a page and the prince's equerry – using a silver ashtray, a brass poker and fire tongs! They then took the basket to the kitchens and drowned the creatures in boiling water.

Naturally, we are to speak of this to nobody. Doyle thinks it may be the work of Fenians. Oscar is inclined to think it the endeavour of a lone lunatic.

He is particularly concerned because the youth who delivered the basket to the door of Marlborough House – dressed as a florist's boy – mentioned Oscar's name, saying the flowers were a gift for the prince from Mr Wilde. That is why they were carried into the royal presence without delay.

I have since had my own unhappy thought about the episode – which I will share with you, my dearest, but only you.

I saw Prince Eddy again on Wednesday night – at 'The Bar of Gold'. I went on Vampire Club business, though none was done. The young prince is in a bad way. He talked, as he often does, of how his father despises and mistrusts him – he claims his father believes he might indeed be Jack the Ripper and has set police spies on him. It's nonsense: we know that. I have no doubt the Prince of Wales loves his son as much as we love ours – but Prince Eddy is quite mad at times, especially as the opium leaves him – and I have a fear that this 'nest of vipers' could be some hideous practical joke of his.

Come what may, Florrie, you are to speak of none of this tonight. Not a word. Not a hint. Dear Constance is in the dark – and must remain so. It is not for us to reveal to her her husband's true nature. She will find out soon enough, poor girl – we can be sure of that. Genius he may be, charmer he is, but, as always, lovely wife of mine, I am so grateful you chose not to marry him.

No later than 7.40 p.m. – please.

Bram

PS. Wear my mother's diamonds tonight. You know, don't you, what the people call you – what the newspapers call you? You know, don't you, that this evening, before the curtain rises, when you step into our box at the theatre, all eyes will be upon you? In the dress circle they will lean over the balcony's edge for a better view. Up in the gallery they will stand on their benches to catch a glimpse of you. You are 'Florrie Balcombe Stoker, the prettiest woman in England'. I am so proud that you are mine.

78

Letter from Professor August Onofroff sent to Oscar Wilde, care of Arthur Conan Doyle at the Langham Hotel, London W.

Empire Theatre,
Leicester Square,
London

20 March 1890

My dear Wilde,

  Thank you most kindly for your letter and your most generous comments. It was a dark night, ending in great tragedy, but I am nonetheless very grateful to you and to His Royal Highness for my engagement. To perform 'by royal command' is a great honour and one I will not forget. You may rest assured that Mr Wilson gave me my fee, as agreed, at the conclusion of the evening. There is nothing outstanding.

  Now, to your two questions.

  1. What did I learn from the seance? The simple answer is: not nearly so much as I would have wished. We were interrupted even as we started. However, we started well – thanks in no small measure to your ingenious ruse. Some would accuse us of 'trickery' – revealing to me beforehand what words you and His Royal Highness planned to write upon your cards was perhaps not wholly 'ethical'! – but I believe that the trick was justified. It gave others in the room confidence. It disarmed the sceptical. It inclined them to suspend their disbelief and 'open up' more quickly and more freely than they might otherwise have done. In short, it made them more immediately susceptible to my powers.

As a consequence, even as we started and I looked around the circle, no mind was entirely closed off to me. What did I see? Surrounding each and every head I saw the yellow cloud of moral turpitude. There was no exception, I am afraid – not one. (This does not mean that every individual in the group is already guilty, but it does mean that each one will fall from grace in the fullness of time.)

The darkest penumbra surrounded the two oldest men in the circle and what I saw, in the brief moment available to me, involved, in each case, the man's oldest child. As to the green aureole of death – it seemed to me to be at its sharpest and most vivid around the head of young Prince Albert Victor. More than that, I cannot tell you.

2. Could a subject under hypnosis be persuaded to commit suicide? I think not – at least not against his or her will. One hundred years ago,

*in the heyday of Franz Anton Mesmer, it was
believed that the hypnotist was possessed of
'animal magnetism' and, as a consequence, that
his subjects were drawn by an irresistible force to
obey his commands.*

*We think differently now. Today, we recognise
that the skilled hypnotist can place a susceptible
subject in a trance and that, in that trance, the
subject will be open to suggestion – but only to
suggestion, not to command.*

*For example, as an hypnotist (and I am not one
of the best; mind-reading is my gift) I might be
able to murder you, my dear Wilde, by persuading
you to drink a glass of wine that (unbeknown to
you) happened to contain poison, but I doubt that
I could persuade you to shoot yourself – let alone
slit your own throat.* Unless, of course, you were
already so inclined.

*This last possibility is why there is talk in
Parliament just now of introducing legislation to
control the conduct of hypnotists and so protect
the unsuspecting and the vulnerable. Faced with
a subject already inclined to self-harm or suicide
through madness or melancholy, an unscrupulous
hypnotist might indeed be able to induce that
subject to a fatal act.*

I trust that this is helpful.

*If I can be of further assistance, do not
hesitate to write to me. And please be assured
of my complete discretion at all times. As I
told His Royal Highness on Tuesday night,
everything that passes between us is entirely*

*confidential and, so far as I am concerned, will
for ever remain so.*

 Yours most sincerely,
  A. Onofroff

79

From the notebooks of Robert Sherard

In the carriage taking us from the Langham Hotel to 40 Grosvenor Square, Oscar read out to us the letter he had received from Professor Onofroff.

Conan Doyle greeted it with considerable excitement. 'Onofroff is telling us that Yarborough could have induced both the Duchess of Albemarle and Mademoiselle Lavallois to take their own lives.'

Oscar smiled. 'Onofroff is also telling us that around each of our heads he has seen the yellow cloud of moral turpitude. That includes your head, Arthur. You may not have fallen from grace yet, my friend, but, according to Onofroff, it is only a matter of time.'

Oscar was in a playful frame of mind. With his tongue he moved his Turkish cigarette from one side of his mouth to the other. Winking at me, he passed me the letter to inspect.

'What do you say, Robert?'

'I say the man's a charlatan. He can no more read minds than I can read Sanskrit. On Tuesday night a woman was murdered within a few feet of him and, for all his professed psychic powers, he failed to "sense" the tragedy taking place in our very midst. There was a murderer in the room – almost within arm's length – and all the great Onofroff registered were yellow clouds and dark penumbra.'

'Do not forget the green aureole of death, Robert. He registered that, also.'

Conan Doyle was not amused. 'Never mind your joshing, gentlemen. Whether the man can read minds is neither here nor there. What he says about the power of the hypnotist over the vulnerable has to be taken seriously.'

'Does it?' I asked. 'The man is a music-hall turn, Arthur.'

Conan Doyle pulled the letter from my grasp.

'Whatever he is, what he says here rings true.'

He sat forward on his seat and addressed us with a passion that defied mockery.

'We know that a strong will can, simply by virtue of its strength, take possession of a weaker one, even at a distance, and can regulate the impulses and actions of its owner. Napoleon proved that across Europe. Henry Irving proves it night after night from the stage of the Lyceum. A powerful personality – by force of personality – can move men to action and to tears. Combine such a force of personality with the art of the hypnotist and what villainy cannot be achieved?'

'Lord Yarborough is neither Napoleon nor Irving,' said Oscar, holding out his cigarette and tipping the ash into his cupped hand.

'No, but he is nonetheless a man of achievement and ambition – a small man with a considerable personality, a strong will, iron determination and high intelligence. And he is a hypnotist. What he wants, he gets – by fair means or foul. To make progress with his research into the nature of hysteria he must explore both the behaviour and the anatomy of his patients. He needs them alive and he needs them dead. By the very nature of their illness, his patients are vulnerable – prone to hysteria and to melancholy, to wild heights of excitement and terrible sloughs of despond. Yarborough does not need to murder them with his own hands. He has only to hypnotise them at their most vulnerable and induce them to terrible acts of self-immolation. The Duchess of Albemarle was Yarborough's patient. Under hypnosis, he could do with her as he pleased.'

'Could he persuade her to take her own life and *subsequently* dispose of the instrument with which she committed the fateful act?' asked Oscar, smiling. 'And could he persuade Lulu Lavallois, first, to kill herself and, then, post-mortem, to hide the instrument of death on the supper table in the adjoining room?'

'Besides,' I added, 'Mademoiselle Lavallois was not Lord Yarborough's patient.'

'So he tells us,' snapped Conan Doyle, 'but she *was* Charcot's. That we know.'

Our four-wheeler was now drawing up outside 40 Grosvenor Square. Conan Doyle looked out of the carriage window.

'There he is,' he cried.

Lord Yarborough was standing on the top step, awaiting admittance to the house. He looked down at our carriage and, recognising us, waved.

'And look over here, gentlemen,' said Oscar, directing our attention to the other side of the street.

A lone figure in a dishevelled raincoat stood lurking by the gates to the garden square.

'It's your old acquaintance from the Dover train, Arthur – the fellow whose sinister appearance so caught your fancy: the man with the twisted lip. All our chickens are coming home to roost.'

'This is Where it Ends'

80

From the journal of Arthur Conan Doyle

Following the hideous business of drowning the
viperidae in the kitchens at Marlborough House, we
took Oscar's four-wheeler across Trafalgar Square
and down the Strand to the Lyceum Theatre.

'In the aftermath of those vile snakes, we need
the security of known relationships,' said Oscar.
'We need the comfort of friends. And we need
food and drink. And I need a change of clothing.
Bram Stoker can supply all these.'

Bram did. He is the best of men. His easy
companionability repaired our tattered nerves. He
sent out for beer and sandwiches – and two bottles
of hock, at Oscar's insistence. And, from the
Lyceum wardrobe, he supplied Oscar with a sober
set of clothes suitable for the Albemarle wake. (It
was a costume for an eighteenth-century
clergyman, but the cut and style fitted Oscar
uncannily.)

We spent almost two hours with Bram – telling
him our news and hearing his, talking of this and

that and nothing in particular – and felt much the better for it.

From the Lyceum we drove back up the Strand, across Trafalgar Square once more, up the Haymarket and along Regent Street to the Langham Hotel. There, in my bathroom (two shillings extra, but worth every penny), Sherard shaved and I changed my tie, while Oscar looked through his post – there were letters and telegrams awaiting him, sent care of me – and admired himself (inordinately!) in the looking-glass.

At six o'clock we set off for our final destination of the day: 40 Grosvenor Square.

'We are going back to where it all began,' I said, as we climbed aboard the four-wheeler, 'only eight days ago.'

'It began a day or two before that, I think,' said Oscar.

'The Albemarle reception was on Thursday the thirteenth of March – a week ago last night,' I said.

'But the wedding anniversary of the Prince and Princess of Wales was three days before – on Monday the tenth of March.'

'Is that significant?'

'Possibly – if I am correct and it is love and loss that lie at the heart of our murder mystery.'

Oscar sat back in the carriage, clutching his correspondence to his chest and smiling enigmatically.

'You have received fresh intelligence, Oscar?' asked Sherard.

'I have – and it includes an interesting letter from the great Professor Onofroff. I wrote to him on Wednesday with a couple of queries. He has been good enough to reply by return of post.'

Oscar read out Onofroff's letter – and I pounced upon it. Onofroff confirmed what I had already considered possible: that a subject *prone* to suicide could be *induced* to suicide under hypnosis.

When we reached 40 Grosvenor Square, we found Lord Yarborough standing on the doorstep. As we alighted from our carriage, Oscar hissed to me: 'Be civil to him – for the moment.'

Oscar paused to give instructions (and further emolument) to the coachman – the long-suffering fellow had been held at Oscar's disposal since the crack of dawn – while Robert Sherard and I climbed the steps together.

Yarborough boomed effusively: 'Good afternoon, gentlemen. How was the Prince of Wales? Did you get to him on time? Did you get your cheese straws? I rode to town in the pony and trap just now – not a good idea.'

I said nothing, leaving Sherard to mumble inoffensive replies on our behalf. I nodded briefly to Yarborough and then stood on the doorstep, looking back over my shoulder, beyond the four-wheeler, to the half-familiar figure that stood watching us from across the street. I saw that Yarborough had noticed him, too.

'Have you rung the bell?' called Oscar, as he climbed the steps to join us.

'I have,' answered Yarborough cheerfully, 'twice.'

As he spoke, the front door was opened. The scene that greeted us was not what we had expected.

The Prince of Wales was standing in the centre of the hallway, at the foot of the main staircase. He was dressed in full mourning and his face was as grey as his beard. In his left hand he held a folded handkerchief. With his right he clasped the hand of the Duke of Albemarle.

'She was a remarkable young woman,' we heard him say. 'So full of life. I offer you my heartfelt condolences, Duke. She was my special friend.'

'Are we late?' murmured Oscar.

'No,' whispered the butler. 'His Royal Highness was early. He was anxious about the possibility of photographers.'

Also standing in the hallway, next to his father, equally ashen-faced and in full mourning, was Prince Albert Victor and, beside him, ranged to the right of the staircase in a solemn row, were General Sir Dighton Probyn, Harry Tyrwhitt Wilson and Frank Watkins, the Prince of Wales's page.

Just beyond the page, standing alone, with his head bowed and his hands held behind his back, was Oscar's young friend, Rex LaSalle.

To the left of the staircase, ranged behind the duke and providing a counterbalance to the royal party, stood the indoor staff of the Albemarle household. As personal maid to the late duchess, little Nellie Atkins, weeping silently, had pride of place at the front of the line.

'Shall we view the body?'

'Thank you, Duke,' said the Prince of Wales. 'I should like to pay Helen my last respects.'

'Very good, sir,' said the duke quietly. 'Parker will lead the way.'

The butler moved from his station by the front door to the centre of the hallway. He bowed low to both the duke and the Prince of Wales and then, sharply, turned his back on them and, in the manner of a mace-bearer marching before a lord mayor, led the procession out of the hallway, along the corridor to the left of the main staircase into the ground-floor morning room where lay the coffin of the late Duchess of Albemarle.

Lord Yarborough turned to me and murmured silkily: 'Will you come to view the body, Dr Doyle? It seems I did not steal it away to chop it up for science, after all.'

'We saw you collect the body on the day of the duchess's death,' I whispered.

'I made the arrangements with the undertakers – on behalf of my friend, the duke. Nothing more.'

He smiled at me coldly and narrowed his eyes.

'If you will excuse me,' he said.

Moving swiftly across the hall, he joined the royal party, taking his place alongside General Sir Dighton Probyn, one step behind Prince Albert Victor.

'We're latecomers,' muttered Oscar. 'And interlopers. We should go last, after the servants.'

It was a curious procession, with at its head, side by side, the late duchess's husband and her royal lover, and, at its tail, her deaf and dumb maidservant and a young man who claimed to be a vampire and had met the deceased only the once and that just a week ago.

Sherard, Oscar and I followed the procession, but kept our distance. As we entered the darkened morning room, about ten paces behind the line of mourners, the duke and the princes, Yarborough, Probyn, Wilson and the prince's page had moved past the coffin and through the double doors beyond into the adjoining drawing room. There we could see Parker already serving wine.

We waited in the doorway and watched as the household staff filed past the coffin and proceeded to join their lord and master in the drawing room beyond. There, they, too, were offered wine. Grief engineered an interesting scene: the Prince of Wales in earnest conversation with a butler; the Duke of Albemarle with a consoling arm wrapped around the shoulders of a weeping lady's maid.

'Let us view the body now,' whispered Oscar. 'We are alone.'

Though the doors to the room beyond were open, we were alone. The drawing room was brightly lit, but the morning room where the coffin lay was in semi-darkness. The gas lamps were turned low and at the four corners of the open oak coffin stood four tall brass candlesticks, each with a single candle lit.

Oscar led the way into the room and stood at the head of the silk-lined casket with his hand resting on it, gazing down at the face of the late duchess.

'She is as beautiful as I remember,' he said. 'Helen, late of Troy, now of Grosvenor Square.'

The lady was indeed beautiful. The embalmers had not robbed her of her loveliness. Her eyes were closed, her lips were sealed, her brow was clear. She looked to be at peace.

'Her nose is more pointed than I recall,' said Oscar.

'Death does that,' I said, 'even in the young.'

His eyes scanned the length of the coffin. 'She is as lovely as I remember, but not so tall.'

'Did you know her well?' whispered Sherard.

'Well enough to be invited to her parties, that's all. We were never alone together. I saw her only among crowds. We never spoke for more than a few minutes at a time. But I liked her. And I admired her fire, her fierce energy. It was wonderfully at odds with her pallor – with her lily-like beauty – and the frailty of her heart.'

Sherard peered closely at the corpse within the coffin. 'Do you think that she was truly "mad" in the way that they say she was?'

Oscar laughed quietly. 'It's possible. From the very first, whenever we met, she kissed me full on the lips. Remember, Robert, when a married woman kisses you on the mouth, it tells you more about her character than it does about your charms.'

He looked down into the coffin, smiled, and with his right hand gently caressed the lady's hair.

'She was guilty of the sins of the flesh. Do they matter?' he asked, moving his hand, his fingers at her right temple. 'She was mad with desire. Is that a sickness? She was mad for love. Is that a crime?'

As he spoke, Oscar leant further over the coffin. For one disconcerting moment, I thought that he was about to lower his head to kiss the dead woman on the lips. Instead, he placed his other hand against her left temple and held it there.

'Take care,' I whispered. 'Your hands will leave a mark upon her flesh.'

'It matters not a jot,' he said, tightening his grip on the dead woman's hair. 'She's dead. She feels nothing.'

He glanced towards the doorway to the drawing room, then turned his gaze back to the coffin.

'And that is perhaps fortunate,' he murmured, his voice suddenly choking. 'For look – she has been beheaded.'

With both hands, Oscar lifted the duchess's head clean out of the coffin.

'My God,' I gasped.

'This is monstrous,' hissed Sherard.

Oscar, with his eyes tightly shut, held out the head towards me. 'What is the meaning of this, Arthur?'

'I do not know,' I said.

I looked down at the serene face of the dead woman and below it at her slender neck. It was entirely blemish-free. The head and neck had been severed with skill and precision just above the clavicle. The cut was quite clean: the work of a fine butcher's knife or a surgeon's saw.

Oscar stood, frozen and blind, gripping the severed head between his hands.

'Put it back,' I hissed.

He did not move. Suddenly I sensed a quietening of the hubbub in the room beyond. I had no choice: with both hands I wrested the head from Oscar's grasp, holding it by the jaw. It was so heavy that I almost let it fall on to the floor.

'In God's name—' cried Sherard as Oscar staggered backwards and I heaved the head back into the coffin.

I placed it accurately, in one fell move – much as, when I was a boy, I would score a try on the rugby field at Stonyhurst.

'Say nothing yet,' stammered Oscar, opening his eyes and steadying himself by taking hold of one of the coffin's brass handles.

Before I could protest, a voice called out from the doorway to the drawing room.

'Gentlemen, come through.'

It was the Duke of Albemarle. He did not venture into the darkened room, but beckoned us towards the light.

'We are about to raise our glasses to Helen's memory. You must join us.'

Oscar, recovering his composure instantly (there is much of the actor about him), led us from the duchess's coffin towards the duke.

'We were saying our farewells, Your Grace,' he said. 'We are privileged to be here.'

The duke shook Oscar by the hand and ushered him into the drawing room. He nodded to Sherard and to me.

'I am glad that you were able to come,' he said pleasantly. 'Your friend LaSalle is here also. I had not realised that he and Helen were acquainted.'

'Nor I,' said Oscar.

We looked around the brightly lit drawing room: the gas lamps were turned high, the candelabra filled with flickering candles. Apart from the butler serving wine, the servants had now all gone.

'I feel we are intruders,' said Oscar. 'I had assumed a larger party.'

'No,' said the duke, stopping his butler and assisting Oscar, Sherard and me each to a glass of pale-green wine. 'This evening is for His Highness's benefit. Royal protocol dictates that he cannot attend the funeral, but he wished to pay Helen his last respects. He honours her memory. We are honoured by his presence. I am honoured by his friendship.'

'We are privileged to be here,' Oscar repeated.

'I understand your interest in the tragedy,' said the duke. 'I appreciate your concern. That is why I invited you.'

He smiled and raised his glass to us.

'I was also anxious that you should finally see that there is no sinister mystery here. There was sickness – and there is sadness. That is all.'

'And secrets?' asked Oscar.

'Certainly,' said the duke. 'And secrets, too, but only matrimonial secrets.' He rested his hand on Oscar's shoulder. 'We all have those, I fear. None of us lives beneath an ever-cloudless sky.'

He turned towards the rest of the room.

'Charge your glasses, gentlemen. Parker, make sure everyone is well supplied.' He smiled at Oscar once more. 'We are drinking German wine, Mr Wilde. It seems more fitting than French somehow.'

Oscar smiled and inclined his head towards the duke, but said nothing.

'I am going to propose a toast,' said the duke.

He looked directly at the Prince of Wales and then at Prince Albert Victor, standing with Lord Yarborough at his father's side.

'With Your Highness's permission?'

The Prince of Wales nodded and removed his cigar from his mouth.

The duke raised his glass and said simply and clearly: 'Let us drink to the memory of Helen, Duchess of Albemarle. May she rest in peace.'

'May she rest in peace,' said the Prince of Wales.

We all raised our glasses and echoed the sentiment.

The duke turned towards our group once more and said, a little distractedly, 'It's a fine wine, is it not? Helen was partial to a good Gewürztraminer. Parker will bring us further refreshments in a moment. I understand from Yarborough that you gentlemen have a penchant for cheese straws.'

As we laughed, Oscar looked at the duke and enquired earnestly: 'In the event of a fire, Your Grace, how would one best escape from the house?'

The duke looked quite bewildered. 'What an extraordinary question, Mr Wilde.'

'Besides the front door, of course,' continued Oscar. 'What are the other means of escape?'

'None,' said the duke, bemused, 'beyond the garden door at the back and the area door from the kitchen. One might be able to escape through the attic to the roof. I don't know. I have no idea. Why on earth do you ask?' He laughed. 'Are you expecting a fire?'

'No,' stammered Oscar. 'No.' He joined in the laughter. 'I'm not sure why I asked.' He looked about him. 'Perhaps it is all these candles. Forgive me.'

'And please excuse me, gentlemen,' said the duke, now looking at Oscar somewhat askance. 'I must attend upon the princes. They will be leaving shortly.'

As the Duke of Albemarle left us, the main door of the drawing room opened and Rex LaSalle came into the room. He looked about until he saw us and then, his hand half raised in greeting, made his way towards us.

'Good evening, gentlemen,' he said. He shook our hands and then touched Oscar on the arm. 'May I have a private word?'

'I always welcome the prospect of a private word,' replied Oscar. 'It holds out so much promise. Robert's first book of poems was entitled

Whispers, you know. Come into this corner by the window, Rex, and whisper to me.'

As Oscar and LaSalle stepped aside and began their whispered conference, I turned urgently to Sherard: 'Whatever Oscar says, however much he protests, we must go to the police – now. We must telephone them at once.'

'Will the prince not have a police guard waiting for him in the street?'

'I think not,' I said. 'He is here on private business. He came by brougham. Besides Probyn and Wilson, he is unattended. You must go to the telephone room, Robert, and call Scotland Yard. Now. Slip into the hall discreetly. I shall stay here and make sure that no one leaves.'

As Sherard made to depart, Oscar returned and caught him by the arm. 'Where are you going, Robert?' he asked.

'To call the police,' I whispered. 'At my behest.'

Oscar raised a quizzical eyebrow.

'At my *insistence*, Oscar. We must. Yarborough must be arrested.'

'Here? Now? In the presence of the Prince of Wales? In the midst of the wake?'

'If needs be, yes. The woman's been beheaded. Albemarle may be implicated. There's no time to be lost. We must summon the police.'

Oscar released Sherard's arm and, taking hold of mine, he steered me towards the window.

'Look into the street, Arthur. What do you see?'

The light was now fading in Grosvenor Square and the street was gloomy and deserted.

I saw nothing but a carriage, leaving the square to the north.

'Isn't that your four-wheeler?' I asked.

Oscar peered into the street. 'Yes. I told the cabman he was free to go if another fare came his way.'

'And where is the prince's carriage?'

'Not here yet – evidently. You see, Arthur, we have time on our side – and His Grace has already alerted us to the most likely means of escape. So long as no one leaves this room and makes for the garden door or the kitchens or the attic, all will be well.'

'We need the police,' I repeated, in growing desperation.

'Look out of the window, Arthur. Look across the street. Can you not see him, lurking among the bushes in the garden square? Yes, there he is, beside the wrought-iron gate: your friend with the twisted lip. He's a policeman – you can be sure of that.'

'I will telephone Scotland Yard,' I persisted. 'I will speak with Inspector Andrews. I will.'

Oscar sighed and, quite suddenly, acquiesced.

'Very well,' he said. 'I will accompany you.'

We left Sherard in the drawing room, standing with his back to the doorway that led to the morning room. We made our way around the edge of the room towards the main door that led from the drawing room directly on to the hall.

We went unnoticed: Albemarle was deep in conversation with the royal princes and Lord Yarborough; Sir Dighton Probyn and Tyrwhitt

Wilson were studying the Romney portraits of the duke's grandparents above the fireplace; Frank Watkins, the prince's page, was assisting Parker, the butler, recharging glasses and emptying ashtrays.

The hallway was empty. Before we crossed it to reach the telephone room, Oscar paused and looked back at the door to the drawing room that we had just closed behind us.

'Did you notice there was no key in the lock, Arthur?' he said. 'No key on the inside of the lock – and, as you see, no key on the outside.'

'Does that signify?' I asked. 'I suppose the butler holds all the keys.'

'It simply means that we cannot lock them in. When we return to the room in just a moment – before the police arrive – you will have to stand guard inside this door and Robert will have to stand guard by the door leading to the room where the duchess's coffin is lying. We don't want any of them running away—'

'None of them will escape,' I said emphatically.

Oscar laughed.

'I fear they will all escape, Arthur. Every one. Love is an illusion and it's an unjust world. They will all escape, but let them at least hear the truth before they do.'

'You know the truth, Oscar?' I asked.

'I do,' he said solemnly. 'And it is very terrible.'

Quietly we walked together across the hallway to the telephone room. Oscar reached for the doorhandle.

'This is where the tragedy began. And this is where it ends. Prepare yourself, Arthur. There will be no more horror after this.'

And so saying, he turned the handle and pulled open the door.

The body of Nellie Atkins, the duchess's maid, tumbled forward and slumped at my feet. The body fell limply, like that of a rag doll, and landed, awkwardly, on its side. The maid's scarlet face stared up at me like a macabre medieval gargoyle: her eyes bulged, her tongue lolled out of her mouth.

I took her pulse, knowing it was to no purpose. I saw at once that she was dead. She had been strangled and her neck was broken.

The Truth

81

From the journal of Arthur Conan Doyle

'How did you know of this?' I asked, looking up at Oscar as I knelt at the dead girl's side. '*When* did you know of this?'

'Moments after it occurred,' he said. 'When it was too late.'

'We must call Scotland Yard,' I said.

'There is no need. LaSalle has called them already – at my instruction. Scotland Yard will be here shortly – and in force. We can tell them everything – or, at least, everything they need to know.'

'Can we?' I asked. 'Do we know it all?'

'I know it all, I think,' he said. 'Indeed, I know too much.'

He gazed down at Nellie Atkins's crumpled corpse.

'I should have acted sooner. I might have prevented this. Poor child. Deaf and dumb. And now dead.'

The clock on the far side of the hallway struck

the half hour. Oscar turned away from the body and looked back to the drawing-room door.

'Bear with me, Arthur – until the police arrive. Let us utilise what time we have to confront our betters with the truth. It may be our only opportunity.'

Against my better judgement, but not against my will, I lifted the poor dead girl's body and moved it back into the telephone room. I closed the door against it and followed Oscar as he crossed the hallway once more.

He looked absurd in his borrowed clergyman's garb of woe and yet there was a grandeur in his bearing that commanded attention and respect. I was ready to do his bidding. The curious charm of his personality, his height, his bulk, his shining eyes, the dome of his forehead, his evident high intelligence, his sympathy, his sense of feeling and his unique way with words lend to Oscar Wilde an extraordinary authority.

Together, discreetly, we stepped back into the drawing room. The gathering was as we had left it two minutes before. Robert Sherard stood sentinel at the doorway to the darkened morning room. The Prince of Wales and the Duke of Albemarle, with Prince Albert Victor and Lord Yarborough, stood together in the centre of the room, talking, drinking Gewürztraminer, smoking cigars, beneath a brilliant Venetian chandelier. Comptroller, equerry, page and butler hovered close by.

'Your Royal Highnesses, Your Grace,

gentlemen,' declared Oscar in full voice, as I secured the drawing-room door behind us, 'forgive this interruption.'

'No speeches now, Mr Wilde,' called out the Prince of Wales, looking towards Oscar in mock reproof. 'We know you can resist everything except temptation, but you don't need to live up to your reputation here. The duke has proposed a toast to his late wife that was perfect in its simplicity. Do not spoil it by trying to cap it now.'

'I have news to share, sir,' said Oscar. 'I don't wish to make a speech.'

'News? Is my brougham at the door?'

'Not yet, sir,' answered Oscar. 'The news is grave and it concerns us all.'

A sudden stillness filled the room.

'Very well,' said the prince, testily. 'If His Grace is content to hear you out, so are we. What is this news?'

'There has been another death, Your Highness – another murder. In this house – this evening.'

The Duke of Albemarle cried out: 'No!'

Sir Dighton Probyn moved at once to the Prince of Wales's side. Lord Yarborough stepped back and shook his head. Prince Albert Victor covered his face with both hands.

'What are you saying, Mr Wilde?' barked the Prince of Wales angrily. 'What melodrama are you conjuring up for us now? Forget your theatrics, man – stick to the truth, pure and simple.'

'The truth is rarely pure and never simple, sir,' said Oscar, with a wintry smile. 'Give me the few minutes, Your Highness, before your carriage arrives and I will do for you what you asked me to do a week ago: explain the death of your dear friend, Helen, late Duchess of Albemarle.'

'For God's sake,' cried the Duke of Albemarle. 'You said there had been another death – here, this evening.'

'Yes, Your Grace,' said Oscar. 'Nellie Atkins, your wife's maid, has been murdered – strangled to death, her body left abandoned in the telephone room.'

Lord Yarborough moved abruptly towards the drawing-room door. 'I must go to her,' he breathed.

I held my ground and blocked his way, placing my back firmly against the door, covering the handle. On the far side of the room, Robert Sherard, I noticed, had closed the double doors leading into the morning room. He stood with his back to them, his arms folded defiantly across his chest.

'There is no need to attend to the maid, my lord,' said Oscar. 'She is beyond help. She is quite dead. Dr Conan Doyle has examined her. We can leave her body to the police surgeon now.'

'Nellie dead?' said the Duke of Albemarle in a hoarse whisper.

'She knew too much,' said Oscar quietly.

'She was deaf and dumb, Mr Wilde.'

'She saw too much.'

'I am lost for words,' murmured the duke.

Sir Dighton Probyn stood at the side of the

Prince of Wales. 'Your Royal Highness, I think the time has come for you to take your leave.'

The prince turned to the old general and spoke, not unkindly: 'No, Probyn. Not yet. Not until we have heard Wilde's story.'

Carefully, slowly, his eyes scanned the room: he looked in turn at each man standing there.

'There are ten of you here and all can be trusted. Eddy is my son and heir – my flesh and blood, after all. You, Probyn, and my staff – Wilson, Atkins – you three are my liegemen and true. Albemarle and Yarborough are my friends – and gentlemen to the marrow. Parker has been with this house for forty years. If he is not to be trusted, there's no hope for the world. And Wilde and his associates have given me their word of honour: my secrets are safe with them until I reach my grave – and then for a hundred years. They have sworn it.'

'We have, sir,' said Oscar. 'We will tell the police only what the police truly need to know to fulfil their obligations to the law.'

'The truth, but not the whole truth?' suggested the prince. 'That's what the police will get, is it?'

'Exactly, sir.'

'But I will get the whole truth from you, will I, Mr Wilde?'

'Entire, unvarnished – if Your Royal Highness pleases.'

'Unvarnished, eh?' muttered Prince Albert Victor. 'That's not something royalty is accustomed to.'

'I will have done with this, Mr Wilde. We are so deep in now that I suspect only the whole truth can save us. It is better, perhaps, to know the worst than merely to fear it.'

The Prince of Wales looked about the brightly lit room once more and waved his cigar in all directions as he spoke.

'If we are all game for this, gentlemen, shall we clear the air? Shall we let Mr Wilde proceed?'

'Is this wise, sir?' asked Lord Yarborough.

'You've nothing to fear, Yarborough, surely?' asked the prince.

The diminutive physician stepped back, lowering his head as he did so.

'Your Royal Highness,' began the Duke of Albemarle – but one sharp look from the Prince of Wales silenced him.

'We are agreed, then,' said the prince, drawing slowly on his cigar. He reached out and touched the duke on the sleeve. 'I did not mean to be harsh, Duke. The truth may be of benefit to us all – who knows? It may even help poor Helen to rest in peace.'

The room fell silent once more.

Oscar stood by the drawing-room door, facing into the room, with the royal party ranged in an arc before him. To the Prince of Wales's right stood Prince Albert Victor and General Probyn; to his left, and one step behind, stood the Duke of Albemarle and Lord Yarborough. Tyrwhitt Wilson, the equerry, Frank Watkins, the page, and Parker, the butler, stood farther back, in the window bay, side by side, upright and quite still, like guardsmen in a sentry box.

From my vantage point at Oscar's shoulder I could see each man's face quite clearly. All seemed to me to show terror in their eyes – all but the Prince of Wales, that is.

The prince seemed oddly at ease, as if suddenly relieved that all the secrecy was about to be at an end and all the lies were now to be exposed.

'Unravel the mystery, Mr Wilde. Get on with it – you've not got long. My carriage arrives at eight. I am dining with the Danish ambassador. Probyn says I must. What lies at the heart of this tragedy?'

'Love,' answered Oscar, simply.

'Oh, Mr Wilde,' snorted the prince. 'I've heard you say love is an illusion – more than once.'

'Even so, Your Highness, it is love that is the true explanation of this world – whatever the explanation of the next.'

'Love,' repeated the prince, with a little growl.

'And pride,' added Oscar. 'And enmity.'

'Very good,' said the prince. 'That's the philosophy done with. Now let us get to the practicalities. The Duchess of Albemarle: you know why she died, do you, Mr Wilde?'

'I do, sir,' he replied. 'She died because she was your mistress.'

If the heir to the throne was discomfited by Oscar's assertion, he did not show it. He seemed almost amused by Oscar's cool impertinence.

'And the death of Lulu Lavallois?' enquired the prince. 'What brought that about?'

'She was your mistress also.'

The prince chuckled. 'I hope, Mr Wilde, that you are not going to suggest that little Nellie Atkins died because she and I were on intimate terms?'

'No. Poor Nellie was murdered because she knew who it was who had accompanied the Duchess of Albemarle into the telephone room on the night of her death. Nellie saw the man – and later the man saw Nellie and grasped at once that Nellie knew his secret.'

'And this man who accompanied the duchess into the telephone room – did he murder the duchess?'

'He intended to murder her,' said Oscar. 'Indeed, he believed that he had done so. But, as we know, the duchess had a weak heart and her heart gave way before her throat was cut. That, at least, is what both Lord Yarborough and Dr Conan Doyle have concluded – that's what the limited amount of blood found on her body and in the telephone room suggests. The duchess entered the telephone room willingly – anticipating an amorous encounter. Almost at once – possibly when the man produced his knife – her heart gave way. He did not know that she was already dead when, a moment later, he cut into her throat.'

'And the marks upon her chest?' asked the Prince of Wales quietly.

'Some were new and some were old. The murderer saw scars already on her breasts and added more – for good measure. He despised her, I am sorry to say.'

'He was not one of her lovers?'

'No, Your Highness, he was not. Lord Yarborough may be right and the late duchess may indeed have been a victim of the condition known as "nympholepsis", but she took no pleasure in being cut about the body by her lovers. That is a perversity too far. Until the night she died, she had no marks upon her neck and the cuts upon her breasts were not the work of one of her lovers . . . They were her husband's doing.'

The Duke of Albemarle said nothing. He gazed fixedly at Oscar and I saw the terror in his eyes turn to anger.

'His Grace is most gracious to his guests and friends,' continued Oscar, 'but he was a brute to his wife. She betrayed him – time and again, with man after man – and he punished her. He scarred her breasts, knowing her breasts would be seen only by her lovers – and by her lady's maid.'

'She was my wife.' The Duke of Albemarle spat out the words.

'And you loved her very much, once upon a time,' said Oscar. 'And for the sake of "form", you told the world you loved her still – and the world believed you.'

'She was unfaithful,' barked the duke.

'So you took your revenge,' said Oscar quietly. 'Is it not a husband's right? You punished her infidelity and you maimed her in a vain attempt to curb her lust. I imagine that Lord Yarborough –

her physician and your friend – knew what you had done and pardoned you – or at least sought to understand your vicious behaviour. He told me that your wife took pride in the cuts upon her body – that she desired them. He sought to protect you, Your Grace.'

Lord Yarborough's eyes appeared to be fixed on one of the Romney portraits on the wall. He said nothing and gave the studied impression that he was paying Oscar's narrative no heed.

'At first I was certain that the Duke of Albemarle had, at least in part, been responsible for his wife's untimely death. He had the means – the knife he carries in his pocket to cut his cigars. He had the opportunity – he could easily have taken his wife into the telephone room on the night of the reception as the pair waited in the hallway to bid farewell to their royal guests. He had the motive – his wife's repeated infidelities. He might have done the deed, alone – or with a co-conspirator. Mr Parker, the family retainer, has been the duke's loyal servant these forty years. He would do anything for his master.'

Oscar glanced in the direction of the window bay.

'It was Mr Parker who told me and Dr Conan Doyle and Mr Sherard, on the morning following the duchess's death, that Nellie Atkins was not available for interview because she had fallen downstairs. Did she fall? Or was she pushed? Or was she beaten by way of warning – beaten either by her lord and master or by his trusty butler? It hardly matters. The effect was the same.'

Parker stepped away from the window. 'Mr Wilde, I protest.'

Oscar raised a hand. 'Do not protest, Mr Parker. I'm not done yet. I think you'll be spared the gallows.'

'If not the gallows humour,' muttered Prince Albert Victor.

'Mr Wilde,' said the Prince of Wales. 'Time is pressing. Are you telling us that in your far-fetched opinion the Duke of Albemarle was responsible for the death of his wife?'

'Men do kill their wives, Your Highness. It is the commonest kind of murder. I was indeed convinced the duke had planned to kill his duchess – until Tuesday night when, together, we were faced with a second death: that of Mademoiselle Louisa Lavallois.'

'Poor Lulu,' murmured the Prince of Wales.

'Poor Lulu – so full of life and laughter, so full of joy. Why did she have to die? She could have been murdered only by someone who had intimate knowledge of the death of the duchess. The wounds inflicted on Mademoiselle Lavallois were precisely those inflicted on the Duchess of Albemarle. Only her murderer – or anyone who had seen her body in the immediate aftermath of her death – could have replicated those wounds so exactly. That fact alone let my friend Bram Stoker off the hook. And Professor Onofroff, of course.

Besides, neither was here on the night of the duchess's death.'

'What about the composer, Dvorak?' asked the Prince of Wales. 'He wasn't here at that reception, was he, but he looked deuced uncomfortable during Onofroff's seance – and Onofroff marked him down as guilty as sin.'

'Guilty of incest, perhaps. But not of murder. He loved his daughter – not wisely, but too well. Onofroff saw Dvorak and the girl silhouetted within what he called "the dark penumbra".'

'Tomfoolery,' snapped the Prince of Wales, tearing off the band from a fresh cigar.

'Quite possibly, Your Highness. Onofroff also saw you and your eldest son silhouetted within the dark penumbra.'

'You told me.'

The prince turned to his son and took the young man's hand in his.

'My boy is not a murderer. He has his weaknesses – as I have mine. But he is not a murderer. I know it in my bones.'

'But once you thought he was – or might be?' asked Oscar.

'Yes – because a foolish fortune-teller put the notion into my head years ago. It was twaddle, moonshine. Why would Albert Victor – my prince, my son, my heir, my soon-to-be Duke of Clarence – wish to harm little Lulu Lavallois? All she had ever done was help introduce him to the arts of love. Why would Eddy murder Lulu? Why would he want to harm Helen Albemarle?'

'Because he's mad,' said Prince Albert Victor, letting go his father's hand.

'He's not mad,' said the Prince of Wales with feeling. 'He is troubled, that is all.'

The prince looked at Oscar and jabbed his cigar towards him.

'Why,' he demanded, 'should my son choose to murder Lulu Lavallois or Helen Albemarle? In heaven's name, *why*?'

'Because he loves you, sir. Because he wants to spare you the pain and disgrace of scandal. Your friends no doubt envy you your mistresses and admire the unbounded vigour of your manhood, but the Great British Public, as it is called, and the verminous British press, lickspittle to a man, take a less charitable and enlightened view of your domestic arrangements. And your son and those who truly hold you dear – your equerry, for example, and your page – know the danger that these wanton women pose to you and your position. These strumpets have distressed the Queen. They have rocked the Crown. Your son will rid you of them before they can ruin you.'

The Prince of Wales shook his head fiercely and sucked hard on his cigar, his small, imperious eyes fixed on Oscar.

'You are insolent, sir, and wild in more than name. Why should my son – or any member of my household – risk the scandal associated with murder to spare me the scandal associated with adultery? The idea is absurd.'

He turned away from Oscar towards Tyrwhitt Wilson in the window bay.

'Has the brougham arrived yet? Go into the street and find another.'

'A moment more, Your Highness,' said Oscar contritely. 'I crave your indulgence.'

'You've been indulged enough. We're getting nowhere, Wilde. I wish to leave before the police arrive. They must be allowed to enquire into the death of this unfortunate lady's maid without the distraction of my presence.'

Oscar looked at the clock on the mantelpiece. 'The police will not be here for ten minutes yet, sir. I know that. Please depart at eight o'clock as you had planned. Allow me ten minutes more of your time – I beseech you.'

The prince heaved a mighty sigh and shook his head. 'Do these unfortunate women have nothing in common besides their association with me?'

'They have hysteria in common, Your Highness,' answered Oscar quietly. 'They have Lord Yarborough and Professor Jean-Martin Charcot in common.'

'Is that relevant?'

'No,' snapped Lord Yarborough, turning his gaze back from the paintings on the wall and confronting Oscar. 'The Duchess of Albemarle was an hysteric. Her sister is one also. I am treating the sister in Muswell Hill. The duke is generously paying for that treatment. That is the end of the matter. There is no more to it than that.'

'Why then,' asked Oscar, 'is the body lying in the coffin in the adjoining room not the body of the Duchess of Albemarle?'

'But it is,' protested Lord Yarborough.

'For God's sake, Wilde,' cried the Prince of Wales. 'Are you quite mad? We've all seen the body – just now.'

'We've seen the head, sir. We have seen the precisely decapitated head of the late duchess placed in the coffin at the top of another woman's body – a shorter woman, a woman without scars upon her chest. The head is the head of the late duchess. The body, I imagine, is that of a lately deceased patient from Lord Yarborough's clinic at Muswell Hill. I am sure the patient died of natural causes.'

'This is outrageous,' cried Lord Yarborough.

'Most certainly,' replied Oscar, 'but, it seems, not outwith the law. Lord Yarborough is a physician with a licence to dissect. He can cut up bodies in whatever way he pleases – so long as those bodies have come his way legitimately. The Duchess of Albemarle was content to leave her body to science. The remains of her body are now in Lord Yarborough's laboratory in Muswell Hill, I assume, assisting him in his researches into the causes of female hysteria.'

The Prince of Wales turned to Lord Yarborough. 'Is this true?' he asked.

Lord Yarborough hesitated.

'Is what Mr Wilde is suggesting true?' repeated the prince.

'It is,' said Lord Yarborough, eventually. 'In every particular.'

'But *why*, Yarborough?'

'Helen had given permission. She knew that her heart was weak. She knew that for her an early death was not an impossibility. And she knew her sister was afflicted with the curse of hysteria, as she was herself. She wished to assist us in our researches in any way she could – for the sake of others like her sister, if not for her own sake. The thought that her body might help us towards a cure for the malady was of some comfort to her.'

'That I understand,' said the prince. 'What I want to know is: why this grotesque charade of attaching one woman's head to another woman's body?'

Lord Yarborough gave a bitter laugh. 'To allay suspicion. I had come to the conclusion that Mr Wilde and his companions had me in their sights as the murderer. Dr Doyle, in particular, convinced himself that I was inducing patients to commit suicide under hypnosis in order to have ready access to their cadavers. When he and Mr Wilde discovered that the Lavallois girl – of whom I had never heard until the night of her death – had once been a patient of Professor Charcot in Paris – albeit it several years ago – they leapt to their conclusion. They decided I was killing these girls to furnish myself with raw material for my research. I was not – and I sought to prove it to them. The open coffin that we filed past just now: that was my idea. The duchess's body is no longer in one piece; it has been destroyed by dissection, but her head remains intact. I thought that if Wilde and Doyle could see the poor woman's apparent corpse laid out before them, they might think twice before turning me in to the police as a murderous body-snatcher.'

'And was the duke party to this?'

'He was,' said Lord Yarborough. 'He allowed me to take the duchess's body away last Friday. He permitted this afternoon's "grotesque charade", as you rightly call it. He invited Mr Wilde and his companions to be in attendance today at my suggestion. His Grace is my friend – and my paymaster. He funds the clinic.'

'And you believed, did you not, Lord Yarborough, that it was the Duke of Albemarle – your friend and paymaster – who had murdered his wife?' said Oscar.

Lord Yarborough looked at Oscar, but made no reply.

'Yet if he had done so,' continued Oscar, 'why would he also have murdered Lulu Lavallois? To create a diversion – to muddy the waters – to throw suspicion on to another? Perhaps.'

The Duke of Albemarle turned to the Prince of Wales. 'I have known you, sir, since you were a boy. One day I will be your subject. I will always be your friend. You must believe me when I tell you that I am guilty of much, Your Highness, but I am not guilty of murder.'

'I believe you,' said the Prince of Wales.

'And I believe you, too,' said Oscar, 'not that, in

your estimation, Your Grace, my opinion need count for much.'

Oscar eyed the clock on the mantelpiece once more and turned his attention to Lord Yarborough.

'And, my lord, you should know that, whatever Dr Conan Doyle may have thought, I never took you for a murderer.'

I said nothing, but glanced towards Robert Sherard, still guarding the doors to the morning room. From where he stood, he could see through the window into the street. He acknowledged my look of enquiry and shook his head.

'So,' said the Prince of Wales, impatiently, 'Lord Yarborough is not the murderer—'

'No, sir,' said Oscar. 'But inadvertently he led me in the direction of the man who is. Lord Yarborough revealed to me that he is a kinsman of my friend, Robert Sherard. They are first cousins – "bastard cousins" in Robert's phrase, but "cousins nonetheless", as my vampire-friend, Rex LaSalle, put it.'

'Your "vampire-friend"?' muttered the Prince of Wales.

'He's not a vampire, sir – nothing of the sort. Even if such creatures exist, he is not one. He claimed to be one to gain my attention – to be amusing, original, *different*. He wants to be "special". He feels it is his entitlement. He has many fantastic claims to his credit. He says he has been an actor, but he can't have been. He speaks of none of his past triumphs. He claims to be an artist, but if he is, where is the smell of turpentine and oil? He even claims to share my birthday, but knows nothing of the great events associated with the sixteenth of October: the burning of the Oxford martyrs, the guillotining of Queen Marie Antoinette of France, the birth of James II of Scotland. And little of my philosophy – though he has studied it. I am one of his curious obsessions. We met – it seemed by chance – in Tite Street, outside my house, on Monday the tenth of March, Your Highness's wedding anniversary. We spoke of that. We met again, here, at the duke and duchess's reception. He contrived an invitation – or perhaps he just arrived and, being correctly dressed and wonderfully well favoured, simply walked through the door. Invitation cards were not collected on the night.'

'This man,' stammered the Prince of Wales, 'this vampire-friend of yours – this man is the murderer?'

'Yes,' said Oscar, gently. 'He told me he was a vampire – to intrigue me, so I thought. I asked him who might be his next victim – and he pointed across the crowded room and said it would be our hostess, the Duchess of Albemarle. I glanced in the general direction in which he pointed, but I did not see the duchess – there were so many ladies there. I simply laughed at what I took to be his pleasantry. Now I see that I was his alibi. He had *already* found the duchess and lured her into the telephone room – he is so very handsome – and cut her throat. He liked to play the vampire, so he left tell-tale incisions in her neck. He ravaged her with his knife, ruthlessly, and then returned to the party to amuse himself in my company.'

'Can this be true?' gasped the Duke of Albemarle.

'I am in no doubt,' said Oscar. 'He murdered Louisa Lavallois, too – but that killing, unlike the first, was not premeditated. He saw Mademoiselle Lavallois. He saw His Royal Highness's easy way with her and he seized his moment. When he caught sight of her returning to join our party after the performance, he slipped unnoticed into the curtained vestibule adjacent to the ante-room to the royal box, followed her into the water closet and murdered her – in exactly the way he had murdered the duchess. He is bold and has nerves of steel. He is fastidious, too. As he went about his work, he made sure that none of his victim's blood was spilt on his person. And when the deed was done, he left the murder weapon wrapped in a napkin among the sandwiches.'

'Where are the police?' I cried. 'Where are they, Oscar?'

Oscar turned to me. 'They will be here shortly, Arthur. Once the prince has gone, they will appear.'

'But LaSalle – he must be stopped.'

'He has been. I've seen to that,' said Oscar. 'Poor Nellie Atkins was his final victim. I should have realised he would try to kill her, too. When, during our enquiries, LaSalle returned with us to this house, we saw Nellie up on the landing carrying linen. She saw us looking up at her and we all saw the terror in her eyes, but I did not realise then, as I should have done, that it was because she had recognised LaSalle as the man she had seen accompanying her mistress into the telephone room.'

'Who is this man, LaSalle?'

'He comes from the island of Jersey, Your Highness. I don't know his name. It's not LaSalle – I do know that. He stole the name LaSalle from a gravestone. There was a lad about his age called Reginald LaSalle – born in October 1863. Our mutual friend Lillie Langtry knew the real Reginald – they played together when they were children. The boy was killed in a fire in the summer of 1870. I received a telegram from Jersey with the dates and details this afternoon. Our murderer – my vampire-friend – adopted the surname to give himself some sort of identity. I imagine his first name was his own invention – since Rex is Latin for "king".'

'Who is this man?' repeated the Prince of Wales.

'I really do not know, Your Highness, but he believes he is your son.'

Case Closed

82

From the notebooks of Robert Sherard

A terrible silence fell in the room. As the clock on the mantelpiece struck the hour, we heard a distant rumbling of metal wheels on cobblestones.

I moved towards the window, from which I saw the lamps on a pair of carriages coming towards the house from the northern corner of the square. They were not police carts.

'I believe this may be Your Highness's brougham,' I said.

'Thank you,' said the Prince of Wales. 'I'm obliged. And thank you, Mr Wilde. I'm grateful to you for your account of these tragic events. I am relieved the culprit is under lock and key. I've been a victim of such lunatics before.'

'Your Highness did visit the Channel Islands in January 1863,' said Oscar.

From his pocket Oscar had produced the small sheaf of letters and telegrams he had collected from the Langham Hotel that afternoon. He rifled through them as he spoke.

'Did I? It's possible. I get about, you know. It's part and parcel of being Prince of Wales.'

Oscar held his handful of papers out towards the prince. 'Rex LaSalle believes you are his father, sir. He believes that you met his mother on the island of Jersey and made love to her – that you proposed to her and "married" her. He believes that he is the fruit of your union – born in wedlock of a kind, conceived before your official marriage to Princess Alexandra of Denmark on the tenth of March 1863.'

'We have heard enough, Mr Wilde,' said Sir Dighton Probyn. 'It is high time His Royal Highness took his leave.'

'This is madness, Mr Wilde.'

'There is madness in all murder, sir – and desperation. Rex LaSalle believes he is your son because that is what his mother told him. She told no one else. It was their secret. The boy was brought up to believe that, once upon a time, his mother had exchanged vows with a prince and that one day he would be king. It was the stuff of fairy tales.'

'It was stuff and nonsense,' said the prince emphatically. Probyn and Prince Albert Victor stood at his side, willing him to leave.

'Of course,' said Oscar, folding the papers and replacing them in his pocket. 'Pure lunacy, wild make-believe – but real to Rex LaSalle, terrifyingly so. He believed he was a prince in all but name. He believed that fate – and Your Royal Highness – had denied him his birthright. You spurned his mother, you broke your vows—'

'I was just twenty-one in 1863, Mr Wilde,' exclaimed the prince.

'And she was just eighteen. And when she died, a month or so ago, according to her son, she died an old woman.'

'I am sorry to hear it.'

'It was her death that provoked these murders. The mother had fed the son her fantasy, but also constrained him – saved him from himself. Once she was dead, the boy had nothing more to lose. He set out on the course of madness that ended tonight in the cruel murder of poor Nellie Atkins. He left Jersey and came to London, bringing his new identity with him. He sought me out. He had read about me in the newspapers and been taken by something I'd once said. He knew that he was "special" and he vowed that one day he would be famous – or, if not famous, at least notorious. If he could not have everything, he would still have something. If he could not be a prince of the United Kingdom, he would be a prince of murderers.'

'Clearly I am fortunate to have been spared,' said the prince, now moving firmly towards the drawing-room door. 'I take it that vile nest of vipers was this man's doing. I'd feared the return of Irish assassins.'

'Yes, it could only have been him, but the fault was mine,' said Oscar. 'Foolishly I had told LaSalle of our appointment with Your Highness: he knew where to send his nest of vipers and at what time.'

Oscar and Conan Doyle moved aside to let the prince pass. The Duke of Albemarle stepped forward to open the drawing-room door.

'At least he didn't try to shoot me in the street. I've had that happen – more than once.'

'He would not wish to kill you, sir. That would be

patricide, that would be regicide – but he would kill the thing you loved. He had no plan to murder Mrs Langtry or any of your past conquests. He wished to hurt you *now* – to avenge his mother and repay your neglect. He came to London to kill your current mistress – and when he chanced to see you with Mademoiselle Lavallois and saw the delight you took in her company, he decided, then and there, to despatch her as well.'

'Extraordinary,' muttered the Prince of Wales.

'And you have stopped this murderer in his tracks, Mr Wilde,' announced Sir Dighton Probyn with finality. 'You have done the state some service.'

The party was now reassembling in the hallway. The page, Watkins, and Parker, the butler, hovered by the two princes with their hats and canes. Tyrwhitt Wilson stood with the Duke of Albemarle at the front door.

The Prince of Wales paused a moment and, taking his cigar from his mouth, contemplated the closed door to the telephone room in the corner of the hallway.

'The unfortunate maid's body is still in there, is it?' he asked.

'It is, sir,' said Conan Doyle. 'The police will be here shortly. They will deal with it.'

'Ah, yes,' murmured the prince. 'The police.'

'We are on our way, Your Highness,' said Sir Dighton Probyn crisply, nodding towards Parker who pulled open the front door.

'Good evening, gentlemen.'

The Prince of Wales stood in the doorway, offering his farewells.

'I'm relieved to find you're not a murderer, Yarborough. I'm patron of your Royal Society, you know. And I've an aversion to scandal.' He laughed at his own joke. 'Good evening, Duke. I shall think of you tomorrow, during the funeral. And we shall dine soon – at the end of next month, when I get back from France. I'm going on Sunday – my little spring break, *en garçon*. You know how it is. I'm hoping Eddy will join me for a few days in Paris.'

He turned to Prince Albert Victor.

'You will join me, won't you, sir?'

Prince Albert Victor clicked his heels and bowed.

The Prince of Wales's pale and watery eyes scanned the remainder of the gathering. 'Thank you, gentlemen. Good evening.'

He turned to go, placing his hat firmly on his head as he did so, then turned back and looked directly at Oscar.

'Good night, Mr Wilde. Thank you for your endeavours. I enjoyed your account of what occurred, but remember what we have agreed. It's not to be written down, not a word of it – not even in a play with me disguised as the Prince of Carpathia or some such.'

'Rest assured, Your Highness,' smiled Oscar. 'Your secrets are safe with me.'

'And LaSalle, whoever he is – believe me, Mr Wilde: he is not my son. I am not the father of a murderer.'

'I believe you, sir – completely. I have never had much faith in mind-readers and fortune-tellers.'

The prince, now descending the steps to the pavement, turned once more. 'What's that you say?'

'What the fortune-teller told you all those years ago – what Onofroff saw in the dark penumbra on Tuesday night – you and your eldest son and the stain of murder . . . All moonshine.'

'Yes,' cried the prince, disregarding Oscar and looking up at the sky. 'It's a fine night. And the moon's just coming out from behind the clouds.'

The page held open the carriage door and the equerry helped the prince climb on board.

'I trust the Danish ambassador will be serving an *English* dinner. We shall speak of my darling wife, of course. It will be very jolly.'

General Sir Dighton Probyn climbed into the brougham behind the prince. Tyrwhitt Wilson closed the carriage door. The prince peered out of the window and waved to us as the carriage moved off.

The second brougham was for Prince Albert Victor, who bade us farewell on the front steps of 40 Grosvenor Square. He looked weary as he left – and sad.

'So I am not a murderer, after all,' he said to Oscar as they shook hands. 'Thank you for that, Mr Wilde.'

'I hope you find your heart's desire, sir,' said Oscar.

'Tonight I'll settle for simple oblivion,' he answered, smiling. 'I'm bound for Limehouse and "The Bar of Gold". Goodnight.'

'Goodnight, sweet prince,' said Oscar.

The royal party gone, we made our way back into the hallway and Parker secured the front door.

'Mr Wilde,' said the Duke of Albemarle, 'would you and Dr Doyle and Mr Sherard be so good as to wait here for the police. I will give Lord Yarborough a drink in the drawing room. We will be entirely at your disposal when the police arrive. Parker will bring you further refreshments. I don't believe you ever got those cheese straws.'

The duke and Lord Yarborough returned to the drawing room. Parker went about his business.

Conan Doyle looked anxiously at the telephone-room door and checked his pocket watch. 'You say LaSalle is secure. Where is he? Is he with the police now? Where are they? It's well past eight.'

'The police will be here soon, Arthur,' I said. 'Rest easy.'

'No,' said Oscar, laughing quietly. 'They won't be here soon. I told a lie. The police have not been summoned.'

'In God's name, man,' cried Conan Doyle, 'what have you done?'

'I let LaSalle take my four-wheeler. Sherard watched it depart – an hour ago.'

'I saw the passenger, Oscar. It wasn't LaSalle.'

'No, the passenger was the coachman. LaSalle was up top, driving the carriage.'

'By all that's merciful,' cried Conan Doyle in a frenzy of distress and confusion, 'you've let the man go?'

'He will commit no more murder, Arthur. He killed Nellie Atkins in a moment of madness and came and told me what he had done. He whispered it to me – in the drawing room, not an hour ago.'

'And you let him escape?'

'To spare him the gallows. I gave him the means of escape and a poetic idea, borrowed from Shakespeare. He will commit no more murders. He promised me.'

'He *promised* you? The *murderer* "promised" you! And you gave him a poetic idea borrowed from Shakespeare! This is lunacy, Oscar. We must telephone for the police – *now*.'

Oscar shook his head.

'We cannot use the telephone. LaSalle tore out the wires. Let us cross the road and fetch our friend Boone.'

'Boone?' Conan Doyle was quite bewildered.

'Inspector Boone of Scotland Yard – your man with the twisted lip, Arthur. He is out there pursuing vice – and missing murder. This will give him something useful to do.'

'I thought he was watching Prince Albert Victor,' I said.

'He has been – among others. And, believe it or not – or so he told me on the Dover train, when you two young gentlemen were fast asleep – I, Oscar Wilde, am one of the "others". While you slumbered, he as good as accused me of unnatural vice. He told me that one day he would prove to be my nemesis. The words these policemen know!'

Oscar reached out to Conan Doyle and put his arm on the doctor's shoulder. 'Arthur, you are too good for this world.'

'Never mind that,' said Conan Doyle. 'Let's get to Inspector Boone. We need the police, Oscar. We need a dose of reality.'

'We do,' cried Oscar and his eyes were suddenly full of tears. 'A dose of reality – and then a bucket of champagne. Who needs cheese straws? We shall dine at the Café Royal on oysters and Perrier-Jouët. Case closed.'

'The man is a murderer, Oscar. Not a prince or a vampire, but a murderer.'

'Yes,' said Oscar, 'I know. And a poor girl lies dead in that room because of him. But he was impossibly handsome, wasn't he? And even men of the noblest moral character are susceptible to the influence of the physical charms of others. Have I said that to you before? It's true nonetheless – as I fear you will discover one day. Even you will discover it, Arthur. Even you.'

83

Telegram sent to Constance Wilde at 16 Tite Street,
Chelsea, at midnight on Friday, 21 March 1890

HOW WAS THE SCOTTISH PLAY? HOW WAS
IRVING? HOW IS BRAM? HOW ARE YOU MY
DARLING WIFE? PARIS PALLS. LONDON CALLS.
RETURNING SUNDAY. ALL WELL. BERNHARDT
DIVINE AS EVER. OSCAR WILDE AS ALWAYS

84

**From the *Evening News*, London, first edition,
Saturday, 22 March 1890**

CURIOUS DEATH IN SOHO

The dead body of a young man was discovered in the early hours of this morning in the stockroom of the Portuguese wine shop at 17 Wardour Street, Soho.

The young man, as yet unnamed but believed to be in his mid-twenties and of smart appearance, had apparently been drowned to death in a full cask of malmsey wine from the Madeira islands, in the manner of the notorious death of the Duke of Clarence in Shakespeare's play, *Richard III*. According to the police, the present case has all the appearance of a tragic accident and foul play is not suspected.

85

Telegram sent from the Langham Hotel, London, to Louisa 'Touie' Conan Doyle in Southsea, at 9 a.m. on Saturday, 22 March 1890

RETURNING TO SOUTHSEA THIS MORNING.
ALL WELL. SO HAPPY. I LOVE YOU DEAREST.
HEART AND SOUL. NOW AND ALWAYS. FOR
EVER AND A DAY. ACD

Author's Note

Arthur Conan Doyle married Louisa 'Touie' Hawkins in 1885. She suffered from tuberculosis and died in 1906. In 1897 Conan Doyle met the second great love of his life, Jean Leckie. He married her ten years later, in September 1907, fourteen months after Touie's death. He had five children: two with his first wife, three with his second. In 1902, in recognition of his services to the Crown during the Boer War, he was knighted. He died on 7 July 1930, aged seventy-one.

Oscar Wilde married Constance Lloyd in 1884. They had two sons: Cyril (1885–1915) and Vyvyan (1886–1967). Constance died on 7 April 1898, aged forty, in Genoa, following unsuccessful spinal surgery. Oscar, having served a two-year sentence of imprisonment with hard labour for homosexual offences, was released from Reading Gaol in 1897 and died in exile, in Paris, on 30 November 1900, aged forty-six.

Robert Sherard, whose father was the natural son of the 6th and last Earl of Harborough and whose mother was the granddaughter of William Wordsworth, was twice divorced and three times married. He wrote poetry, short stories and detective fiction, and biographies of Emile Zola, Alphonse Daudet and Guy de Maupassant, as well as Oscar Wilde. He died on 30 January 1943, aged eighty-one.

Bram Stoker married Florence Balcombe in 1878. They had one son and a marriage lasting thirty-four years. Stoker was Henry Irving's manager at the Lyceum Theatre in London for twenty-seven years. He published *Dracula* in 1897 and died on 20 April 1912, aged sixty-four.

Jean-Martin Charcot was the foremost neurologist of his time and the first to describe and name multiple sclerosis, among several other conditions. He died on 16 August 1893, aged sixty-seven.

Jane Avril was under Charcot's care at the Pitié-Salpêtrière Hospital in 1880s, but her claim to fame lies in the posters of her created for the Moulin Rouge by Henri de Toulouse-Lautrec in the 1890s. She died on 16 January 1943, aged seventy-four.

Albert Edward, Prince of Wales, married Princess Alexandra of Denmark on 10 March 1863, when he was twenty-one and she was eighteen. They had six children, the oldest of whom was Prince Albert Victor, known as Eddy, who was created Duke of Clarence and Avondale in the summer of 1890 and who died of pneumonia on 14 January 1892, aged just twenty-eight.

The Prince of Wales succeeded Queen Victoria as King Edward VII on 22 January 1901. Ever tolerant, Queen Alexandra allowed the last of her husband's many mistresses, Alice Keppel – great-grandmother of the Duchess of Cornwall, the present Princess of Wales – at his bedside as he lay dying. He was succeeded by his second son, King George V, great-grandfather of the present Prince of Wales.

Edward VII died on 6 May 1910, aged sixty-eight. One hundred years later, the manuscript of *Oscar Wilde and the Nest of Vipers* was delivered to John Murray of London, sometime publisher of Arthur Conan Doyle.

For further historical information and for details of the other and forthcoming titles in the series, for reviews, interviews and material of particular interest to Reading Groups, etc., see:

www.oscarwildemurdermysteries.com

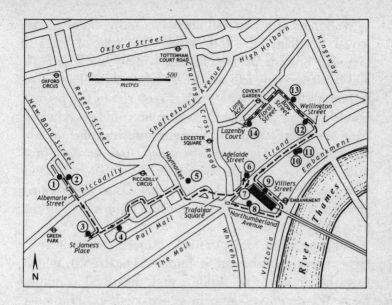

A Walk in
Oscar Wilde's West End

When you are next in London, you can take this hour-long walk through Oscar Wilde's West End, visiting several of the locations featured in the *Oscar Wilde Murder Mysteries*.

The walk begins in Mayfair, at the north end of Albemarle Street, London W1, home of **Brown's Hotel** (1), from where Oscar Wilde made phone calls, and where Alexander Graham Bell made the first telephone call in England. Opposite, at number 13, is the site of the old **Albemarle Club** (2) where Oscar was a member. It was here that the Marquess of Queensberry, so enraged by Oscar's romantic involvement with his son Bosie, left his visiting card accusing Oscar of 'posing as a somdomite' (*sic*). It was Wilde's libel action against Queensberry that ultimately led to his downfall.

Walking south you will cross Piccadilly, home of the Royal Academy, the Café Royal and one of Oscar's favourite bookshops, Hatchard's. Walk down St James's and before turning left into King Street, take a look at 10 **St James's Place** (3), where Oscar took rooms in a private hotel (now an art gallery) so that he could work away from the distractions and interruptions of home in Tite Street, Chelsea. He wrote *An Ideal Husband* here in a little over two months between November 1893 and February 1894. It was also here that Oscar entertained young men, some of whom testified against him in his 1895 trial.

On King Street look out for St James's House on your right, the site of the old **St James's Theatre** (4), which saw the premiere of Wilde's first theatrical triumph, *Lady Windermere's Fan*, in February 1892. His most celebrated play, *The Importance of Being Earnest*, opened at the theatre in February 1895 to rapturous applause, despite the Marquess of Queensberry's best efforts to sabotage the event with a public denunciation of Oscar. Arriving with a prizefighter, he tried and failed to gain admission by the stage door. It was only a few days later that Queensberry famously left his card at the Albemarle Club. The St James's Theatre was demolished in 1957 to make way for an office block; Laurence Olivier, Vivien Leigh and Winston Churchill led the campaign to save it.

Continue west until you reach Haymarket, where you will see the **Theatre Royal** (5) straight ahead of you. It was here that *A Woman of No Importance* opened in April 1893, followed by *An Ideal Husband* in January 1895. Charles Brookfield played the small part of a servant, Phipps, despite his rocky history with Oscar. Now head down Haymarket, left onto Pall Mall and, after crossing Trafalgar Square, pause at the foot of Adelaide Street to admire **A Conversation with Oscar Wilde** (6), created by Maggi Hambling in 1999 and the only statue of Oscar Wilde in England. The inscription reads, 'We are all in the gutter, but some of us are looking at the stars', a line from *Lady Windermere's Fan*.

From here cross the Strand, passing **Charing Cross Station** (7), where Oscar regularly took the Underground home to Sloane Square. When Oscar arrived in London in 1879 the city's population was about 4.7 million; when he left for France in 1897 it had increased by about fifty per cent. The new Tube network made it possible for the growing mass of Londoners to escape crowded slums into new suburbs – including that of Conan Doyle's South Norwood – thereby relieving the pressure of overcrowding and ugly tenement development from the city centre.

Now turn left down Northumberland Avenue, stopping for refreshment in the **Sherlock Holmes pub** (8) where, in the upstairs bar, Holmes's rooms from 221b Baker Street have been recreated. (Look closely and you will spot Oscar's photograph and visiting card on Holmes's mantelpiece.) Continuing up Villiers Street, look out for the New Players Theatre on the left. This was once home to **Gatti's-in-the-Arches** (9), the celebrated music hall built by Carlo Gatti in 1867 in the undercroft of the new Charing Cross Station. Originally a working-class form of variety entertainment, music hall was at the height of its popularity in Oscar's day, attracting audiences from all walks of life. By 1895, Gatti's boasted a grand café and billiard saloon, and counted Rudyard Kipling (a Villiers Street resident) among its patrons.

Turn right onto the Strand, a smart promenading street in Oscar's day, taking in the **Savoy Theatre** (10), the first public building in the world to be lit by electricity, and home of Gilbert and Sullivan. Their 1881 opera *Patience* was a satire of the Aesthetic Movement, and particularly of Oscar Wilde. But rather than damage his reputation the play served merely to propel Oscar even further into the limelight. Adjacent to the theatre, and built on the back of its great financial success, is the **Savoy Hotel** (11), where Oscar frequently stayed on his nights away from home. It was evidence from one of the chambermaids at the Savoy that helped lead to his conviction on charges of gross indecency in the notorious trials of 1895.

Crossing the Strand and heading north on Wellington Street you will pass the **Lyceum Theatre** (12), home of the great Sir Henry Irving, the first actor to be knighted. Irving and his general manager, Bram Stoker, were both friends of Wilde. Heading north, pause at **Bow Street Police Station** (13) where, following the collapse of his libel case against Lord Queensberry, Wilde was arrested and formally charged at the beginning of April 1895.

Turning west down Floral Street, continue for 200 yards before cutting left down Lazenby Court to the small wooden-fronted **Lamb and Flag pub** (14), also known as the 'Bucket of Blood' because of the bare-knuckle boxing held there, largely in secret. The sport was bloody, crude, illegal and notoriously corrupt until 1892 when the Marquess of Queensberry's rules – introducing gloves, rounds and protecting the injured man – were finally accepted, and boxing began to enter the realms of respectability.